'A magnificent crime novel, at least as good as his stunning 2014 debut . . . His portrait of an edgy, sexy, corrupt, dangerous, deeply racially prejudiced city, where savage violence cohabited with exciting music, is totally absorbing' Marcel Berlins, *The Times*

'Celestin certainly doesn't short-change us on plot as his book centres on investigations into the disappearance of a celebrity heiress, the brutal murder (complete with gouged-out eyes) of a gangster and an attempt to poison a group of pro-Capone city dignitaries . . . He writes so vividly that at times I was convinced I could see 1920s Chicago in front of me and, even more impressively, he writes so well about music that I could virtually hear it. His first book was one of the best crime novels of its year and this sequel is even better. VERDICT: 5/5' *Daily Express*

'Captivating . . . Under the constant threat of bloodshed, the three stories gradually weave together into an intriguing portrait of a time and a place . . . The young Louis Armstrong turns up, and his powerful, searching, explosive jazz pulses through the pages'
Spectator

'Celestin's promise of two further instalments of this lively, jazz-based series can only be cause for celebration' *Sunday Times*

'As he did in his first novel, *The Axeman's Jazz*, Celestin perfectly captures the jazzy street rhythms of this proudly pugnacious city and its peculiar characters' *The New York Times*

'An enthralling and evocative race through gangster-filled twenties Chicago'

Malcolm Mackay, author of *The Necessary Death of Lewis Winter*

Praise for *The Axeman's Jazz*

'Intoxicating'   *Sunday Mirror*

'The best debut I've read this year . . . A serial killer tale that captures its time and place with real style'
Scotsman, Crime Books of the Year

'Celestin has skilfully woven around the facts a clever story of three detectives who, in different ways and for different motives, set out to find the murderer. He brilliantly portrays the mood of a city under a siege of fear'   *The Times*, Crime Books of the Year

'Outstanding'   *Daily Telegraph*,
Top Ten Crime Books for Summer

'*The Axeman's Jazz* manages to be both a fascinating portrait of a vibrant and volatile city and a riveting read'   *Guardian*

'Beautifully written, the evocative prose brings the jazz-filed, Mob-ruled "Big Easy" of pre-prohibition America to life in glorious effect with a story full of suspense and intrigue. Stunning'
Sunday Express

'An absolute must for true crime fanatics'   *Refinery29*

DEAD MAN'S BLUES

Ray Celestin is a novelist and screenwriter based in London. His debut novel, *The Axeman's Jazz*, won the CWA New Blood Dagger for best debut crime novel of the year, and was featured on numerous 'Books of the Year' lists. His second novel, *Dead Man's Blues*, won the *Historia* Historical Thriller of the Year Award, and was shortlisted for a number of other awards, including the CWA Gold Dagger for best crime novel of the year. The novels are part of his City Blues series, which charts the twin histories of jazz and the Mob through the middle fifty years of the twentieth century.

Also by Ray Celestin

The Axeman's Jazz
The Mobster's Lament

RAY CELESTIN

Dead, Man's Blues

PAN BOOKS

First published 2016 by Mantle

First published in paperback 2017 by Pan Books

This paperback edition first published 2021 by Pan Books
an imprint of Pan Macmillan
The Smithson, 6 Briset Street, London EC1M 5NR
EU representative: Macmillan Publishers Ireland Limited, 1st Floor,
The Liffey Trust Centre, 117-126 Sheriff Street Upper, Dublin 1, DO1 YC43
Associated companies throughout the world
www.panmacmillan.com

ISBN 978-1-5290-6562-6

5 7 9 8 6 4

A CIP catalogue record for this book is available from the British Library.

Printed and bound by CPI Group (UK) Ltd, Croydon, CR0 4YY

Visit www.panmacmillan.com to read more about all our books
and to buy them. You will also find features, author interviews and
news of any author events, and you can sign up for e-newsletters
so that you're always first to hear about our new releases.

For Mum

PROLOGUE

CADENZA

'Jazz has come to stay because it is an expression of the times, of the breathless, energetic, superactive times in which we are living.'

LEOPOLD STOKOWSKI, 1924

New Orleans, August 1922

Louis Armstrong ran down the platform as the *Panama Limited* was departing, his cardboard suitcase in one hand, his cornet case and tickets in the other. He waved the last of these at the platform attendant who didn't even look on account of him being too busy laughing at the boy, chubby and sweating and overloaded with luggage, trying to run along the train, trying to overtake the whites-only carriages, get to the ones he could jump on without fear of catching a beating.

The train blew its whistle and Louis redoubled his efforts, dodged past a stack of luggage, past a bemused-looking porter, reached the first carriage marked *Colored*, threw his suitcase on board, put the tickets in his mouth, grabbed the handrail and swung himself onto the train as the driver increased the heat and the train soared out of the station and blasted into the burning southern skies.

He collapsed into a heap on the floor and stayed there a moment, trying to get his breath back, lungs burning from too little exercise and too many cigarettes. He rummaged around in his pockets for his handkerchief, wiped the sweat from his face, tried to make himself look presentable, and made his way to his compartment. When he found it, he saw it was cramped and close and occupied by a large woman and a brood of young children, all of them sitting on the two bare wooden planks that passed for seats. Louis smiled at the woman and she screamed at the children

3

to make room for him and he swung his suitcase onto the flax netting above the seats.

'What's your name, boy?' the woman asked when Louis had squeezed himself into a corner.

'Louis Armstrong, ma'am.'

'You Mayann's son?'

'Yes, I am.'

'I've known your mother years,' she said, her tone suggesting she was for some reason proud of the fact. 'Where you headin'?'

'Chicago.'

'Us too. You got work that way?'

'Yes, ma'am. Playing with Joe Oliver's band. Second cornet.'

'Joe Oliver?' repeated the woman, rolling the name round her memories for a few seconds, trying to see if it would stick. Then she shrugged. 'Well, good luck to ya'. You eaten?'

'No, ma'am.'

'You brought food?'

'No, ma'am.'

In his rush to get to the station he hadn't had time to stop off at a grocery and now the woman was looking at him slant-eyed. The train contained three dining cars, one serving French food à la carte, one serving cafeteria food, and one serving lounge snacks, but black people were allowed in none of them. The woman tutted, then shouted at the eldest of the children to get the basket, and when the child had retrieved it from the netting and placed it on the floor in the center of the compartment, she took the gingham off it and passed out pieces of fried chicken and cat-fish, corn on the cob, breaded okra, johnnycake, and bottles of lemonade, and Louis felt, five minutes out of New Orleans, that he'd already found a new family.

After they'd eaten they collected the leftovers in the basket and Louis played with the children, stared out of the window, chatted, smoked, fell asleep, and the day turned to night and at some point he awoke to see a galaxy of city lights streaking past the window, daubs of neon against the blackness, the sense of a great hustling on the streets below, and then the sodium buzz of Chicago's 12th Street station.

Louis helped the woman down and they walked along the platform and into the center of the station. He looked around at the people there, and saw how quickly they were walking, how they rushed, how sharply they were dressed, how streamlined, sleek and modern everything seemed. He wondered if it was just his eyes, and he turned back to look at the train, at all the Southerners collecting their bags, and the difference leapt out at him: the ragged, unfashionable clothes, the battered baggage, all of it caked in poverty and the dust of the southern plains.

Compared to the Chicagoans, Louis' people looked like refugees from some far-away, famished country, and in that instant he realized that his notion of home would be tested in these new surroundings, that it would be a struggle to not let himself be influenced by the contrast. Getting out of the South was battle enough; black folks had been lynched just for being seen at a counter buying train tickets North, mothers poured pepper into the shoes of their children making the journey, in the mistaken belief that it threw hunting dogs off their scent. But now Louis sensed there was another battle looming for all these people, a battle to fit in, to not be taken advantage of, to not lose who they were in the attempt.

'You sure you got somewhere to go?' the woman asked.

'Sure, ma'am. Joe Oliver's sending someone to pick me up,' Louis said.

The woman stared at him, unconvinced, then she nodded and gathered up her children and wished him good luck, and the moment she had disappeared into the ever-shifting crowd, Louis regretted having lied to her. He turned around and took in the immensity of the station and the city beyond and he remembered the stories of jazz musicians leaving New Orleans and ending up stranded in strange places, fleeced by promoters and record-company men, left without a friend or a cent, begging on the streets for enough to buy a train ticket home.

He tried to shake the thought, looked for a restroom to go and freshen up in, so he could continue the journey feeling vaguely clean. He saw a sign and followed the arrow to a set of marble steps leading down to a pair of doors, the usual symbols for men and women over each. But he couldn't see any signs for whether the restrooms were for white people or colored, and so he stood there a minute, hesitant.

'Boy, you look loster than a snowflake in hell,' said a voice behind him, and Louis turned to see an old Negro dressed in a Red Cap's uniform standing behind him, grinning. Something about the man's manner and approach suggested he'd done this before, that working in the station often involved helping out newly arrived Southerners looking dazed by their own situation.

'Where you from now?'

'N'awlins.'

'N'awlins?' repeated the man with a sour look on his face. 'I ain't got much time for N'awlins. Can't stand the smell of beer.'

Louis frowned, unsure what to make of the comment.

'Where you need to go?' asked the man.

'Southside.'

'Every darkie getting off every one of those goddamn trains is going to the Southside, boy. Whereabouts in the Southside's the question.'

'The Lincoln Gardens. I'm here to join Joe Oliver's band.'

'*King* Oliver?' said the man, suddenly animated. 'You the new cornet player everyone's talking about?'

Louis frowned, guessing there'd been some mix-up, wondering since when was Papa Joe called *King*?

'Come on, boy. Let's get you a car.'

The Red Cap led him outside and put him in a taxi and told the driver to take him straight to the Lincoln Gardens and Louis sat on the edge of the seat and watched the city whistle by. They drove out of the station, down State Street, past what looked like a red-light district, and in no time at all Louis got the feeling they were in the heart of the Southside, in Bronzeville, the Black Belt, the new home of jazz. It was gone ten on a work night, and the streets were as packed and alive as a Saturday on Bourbon Street. The cab passed jazz clubs and blues bars and chop-suey joints and pool halls and cinemas and vaudevilles, all lit up with every shade of neon shining bright and lurid in the darkness.

They passed under elevated railroads, and alongside street-cars; and in the distance, row upon row of skyscrapers gleamed in the night, giving Louis a sense of a whole city riding a spark, shining with electricity, chrome and speed. From the black people rushing down the streets in sharp suits and dresses, to the traffic and trains zooming past, to the flashing of the neon signs, all of it pulsed with new realms of possibility.

The cab swung a left onto 31st Street and dropped him off outside the Gardens and Louis looked up at the building and caught sight of the sign above the doors: *KING OLIVER AND HIS CREOLE JAZZ BAND*.

And then he heard the unmistakable sound of his old mentor's cornet cutting through the walls of the building and soaring out onto the street. It was the same, lowdown blues from back home, but different somehow. It took a moment to figure it out: the speed. It was much, much faster, just like the people he'd seen rushing through the streets; it had a more frenetic tempo, made breakneck to suit its new home.

'It's the King's new boy,' shouted the cabdriver over the noise to one of the bouncers at the door, swinging a thumb in Louis' direction. The bouncer was huge, and despite the heat he was dressed in a wool overcoat, with velvet lapels and a fur collar. Louis stepped out of the cab and the bouncer eyed him, and he felt conscious once more of his clothes and his battered cardboard suitcase.

He paid the driver and as the cab screeched off Louis took in the men walking up and down the sidewalk, hawking pints of gin or wraps of marijuana or heroin or cocaine. And in the queue outside the club, he saw something that made him stop: white people. A group of awkward young men, studious-looking, skittish, listening to the music like they were listening to some kind of god.

The bouncer stared at Louis and inclined his head a whole eighth of an inch toward the entrance; Louis walked to the front of the queue and the bouncer swung the door open and that's when the music really hit him, like a freight train, ear-splittingly loud and unrelenting.

They stepped through the foyer and onto the dance floor and Louis saw it was packed with hundreds of young slickers, dancing to the sound of Papa Joe's freak music, his horn growling and moaning and bending its timbre and pitch. The place was thumping with jazz, swirling in a current of optimism and hedonism, crazed by the here and now. And in that moment, a realization flared through Louis' mind – despite the difference in tempo, all these sophisticated Northerners were flocking there to listen to Southern music, to New Orleans music, to *his* music. And he thought of that ragged-looking army of refugees getting off the train at the 12th Street station. They might have been impoverished, but they were giving the city something it craved, something it worshipped.

And a smile cracked his lips. He wasn't sure what was going on, some exchange between people from different ends of the country, between fast and slow, black and white, old and modern, some forging of something new and important. Something was happening in Chicago, and he grinned from ear to ear at the beautiful bizarreness of it all.

PART ONE

FIRST CHORUS

'We have reached a time when a policeman had better throw a couple of bullets into a man first and ask questions afterward. It's a war. And in wartime you shoot first and talk second.'

DETECTIVE WILLIAM SHOEMAKER,
CHICAGO PD, 1925

'The only effective rule in Chicago is that of violence, imposed by crooks and murderers. The ill fame of Chicago is spreading through the world and bringing shame to Americans who wish they could be proud of that city. They are forced to apologize for America's second-largest city and to explain that it is a peculiar place.'

WASHINGTON POST, 1928

1

Thousands thronged the streets, blocking traffic, locking down whole neighborhoods, pretty much all of the commotion centered on the Sbarbaro & Co. Undertaking Rooms at 708 North Wells Street. People filled the roads and sidewalks around the building, others lined the procession route, others still took up positions at the gates to Mount Carmel, or climbed lampposts or hung from awnings. Families arranged chairs around upper-story windows. In the sky, a black fuzz of mourners sprouted like mold along the rooftops, crowning the proceedings.

Only a tiny fraction had actually known the deceased, a high-level politico with a history of rumored Mob connections, who wore suits with pockets tailored especially large to accommodate his bankroll, who distributed turkeys and coal to the poor at Christmas, even to Negroes. But a gangster's funeral provided spectacle: thousands in the streets; celebrities and politicians; a parade of flowers and luxury cars; a casket costing more than most people's houses; mobsters who would kill each other on any other day, walking side by side, respecting the funeral-day truce. And so the ceremony became an event: Chicago, restless city, dynamo, home of the skyscraper and the twenty-four-hour factory, only ever stopped for the funeral of a gangster.

Among the crowds thronging the streets that morning, one man was making a particular nuisance of himself, jostling past people as politely as he could . . . *Excuse me, ma'am . . . I hate to be a pain . . . Would you mind . . .* heading as straight as he could for the center of the spiderweb, the front door of Judge John Sbarbaro's funeral parlor. The people he slipped past looked at him funny, wondering if he had an invite to the ceremony. He didn't look like a gangster or a politician, and although he had the good looks of a film star, no one could recall him from the screen of the Uptown, or the Tivoli, or the Norshore. Plus he wasn't really dressed for a funeral, but rather in a summer suit of buttermilk linen, which, if a little rumpled, was impeccably cut.

The man, Dante Sanfelippo, was a little into his thirties, of medium height and slender build, with Mediterranean features and striking eyes. He had a leather overnight bag slung over one shoulder, and the tired, muddled look of a traveler, having a few hours earlier gotten off the *Twentieth Century Limited* – the overnight train from New York – and made his way northwards through the throngs after a brief stop at the Metropole Hotel.

Back in New York, Dante was a rum-runner, a gambler, a gentleman bootlegger, a needle man, a fixer, and something of an enigma, a man of many acquaintances and very few friends. He had grown up in Chicago, but had fled the city six years earlier and today was his first day back in his hometown; a hometown which Dante had realized, in the few hours since his return, was nothing more to him now than a ghost town.

After a few more minutes of fighting through the crowd, he finally made it to the cordon that had been formed around the block where the Sbarbaro was located. Pressed up against the barriers were hordes of street kids, urchins who'd had all day to stake out a spot from which to peep at the gangster legends whose names travelled the city in whispers and gunshots; kids to whom Capone, Moran, O'Banion, Genna were a royalty of sorts, the grandest, most glamorous men who would ever shine in their neighborhoods.

Dante studied them a moment, then turned to look over the cordon, and was shocked by what he saw; an ocean of blue flowers laid out on the ground in front of the building in so great a number that not an inch of asphalt was visible anymore. A whole city block covered in wreaths, chaplets and bouquets. The wash of blue broke through the railings between the shopfronts, flowed past fire hydrants, lampposts, garbage cans, lapped against porches and walls. Every blue flower that could be purchased in the state of Illinois, arranged into myriad tributes that must have cost tens of thousands of dollars to order, make up and deliver.

Dante let out a whistle, impressed, then he looked for some way through the flowers, and after a moment he spotted it: a thin sliver of paving stones, heading to the front steps of the parlor, where three gunmen wearing suits and blank-slate expressions were standing guard. Dante sighed and slipped under the cordon and there was a gasp from the crowd, the people guessing he was a trespasser, unhinged, a man with a suicide twitch.

He threw his bag over his shoulder and strolled through the field of cornflowers, campanulas, forget-me-nots. As he approached, the gunmen tensed, their slouches dissolving, hands moving steadily into their jackets. When Dante was a few yards from the bottom of the steps he stopped, and smiled, and nodded, and the men glared back at him with practiced looks.

'I'm here to see Mr Capone,' Dante said, and the closest gunman gave him the twice-over.

'He's busy,' the man replied, punching at the words.

'Tell him it's Dante the Gent.'

At the mention of the name the gunman frowned, as if a ghost had just introduced himself, then a look of realization was chased across his face by a look of worry. The gunman nodded at one of his colleagues, who nodded back and slipped through the glass door into the funeral parlor.

Dante smiled at the remaining guards and lit a cigarette. He heard a roaring noise in the air, and along with the rest of the throng he looked up to see two planes soaring like a scream against the sky. The crowd gasped and rippled as the planes swooped low, then the pilots turned the machines upwards and flew toward the sun, disappearing into its blaze.

The crowd set to wondering what was going on, and Dante turned his eyes back down to earth, took off his hat and wiped some sweat from his brow, hoping the gunman would come back soon and he'd be admitted to the funeral parlor, to get out of the heat. He had been hoping that by leaving New York he would avoid the sweltering temperatures there, but if anything, Chicago looked like it would be even worse for it this summer.

Four days earlier Dante had been on his rum-runner boat in the waters off Long Island. Ever since the start of prohibition, three miles off the coast, just far enough away to be in international waters, a daisy chain of boats selling liquor had sprung up. Going by the name of Rum Row, it ran from Florida in the south to Maine in the north, and the busiest knot of boats on the whole line was the *Rendezvous*, to which the restaurateurs and cabaret men of New York caught speedboats each night, in search of high-quality imported booze.

Among the flotilla of boats that made up the *Rendezvous*, Dante had the reputation for selling the best liquor of all. He personally tested every crate – at great risk considering some of the poisons that were passed off as alcohol. And it was there off Long Island, among the floating warehouses, that a motor launch had approached one night and Dante had been informed by the men on it that his presence had been requested back in Chicago by his old friend Mr Capone. Dante's mind had raced to the city of his birth, a city on fire with gangland murders and bombings, a beacon of urban chaos, burning like a sunset over the Midwestern plains. He left his business operation in the hands of the two men he worked the boat with – a grizzled former crab fisherman from Florida and the man's grandson – and he packed his bags for Chicago.

Four days later, standing outside the Sbarbaro & Co. Undertaking Rooms, he was still none the wiser as to what Capone wanted. He had put feelers out in New York before he left; subtly, trying to gauge what might be the reason, but all he got back was what he already knew – that the tit-for-tat bombings and killings had quietened down after the elections in the spring, that the deadly gang war between Capone and Bugs Moran had abated, and that the city was on the edge of an uneasy truce; still split down the middle between the two, with both armies on standby, a pair of cymbals ready to crash. And Dante had been dragged to the center of it all by a draft it was impossible to dodge.

As he dwelled on it, the door to the funeral parlor opened, the gunman exited and nodded at his colleague, and the colleague turned to look at Dante.

'Mr Capone will see you now.'

2

Ida Davis stood at the window of her office on the ninth floor of the Pinkerton National Detective Agency building and tried to catch something of the tepid breeze that was wheezing in from outside. A thin sheen of sweat was prickling the skin between her shoulder blades, threatening to drip down her back and soak through the cotton of her blouse. The sun had only been up a few hours and already the skies were silky with heat, the city roasting, set to endure another day in the endless heatwave that was unfurling through the summer.

On the avenue far below, the morning traffic was crawling along. Sunshine glinted off running boards and grilles, and even the road itself was shining with unusual ferocity, a ribbon of blazing light stretching away in either direction, making blotches of Ida's vision, forcing her to squint.

On the corner opposite, a homeless Negro woman was screaming to no one in particular in a thorny, worn-out voice that the unnatural heat of that summer was the beginning of the end of times, that Chicago – modern Gomorrah, city of wicked and greedy men – was about to burn in the sweep of the Angel Gabriel's fiery blade. A little further along the sidewalk, two beat-cops were approaching her with their hands on their nightsticks, shoulders hunched like boxers.

Ida closed her eyes a moment and hoped for an end to the hot spell, for the coolness of autumn, the blue light of winter. Somewhere in the distance she heard a church bell tolling nine, but the sound was weak against the roar of the city. She had lived in Chicago for almost ten years, but the constant noise of the metropolis, the unearthly growl of it, was something she could never quite get used to.

Then in the distance she heard a mechanical whine and opened her eyes to see two planes arcing through the sky like a pair of iron lovebirds. She frowned, watched them a moment, then turned her gaze back down to see what had happened with the raspy-voiced prophet, but neither the woman nor the policemen were anywhere to be seen, just the unstoppable flow of pedestrians cascading along the sidewalk, the traffic unleashing its miasma of pollution into the air, where it swirled and shimmered in the heat, warping and distorting the view.

'You all right?' asked a voice from inside the office.

Ida turned to see Michael, who was seated at his desk, looking up at her from some paperwork.

She nodded. 'Just soaking in the car fumes.'

Michael smiled, then there was a knock at the door and they both straightened up.

'Mrs Van Haren,' announced the receptionist, poking her head around the edge of the door frame. She backed out of the room and a tall, thin, middle-aged woman stepped into the space vacated and strode toward them. She was dressed in a suit of gunmetal grey that hung off her frame in a way that suggested recent weight loss, recent grief. On her head was a cloche hat with a peacock feather tucked into its brim, and as she approached, the feather wafted in time with her step, a jauntiness that seemed at odds with her otherwise somber demeanor.

'Mrs Van Haren,' said Michael, standing and holding out his hand to the two seats opposite him.

The woman sat in one chair, and Ida sat in the other, and when they were settled an awkward smile ricocheted between the three of them.

'I'm Michael Talbot and this is my colleague, Ida Davis,' said Michael, and the woman eyed them both before a flummoxed expression crossed her face. Ida knew the look; the woman was unsure of the etiquette involved, having never before consorted with anyone as outlandish as a pair of detectives, especially a pair as outlandish-looking as Michael and Ida.

'Thank you for your time,' the woman said, in a voice as prim as her appearance. 'Do you mind if I smoke?'

Michael shook his head. As Mrs Van Haren took a cigarette case from her handbag, Ida took in the woman's platinum rings and manicured nails. She lit her cigarette with a shaking hand and inhaled deeply. There was something cold about her, something poised and severe, an icing of rigidity with which she was trying to hide her jitteriness.

The previous day, when they'd heard that a Mrs Van Haren had booked an appointment with them, Ida had done a little digging, had found out it was one of *the* Van Harens who was coming to visit; one of Chicago's most distinguished families, and until recently, one of its richest. There was talk in the financial press of the family business being mismanaged, of plummeting earnings per share, profit warnings, investor unrest. There was also talk in the society pages of the family's heiress daughter becoming engaged to a Charles Coulton Junior, a man from a family of greater, but more recent, wealth whose new-money status caused the articles Ida had read to be laced with jibes and snobbery.

'You're the detectives that solved the Brandt kidnapping?' Mrs Van Haren asked, and Michael nodded.

'And the First National gold robbery?' she continued, and Michael nodded once more. They'd also solved dozens of other cases over their years in Chicago – blackmails, burglaries, murders, heists – most of which had never made it into the papers, much to Ida's relief. The woman must have asked someone who the best detectives in Chicago were, and been pointed in their direction. And now she was trying to match up the two unlikely Southerners before her with whatever notions her imagination had conjured up from the press reports she'd read.

Michael, the non-imaginary version, was somewhere past fifty years old, as tall and thin as Mrs Van Haren; his face had been heavily scarred by smallpox, something that made him look ghoulish in a certain light, pitiful in another, and had the benefit of giving him a strangely ageless quality. Ida was twenty-eight and unusually beautiful, if a little awkward, a girl whose defining characteristic was that she was a Negro light-skinned enough to pass for white, a trait that had left her feeling like a misfit for most of her life. The pair of them spoke with New Orleans accents, the easy-flowing cadence marking them out as migrants from that dark city at the other end of the Mississippi from Illinois, brought to Chicago on the same river that before them had brought voodou and jazz, cholera epidemics and tens of thousands of the South's poor.

Ida met the woman's gaze as it lingered over her and she smiled, and the woman smiled back in a strained way before taking another fierce drag on her cigarette, the grey of the smoke swirling about the grey of her dress. Ida usually felt uncomfortable in the company of those born into great wealth; it had been her experience that behind the gentility there always lurked a contempt, a sense of entitlement, a confident belief that the world had been especially reserved for them. But with this woman, she wasn't so sure.

'My daughter has gone missing,' she said eventually, a tremor in her voice.

'When?' asked Michael.

'Three weeks ago.'

'And the police?'

'The police have made no headway into finding her, and knowing the police in this city, I doubt they ever will.'

Michael shared a look with Ida. Police incompetence and laziness were to be expected in Chicago – but not when the family being dealt with was the Van Harens.

'Where was she last seen?' asked Ida.

'Marshall Field's. One of our drivers dropped her off outside the store and that was the last anyone saw of her.'

'Had she been acting unusually in the days before she disappeared?' asked Michael.

'No, Mr Talbot,' the woman said. 'There was no unhappiness, no fretting, no angst.'

Ida thought back to the society pages she had read the previous day. Judging from the articles, the daughter seemed to split her time between the usual high-society events and putting in long shifts doing charity work at Jane Adams House and a project in Hyde Park helping young Negroes from the Southside.

In the photos, Ida had spotted something odd – a clue in the missing daughter's clothing – that made her question whether Mrs Van Haren was telling the truth about her disappearance.

'My daughter was about to get married,' she continued. 'And that, perhaps, is the strange thing about this – her fiancé has also disappeared.'

'And you don't believe they eloped?' asked Michael.

Mrs Van Haren shook her head.

'We approved of the marriage. The wedding was to be one of the highlights of the summer. And then a few weeks before the ceremony, both of them disappear. From different places. On the same day.'

'And the fiancé?'

'Still missing also,' she replied flatly, looking down at the cigarette in her hand. 'I've been over it a million times. If it was kidnap then why no ransom note? If she has wound up in a hospital, or God forbid, a morgue, then why hasn't she been recognized? If she was being blackmailed, then why didn't she ask for money? If she ran away with some lover, then why did her fiancé also disappear? It doesn't make sense. How can one of the richest, most beautiful girls in the city disappear off a sidewalk in the middle of the day?'

Mrs Van Haren looked at them as if she'd asked them a riddle, a crossword clue that was infuriating her.

'It doesn't make sense,' she repeated, desperation seeping into her voice. She mumbled something, then started shaking, and Ida could see the ice was cracking; a moment later she burst into tears, and her previously grey face was suffused with blood. She fumbled a handkerchief from her purse, more to hide behind than to dab away tears, and Ida leaned over and put her arm around her, felt the woman's body shake and convulse.

'Gwendolyn is my only child,' she continued. 'Can you imagine the terror of not knowing what has happened to her?'

She opened up her handbag, took a photograph from it and passed it to Ida. It was a studio shot showing a woman in her early twenties seated in front of a floral screen, wearing a Canton dress of printed crepe, her hair marceled into a wave and dotted with pearls. Ida recognized the girl from the social pages of the newspapers. Gwendolyn Van Haren was strikingly beautiful, a gracious kind of beauty, containing as it did a hint of strength in the high cheekbones and forthright stare.

She passed the photo to Michael, who looked at it for a few seconds, then put the tips of his index fingers together, and Ida, seeing the sign, nodded back at him.

'We'd be happy to look into your daughter's disappearance,' he said and Mrs Van Haren stared at him for a long moment, almost in disbelief, before a smile scrabbled onto her face, a weak-looking smile that was out of practice, unsteady on its feet, a smile that got Ida's sympathy purely because it seemed to be struggling so very hard just to exist.

'Thank you, Mr Talbot, Miss Davis,' she said, her voice warmed by a rekindling of hope. 'Thank you.'

She sniffed and dabbed at her tears again, and the peacock feather in her hat moved about jauntily; Ida looked up at it, and the eye at the center of the feather seemed to stare back at her in an accusing sort of way.

'May I ask where your husband is?' Michael asked.

'He's away overseeing business out west,' she replied stiffly.

Ida wondered exactly what she meant. The family had made its money on the railroads, helping set up Chicago as the nation's main transportation hub. But now the family money seemed to rest solely in investments, and bad ones at that, and Ida wondered what business could be more important to a man than the job of finding his own daughter, and consoling his tormented wife.

'What are the next steps?' Mrs Van Haren asked.

'We'll see what the police reports have to say, and take it from there.'

'You'll be consulting with the police on this?' she asked, and for the first time there was an edge in her voice, and the handkerchief in her hand increased its trembling ever so slightly.

'We have friends in the Police Department,' said Michael, using as vague a terminology as possible for the army of corrupt cops the agency had arrangements with. 'Under the circumstances, I'm sure they'll be willing to grant us access to the case files.'

He smiled and Mrs Van Haren smiled back, uncertainly.

'I'd like to ask for your discretion in this,' she said. 'The police, despite their many failings, have kept quiet.'

'We keep all client information confidential,' said Michael, and Mrs Van Haren nodded.

'After we realized she was missing,' said the woman, 'we – that is, my husband and I – put together a reward for her safe return. Fifty thousand dollars. We were to go to the papers with an announcement, but the police warned us against it. That money is still earmarked for whomever it is that finds my daughter, including you. I need to know what happened to her,' she said, the pleading tone returning to her voice. 'I need to know where she is.'

'That's a generous offer, Mrs Van Haren,' said Michael, 'but it's against company policy to accept enticements.'

She nodded, and fished about her purse for another cigarette.

A few minutes later, after they'd taken some further information, they were all standing and saying goodbye and Mrs Van Haren was walking out, face ashen once more, the feather bouncing resolutely in her cap.

'What do you think?' Michael asked after she had left.

'She's hiding something,' said Ida. 'And I'm guessing that fifty thou she mentioned was supposed to be hush money. She doesn't want the police involved and her husband's suspiciously absent.'

'As is the fiancé.'

Ida nodded and walked over to the window to catch the breeze once more. She thought again of the photos of Gwendolyn Van Haren she'd seen in the magazines and how they didn't tally with the story her mother had told. She peered out of the window a moment, and was glad to see that the homeless woman was on the street corner once more, screaming about the opening of the Seventh Seal, the throne of God, the devastated earth.

Ida turned and sat on the windowsill and looked at Michael.

'How *does* one of Chicago's most famous heiresses disappear off the street into thin air?' she asked.

'I don't know,' said Michael. 'Let's find out.'

3

The blood trail started in the heart of the Federal Street ghetto, on a cobbled road near the Rock Island and New York Central Railroad lines. In drips and splatters, it skipped northwards and turned a corner into a narrow alleyway, past broken crates, garbage cans, grease stains and scraps of rotting food, until it eventually stopped a few yards from the alleyway's other end, in a rich, syrupy puddle, on top of which lay the source of all that blood: the body of a middle-aged white male, finely dressed, spread-eagled, mutilated and dead.

There were two people in the alleyway with the corpse, a beat-cop and a crime-scene photographer. The rest of the officers had been sent out to canvass the locals, or man the cordon at the mouth of the alley, and the detectives who'd caught the case had gone to the pool hall around the corner to use the phone and await the Coroner's physicians.

The beat-cop, a lazy, scuffed-knuckle type, was supposed to be keeping an eye on the evidence, but was instead rolling a cigarette whilst leaning against the service entrance to the kitchen of the Mai Wah Noodle Palace, whose wall made up one half of the alleyway.

The photographer, who went by the name of Jacob Russo, was in the process of setting up his camera on a tripod to catch a close-up of the dead man's face.

Jacob was in his thirties, tall and rumpled, and he went about his business with the world-weary manner of a war correspondent. He locked his camera, a Voigtländer Bergheil, onto the base plate of the tripod; then he looked at the light around him, and tried to guess at the right exposure settings. The alleyway was so narrow, and the buildings either side of it so tall, that they managed to cut out all the sunlight, leaving the slender strip of asphalt they were on as shadowy and dark as an underground sewer. On top of that, the chop-suey joint whose wall the beat-cop was leaning against had a huge neon sign running down its corner, and the light from the sign was flooding into the alleyway from State Street, flashing purple and red in two-second intervals, washing over the dead body like an electric tide, ebbing and flowing: purple . . . red . . . purple . . . red . . .

'Like a goddamn carnival,' said the beat-cop, grinning at Jacob and popping his cigarette into his mouth. Jacob nodded back, though he'd thought the neon looked more like a warning beacon, an echo of things to come.

He turned to look at the mouth of the alley, at the sign stretching thirty feet up the corner of the building: *CHOP SUEY . . . NOODLES . . . CHOP SUEY . . . NOODLES . . .*

The words alternated with the image of a Chinese dragon, looking lost in its electric body, pondering the foreign soil below.

Jacob turned his attention from the sign to the corpse and studied it a moment. The victim was in his fifties, he guessed, and was dressed like a gangster – double-breasted suit adorned with a buttonhole carnation and a breast-pocket handkerchief, shoes patent leather, covered by spats. Not the type of man you'd expect to find dead in an alleyway in the most crime-addled part of the crime-addled Black Belt.

Stab wounds littered the man's sizable belly and chest, but it was his face – a tough, lined, mustachioed face – that caught Jacob's attention. The man's eyes had been gouged out. The eyeballs placed, quite daintily, a few inches from the head, where they lay atop the greasy asphalt like a pair of peeled lychees, catching the reflection of the neon sign, the dragon appearing at intervals on their glossy white domes.

After the stabbing and the gouging, the man had been finished off with hands around his throat – where there was a ring of blue and yellow bruises. What was left of his face bulged unnaturally, the blood having rushed into it during the strangulation, causing lips and nose and cheeks to swell, veins to pop, making the face less human and more like a plastic Mardi Gras mask, half melted in a fire. And on top of all of that, the face was flashing purple and red in two-second intervals.

The man's left hand was thrown back behind his head, the right stretched out sideways, almost touching the restaurant's trash cans, which were lined up along the wall and giving off a rich, pungent smell of rotting meat and fish sauce.

There was something peculiar about that hand.

Jacob shuffled over to get a closer look, lowering himself down onto the asphalt which felt strangely warm to the touch. He took a flashlight from the messenger bag at his hip, switched it on and shone it over the hand. There were shards of dark green glass buried deep in the skin of the man's palm and fingers, dozens of them, peppered all over. Then Jacob smelled it – the tang of champagne wafting off the glass-embedded skin, and beneath it, a chemical smell, sharp and burning. It had been years since he had smelled it, but he knew in an instant what it was – the scent of chemically altered alcohol.

He paused a moment to breathe, and a searing pain shot through his foot that brought him back to the here and now. He rose and stretched out his leg, flexing the wasted muscles around his ankle. He looked up to see the beat-cop smirking at him, but Jacob, accustomed to being treated like a joke by the Police Department, ignored the man and set about moving his tripod over to catch a shot of the victim's hand.

He readied the Voigtländer, then poured some magnesium powder into his flash lamp and raised it above his head. He pressed the shutter release and when he heard the camera's timer whirring he set off the flash lamp and there was a fireworks thump as the magnesium exploded and sent a wave of whiteness cascading around the alley, transporting them for an instant into a realm of dazzling nothingness.

Then the purple-red reality faded back into view and Jacob watched as the powder sent a cloud of smoke into the air which wafted toward the beat-cop and sent him off into a coughing fit.

'Goddammit,' the man said, shooting Jacob a venomous look through the gloom, wiping pearls of spittle from his lips.

Jacob suppressed a smile and made like he hadn't noticed. He slipped a dark slide into the camera and took out the plate, tossing it into his messenger bag. Then he leaned against the wall, lit a cigarette and looked again at the body: the two nightmarish craters where the eyes should have been, the third crater of the man's mouth, open as if he was still surprised at what had happened to him.

Jacob heard a noise and looked up toward the pale nickel of sunlight at the mouth of the alley. A car had pulled up on State Street and two men from the Coroner's Office hopped out, bulky leather Gladstone bags in their hands. They met the detectives, who were stepping out of the pool hall at about the same time, and after conferring a moment, they ducked under the cordon rope and headed into the alley.

'Ain't there no goddamn lights in here?' said the older of the two Coroner's physicians, squinting through the gloomy neon haze, prompting his assistant to take a flashlight from one of the Gladstone bags. He turned it on and as its beam cut an angle through the gloom the men got to work on the body.

'What's the nearest funeral parlor to here?' asked the lieutenant.

'Gracie's. Two blocks away,' replied the younger of the two doctors without looking up. 'It's a coon place.'

'It'll do. Let's get wrapped up here quick. Before the Chinks next door put the body on the menu.'

The lieutenant grinned at his own joke, and Jacob made eye contact with the younger detective. They nodded at each other.

The young detective turned and headed back toward the mouth of the alley, and Jacob followed him. They stepped out onto State Street, and were blinded by the sunlight a moment; then the young detective – Frank Lynott – produced a pack of cigarettes from his jacket pocket.

'Your limp's worse,' he said. 'You okay?'

Jacob nodded. It always happened when he kneeled for too long. If he did his stretches and stayed mobile, people hardly noticed his limp, but after sleep, or after crouching, or after any period of inactivity, he moved with a noticeably uneven gait.

Lynott lit up and they surveyed the scene on the street: a group of young men were milling about the cordon at the mouth of the alley; others were heading into the pool hall or the noodle parlor; taxis were looking for fares.

A few hours earlier, when the man was being killed in the alleyway, just a few yards away State Street would have been alive and jumping, with the clubs open, and music blaring, and gin hawkers working the queues. But no one had noticed the asphalt tango going on in the alley. Or if they had, they hadn't concerned themselves with it.

'You manage to get anything good before the Coroner's men got to work?' Lynott asked, turning to look at Jacob with a sly grin.

'Sure,' Jacob replied, wiping a sheen of sweat from his brow.

Coroner's physicians were appointed on the Coroner's personal recommendation, and the recommendations had long since become an opportunity for backhanders. So of the twenty-six currently working in Chicago, not a single one actually had any experience as a pathologist, and only one was affiliated with a hospital: a consultant on a children's ward. All of which meant it was only a matter of time before the two doctors in the alleyway compromised, contaminated or destroyed any evidence remaining. And both Jacob and Lynott knew it.

'The attack started somewhere nearby,' Jacob said. 'In an

alcohol stash spot between here and the Rock Island railroad tracks. He was stabbed there, but he managed to get out, probably by smashing a champagne bottle into his attacker's face. He stumbled all the way here, by which point he'd lost too much blood from the stabbing, so he collapsed. The killer followed the blood trail, caught up with him, pulled that trick with the eyeballs, then strangled him.'

'Jesus. He gouged his eyes out while he was still alive?'

'I think so. Strangler victims' eyes fill with blood from the pressure. Those ones on the street are as white as marble.'

'And the rest of it?' asked Lynott.

'He's got glass embedded in his hand. Dark green glass, thick. And his hand smells of champagne. Means he was attacked somewhere there were champagne bottles nearby. He picked one up and retaliated. The blood trail leads back to the railroad tracks. There's no bars or cathouses down that way, so the only other places there'd be champagne at hand would be a bootlegger's stash spot. Plus the man's dressed like a gangster, so he was probably down here doing business and something went wrong. I'd check the hospitals for anyone admitted looking like they'd had a bottle wrapped into their face. If they're not the killer, they're at least a witness.'

Jacob paused and thought of telling Lynott about the caustic smell on the dead man's hands, but after a moment he decided against it, not sure if a faint, almost indiscernible scent that he might have imagined really constituted evidence. They both smoked silently and stared out at State Street a while.

The two men had grown up on the same block, had both dreamed of becoming detectives. But Jacob had been barred from entrance because of his leg, so Lynott had put him forward for the job of crime-scene photographer, and Jacob had landed it. He visited crime scenes, developed the prints, studied the minutiae, cultivated an eye for what was important. And this was the reason why he was a standing joke in the Police Department – Jacob was an outsider with a limp and more talent than any detective in the division.

On the opposite sidewalk, the door to one of the cheap hotels that lined the street opened up, and a couple stepped out into the glaring sun, rubbing their eyes, looking dog tired and sleepless. The man, a Negro, and the woman, a blonde, nodded at each other and wordlessly went their separate ways. That was something else about the Black Belt – black men with white women, white men with black women – the mixing that occurred in the city's 'Black and Tan' interracial jazz clubs often ended up in the flea-ridden hotel rooms that overlooked the strip.

Something about the scene tugged at Jacob's thoughts, a memory waiting in the shadows, just outside the spotlight of his consciousness.

'What is it?' asked Lynott, who'd noticed him frowning at the hotel front.

'I dunno. Something about this reminds me of something. Like I've seen it all before.'

'You seen a guy get stabbed, have his eyes gouged out and strangled?'

'When you put it like that, you'd think I'd remember.'

They grinned at each other and carried on smoking.

'There's something else bugging me about those eyeballs,' said Jacob.

'That they're looking at the trash cans?'

'The vic got killed in the middle of the night. He's been there hours. How comes no rats ran off with them?'

He turned to look at Lynott, and Lynott shrugged, and Jacob continued to mull over the murder. As hellish as the crime scene was, what tugged at his thoughts was the image of the couple leaving the hotel. He had a sense it was connected, and he wanted to know how.

'I'll get someone to see where those blood trails start,' said Lynott after a moment. 'We better get back.'

Jacob nodded. They stepped out of the sunshine of State Street back into the shadow of the alleyway, becoming shadows themselves except for the tips of their cigarettes, which glowed red in the gloom.

4

Dante sat at the back of the funeral parlor's viewing room alone but for the corpse, which had been laid out in a casket at the front, surrounded by a few thousand dollars' worth of delphiniums and irises. The casket lid was latched back and open – a big deal for Sicilians: the casket had to be open for two days and two nights for the soul to ascend to heaven. The belief had led to some of the underworld's more moronic hitmen finishing off their victims with a shotgun blast to the face, ensuring a disfigurement, a closed casket, purgatory, hell.

This old man's face, though, was damaged by nothing more than the buffeting of life – a few wrinkles, grey hair, a smattering of liver spots. The casket was lined with blue velvet, and the corpse was dressed in a blue suit with a blue rose in its lapel. Dante wondered if the color theme was some dying wish, or if the man's friends had simply gone overboard.

In the silence, he heard the drone of the planes overhead once more, then something closer, footsteps, and he turned to see three men enter the room: Al, his brother Ralph, and his bodyguard Frank Rio. Al grinned when he saw Dante, and Dante grinned back, trying to cover up his shock at how much Al had changed in the six years since they'd last met.

They crossed the room and embraced, then Al stood back and they regarded each other. Al was much fatter than Dante remembered, balder too, and strangely pale, looking ten years older than he actually was. The fine food, cigars, booze, cocaine, the stress of forever having to guard against assassins and intrigues – all the ingredients of *la malavita* were taking a devastating toll on Al Capone.

'Long time, Dante,' said Al in his trademark soft-spoken voice, barely louder than a mumble. 'How's the Big Apple?'

'Ripe for the picking.'

Al flashed him a grin, and slapped him on the back.

Dante and Al had run together years before, both of them up-and-comers in Torrio's Mob. But while Dante had left Chicago and wandered across the country like a haunted ghost, Al had stayed in the city and become the overlord of its underworld, ending up in charge of an organization that controlled most of the booze, gambling and prostitution in the city, that turned over a hundred million dollars a year, out of which Al paid for the elections of mayors, governors and senators. Prohibition had un-leashed the biggest crime wave in American history, and Al had ridden it all the way to the top. If there was an undisputed winner of the Volstead game, it was the prematurely aged twenty-nine-year-old standing in front of Dante, five foot seven, grey eyes, hair the color of bark, a knowing smile playing on his lips.

Dante said hello to Frank, and then to Al's brother Ralph, who coldly nodded back a greeting. Ralph 'Bottles' Capone was just one of the brothers involved in running the organization. While Al was the Outfit's outer face, always dressed to perfection in dazzling suits, smiling for photo shoots, turning up at galas and sporting events and political rallies, Ralph took care of beer dis-tribution.

'Condolences on your loss,' said Dante, nodding toward the casket.

'He had it coming,' said Al. 'Last viewing's about to start, let's talk.'

They pulled some chairs into a horseshoe and sat, and Al leaned back, moving into a beam of light coming in from the windows, casting the scars on the side of his face into bright relief. Al was painfully conscious of the scars, three of them, bumpy and purple, raked from his ear to under his chin. He'd caught them years before in a barroom brawl in Brooklyn, and he used a mix of talcum powder and concealer to cover them up. This attempt at controlling his image didn't work, so among Al's numerous nicknames – Snorky, King Alphonse, Al Brown – was the one he detested, Scarface.

Al looked at Dante a moment before he spoke.

'We got a traitor in the Outfit,' he said. 'I want you to smoke him out.'

Dante thought a moment, surprised by the request, but trying not to let it show on his face.

'Ralph,' said Al, nodding to his brother, 'you wanna fill Dante in?'

Ralph nodded and cleared his throat.

'About three weeks ago there was a poisoning at the Ritz. Some of Big Bill Thompson's group booked out a private room for a shindig. Food, girls, cards, booze. The mayor was there, the governor, two former senators, the State's Attorney, the head of the Employers' Association, a judge at the municipal court. They got served a round of champagne before the meal and an hour later two of them were in the morgue and the rest were in hospital having their stomachs pumped.'

Dante nodded. The list of men was a who's who of the Capone-sponsored end of the Republican Party. If the booze had done its work more thoroughly, Capone's political base would have been all but wiped out. And worse still, the press and the government would have turned their attention onto the Outfit, and special censure would have rained down from the murky agencies in Washington being set up to deal with exactly this kind of organized crime.

'Poison booze?' asked Dante.

Ralph nodded, and Dante pretended to think.

'Our boy at the hotel ran interference on any press stories and tried to figure out where the batch they'd been served had come from. He traced it through front-of-house into the kitchen and from there to one of our deliveries.' Ralph jabbed at his own heart, indicating that someone in the Outfit had supplied the killer alcohol.

'I picked it up at our end, traced the delivery. The batch had come from one of our warehouses. It had been driven out to the Ritz in one of our vans, by two of our boys, and the two boys and the van were nowhere to be seen. Until three days later when they turned up in a field outside Lockport, burned to a crisp with bulletholes in their heads. We've been digging into it from every angle, and none of it makes sense. Like Al said, it looks like someone on the inside is trying to take us out, but we ain't got a clue who.'

Ralph held up his hands and Dante nodded.

'And it's not Moran?' he asked, turning to look at Al.

Bugs Moran was the head of the Northside Gang, Al's main rivals in the city. He had a penchant for leather jackets and was nicknamed 'Bugs' because he was buggy, crazy, homicidally violent and not very clever. Moran had made more than a dozen attempts on Al's life in a little over a year and a half, until Al had called a peace conference at the Hotel Sherman and they'd agreed to divide the city between them. The truce was still holding, shakily, but everyone knew the slightest tremor could send it tumbling.

'If Moran was behind it, someone would be bragging,' said Al, shaking his head. 'I put out feelers and no one's talking. Plus it ain't his style and he ain't got nothing to gain by doing it on the down-low. I can't start another war without knowing for sure.'

'And the two casualties?'

'Borelli and Scanlan copped it. Borelli was a two-bit alderman in one of the river wards, Scanlan worked for the Board of Trade. Small, Ford and Crowe ended up in hospital.'

'And the mayor was all right?'

'He had his stomach pumped,' said Ralph. 'He's fine now, but his presence there complicates the situation.'

Mayor 'Big Bill' Thompson – one of Chicago's most corrupt politicians – had backed Capone for years, and Capone had backed him. But when Thompson had been re-elected the previous spring, he'd got it into his head that he could make a run for the presidency. He'd started building bridges and roads, an airport, creating jobs, and clamping down on his former mobster friends, raiding nightclubs and breweries, despite the fact Capone had contributed over a quarter of a million dollars to his re-election campaign, and Bugs Moran fifty thousand. Now that he'd been poisoned in a Capone-supplied hotel, the mayor might have every reason to suspect Capone himself had been behind it.

Al stared at Dante, and Dante's eyes again flicked to the makeup and scars, and he thought of Red Indians painting their faces before battle.

'What do you think?' Al asked, and Dante blew air through his teeth.

'It could be someone with a grudge against one of the people at the party came up with a bullshit plan for poisoning them. Or it could be what you're worried about . . .' Here he stopped to look at the three of them and noted the concern on their faces. The second possibility was that the poisoning was an attack on the politicians because, the mayor excluded, they were paid-up Capone lackeys; then Al was facing an out-and-out attack on his organization.

'If it was aimed at you,' continued Dante, 'then I think you got a helluva mess to deal with. And seeing as you've asked me all the way out here to Chicago, I'm guessing I've got a helluva mess to deal with, too.'

Dante smiled and Al stared at him a moment, and Dante got worried that maybe his levity had been misplaced. Good moods were delicate things with Al, ripped apart on the slightest snag. Al could be charming and courteous one second, murderous the next. For all his refinement and elegance, back in the Torrio days, it was Al who had run the torture chamber in the basement of the Four Deuces Club. And recently Dante had heard rumors back in New York from his friends Lansky and Luciano that Al had been behaving ever more erratically, ever more unhinged.

But then Al flashed a smile back and shrugged his shoulders, and Dante relaxed a touch.

'Yeah, that's about the size of it,' he said.

'Why me?' asked Dante.

'Ain't no point having an insider look for a traitor. You wanna audit, you call someone from the outside. You built up a good reputation for being a fixer out in New York. I'll pay you, and when it's all over, I'll cancel your debt. We got a traitor in our midst, Dante. I need you to find him. What do you say?'

Dante paused a moment to take in his situation. He had already reconciled himself to accepting the job. He was in hock to Al from six years earlier, when he had rushed out of Chicago, and now Al was calling in the debt. He tried to gauge his slim chances of finding the traitor, his slimmer chances of getting through it alive, and the slimmest chance of all – that through the whole operation, Al wouldn't discover Dante's secret and take him out himself. Between Dante and his goal was an unfathomable void where the future would play its tricks, but his only choice was to make the leap.

Ten minutes later, he stepped out of the funeral parlor and into the heat and verve of the scene outside. The crowds had been pushed back for the cortege to assemble, workers were loading the wreaths onto carriages, a fleet of policemen on motorcycles were arranging the escort. Dante stopped a moment in the shade of the funeral home's entrance, lit a cigarette and turned to look at the gunman by his side.

'You really Dante the Gent?' asked the gunman.

'Why d'you sound so surprised?'

The gunman shrugged, suddenly looking youthful and naive.

'Cuz everyone thought you were dead.'

Dante thought a moment.

'Stick around,' he said, and the gunman laughed.

Then the doors behind them opened up and they stood aside as the pallbearers walked out, straining under the weight of the platinum casket. They negotiated the steps and placed the casket on the horse-drawn carriage at the head of the procession, passing by a quartet of men wearing silk sashes identifying them as members of the Chicago Opera Company. Dante watched them a moment, then he craned his neck to see how far back the cortege went.

When a gangland war was underway, tit-for-tat killings were followed by tit-for-tat funerals, with each gang trying to make their buddy's send-off more impressive than their rival's from the week before. And so Mob funerals spiraled in their opulence, becoming ever more monstrous and bloated with flowers.

'Twenty-five carriages just for the bouquets,' said the gunman. 'Thirty limousines too. Sbarbaro said the cortege would be a mile and a half long.'

Dante nodded. 'That's not a cortege, that's a homecoming parade.'

The gunman laughed, and Dante imagined the disruption the cortege would cause as the fifteen miles of road between the Sbarbaro and the Mount Carmel cemetery were closed down.

'So you really Dante the Gent?' the gunman asked again.

'Maybe I am,' said Dante, and he raised his hat to the boy and ambled onto the sidewalk. He passed the motley mix of mourners assembled there – bootleggers, racketeers, aldermen, assassins, congressmen, pimps and priests – so tight-knit that any person watching was left in no doubt as to the level and extent of the corruption eating away at the city. Even the undertaker himself embodied it. John Sbarbaro, as well as being the funeral director of choice for the city's gangsters, was also one of the city's judges.

Dante slipped through the crowd, which seemed to have grown denser, and as he reached the corner of Grand Avenue, the marshal blew his trumpet to signal the procession was underway, and the two planes came back, flying overhead, swooping down so low the crowd let out worried cries, and everyone looked up, and the planes were already blocks away.

Then they banked, and turned and headed back over the procession, and when they were above the throng once more, the bottoms of the planes opened up, and from their bowels was unleashed a downpour of blue flower petals. It was as if the airplanes' propellers were churning up the sky itself, slicing it into blue flakes which waltzed their way to earth.

When they realized what was happening, the crowd gasped as if they were at a fireworks display. Dante shook his head and wondered again what it was about gangsters and flowers. And even as he turned his back on it all and headed east, the petals were covering hats and clothes and smiling faces, as if the city had been caught under a sudden storm of blue snow.

5

Like many of Chicago's twenty-five thousand speak-easies, the saloon on the corner of Madison and Wells Streets was technically a 'cordial store'; a place where adults went to drink sodas, seltzers and colas till four o'clock in the morning. 'Cordial stores' became so widespread that the notion of them stopped being preposterous and they became instead an accepted aspect of city life, bothering no one except Chicago's few remaining Anti-Saloon League members.

To stop people in the street from looking into the store, the front windows were packed thickly with a display of the bottled drinks it was supposed to be selling: Coca-Cola, Dr Pepper, Canada Dry ginger ale, root beer, lime cordial. On a sunny day like today, the display of bottles created a stained-glass effect which washed over everything in the place: the bar, the tables, the afternoon crowd, all of them glowing with blotches of garish color, adding an air of impishness to the illegal drinking going on inside.

Michael was seated in one of the booths along the back wall, waiting for Ida while she got them their drinks. He happened to be sitting in a patch of purple light beaming in through a grape-soda bottle and it caused the people walking past to cast him wary looks. For some reason purple made the smallpox scars on his face seem especially freakish. He lit a cigarette and watched Ida through the mirrors behind the bar as she waited her turn, standing next to some office girls who were howling at the jokes of a few clerks trying their luck.

Men and women drinking together in bars was one of the

ironies of prohibition. Back in the old days saloons looked to distance themselves from accusations they were brothels by refusing women entry. But speak-easies, by definition already illegal, had no reason to stop them, and so women flocked to the new drinkeries, meaning the law which was supposed to drag men out of the bars, ended up dragging women into them. Michael had heard from numerous saloon-keepers that the reason the number of bars in the city had trebled since the start of prohibition was the presence of women; and he had heard from numerous policemen that the reason the number of murderesses had trebled in the same time, was the presence of bars.

Ida ordered three schooners of beer, paid, and headed back to the table, moving through the crowd slender as a knife. Michael was proud of his protégée, the best, most natural detective he had ever worked with. He thought about the nineteen-year-old slip of a girl he'd met almost a decade ago, a shivering, uncertain Southerner in the big city for the first time. The Pinkertons had taught her how to shoot a gun, pick a lock, drive a car, shadow a suspect; how to interrogate, bribe, coerce, coax, calculate – but all those skills were just refinements of a natural talent.

She reached the booth, sat and passed him a glass, and they both drank. Then Michael took the photo of Gwendolyn Van Haren from his pocket and placed it flat on the table.

'She's not the kind of woman who melts into the background,' said Ida, picking up Michael's silver cigarette case from the table and helping herself to a Virginia Slim. Michael nodded and looked over the photo once more: the heiress in her perfect dress, beautiful, elegant and regal. But despite her natural bearing, there was something haunting her features, a melancholy, a forlornness, a distance, that oddly reminded him of Ida.

There was an eruption of laughter from the bar, and Michael and Ida looked up to see the office girls cackling once more and the clerks patting themselves on the back. Then the front door opened and a man in a brown cotton suit entered. He spotted them through the crowd and headed their way. Lieutenant Ralph Stockman was short, pudgy and easygoing, and worked missing persons in the Detective Division.

'How's my two favorite Pinks?' he said, flashing Ida a smile.

'Doing good, Ralph. We got you a beer,' said Michael, sliding the drink across the table. Ralph sat and took a long swallow.

'This goddamn heat,' he said, taking off his hat. 'I think it's making me lose my mind.'

He sighed and passed them over a slim paper folder: the division's investigation into Gwendolyn Van Haren's disappearance.

'Mullens and me caught the case,' he said.

'And?'

'And it's an odd one, even after you've accounted for the pedigree of the girl. She woke up one morning, asked the family driver to take her shopping, stepped onto the sidewalk in front of Marshall Field's in the middle of the midday rush and disappeared. Into thin air.'

Ralph made a waggling motion with his fingers, a magician casting a spell.

'We spoke to the people at Marshall Field's and no one remembers her entering. The Van Harens have an account there – when one of them visits, they know about it. We canvassed the locals and no one remembers seeing her. Took her photo up one side of the Loop and down the other. Not a thing. Then we drove over to chez Van Haren, and that's when things got interesting. We didn't get any leads, but there was a damn strange atmosphere in that house. Mullens and me both picked up on it.'

'Strange how?' asked Ida.

'I dunno. It wasn't just the usual unhappy-rich-folks strange. I can't put my finger on it. But it was like every one o' them had something to hide – the mother, the father, the driver, that goddamn butler. Couldn't get a bean out of one of 'em. So we came back to the division, typed up our reports, and the chief took the file off us before the ink was dry.'

Ida and Michael shared a look. Captain Hoban, the chief of the division, was a notorious Capone shill, and had for the last few years been looking to make a move into politics via a job opening in the State's Attorney's office – a job opening that never seemed to materialize.

'I'm guessing someone in City Hall leaned on him,' said Ralph, voicing what all three of them were thinking. 'Anyway, my take on it was the girl wanted to disappear. She got in a jam, went on the run, and now she's either drinking Margaritas in a Havana hotel, or the real world got the better of her and she's dead and buried in a coal cellar somewheres. Until anything new surfaces, the case is unofficially shit-canned.'

Michael nodded. The Van Harens had the political clout to get every cop in the division fired if they wanted to, and yet the captain was letting the case slide, and the mother had come to them begging for answers.

'You get anything on the fiancé?' Ida asked, and Ralph shook his head.

'None of our lot caught the case. If the fiancé did disappear, no one's reported him as an MP.'

Michael thought a moment.

'Thanks for this, Ralph,' he said.

'No problemo.'

'How's everything else at the station?'

'Jittery as hell,' said Ralph. 'Everyone's waiting for Capone versus Moran part two to kick off.'

He raised his eyebrows, then finished his beer in a long gulp, and picked his hat up off the table. Michael passed him an envelope stuffed with five-spots. Ralph nodded his thanks, then gestured to the folder on the table.

'I'll need that back first thing tomorrow morning,' he said.

'Sure thing,' said Michael.

Ralph smiled at them both, his eyes lingering on Ida a little too long, then he shimmied his way out of the booth and, as he headed off into the crowd, the gaudy spots of color beaming in from the windows shifted over his form.

Ida turned to look at Michael. 'What do you think?' she asked.

'First thoughts would be the fiancé killed her and ran away. That'd explain the simultaneous disappearances.'

'Or maybe it was the other way around.'

'Maybe, but she looks a little too delicate for that.'

'Maybe they both committed a crime and they ran away together,' Ida suggested.

'Maybe,' replied Michael, 'but that doesn't explain the jittery mother, and the jittery police captain, and the house full of people with secrets. And then there's what you found in your trawl through the gossip magazines.'

Ida had told him about her discovery, how at some point the previous Christmas, in all the photos in the press, Gwendolyn had started wearing long-sleeved gloves to every event she'd been photographed at. It made sense in the winter, but when spring rolled around, she was still wearing the gloves, even at the engagement party where she'd been showing off her diamond ring. Long gloves, needle marks, the scars of slit wrists.

'Suicide doesn't explain the missing fiancé,' said Ida.

'Neither does an overdose.'

'Maybe they're in hock to a gang of dope peddlers.'

They both went silent a moment. Then Ida finished her beer and stared at the empty glass.

'So, shall we discuss the fifty-thousand-dollar elephant in the room?' she asked, looking up at him.

Michael had been hoping she wouldn't bring it up.

'What's there to discuss?' he said. 'If we accept the money and anyone finds out, we lose our jobs. So we put the fact she made the offer in our meeting report, and refuse any payment.'

'Or,' said Ida, 'we don't put it in our report and keep the money if it's offered us . . .'

'I wouldn't be so certain the mother's going to pay out, even if we do find the girl. What if we find out she's dead? Or it turns out she killed herself because the father was abusing her? You think Mrs Van Haren's gonna pay to hear that?'

'Maybe not,' Ida conceded, 'but it's worth a shot. Fifty thousand, Michael. We can finally get out of the Pinks, start our own office, retire even. You could send your kids to college, move out of the Black Belt.'

He registered the exasperation in her voice. Both of them were getting sick of working for the Pinkertons. Interesting cases came along now and then, but much of the company's work was odious at best – breaking strikes, coercing witnesses, acting as political security. On top of that, the company stifled Ida's ambitions, always underplayed her role in their successes, despite Michael's protestations. But with a family to support, and no savings, Michael couldn't quit the job, as trapped as any of the other million or two wage slaves whose spirits the city harvested.

'This is a once-in-a-lifetime deal,' Ida continued. 'Fifty thousand dollars won't turn up again. Not for people like us. I say we risk it all. Keep the offer off the report and see what happens.'

'And if someone finds out and we both get fired? Detective jobs ain't exactly easy to come by.'

'They're a lot easier to come by than fifty thousand dollars. We don't have to file the report till tomorrow,' she said, in a softer tone of voice. 'All I'm saying is – think on it till then.'

He looked at her and saw her frustration, saw all the opportunities that had been denied her through her life, as a woman, as a Negro, frustrations Michael could only just appreciate. And now a rich white lady had turned up and dangled more money than they could make in a lifetime in front of them, and the only thing standing between them and it was Michael's skittishness.

'All right,' he said, 'I'll have a think on it.'

'Talk to Annette about it too,' she said with a mischievous smile, guessing Michael's wife would take Ida's side in the argument. Michael gave her a look, then smiled and shook his head, already getting the feeling he was being backed into a corner.

'So when do we go round to the Van Haren residence?' she asked.

'Tomorrow morning,' Michael replied. 'Let's spend the afternoon ringing around the hospitals, asylums and morgues. Maybe give someone in Narcotics a call. You never know, this case might be over before it's started.'

He finished his drink and they left the cordial store, stepping out into the heat and haze of Madison Street, where the cabs, carriages and touring cars were all caught up in a snarl of traffic that was somehow worse than usual. The sidewalks were overflowing with people, thousands of them, and Michael thought how hard it would be to find a girl in a city the size of Chicago. He put on his hat and thought of his own daughter and the pit of despair he'd face if she ever went missing. Why was it the older he got, the more easily his mind wandered down the path to hell?

His thoughts were interrupted by a whining noise far above them, and they looked up to see two planes flying south, heading toward the airfield near the lakeshore. They watched them a moment as they flew by, then a speck appeared in the air, something small and delicate swirling in the heat. Michael frowned at it, trying to figure out what it was, and after a few seconds, when it had wafted nearer, he realized – it was a single blue rose petal, a lone piece of confetti. Michael and Ida shared a look, confused as to where it could have come from. Then they watched as it floated the last few feet to earth, landed on the sidewalk, and was instantly turned to oil by the unceasing march of the pedestrians.

6

Jacob worked the crime scene till noon. Then he packed up his camera and tripod and left Bronzeville, catching a trolley north across the city through streets choking with traffic. He rested his head against the window frame and closed his eyes and imagined the heat becoming so strong it melted the road and the buildings too, the stone turning gooey, the whole city falling to earth in a great, grey sludge of cement. Then he opened his bleary eyes, realized he'd fallen asleep, and tried to stay awake till he reached his stop on Taylor Street.

Eventually he arrived, lugged his tripod and camera off the trolley, and walked the last few blocks to his building. He climbed the stairs, opened the door to his apartment and stepped into the living room. He put down the tripod and the camera, headed over to the windows, opened them up, then left again, descending five flights to the super's room in the basement. Like many of the building's residents, he rented a shelf in the super's refrigerator. He knocked and the super's daughter opened up, a teenaged, red-haired girl, listless and antsy in the heat.

He asked her to grab him a couple of the cold beers he had in the cooler, and he leaned against the door frame and watched as she approached the hulking white metal icebox in the apartment's kitchen, yanked open the handle and took the bottles out. Everywhere Jacob looked there were new and wonderful gadgets pushing them forward into the future – refrigerators, radio sets, vacuum cleaners, electric razors. But Jacob could afford pretty much none of them, not after he'd paid for his photographic equipment. The girl turned to see him staring in her direction, and

47

she smiled to herself, returned to the door and languidly held out the bottles for him to take. He thanked her and made his way back up the stairs.

By the time he'd returned to his apartment his ankle was throbbing, so he sat on the sofa and cracked open one of the beers. He waited a moment, then smelled the beer, and the beer smelled okay, so he took a sip. He lit a cigarette and looked across the room at the huge copperplate map of the city he'd pinned to the wall there – the only picture he'd ever brought into the apartment. He'd put it up when he'd got his first job as a crime-scene photographer. He'd started sticking little red pins in it, one for every scene he'd attended. But within a few months there were no spaces left around the areas that he was usually called to, so he'd abandoned the project, taken out the pins, and now there were just holes scattered across the map, perforating most thickly the neighborhoods that were highest in violence.

There was something a little uneven about the layout of the city, with the shoreline running top to bottom, the lake on the right, the city on the left, as if the whole of it was split into two ill-matched halves. His eye ran over the neighborhoods one by one: Bronzeville in the south, full of poor Negroes; the Gold Coast in the north, full of rich whites; the Loop in the center, with its banks and offices and fancy hotels; and next to it the Stockyards and the railyards; through to the jumble of ghettos beyond.

He looked again at the places where the pinholes were clustered most thickly and noted how the neighborhoods richest in crime also had the most colorful nicknames – the Black Belt, the Spaghetti Zone, the Bloody Nineteenth, Little Hell.

Chicago was the world's third-largest city, but it led the way in murders, bombings, hijackings, graft, bootlegging and kidnaps. Police officers only received a month's training before they were let loose on the streets, and as the department was short of detectives, those untrained men were as quickly promoted. It meant a third of all murders went unsolved, convictions for gangsters were non-existent, and the Police Department managed, on average, to accidentally kill an innocent citizen every week.

The situation left Jacob feeling as if every fool, robber and good-for-nothing had a job on the police force, while he – an intelligent, talented war hero – was barred from entry, all because of a bad leg. It was hard not to let the unfairness of it fill him with resentment and anger. Every now and then he caught himself composing rants in his head about the injustice, the stupidity. He tried to train himself out of it. He'd figured long ago the only way to deal with the situation was to work on cases regardless, ignore the fact that he wasn't allowed to have a badge and just do what he was good at. He picked crimes that he knew he could make a difference on, the unsolvable cases actual detectives couldn't be bothered with, the ones where the relatives were left feeling shortchanged.

In the years since he'd returned from the war he'd supplied the evidence that had led to dozens of convictions, all on cases the division had left to grow cold, and perhaps better than that, he'd helped prevent miscarriages of justice – he'd helped set free innocent men whom lazy or hateful cops had decided to frame. Every unusual case that came along was an opportunity to prove them all wrong, to assert himself against a system that wanted to keep him down.

He finished his beer and went into the darkroom. He pulled down the blinds, and hooked sheets of plasterboard over the sills to stop out the light. Then he switched on the overhead, and the room was flooded with a garish mix of red light and thick shadows. He closed the door, shoving a draft excluder against it, and got to work.

In the darkroom's stifling heat he conjured up, as if from the grave, the images of death he'd recorded that morning, bringing the horror back to life, extending its scream beyond the confines of the alley, releasing it back into the world by the magic of developing chemicals and fixative onto photographic cards in a palette of pearly white and grey. Then he took the photos out of the wash bath one by one, and hung them up with wooden clothes pegs onto the wires that criss-crossed the space.

By the time he was finished, over an hour later, he was drenched with sweat and feeling woozy. Nothing to do now but wait for them to dry. He stepped out of the room into the relative coolness of the rest of the apartment. He took a long, cold shower, changed into cotton trousers and a white vest, brushed his teeth, and went back to the living room. He grabbed the second beer and stepped through the window onto the fire escape, sat, lit a cigarette, and opened up the beer. He waited, then he drank and chained Lucky Strikes and passed the afternoon watching the view: the tenements close by, the elevated trains snaking between their rooftops, the pale skyscrapers beyond them, and the steam cranes raising yet more towers into the sky.

He watched the children playing in the street below, the housewives gathered around the porches. In the heat, people rushed to get outdoors. Some went to the park or the lake, or bought tickets to the cinemas which were air-cooled, or they sat on trolleys, by the windows, hoping for an artificial breeze as the cars looped through the city. But most just sat on front steps, or took chairs out onto the sidewalk, or laid down picnic blankets on paving stones and the wisps of grass that grew up in the cracks, the last sorry vestiges of the prairie.

And when evening turned to night, people dragged their mattresses out onto the fire escapes or rooftops to sleep in the cool there. In New York, which was sharing the dangerously hot weather, hundreds of people were decamping to Central Park every night – mattresses, blankets and alarm clocks in tow – and come six the next morning, the park was a-roar with alarm clocks going off. Jacob knew how it would pan out here; the communal feeling of the women and children in the afternoon would give way to drunken fights between the men in the night, the weather and the drink heating their anger to boiling point.

Someone somewhere switched on a radio and light music, crooning, wafted through the air. That was the other thing about the heat – open windows everywhere meant one radio, one record player, one piano, could infuse a whole neighborhood.

Jacob checked his watch and went back into the darkroom and separated out the prints. He'd made three sets: one for himself, one for the cops, one for the *Tribune*. Like most of the city's crime-scene photographers, he moonlighted with Chicago's bloodthirsty press. It was a conflict of interest that no one much minded – the newspapers got to print an unending stream of gore, and the police received backhanders and help from the editors if they ever needed it.

When the photos were in three neat piles Jacob flicked through them all, studying them one by one, looking for clues amongst the carnage, but all he saw was a parade of images both ghastly and mundane; blood splatters; a pinstripe suit; glass embedded in skin; a homburg hat lying in the bull's-eye of a white chalk circle; the eyeballs, also outlined in chalk, making them look oddly cartoon-ish.

Jacob sighed and carried on, checking the data that filled the frames, the cards placed next to each piece of evidence with reference numbers on them, dates, hours, distances. But nothing jumped out at him, and after more than a dozen rounds through the set, he laid them all out in a grid on the floor and checked them again; then when that didn't work he jumbled them up in a black-and-white confetti, hoping the randomness might spark something.

But it didn't.

As he stared at the dead man's image, he noticed a song coming in through the window – Ma Rainey's 'Deep Moaning Blues'. He closed his eyes and listened to the music, and couldn't help but feel that those blues had been written specially for this dead man, this unknown victim of the city.

In the darkness he saw once more the couple leaving the hotel. He knew the place well, had been called there often enough. It was only a hotel in the loosest sense of the word, more a flophouse for drunks and junkies and gangsters down-at-heel, for newly released convicts and transients of every description, a place where alcohol, firearms and fragile egos mixed together in a way that kept crime-scene photographers like Jacob in work, documenting the aftermath. The place also rented out rooms to hookers by the hour, or eager couples that had nowhere else to go.

And as Jacob thought on that, realization washed through his mind like a flood.

He jumped up and ran into the poky bedroom in which he stored his archive of old photos, started ripping open the envelopes in which they were kept. Four years earlier he'd attended another crime scene in the Black Belt where a man had been stabbed to death and had his eyes gouged out. A Negro man this time. In the flophouse on State Street.

Eventually he found the set he was looking for. Paul Kellett. The man had gone to the hotel with a white woman he'd picked up in a nightclub in the early hours of a Saturday morning in November. And another man had broken in on them, killed Kellett and nearly killed the girl, had left Kellett's eyeballs on the mattress, pupils pointed at the wall.

Jacob stared at the photos, a little faded, a little yellow in the corners, but there it was, an almost identical attack.

He shot into the living room and put a call through to the Detective Division at the 2nd District station, police HQ.

'Frank? It's Jacob.'

'What's up?'

'Paul Kellett.'

'What?'

'Negro. Killed in a State Street flophouse four years ago. Someone broke in and stabbed him to death and gouged his eyes out. It's identical.'

There was silence on the line for a few seconds before he heard Frank's voice again.

'Shit. I'll pull the files.'

Lynott hung up and Jacob put down the receiver, drumming his fingers on it, thinking how he could pass the time. He went back to the bedroom and fumbled all the envelopes back into place, save for the ones from the Kellett murder, all the while cursing himself for not having made the link earlier, worried that maybe forgetting such a gruesome case was a sign he'd seen too much murder and cruelty in his life.

Then his phone rang.

'You're not gonna believe this,' said Lynott when he'd picked up. 'A man named Anton Hodiak was convicted of the crime. A killing-floor worker. Hated blacks, especially ones that slept with whites. Killed Kellett and nearly killed the blonde he was sleeping with. Pulled the same trick a few days later on a different couple. Except this time he kidnapped the girl too. Kept her locked up in his apartment for a few weeks. Tortured her. Neighbors called the police on him after they heard her trying to break out. He received a death sentence in 1925, commuted to life a year later. Then he was pardoned by Governor Small last year and was released from Joliet in January. He's been on the loose in Chicago ever since.'

7

Michael stood amongst a clutch of straphangers as the streetcar rattled its way south, feeling faintly weary from his afternoon's work. He'd called all the morgues, hospitals and asylums in the city and its surroundings, checking with his people for any stray young blondes that had arrived in the last few weeks, claimed or unclaimed, but he'd drawn a blank with all of them. And the whole while he'd been thinking about Ida and Mrs Van Haren and the money, and whether to accept it. Even though he knew he couldn't make a decision till he got home and spoke to his wife.

He stretched out his back and rolled his head left and right to ease the tightness in his neck. Age was spreading through his body like a stain, making it feel bulky, unwieldy. Nowadays every bone had a fault, every tendon a kink, every muscle a knot. God only knew what would happen when the rest of it started to go.

As the streetcar moved ever southwards, more of the white passengers disembarked, and more Negroes boarded, until Michael was the only white left. When they reached the stops to the west of the Stockyards, the streetcar filled with workers knocking off their shifts, hard men, killers of cattle, life-beaten and worn-looking, swathed in the stench of dried blood. The smell mixed with the terrible heat of the day and soon enough the streetcar reeked like an abattoir and Michael had to fight the urge to put his free hand to his nose.

When they arrived at 47th Street he fought his way off and began the short walk home, moving from the grand buildings of the strip to the more run-down streets beyond, passing by dilapidated greystones and housing complexes, crumbling churches and foul-smelling trash cans, left to grow rancid in the summer heat.

Being one of the only white people to live where he did made Michael an object of suspicion, of sideways glances and frowns. But he was always smartly dressed, and with his razed red face, something of a fearsome prospect. The locals who knew him didn't mind him, and the others assumed for a white man to be that far south, he must either be a policeman or a madman or a gangster, all good enough reasons to leave him be. Any animosity directed toward him never went further than dirty looks and jokes behind his back. If anything he felt a sense of pity from the people who knew his story: *There goes the white man who was fool enough to marry a black woman, and now he has to live here, with us. Used to be a policeman too. Had to quit the job and head up north.* When people heard the couple were from New Orleans, there were rumors, too, of witchcraft, of voodou, of her putting a spell on him, and him marked like the devil for his troubles.

It was a strange place to live after growing up in the Big Easy. The neighborhoods back in New Orleans were poor, but they had always been poor; the slums were composed of shacks built in the mud. But in the Black Belt, the run-down houses had once been luxurious, with ornamental stonework, columns and railings, all built along grand avenues. Rich people had made these streets, lived in them, then moved off somewhere better, and their abandonment still haunted the area, leaving a sense of desolation in the air, of having missed the exodus.

Even after nearly ten years there, Michael hadn't quite gotten used to it, and neither had Annette. There were enough similarities between New Orleans and Chicago – both cities founded by French traders, both lying between a river and a lake, both filled with blues and jazz and beautiful architecture, the Paris of the South and of the Midwest respectively – but the similarities were never enough to make the place truly feel like home.

Just as he was turning the corner onto his street, he heard a commotion down an avenue, turned onto it to investigate and came across a crowd loafing about a tall, four-story, redbrick building. Three Black Marias were parked up outside the place, a clutch of Negro men were sitting on the sidewalk in handcuffs, and a group of locals had stopped to watch the show. The front door of the building had been broken open, and policemen were coming and going. On the top floor, where all the windows were open, Michael could see more officers milling about.

He had passed the building often enough, had noted the steam coming from its vents even on the hottest of summer days, had noted the pigeons lining up on the roof in the dead of winter, had smelled the rye vapor on the air. It was only a matter of time before the operation was busted.

A policeman poked his head out of one of the top-floor windows.

'We're ready!' he screamed.

The officers on the street formed a cordon and pushed everyone back to the opposite sidewalk, and a handful of photographers with press cards tucked into the brims of their hats kneeled down at the curb and pointed their cameras upwards. When the officer in the window saw the road was clear, he disappeared inside and then there was a sound like an explosion, and a torrent of whiskey burst from the top-floor windows, gushing like a waterfall down the front of the building, thousands of gallons clattering onto the sidewalk, where a lake of whiskey quickly formed, engorging the gutters and grates.

And then the torrent slowed to a stream, a trickle, a drip, and a heavy quiet descended on the crowd, everyone silent except for the photographers, who continued to snap away. Great wet streaks stained the brickwork below the windows, leaving the building looking like a tear-stained face, its eyes gouged out, its mouth agape; and the vapor rising off the whiskey lake was enough to get them all drunk.

Then the policemen lifted the handcuffed men off the sidewalk and stood with them in front of the paddy wagons while the photographers took their pictures. The handcuffed men didn't look dishonest or menacing. If anything they reminded Michael of the abattoir workers from the streetcar. And the policemen holding them up looked just as embarrassed, wearied by the pointlessness of it all. By the next morning the proprietors would be free and the distillery would be undergoing repairs.

Michael remembered his own time as a cop and he lamented the stupidity of banning alcohol in a country run by an Irish police force, the stupidity of placing America's fifth-largest industry into the hands of criminals, gifting them two billion dollars a year, daintily wrapped up in a tax-free bow.

Michael turned and headed home. He let himself into his apartment and walked through the living room into the kitchen. Annette was at the stove, making their dinner, still wearing her nurse's uniform. Michael walked up to her and kissed her on the back of the neck and she turned to him and smiled. They were always happy to see each other after even the briefest separation, the world being so against them.

'Telegram arrived,' Annette said, nodding at the kitchen table. Michael frowned, walked over and picked it up: CALL ME TONIGHT LAKE VIEW 137586 WALKER.

Jim Walker was an assistant at the State's Attorney's office, someone Michael traded information with now and again. A telegram at home was highly unusual. He tucked it into his shirt pocket and decided to call him after dinner. He went into the bathroom and took a cold shower, changed into clean clothes, and when the children had come back from playing with their friends, they sat down to a meal of corn on the cob and smoked ham.

As Michael watched his children eat, he thought of Mrs Van Haren's money once more. He had always lived with the sad fact that the opportunities afforded to his children were fewer than those given to him purely because they were a different color. Now Thomas would be finishing school soon, and Mae not too far behind, and Michael feared for what would become of them. Chicago didn't offer uneducated Negroes much in the way of a decent wage, but plenty in the way of blue-collar drudgery and crime. With money to get them educated, to send them to the University of Chicago or Northwestern – both of which admitted colored people – they could become doctors or lawyers, safe in the ranks of the black middle class. Otherwise, the only options for Thomas were ending up broken and aged like the Stockyard workers on the streetcar, or in the back of a police wagon like the bootleggers.

There was laughter around the table and Michael looked up to see smiles and grins and he realized he had missed a joke. Thomas was saying something, leading the conversation, confident as always. Mae was acting coy. Annette was looking over them with a stern and motherly eye. And Michael was worrying about the future.

After dinner they set about clearing the plates and Michael stepped out to the store to use the phone there to call Walker. He turned onto the avenue where the grocery was, passed a group of girls playing hopscotch, a gaggle of old women sitting on kitchen chairs, fanning themselves with newspapers. Over the years the neighborhood had gotten busier, bursting at the seams with newcomers from the South, all of them moving to these few overcrowded blocks, and the influx had only grown larger with the Mississippi floods the previous year. And all these newcomers had no choice but to move to the Black Belt, due to the prejudice and violence they encountered if they tried to move anywhere else.

The high demand for space meant the landlords could raise their prices extortionately, so while Negroes got paid the lowest wages in the city, they had to pay the highest rents, and Michael, having a black wife and two children with her, was similarly gouged. And in this was the root of the neighborhood's slow deterioration – was it any wonder the tenants there had neither the means nor inclination to repair the buildings their landlords were leaving to rot, to put their own meager money into improving the assets of the men who were exploiting them?

Southerners in the big city had to negotiate all these problems, and as they did so, they were depicted as slow, bumbling, un-cultured, cluttering up the sidewalks that people with jobs were busy rushing down. The *Broad Ax*, one of Chicago's most popu-lar Negro newspapers, even printed a column, 'The Wise Owl', offering advice to new arrivals on how to stop acting like country bumpkins: *Refrain from wearing head-rags and other signs of slavery in public.*

Michael turned a corner and passed a shoeshine stand, a front for a drug-dealing operation, at which a pale-looking white man in a linen suit was buying a wrap of heroin. Michael nodded at the shoeshine man, who grinned and nodded back, then he reached the grocery and said hello to the old-timer who ran the place. He stepped into a glass-paneled booth, lifted the receiver, pulled the telegram from his pocket and gave the operator Walker's number.

'One moment, please,' said the operator, and as Michael waited he got steadily more parched in the sauna-like booth. A few seconds went by and the call was connected.

'Walker? It's Talbot.'

'Michael! Glad you called. I heard you had a visit from a cer-tain rich lady today. I need to talk to you about it before you take the job.'

'I've already taken the job.'

'Maybe you're gonna have to *un*-take it. You free tomorrow afternoon?'

'Sure.'

'You know Delano's by Comiskey Park?'

'Sure.'

'Meet me there at five. And don't tell anyone we spoke.'

Michael put the phone down and stepped out of the booth. He dropped a coin on the counter for the old man, and as he made his way out of the store he noticed on the racks outside the shop there was a bucket full of cantaloupes resting in ice-water, the sign above it informing him they were from Louisiana. He paused and looked at them, the pale yellow globes bobbing about in the ice-blue water, promising sweetness and coolness and a taste of back home. He searched about for a ripe one.

When he got home, he cut it up and shared it out. The children went off to their rooms, and Michael and Annette sat in the living room and he told her about Mrs Van Haren's money, and Walker's telegram; and as they discussed it, they watched through the window as the roaring sun passed behind the silhouettes of the steam cranes in the distance and sunk into a thin strip of sky between two high-rises, as if the city had captured the great orb, and was squeezing out its life like an orange in a press.

Then night came on, a jungle of neon and cement turned shadowy blue, oceans of electric lights all over the city: the arcs of the cinemas downtown, the skyscraper beacons warning aircraft of their height.

They dwelt on the possible future paths their children might take. Michael tried to assess his chances of finding the missing girl. They talked about the dangers the case might pose for the family. Images flickered in Michael's mind's eye, of Thomas as a Stockyard worker, a bootlegger, a shoeshining drug dealer, a university graduate.

Sometime after eleven he left the apartment and went back to the store, and placed a call to Ida who'd had a phone line installed at her home the previous year.

'It's me,' said Michael.

'What's happened?'

She sounded sleepy, her voice muddled and rasped.

'When I got home this afternoon I had a telegram from Walker at the State's Attorney's. Wanted to talk to me about the Van Haren case.'

'Someone's moving quick. She's being followed.'

'Her or us.'

'Maybe Ralph let something slip at the division. Or someone noticed the case folder was missing.'

'Or maybe one of Van Haren's servants is informing on her.'

They stayed silent a moment as they mulled over the possibilities.

'There's something else,' said Michael. 'I spoke to Annette. About Walker. And the money.'

'And?'

Michael wiped the sweat from his brow, the heat in the booth having closed its fingers round him.

'I'm in.'

8

Al had arranged for a room at the Drake Hotel so after the funeral Dante caught a taxi there, and checked in under the suspicious eyes of the reception staff. The Drake was a lavish place, fashionable with celebrities and the upper crust, and a man like Dante, in his rumpled suit, sweating and pale, clearly looked out of place. He caught the elevator to his floor, and walked into a suite of rooms so large it took the bellboy a couple of minutes to show him around.

Dante took a shower, sat on the sofa, smoked a couple of cigarettes and leafed through the room-service menu while he waited. Then there was a knock at the door and the man entered, a balding Chinese man in a summer suit and bow tie, a blue anemone in his lapel. Dante stared at the flower a moment, then shook his head and let him in.

The man delivered what had been agreed upon at the funeral parlor: a .45 Colt service revolver, a .38 snub-nose Beretta, a Maxim silencer, five boxes of ammo, a lock-picking kit, five hundred dollars in cash, the number of the direct line through to Al's suite at the Metropole, and the keys to a Stutz Model BB Blackhawk roadster, which the man informed him was parked up in the hotel's lot – license plate 286-515.

'You mind me asking something?' said the man when they had concluded their business. 'What's with the Beretta?'

He nodded to the tiny gun laid out on the table. Cheap European imports like the Beretta had become popular over the decade, despite being shoddily made and inaccurate, and so low-caliber they had almost no stopping power. The guns had numerous nicknames: British Bulldogs, Pocket Revolvers, Saturday Night Specials, Suicide Specials – the last two on account of the circumstances in which the guns were often fired. They were sold to women mostly, as they fitted inside a purse, and no gangster or policeman would be caught dead with one.

'I mean,' said the gun dealer, 'you probably can't even kill anyone with it.'

'Suits me,' said Dante. 'I can shoot first and ask questions later.'

He grinned and the gun dealer grinned back.

'Fair enough,' the man said. 'Now, can I interest you in any hand grenades, nitroglycerin, marijuana or cocaine?'

'I don't think so,' said Dante.

The man smiled again, nodded, and went on his way.

After he'd gone, Dante went down to the parking lot and looked about for the Blackhawk. He found it easily enough – it was large, sporty, boat-tailed and painted black with a red trim that gleamed in the sunshine. What it lacked in subtlety it made up for in speed – the car had hit over a hundred miles per hour in Daytona the previous year. Dante wondered exactly what Al was thinking in getting him such a conspicuous vehicle; then he grinned, got in and hit the ignition.

He drove south through mid-afternoon traffic to the Black Belt, a neighborhood of jazz and blues and other subtle riches, and he sought out the name he had been given by his friend back in New York. He found the man at a corner on State Street, manning a shoeshine box. Dante parked up, paid a kid a dollar to mind the car, and sat at the shoeshiner's and ordered 'the special'.

When the man had finished, Dante handed him his money, and the man handed Dante in return a small brown block wrapped in cellophane. Dante bid the man good-day and drove back uptown, stopping off at a medical-supplies store, and a grocery. He didn't take a direct route, he drove about, taking it all in, getting reacquainted with the city of his birth, shocked at how much it had changed in just a few short years. From the Gold Coast to Bronzeville, from the lakefront to the river wards, the city was abuzz with transformation.

Even in the slums outside the Loop things had undergone a drastic modernization. The city had always been a patchwork quilt of old-world neighborhoods, memories of foreign hometowns transported to the Midwestern plains. Now that farrago of communities was being cut through with lines of modernity, slashed at by the gods of progress, leaving across it perfect scars of elevated railroads, high-rise blocks, grand avenues as precisely straight as the drawings of the city planners who dreamed them up. And Chicagoans had no choice but to make do with this gouging of their city, a city forever stretched between an imported past and an imagined future.

He headed north again up the Magnificent Mile, where skyscrapers were being hoisted up by the dozen, their unfathomable weight of steel and rock screaming ever upward. Chicago had invented the skyscraper, had foisted it on the world, and now it was almost as if the city felt a duty to keep replicating its invention, in a million different forms, across its increasingly cluttered skyline. The low sun was sending girders of light slanting onto streets through the gaps in the skyscraper canyon, so as he drove, he passed alternately through stretches of golden sunlight and pale blue shade.

Eventually he passed the city limits, still heading north, to the place where he and his wife would go when they skipped off school – an isolated beach in a tiny cove in a not much frequented part of the lakeshore. Although in his absence the city had spread itself ever further into the prairies, devouring more and more of the lakeshore, he was glad to see when he arrived at his destination that the city's assault on the earth had not yet destroyed the part he loved.

He pulled up to the same sandy piece of ground he used to park on when he stole his father's car to drive Olivia out there, and took a moment to look out over the waters and the city clinging to the hem of the lake. He could have sought out her grave, to pay his respects there, but he had already been to a funeral once that day, and the sad truth was, he didn't know where she was buried. Coming to the beach where they had misspent the tender afternoons of their youth seemed like something she might smile at.

He fixed his eyes on Lake Michigan in front of him, its waters as immense as a sea, and he watched as they changed color with the setting sun. Further down the beach, in the midst of the urban sprawl, rich folks were sucking down oysters and champagne, couples were promenading on the boardwalks, kids were getting into trouble, but all the way up here, there was just the vastness of the prairie meeting the vastness of the lake. The only sounds were the soft lapping of the waves, the rustle of the wind in the grasses, the distant barking of dogs.

When the sun had set and darkness come over the land, dots of light appeared in the gloom, from the city to the south, and the ships far out on the lake. Dante switched on the light in the car, unwrapped the cellophane from the block and inspected what he had bought. He could tell by the color, the texture, the firmness, that it was the same stuff he got back in New York – Turkish, by way of processing plants in Marseilles, shipped across the ocean to Canada and smuggled into the country by bands of enterprising young men like his friends Lansky and Luciano back in the Big Apple.

Dante crumbled some of it onto a spoon he'd grabbed from the hotel, scraped the flint on his lighter and watched as the mixture bubbled and popped and turned to liquid, and his mind drifted back to the ghosts he had run away from six years earlier, and the strange irony of the job Capone had tasked him with.

When Dante was a young bootlegger in the city, his business partner, Saul Menaker, had told him of a man that had a connection to two chemists over in the Caribbean. The chemists had invented a method of changing the chemical structure of alcohol, just a slight rearrangement of the molecules, which meant the alcohol would pass the alcohol-level checks at the border on a technicality, whilst retaining its taste and its ability to intoxicate. To drum up interest from distributors, the chemists had cooked up a sample, and with a showman's touch for ballyhoo, had distilled it into a batch of champagne.

It seemed like a good deal to Dante and Menaker, a good way to avoid the poisons other producers derailed their alcohol with – aftershave, antifreeze, embalming fluid, paint thinner, coal-tar dye, sulphuric acid, formaldehyde. Of all of them, fusel oil was the worst. A by-product of fermentation, it was put into clear liquor to give it the color of whiskey, and caused people to go blind and insane.

Around a thousand people died each year from drinking tainted booze – more deaths than the gunmen ever caused. When a batch did the rounds, the rumors surrounding what had happened to the drinkers read like a dispatch from a battlefield – deaths, blindness, insanity, paralysis, lost limbs, muteness. The drink got so poisonous and strong that doctors began prescribing morphine to people as a way of coping with hangovers, causing a spike in narcotics addiction, too.

This champagne, on the other hand, the chemists' representative informed them, was only different to regular alcohol in the after-scent it gave off when it had been exposed to air, a slight, almost unnoticeable, caustic tang.

Dante and Menaker had picked up a dozen cases to see if they were any good, not knowing that the chemists had overstated their qualifications, and the process, more often than not, turned the alcohol toxic, more toxic than any of the other adulterated booze on the market. By the time Dante had realized the alcohol was poisonous, he had already given away most of the bottles, inadvertently killing six people in the process, including three members of his own family.

It was a stroke of bad luck that it was his little sister's high-school graduation day; the girl having received a scholarship to study literature at UC, Dante's parents had decided to throw a celebratory meal and they had asked him to get them some alcohol. He'd dropped off a case of the champagne at his old family home on his way to another delivery and promised to pop back there when he was done. While he was gone, his parents had opened up the champagne, toasted his sister's success, and within a few minutes they were vomiting blood. By the time they got to the hospital Dante's mother and sister were dead, and his father and brother were both invalids.

In a daze he'd run around town frantically trying to trace the remaining bottles, and he'd returned home in the early hours, selfishly expecting to find some solace in the arms of his wife. But he hadn't accounted for the bottle he'd left in his own kitchen, and he came home to find Olivia and her sister splayed out on the linoleum in a pool of vomit, bloodied urine, broken glass and the fatal champagne.

He had rushed Olivia and her sister to the hospital, feeling sick as he entered the place for a second time that day, the doctors asking what they'd had to drink and where they'd got it. He remembered sitting next to his wife in the hospital bed as she'd died, and coming back home the next morning, sleepless and dazed, responsible for the destruction of his whole family.

He'd climbed to his apartment, sat on the sofa, staring for what seemed like hours at the stains on the kitchen floor. Then he had gotten up and, still in a daze, had walked to the Illinois Central station. He'd left the door to the apartment open, his car in the street, the bank accounts, the bootlegging operation, his other business interests. At the station he called Al, telling him he was going on the lam, telling him he'd owe him one if he could clean things up, keep the police from tracing him. Al agreed, asked him where he was going, and Dante had hung up, got on a train and never looked back. Until now.

The mix in the spoon reached a liquid state, and Dante snapped his lighter closed. He grabbed the syringe he'd bought at the pharmacy and placed the needle into the mixture and pulled the plunger up, and then he lifted the syringe to his eye, inspecting the liquid trapped in its thin, glass prison. He got out of the car and sat on the sand in front of it, leaning his back against the fender. He stared out across the lake and watched the glow of a night train moving along the horizon, its line of lighted windows like an illuminated dragon. Wind rustled through the dune grass, water sloshed, all of it hypnotic and calming.

He wrapped his belt around his upper arm, found a vein amongst his scarred skin and slipped the needle in, the city lights reflecting on the glass of the syringe. When he had finished he pulled the needle out and looked up at the dragon of the night train pushing silently through the moonlight, and he felt the cool warmth rushing through him, his muscles relaxing, his mind at ease, his self dissolving till he was nothing but a collection of sensations and responses, nerve-ways warm and tingling, and in that nothingness he found peace at last, and he listened to the movement of the waves as if they were lapping inside his own soul.

In the distance the dragon train had disappeared, but he could still see the lights of ships far out in the lake, plowing a course north to the freezing waters of St Ignace, Lake Huron, Canada. He closed his eyes and wondered if he should go back to see the people he had run away from all those years ago, go and see what remained of his ruined family.

He had wandered around the country shadow-like after he'd left Chicago: a hobo riding boxcars, scavenging food, stealing. He'd tried to end it all a few times, but something had always pulled him back. He fell in with a pack of needlers on a train through the Appalachians and in the clean, crisp mountain air he had learned the habit. After a few years he wound up in New York, in the depths of winter, and had collapsed from lack of food, frostbitten, in a park opposite a church in the Bronx. A priest had rescued him, fed him, gave him work and a place to stay, and from there he'd managed to build a life, but it wasn't really him anymore, now it was just a bandage he'd hoisted over his wounds, and he often found himself watching himself acting the part of being himself.

Aside from the operation on his boat off Long Island – the operation that involved him personally testing every crate he sold – he started trying to help people out, and further gained a reputation as a fixer: he intervened in disputes, found runaways and missing product, made news stories and blackmail notes disappear. If people had a problem that needed fixing, they came to Dante, guessing him to be the image he cultivated – easygoing, debonair, a man with panache, not realizing he was just a washed-up excuse for a human being who'd run away from killing six people and destroying his own family, who was too weak to do away with himself, a man who could only silence the horde of demons running around his soul by injecting himself with dope every few hours.

And whenever he came across bad booze in New York he chased it down zealously, and built a reputation for that as well. He guessed maybe that was part of the reason Al had asked him back, aside from his reputation as a fixer, aside from him being an outsider.

He wondered again if Al knew about his dope habit and he thought back to the meeting that morning. Maybe he'd blamed Dante's sweat on the heat, the bags under his eyes on tiredness from the journey. Despite his cocaine use and drinking, Al hated heroin and the people who used it, equating it with weakness, femininity, untrustworthiness. It was why he didn't deal in the stuff, missing out on all the money Dante's friends – Luciano and Lansky – were making from it back in New York. Al refused even to employ dope heads, had them beaten and thrown out of the Outfit if they were ever discovered within the ranks.

It was only a matter of time before he found out about Dante, discovered that the man to whom he'd entrusted this most delicate mission was weak and couldn't be trusted. Dante wasn't sure what would happen when Al found out about him. Maybe he would send his bodyguard Frank after him, or maybe 'Machine Gun' Jack McGurn or any of the other psychopaths on the Outfit's payroll. Dante had entered a new world back here in Chicago, a dangerous and changed world it would take all his wits to navigate.

In the distance, the barking of the dogs got louder and angrier, accompanied by howls and yelping. He heard a rustling in the reeds and he broke off his reverie, opened his eyes and looked behind him. Something was moving in the undergrowth, scrabbling about. He padded around to the driver's side of the car, reached in and took the Colt from the pocket in the door. Then he inched over to where the reeds were rustling about, and used the nose of the gun to part them. In a splash of moonlight, he saw a stray dog licking its wounds, young and small, with straggly brown fur. The dog had a cut along its face, hair ripped out of its back. It looked up at him with fearful eyes, wondering if it was about to get into another fight.

Dante got down on his haunches and inspected the dog more closely.

'It's okay, boy. It's okay,' he said softly, but the dog still cowered.

He thought for a moment, went back to the car and returned with a water canister and a cloth. He poured some water into the canister cap and put it on the sand in front of the dog. The dog thought a moment, then came forward and lapped up the water. Then Dante poured some of it onto the cloth, and took hold of the dog and wiped the wounds clean.

When the work was done, Dante stood and looked at the dog, and the dog looked back at him with an expression Dante couldn't quite fathom. Then Dante smiled, tipped his hat and returned the canister and the cloth to the trunk. He sat in the driver's seat with both the doors open, catching the breeze. As he was lighting a cigarette he heard a noise and turned to his side to see the dog sitting on the ground by the passenger-side door, its black eyes gleaming, fixed on him, looking grateful, masterless, lonely. Dante thought a moment before patting his hand on the passenger seat, and the dog jumped into the car and sat down next to him. Dante smiled, stroked the dog's head and the two of them stared out at the lake.

In the morning, the sun would beat down mercilessly on its surface and a haze of moisture would rise into the air and drift over the beachfront, peppering the city with lake water and corrosion and suffocating humidity. No respite for Gomorrah. Except here, now, in these few dark hours of cool, in the no man's land between the prairie ghosts and the lake nymphs, with the last light of the dragon rushing through him. He stared out at the black mass of water, to the vastness of Canada and the Arctic beyond, to the black mass of the sky above, in which the world was just a suspended mote, and in his oblivion he thought how much better it would be if every void was strapped with stars.

PART TWO

DUET

'All the tints of the racial rainbow, black and tan and white, were dancing, drinking, singing, early Sunday morning at the Pekin Cafe. At one o'clock the place was crowded. Meanwhile a syncopating colored man had been vamping cotton field blues on the piano. A brown girl sang. Black men with white girls, white men with yellow girls, old, young, all filled with abandon brought about by illicit whiskey and liquor music.'

NEWSPAPER REPORT QUOTED BY THE
CHICAGO COMMISSION ON RACE RELATIONS, 1922

'Slumming parties are apparently pleased with the atmosphere of sensuality in Chicago's nightclubs and find delight in seeing the intermingling of the races.'

THE JUVENILE PROTECTIVE ASSOCIATION,
CHICAGO, 1923

9

The morning after their meeting with Mrs Van Haren, Ida and Michael booked out a car from the car pool in the basement of the Pinkerton building and drove across town to the Van Harens' mansion.

'What did Annette have to say?' Ida asked Michael when they had left the Loop, and were heading north up LaSalle Street. She'd been surprised by Michael's call the previous night, and even more surprised that he'd agreed to risk their careers in not reporting Mrs Van Haren's offer of money.

'She said new jobs were a lot easier to come by than fifty thousand dollars,' said Michael, turning to smile at Ida.

She nodded, then turned to look at the road ahead with a sense of optimism. She'd realized long ago that even when her apprenticeship with Michael was over, she wouldn't be getting promoted, that she'd never be a lead detective, that the men at the top of the organization were of the opinion that the only role for a Negro girl in the company was as an assistant, a footsoldier, someone who was good for getting information out of Negro witnesses and nothing more. After nearly ten years of being a Pinkerton she was starting to feel trapped. If she wanted to move up in the world, she and Michael had to strike out alone and start their own business. But they couldn't do it without money.

Now, however, with Mrs Van Haren's reward, there was a chance for independence, for being everything she could be. 'Self-determination' the commentators in *The Chicago Defender* called it. As she sped through the sunshine that morning with Michael, she could feel the new possibilities as palpably as the lake breeze whistling through the car, and almost against her will, a smile formed on her lips.

'Objectives for today?' Michael said, bringing her back to the here and now. She turned to look at him and he gave her the grin he used whenever he was testing her.

Ida thought. 'One, interview the driver that dropped off Gwendolyn on the day she disappeared – see if there's any holes in his story. Two, try and figure out what's going on with the missing father and why he ain't around. Three, see if we can pick up on the atmosphere in the house that Stockman and Mullens noticed. And four, in light of the phone call with the State's Attorney's last night, try and figure out how they found out so quickly that Mrs Van Haren had employed us. I miss anything?'

'If you did, I can't think of it.'

Soon enough they were sailing down roads lined with luxury apartment blocks and bloated Queen Anne-style mansions, all of them set in spacious grounds and so sun-soaked Ida imagined they could be in Florida or California. The Gold Coast was the city's millionaire district, a neighborhood of sandy beaches and gilded bank accounts populated mostly by Chicago's merchant princes. It was located on the northern lakeshore and perched where it was, it somehow felt detached from the rest of the city, untainted by the smoke of the forges and the blood of the Stockyards. But perhaps even that wasn't quite enough; if the Gold Coast could have detached itself from the rest of Chicago and floated a mile or two out into the lake, it probably would have done so.

Ida checked the address and they turned off the main road and onto a cross-street and Michael parked up outside a great house whose white walls shimmered in the sunshine. They got out of the car and walked up a long, curving driveway that cut through vibrant lawns, sparkling and jeweled, an effect that made the house look like an island floating in the middle of a green sea. Further on a row of high fir trees ran along the property's boundaries, demarcating the land, isolating it.

The house itself was three stories high and along its front was a row of Doric columns and to its side a porte-cochère, where a stocky man was washing a collection of luxury cars. The man paused in his work when he saw them approaching, and Ida wondered if he was the driver who had dropped off Gwendolyn at Marshall Field's.

They reached the front of the house, climbed a stone staircase and rang the bell. A few moments later an old man in a butler's uniform opened the doors, an ancient Negro with a gnarled body, half bent over, shoulders misaligned, a smile on his face that seemed to be frozen into place.

'Yes?' he said.

'Good morning,' said Michael. 'Is Mrs Van Haren in?'

'Mrs Van Haren is indisposed.'

Michael and Ida frowned and shared a look.

'We had an appointment.'

'Yes,' said the butler, as if remembering something, 'you must be the two detectives. You're here to talk to Mr Meeghan, our driver?'

The butler held up a hand and they walked back the way they had come, then to the side of the house where the man had been cleaning the cars.

'George, the detectives,' said the butler, before taking up a position under the porte-cochère, within earshot, his hands dangling by his sides, one hanging shorter than the other on account of his oddly sloped shoulders. Michael introduced himself and Ida, and the driver nodded back. He had a ruddy complexion, with thinning hair colored a Saharan yellow, and the kind of build that suggested bodyguard more than driver.

Michael ran the questions, and Ida watched. They always split their interviews up like this – one talking, the other scrutinizing the interviewee's face and body for any disturbances at anything mentioned. Michael had trained her in how to study humanity closely enough to spot these things, and now she never missed even the grain of a lie.

The driver repeated the story they'd already read in the police reports. He'd picked up Miss Gwendolyn in the Duesenberg and had driven her from the house down to Marshall Field's; the last he'd seen of her, she was disappearing into the crowds outside the store on North State Street.

'Did she look anxious or perturbed on the way over there?' Michael asked.

'No.'

'Did she do anything unusual on the days leading up to her disappearance?'

'No.'

'Do you have any information you think might be useful?'

'No.'

And just for a second, the man's eyelids flitted, as swiftly as mosquito wings.

'What was Miss Gwendolyn like?'

And now something else disturbed him; a niggle of energy flickered through his face, a by-product of the effort involved at having to come up with a lie.

'Beautiful and happy.'

Michael managed to tease a few more details out of the man: after he had dropped her off at the store he had driven back to the house and stayed there till the evening when he had taken Mr and Mrs Van Haren out to the opera, driving them back around one o'clock. No one realized Gwendolyn hadn't come home from her trip till the next morning.

As they spoke, Ida had a notion that someone other than the butler was watching them. She broke off from keeping her eyes fixed to the man and looked about her, and caught sight of a figure standing in one of the upper windows: a chubby young Negro girl in a maid's outfit, peering down at them. Their eyes met and a worried look came over the girl's face. She jumped back from the window and disappeared into the darkness so quickly Ida wondered if what she'd seen had been an apparition.

Then Michael wound down the interview and he looked at Ida and she inclined her head to the left a little to indicate the driver had lied. Then the butler walked over to them and they headed back along the path.

'I'd like to interview the maid, please,' Ida said to the butler.

'Mrs Van Haren said you were only to interview Mr Meeghan,' the man replied, still smiling.

'I know and I understand that, but it's important I speak to her,' said Ida. 'If Mrs Van Haren were here, I'm sure she'd agree.'

The butler looked at her again with that smile still stuck to his face like it was a permanent fixture. 'I'm afraid that's impossible. I'll walk you to your car.'

He continued on down the driveway, and Ida tried to get a handle on the situation, eventually figuring that maybe the absent Mr Van Haren had given the butler instructions to allow no one into the house.

'I understand your position,' she said. 'Mr Van Haren told you not to let us inside.'

'I don't know what you're talking about.'

'Here's the thing, though,' she continued. 'If you don't let us in, we'll tell our friends in the Police Department about it. Lieutenants Stockman and Mullens – the two men that visited here a few weeks ago. They'll have to come back to see what you're hiding, and maybe they'll make a racket this time – squad cars, Black Marias, gongs blaring. Maybe they'll do it at five in the morning. Maybe they'll have to take you into custody. And all because you didn't help us.'

She looked levelly at the man, and noticed how his smile was still managing to hang on to his face by its fingertips.

'But if you let us in to talk to the girl, we won't tell Mrs Van

Haren, and we won't tell the Detective Division, and Mr Van Haren'll never find out, and things'll go back to just how they were. So what do you say?'

Two minutes later they were inside the house, walking through an air-cooled hallway, shoes clacking on a milky-colored marble floor, the sound echoing shrilly around the vastness of the place. They approached the bottom of a grand staircase and stopped.

'Wait here, please,' said the butler. 'I'll go and fetch her.'

When he had gone, Michael turned to look at Ida with a quiz-zical expression.

'She was watching us from a window,' she said. 'Looked scared as a rabbit.'

Michael nodded. 'And the driver?'

'Lied about having any information that might prove useful, and about the girl being happy.'

'Suicide?'

'That'd explain why Mr Van Haren ordered the butler to keep us out of the house.'

'You want me to stall the butler?' asked Michael. 'Give you some time alone with the girl?'

'Sure.'

'It might give me the chance to have a look around the place. Good work, by the way – coercing the butler.'

'Yeah,' said Ida. 'I suppose it was.'

They smiled at each other and as they waited for him to return, they looked about the hallway; despite the fact it was filled with antique furniture and oil paintings and *objets d'art*, Ida felt it looked empty somehow, sterile. It possessed the same coldness she'd observed in Mrs Van Haren the day before, the sense that the place, and the people in it, had developed a layer of frost.

'A whole new world,' Michael said, and Ida nodded.

She heard the sound of footsteps approaching and looked up to see the butler return.

'You can talk in the drawing room,' he said.

He led them down a corridor, then another, then another, over what felt like acres of ash-wood parquetry. Eventually they reached a door and the butler opened it, holding up a hand for them to enter.

'May I use the restroom before we start?' asked Michael and the butler gave him a funny look.

'Very well. This way, please.' And the two men walked off back down the corridor and Ida stepped into the drawing room.

It continued the theme of the hallway – large, high-ceilinged, full of high-ticket furniture and air-cooled to freezing point. There were a couple of tall windows on the far wall, through which the morning sun was shining. At the bottom of the windows was a pair of armchairs, and standing next to them was the girl Ida had caught spying on them earlier, the same scared-rabbit expression on her face. Ida crossed the room to greet her, smiling as she did, trying to relax the girl.

'Glad to meet you. My name's Ida.'

'Glad to meet you too, ma'am. I'm Florence,' said the girl in a Southern accent.

She looked even younger in the sunlight streaming in from the windows; a little chubbier too, the blue-and-white maid's uniform straining against her hips.

'Where are you from?' Ida asked.

'Ocean Springs, Mississippi.'

'Well, I'm from just down the coast, New Orleans,' said Ida, hoping to create a sense of sisterhood. But the girl's manner was cautious and guarded, and on her face was a flummoxed expression Ida had seen countless times: she was trying to figure out Ida's race, and by extension, exactly how formal she should be.

Ida took a moment to look around and think of a way to buy herself some time. Outside on the lawns she could see a pair of

RAY CELESTIN

tennis courts, wrapped in a dark green wire-frame fence, looking as empty and unused as everything inside the house. And beyond them, a path, disappearing through a gap in the tree line.

'Say, Florence, you been outside today?'

'No, ma'am.'

'Well, it's such a lovely day and all, how about we talk in the garden? Does that door over there open up?'

'Yes, ma'am.'

Thinking nothing of it, the girl stood and went over to the French doors that opened onto the lawns at the rear of the house, and the two of them stepped outside. Ida closed the door behind them, and guessed they could make it to the tree line before the butler came back, and despite herself, she smiled at the thought of the man returning and finding them gone.

'You been in Chicago long?' Ida asked as they skirted the tennis courts.

''Bout two years,' said the girl with something approaching a sigh. Ida knew well enough the feeling of being far away from home, how difficult it was to adjust to somewhere new, with its own strange rules and particular forms of love and hate. Back South people like her and the girl only had to deal with white prejudice – which was prejudice enough – but up here, they got it from other black people too, for the fact that they were new-comers from the South. And the stratifications continued further down the lines, divisions arose between Southern blacks that had recently arrived, and those that had been there a while, and between those that were from the upper Southern states as opposed to those from the lower Southern states. Florence was at the bottom rung of all these social ladders, and yet she was working in a good position, as a live-in maid for one of the most prominent families in Chicago.

'How'd you get the job?' asked Ida.

'The cook's husband's a cousin o' mine. He sent me up.'

'And you like it here?'

82

'Sure. Work's not too bad, and I get my own room.'

'And what about Miss Gwen? You like working for her?'

'Oh, sure. She's real nice. Ain't dicty or bossy or nothing. She was getting me lessons at that charity she worked at. Reading and writing.'

'The charity in Hyde Park?'

'Yeah. They got classes for Negroes. She was there every day. Didn't do it just for show, you know, like some of those other rich girls. She believed it. All that change-the-world stuff.'

Ida smiled and tried to imagine what life was like for Florence and Gwendolyn. The two girls, not much different in age, were both sheltered in their own ways, both adrift in a house that was empty except for a handful of distant, older folks. If Gwendolyn had confided in anyone, it would have been her maid.

'She sounds nice.'

'She is,' said the girl a little wistfully, as if she realized halfway through talking that she should have been using the past tense. Then a thought seemed to pass into the girl's head and her face brightened and she smiled.

'I remember once we went to a dress shop in the Loop. I'd gone with her downtown on account of I needed to pick up some tickets from the station for Mr Van Haren. Well, the shop owners wouldn't let me through the door. Said colored servants had to wait on the street, or better yet, around the corner. I weren't fussed but it was winter and it was snowing something fierce. That was my first Chicago winter. Didn't really know what cold was till I left Galilee. Well, Miss Gwen kicked up a fuss. I mean, a real fuss. Refused to leave the shop or spend another cent there till they let me in with her. Told 'em she'd close the family account at the place.' Here the girl smiled. 'They put me by the fire and even got me a chair to sit on.'

Ida smiled back and they reached the tree line and turned down it, onto a long shaded avenue.

'She seem different to you before she disappeared?'

The girl paused. 'No, ma'am,' she said, her words flecked with falsity.

'Tell me about the day she disappeared.'

The girl flinched, then composed herself and told Ida her own version of what had happened, and it dovetailed well enough with the other accounts, but Ida could see the girl was holding back and an idea formed in her mind.

'What did Miss Gwen say to you the morning she left? About where she was going?'

'Just that she was going out shopping.'

Ida nodded, making out like she hadn't picked up on the massive hole in the girl's story. She wondered how pampered Gwendolyn was – if she could have run away without Florence's aid, without help packing her bags and arranging tickets.

'What about the night she disappeared?' asked Ida.

'What about it?'

'Well, Mr Meeghan said Mr and Mrs Van Haren went out to the opera and then they got home late and they didn't realize Miss Gwen hadn't come home till the next morning. Isn't that odd? That it took them so long to notice?'

'I suppose so.'

'You didn't say nothing to them?'

The girl shook her head.

'But Miss Gwen told you she was just going out shopping in the morning. You were at home that night. You knew she hadn't come back, but you didn't say anything to anyone?'

The girl stayed silent and Ida could see her clamming up, drawing in her shoulders as Ida circled around the lies.

'Did Miss Gwen know how to drive?'

'No, ma'am,' said the girl, a new formality in her voice.

'Out of all the servants, who stays over each night?'

'Just me and Mr Richards, the butler.'

Ida stopped walking and turned to look at the girl.

'Listen, Florence, I'm gonna level with you, because I like

you, and you remind me of me ten years ago, and I'd hate for you to lose your job when all you were doing was trying to help out Miss Gwen.' As Ida spoke she could see the tears welling up in the girl's eyes, and she felt a sharp pang of guilt for manipulating her emotions. She thought about the distance of the house from anywhere there was a transport connection, how Gwendolyn couldn't drive, how no one was home that night apart from the two girls and the butler, who was probably in bed. Ida came up with the most likely explanation that fitted the lies: Gwendolyn had come home from the city that night, when no one was around except Florence, and then she'd run away. Without any stations nearby or a car to drive, she'd had to call a cab. Ida decided to gamble and unleashed a lie.

'We spoke to the neighbors,' she said. 'They told us they saw a taxi that night, come to pick up Miss Gwen, and that you were with her. You're in trouble, girl. Why don't you tell me what happened?'

The two of them stood there a moment, pressed in between the two rows of fir trees. And the girl burst into tears, and Ida reached over and hugged her.

10

After Jacob had made the connection between the murder in the alleyway and the murder in the hotel years before, Lynott had gone searching for info on the perpetrator of the former crime. He had found Anton Hodiak's file in the Bureau of Identification, but the details it contained were scant – it listed no known associates, and his former address no longer existed, having been demolished to make way for an apartment block. It did list, however, the address of Hodiak's former employer, and they figured it was as good a place as any to start looking for him.

They met the following morning on Halstead and 42nd Street and as they walked toward the Stockyards entrance, Lynott passed Jacob a folder.

'That's your boy,' said Lynott.

Jacob opened the folder and saw it was Anton Hodiak's ten card – his file from the Bureau of Identification. Clipped to the front page was a photo of the man they were looking for. Hodiak was stocky, with a thick neck, close-cropped hair, and small ears that projected awkwardly from the side of his head. But the thing that was most noticeable was the scar on the side of his face; it ran from his eye to his ear in the shape of the smile that was missing from the man's lips. It gave him a disjointed air, as if Jacob were looking at him from multiple angles all at the same time, like those Cubist paintings from France he'd seen in the *Tribune*.

They stepped through the Romanesque arch which marked the entrance to the Stockyards and approached the guard-house just inside it. Lynott spoke to the guards and one of them consulted a map and found the company they were looking for, a

86

small concession on the west side. He announced that he would accompany them as it was likely they'd get lost without him. The Union Stockyards took up a whole square mile in the very center of the city, and was, by any definition, the largest abattoir in the world, home to over fifty meat-processing companies and twenty-five thousand workers, who in combination produced more than three quarters of America's meat.

They thanked the man and he sauntered out of his guardhouse and took them into the heart of the slaughter. They walked along a wide track of caked mud, passing by drovers herding cattle and armies of blood-soaked men. It was a multiracial workforce, and the guard explained the divisions.

'The East Europeans and the Negroes work on the killing floors,' he said, 'the Mexicans work the freezers and hide cellars, and the Irish handle the livestock. Germans run the trains and the boats. The different groups are always trying to kill each other. Works out well for the bosses though.'

'How so?' asked Jacob.

'Whenever the workers try to unionize it fails because they can't organize across race lines, so the pay and conditions never improve. Divide and rule, boys.'

He raised his eyebrows and smiled ruefully, and they carried on trudging through the dust. They passed by mammoth warehouses, manure mounds, railroads and canals, elevated walkways that rattled with the footfall of cows and pigs. As they journeyed the air became ever thicker with the shrieks of animals, the smells of blood and manure, disinfectant and diesel. Jacob started to get the sense that they were traversing somewhere different, an inner circle of Chicago, a city within a city, a more hellish, more distilled version of the one outside.

And in amidst the stench and excrement and industrial killing, Jacob noticed something bizarre: tourists – groups of them being led about the place by tour guides as if they were visiting a Hollywood studio. They skirted by a gaggle of them and the guard smiled.

'We've been on the sightseeing trail for years,' he said boastfully.

The killing fields may have given birth to one of Chicago's many nicknames, the Abattoir on the Lake, but behind the name was a truth the city took pride in: it was Chicago that fed the nation.

'This is it,' said the guard, when they reached a long barn-like building with a roof made of corrugated sheets. 'You gonna be long?'

'Not too long,' said Lynott.

'I'll wait here to take you back,' the guard said, leaning against a fencepost, lighting a cigarette, and pushing his hat down in front of his face.

Lynott and Jacob stared at the man a second, then they stepped into the building, taking a moment to adjust to the dimness and the monstrous heat inside. The place was long, tunnel-like, and taken up by rows of men standing in front of rows of carcasses hanging upside down from hooks in a tight, precise grid formation.

Behind the nearest section of the grid a man was walking up and down, keeping an eye on things, looking vaguely as if he might be in charge of the operation. Lynott approached him and they spoke, and as they did, Jacob watched the workers on the killing floor.

As each row of men approached a row of dead cows they lifted long-handled meat cleavers into the air and sliced downwards, driving deep gashes along the animals' undersides. After each stroke, there was a pause, then the bellies of the cows emitted a hissing sound, and the slashes spread wide, as if of their own accord, and the animals' intestines, stomachs and other organs flopped from their carcasses and into the trays waiting for them on the ground with a great smacking sound.

The trays were on wheels and youngsters, half bent over, scurried along the blood-soaked floor, pushing the trays over to a group of men who sifted through them, and the cattle on hooks were pushed along by some unseen force, and another set of carcasses arrived on the moving-chains for the men with the cleavers to step forward and disembowel.

The whole process took no longer than ten seconds, start of loop to end, and Jacob thought what it must be like for those men to stand there and perform that same slicing action six times a minute, for twelve hours a day, six and a half days a week, for the rest of their lives.

He remembered hearing somewhere that Henry Ford got his idea for a car-assembly plant by watching the workers at the Chicago Stockyards, how intricately the jobs were divided for maximum efficiency, though as the person who told him had quipped, the Stockyards were less an assembly plant, and more a *dis*-assembly plant.

Jacob heard Lynott say something, and he looked up to see him and the overseer heading toward a huge metal door. The overseer swung the door open and they stepped through into a cooler – a vast, refrigerated space from whose ceiling hung hundreds more animal carcasses. The man nodded to a desk and chair in the corner, where a second man was sitting, then left, closing the door behind him, and the roar of the slaughter dimmed to nothing. That was when Jacob felt it, the blissful coolness of the place.

Jacob and Lynott walked through the frozen carcasses toward the desk where the man looked up at them and smiled. They saw he was wearing gloves and a scarf over a suit and tie.

'Coolest place in the building,' the man said. 'How can I help you?'

He reached into his pocket and pulled out a pouch of Bull Durham tobacco, took off the gloves and began rolling himself a cigarette. As he did so, Jacob took the opportunity to look the man over. He was in his fifties, short and round with eyes too far apart, granite-colored hair, cratered skin.

'You used to employ a man named Anton Hodiak?' asked Lynott, flashing his police badge.

'Anton?' asked the man. 'For fifteen years. What's happened?'

'What did he do for you?' asked Jacob.

'Killed cattle, what do you think? Did it with a smile on his face, too. And I don't mean the scar.' The man grinned and made a looping motion in front of his face with his index finger.

'You know he was convicted of murder, right?'

'He got a bum break. He was wrongfully convicted and pardoned.'

'You seen him since he was released?'

'Sure. I gave him his old job back.'

At this Jacob and Lynott shared a look.

'He's here?' asked Lynott.

'He was. He left town a couple of months ago.'

'Where'd he go?'

'Florida,' said the man. 'Said he wanted to see if he could make a go of things down south. That's why he came back here after he got released, to save up money for the trip.'

'So after he was released from murdering two people, you gave him his old job back?' Jacob said.

'He was pardoned,' said the man defensively, lighting the cigarette he'd rolled. 'The Lord God says forgive. And what did he ever do except kill a couple of niggers that slept with white women? They should've given him a goddamn medal.'

'He also *tortured* one of the white women,' said Jacob.

The man thought about this a moment, then shrugged and took a drag on his cigarette, and the smell of tobacco wafted through the frozen air, and in the stillness, Jacob realized how cold he was getting, the freezer making the sweat all over his body feel like ice.

'You got his address on file?' asked Lynott. 'Here or in Florida?'

'Nope,' said the man. 'What's he done?'

'Nothing. We just wanna talk to him. You know anyone that could help us?'

'I done told you he left town,' said the man, shaking his head, returning the pouch of Bull Durham to his pocket.

'Let's just say we wanna verify that,' said Lynott. 'You know where we can get hold of any friends or family?'

The man shrugged.

'Says in his file he got arrested for assaulting another worker here in the Yards. You know anything about that?' asked Jacob.

'Sure. That was years ago. On account of his little sister,' said the man, smiling. 'The girl got herself knocked up by a coon that worked on the killing floor for Armour and Co. She screamed rape, but you know what girls are like these days. Anton pressured her to get rid o' the thing and the doctor ended up killing her. So Anton went about setting things right. Put the coon in hospital but not before he ripped Anton's cheek open with a cattle hook. Hence the scar.'

Jacob flipped through the folder, looked through the dates. The attack on the co-worker had been a year or so before Hodiak started attacking other Negroes he'd seen around town in the company of white women.

'If he contacts you again, or you find out he's still in Chicago, you give us a call,' said Lynott, handing over a contact card.

'Sure,' the man said sarcastically, raising his eyebrows. 'Now unless you've got any other questions, the door's over there.'

Twenty minutes later Lynott and Jacob were standing outside the Stockyards on Halstead Street once more, where the sun was sparkling gold onto the paving stones and cars and storefronts.

'I'll send a wire down to Florida,' said Lynott, 'see what I can find, but the more I think about it, the more I figure Hodiak ain't our guy.'

'The deaths are identical,' said Jacob. 'His little sister dies cuz she slept with a Negro and now he's running about town killing anyone that crosses the race line.'

'We don't know the dead guy in the alley was crossing the race line. And even if he did, it doesn't make sense. All the attacks before were on Negroes with white women, like his little sister. But a white guy with a black girl? No one gives a shit about that except Negroes.'

'Come on, Frank. You know how it is with these screwballs. They start on one thing and get worse and worse. And what if he's seen another white girl on the street with a Negro and he's kidnapped her and got her holed up somewheres, like the last time?'

'Then that's Florida's problem, cuz that's probably where he is. Let's wait to hear back from them, okay?'

'Can I keep the photo?'

Lynott stared at him, and then there was a noise behind them and they turned to see a man in uniform lead a gaggle of noisy tourists out of the Stockyards and down the road toward a motor-bus. They waited till the group was a few yards away, then Jacob turned to look at Lynott.

Lynott sighed, unclipped the photo from the ten card and handed it to him.

'Don't do anything stupid, Jake.'

11

After the butler had led Michael to the restroom, he told the man, curtly, that he could find his own way to the drawing room, and the butler had left him alone, probably wanting to rush back to Ida and the maid. Michael gave it a few seconds before he padded off down the corridor in the opposite direction, found a staircase and ascended it. He walked along another corridor, checking doors. Most of them gave on to guest bedrooms, many of them covered in dust sheets. What good were all these rooms, he thought, without people to live in them?

After a while he arrived at a set of double doors, opened them gently and peered into a large bedroom murky on account of its curtains being drawn. Through the gloom he could see it was a fussed-over room, draped in doilies and fabrics, as if the owner was making every effort to soften their world. And lying in the bed was Mrs Van Haren, asleep, completely still. Michael frowned, noted the bottle of pills and the glass of water on the bedside table. He walked over and checked the bottle: Pentothal, sleeping pills. Had she taken them herself or had someone used force, keeping her out of the way for the duration of Michael and Ida's visit? The butler's words floated into his head – *Mrs Van Haren is indisposed* – then he stepped back out and closed the door.

A few yards down the hall, he found Gwendolyn's room, identifying it by the pictures dotted around the place. He entered, looked about, then crossed to the dresser to inspect the photographs lined up in silver frames. There were a few shots of Gwendolyn with her parents, looking bored on holidays or dressed stiffly at formal events. There was one of her and some matronly, rich-looking white women standing outside what looked like a school with a group of young Negro students. But most of the photos were of the girl and her friends, a set of flappers, all of them tall and blonde and moneyed-looking. Michael put down the last of the photographs and noted what was missing: not a single shot of her fiancé.

There was a door to an adjoining room and he stepped through it into a long, bright bathroom covered in emerald-green tiles. In the middle of the room was a huge claw-foot copper bath-tub, buffed up to a high golden brown. Under a frosted window was a dressing table with a mirror above it, ringed with light bulbs. Michael looked through the items on the counter: Max Factor face powder, perfumes by Isabey and Charles of the Ritz, dozens of lipstick tubes with the new swivel-top design – all of them perfectly clean of dust. If the girl had had a bottle of mor-phine in the dressing table, a vial of cocaine, a few of her mother's sleeping pills, they had long since been cleaned away by the staff. Then he noticed that something else was missing – no razor-blades.

He went back into the bedroom and rifled through the girl's wardrobes – they'd even taken away her belts. No photos of her fiancé, and no means by which to kill herself. Michael thought on that, and on the girl's mother passed out in a room further down the hall, and the house began to feel like a gilded cage. He checked his watch and figured he still had enough time to search both rooms for hiding places, for stashes of whatever it was Gwendolyn might have been hiding. He walked back into the bedroom and got started.

'I didn't know I was doing wrong,' Florence said through her sobs, and Ida soothed her with a hand on her back like a child. They were still alone, standing in the avenue of fir trees at the rear of the house.

'It's all right. I won't tell anyone. Just let me know what happened.'

'Miss Gwen came home that night, when everybody was out, and she was in a mess. Crying and upset.'

'Where'd she been?'

'Bronzeville.'

'The Black Belt? What was she doing down there?'

'She'd gone looking for Chuck – Mr Coulton – that's her fiancé . . . to find him, to tell him she was breaking it off.'

'What was Chuck doing in Bronzeville?'

'He wasn't there. See, Chuck hadn't been around the last few weeks. He'd kinda gone missing. He does that. Miss Gwen wanted to find out where he was, she . . . she'd found something out about him and she hadn't been sure about the whole thing anyway, and she'd finally decided to track him down and tell him it was over, break off the engagement. But she couldn't break it off cuz Chuck had gone missing. But there's a man in Bronzeville, a Negro, Randall Taylor. He's connected with Chuck. I don't know how. Miss Gwen went down there to see him, to find out where Chuck was. She'd got it in her head that Taylor could tell her. So she was going to meet him, find out where Chuck was, then go over to see Chuck and tell him she was breaking it off. But . . .' The girl let out a sob, and Ida waited.

'Something happened that night. Wherever she'd been. Something awful. She'd seen something.'

'Seen what?'

'I don't know. She wouldn't say. She wasn't making any sense. She kept saying something about blood and bloody hands, and having blood on her hands. She was so scared. Said she had to get out of town or someone was gonna kill her.'

'Someone meaning who? Coulton? This Taylor character?'

'I don't know. I told you, she wasn't making much sense. She said she'd catch the train on out to Montreal, that she'd leave while no one was around and that I wasn't to tell anyone. Not her folks, not anyone. She said she'd call Miss Lena when she was safe, and Miss Lena would call here and let me know.'

'Miss Lena?'

'Lena Jansen. She's a friend of Miss Gwen's. Then it's just like you said it was. She asked me to pack her things and to call the station and book her a suite on the train out to Montreal via Detroit that night. Then I called a cab and when it arrived she got in it and that was the last time I ever saw her.'

'What name'd you use to book the train?'

'Mine. Florence Smith.'

'What was the time of the train?'

'I can't remember what time it left. Eleven, eleven-thirty. It was the overnight from Illinois Central.'

'And what was the name of the cab company?'

'Gold Coast Cars.'

'All right, you're doing good, Florence. Just one last question – what was it that Miss Gwen found out about Coulton? The thing that made her want to call off the engagement?'

'I don't know, Miss Ida. I honestly don't,' Florence said, sniffing back tears. 'I did wrong, didn't I? I let her go and didn't tell no one and now Miss Lena ain't heard from her at all. Nothing in three weeks.'

'You've spoken to Miss Lena?'

Florence nodded. 'She's good. Miss Gwen, I mean. She's a real good person, you know. Not a bad bone in her body. Why's it always the good people bad things happen to?'

'I don't know.'

And just then they heard a rustling at the end of the path, and Ida looked up to see the butler and the driver turn the corner into the avenue and angrily head toward them.

12

A couple of hours after Jacob had returned from the Stockyards he received a call from Lynott.

'The dead man from the alley's been identified. Benjamin Roebuck. I pulled his file.'

'And?'

Lynott gave him the broad outline of Benjamin Roebuck's life, one that had been spent bumping along the bottom of Chicago's criminal ladder.

'There an address?' Jacob asked.

'Yeah, it's six years out of date. I already put a call through. No joy.'

'What about known associates?'

'One. Basil "Three-finger George" Georgiev. The two of them got arrested together a couple of times, rousted once in a brothel sweep and then on a safe-cracking job. You wanna hear about it? It's a peach.'

'Sure,' said Jacob.

'They were trying to blow a safe in the headquarters of the Typographical Union on Halstead, but Georgiev fucked up measuring out the nitroglycerin and he lost half his hand in the explosion. Hence the nickname. After they got released Georgiev had a string of drunk-tank arrests and nothing more. Meanwhile Roebuck got a job doing muscle work for Capone. I can't quite figure out yet which one of the two was the brain cell of the operation.'

'The dead man worked for Capone?'

'For the Outfit, yeah,' Lynott replied.

'Are you gonna pay Georgiev a visit?' Jacob asked.

'No, cuz Roebuck's murder is now being pursued by the Detective Division as a street robbery gone wrong.'

Jacob paused and rubbed his temples.

'He still had his wallet and jewelry on him, Frank. He had his eyes gouged out.'

'Maybe that's why it went wrong,' said Lynott.

'You got any idea what's behind it?' asked Jacob, perturbed by the news that someone in the division was trying to cover up the crime.

'Gimbrel.'

Jacob nodded. Pete Gimbrel was a thug of a cop in the Detective Division, a captain who beat confessions out of suspects with a set of brass knuckles engraved with a quotation from Ecclesiastes: *Whatever your hand finds to do, do it with all your might.* An interesting choice of agent for whoever it was trying to cover up the crime.

'Maybe Capone put the word out he wants it buried,' said Frank. 'Anyway, I shouldn't even be talking to you about it. Something about all this stinks, Jake, and I ain't in a position to follow it.'

'You got the KA's address?' Jacob asked.

'Sure. You got a pen?'

Jacob wrote down the known associate's address on a piece of paper and slipped it into his breast pocket.

'You get any witnesses come forward for the murder yet?' he asked.

'It's the Black Belt, pal, what do you think? And the hospital angle's not working out great neither. The reports came in while we were at the Yards. We found six people with matching wounds admitted the night before last. But none of them fit. Everything's looking like a dead end.'

*

After they'd finished speaking, Jacob left his apartment and caught an electric to Little Poland, hoping the victim's known associate, Basil Georgiev, might be able to provide some clues as to why Benny Roebuck had ended up eyeless and dead in a Bronzeville alleyway. He got out at the end of the line and walked the last few blocks to Augusta Street. It was a wide road, well maintained, dominated on either side by towering, residential buildings whose wood-paneled design made the street look like it was bordered by two rows of giant barns, transplanted from the prairies and dumped in the city to grow monstrous.

Jacob arrived at the address and rang the bell and a middle-aged woman answered the door, wiping her hands on her apron, looking harried and perplexed. Jacob asked for Basil Georgiev, and the woman, a bitter look crossing her face, told him to try his luck at one of the neighborhood bars, reeling off a list of local drinkeries in an irritated, skittering voice before slamming the door in Jacob's face.

He did the rounds and found the man in bar number three, a Polish beer hall that had made it through eight years of prohibition with not the slightest compromise to the Volstead Act. Jacob walked in and asked the barman if Basil Georgiev was there, and when the barman gave him a blank look he tried the nickname – Three-finger George – and the barman pointed to a sodden man at the end of the bar, stooped over the counter with a liquor lean, disillusion written all over him. Jacob made his way over, and when he got close, he could smell the alcohol sweats rolling off the man in plumes. He sat on the stool next to him and the man looked up and Jacob smiled hello.

'You've got that look in your eye,' said the man, in a clear voice that surprised Jacob with its lack of slur or tremor.

'What look?'

'The look of someone who wants something. What is it?'

'I'm a reporter. I wanted to ask you some questions about Benny Roebuck.'

Jacob took the press pass he'd wangled from his editor at the *Tribune* out of his pocket and showed it to the man. 'There's a couple of drinks in it for you.'

Georgiev stared at Jacob as if he was insulted by the offer, then a sour grin crossed his face. He nodded, and downed what was left in the glass in front of him.

'I'll have a large Canadian Club. The real stuff.'

Jacob called the barman over and ordered them a couple of glasses. He took out his cigarettes and offered one to Georgiev, who accepted, taking it from the pack with his damaged hand, a hand split right down the center: thumb, fore and middle finger in place, then nothing, just a jagged line disappearing into the darkness of his sleeve.

Georgiev caught Jacob staring, and Jacob flicked his eyes away, feeling something of the embarrassment he guessed other people felt when he caught them eyeing his limp.

The two men lit up and the drinks arrived and Jacob looked about the place. It was cavernous and dusty, with a rustic smell to it – barley and hops – that made Jacob wonder if they weren't brewing beer in the basement. Planks of rough, unvarnished wood covered all the walls, making the place feel dim, like he'd stepped inside the stomach of a wooden behemoth. Aside from Jacob and Georgiev, there were only two other customers in there, both of them at a table in the shadowy depths, hunched over a chessboard.

'I haven't seen Benny in a good few weeks,' said Georgiev after taking a drink. 'I heard he got turned into a stain on the sidewalk.'

Jacob nodded, surprised at the flippancy, and he wondered if the two friends had fallen out.

'That's why I'm here,' said Jacob. 'I was trying to figure out what Benny was doing down in the Black Belt in the first place.'

'Half of Chicago's down in Darkietown. Dancing to that jungle music.'

'But Benny wasn't on the strip.'

'The newspaper said they found him on State Street,' Georgiev replied with a quickness that surprised Jacob.

'He was found just off State Street, but he was attacked out in the Federal Street ghetto. That's not near the clubs. No one's going down there unless it's on business.'

Georgiev thought a moment, and as he did Jacob stared at him, at the red veins spiderwebbing across his glassy eyes, at his discolored skin, a shade somewhere between Jack Daniel's and bile. The man was ill, Jacob realized, dying.

'He had a girl out that way,' Georgiev said. 'Nigger girl. Worked the cabarets.'

Jacob frowned and Georgiev grinned.

'Old scams and new fools,' he said.

'She was after his money?'

Georgiev laughed. 'He didn't have any. Benny and money were never together for long. What's the matter, you don't drink?' Georgiev said, pointing a finger at Jacob's untouched whiskey.

Jacob lifted the glass, swilled the whiskey about, smelled it, then downed it.

'So why was she with him?' he asked, putting the empty glass back on the bar.

'I don't know. All I do know is it was strange. She was a good-looking girl, half his age. I tried to tell him but he wouldn't listen.'

'How long were they seeing each other?'

'Not long.'

'What kinda angles was Benny working when he died?'

Georgiev shook his head. 'I don't know. He always had a hundred things on the go, every one of them a four-flush.'

'Anything that might make someone want to kill him?'

'Maybe.'

'I heard he worked for Capone sometimes.'

At this Georgiev frowned and paused a moment. 'He worked for a lot of people.'

'Was he working for Capone when he died?'

'I don't know, and I don't like questions about Mr Capone. Why don't you ask him yourself?'

'I'm asking you.'

'Look, Benny never did nothing big for anyone. Slug jobs for the union, twenty-five dollars apiece. Pineapple-throwing, finger-snapping, pulling out nails. Ugly things. Uglier still the look on his face when he did them. Like the grin a man gets with a woman. Maybe something he did ended up getting him killed, maybe not.'

Georgiev shrugged and stared at Jacob, his face hardening, and Jacob realized he was starting to annoy the man.

'You know how I can get ahold of the girl?' he asked before he lost Georgiev in a cloud of ill will.

'She's on the act list at the State-Congress Theater. The Cotton Candy Girls, or the Lollipop Girls. Something like that.'

'She have a name?'

'Esther something.'

Georgiev turned away from Jacob and downed what was left of his Canadian Club.

'You offered me two drinks if I answered your questions,' he said, his tone leaving Jacob in no doubt that the interview was over. Jacob ordered another large whiskey and in the silence between the order being made and the drink arriving, Jacob watched as Georgiev stared at the bar, at the grain of the wood, the rings of that morning's glasses fading inexorably into noth-ingness.

'Did he suffer?' Georgiev asked suddenly, looking up at Jacob, concern and tenderness in his voice, and Jacob was again sur-prised by the man.

'He was dead before his head hit the pavement,' Jacob lied, and Georgiev nodded and turned quiet, and in the silent void that followed, Jacob studied his face, the jaundiced skin, the seared eyes suffused with a piercing sadness, and he felt pinpricks of guilt for having questioned the man.

The drink arrived and Jacob paid, said his goodbyes, and left Basil Georgiev in the dank, wooden belly of the beer hall, with his large Canadian whiskey, to continue his rush into the void alone.

As he was heading back to the tram stop, Jacob noticed a Cadillac slow-rolling down the street, then pulling up a few feet from the entrance to the beer hall. He hustled along the sidewalk, guessing that such an expensive car in such a down-at-heel location could only mean one thing – gangsters. He reached the corner of the block and turned around to see what was going on. The car idled on the street a moment, then the back doors swung open and three men exited, and Jacob recognized the third of them by his leather jacket: Bugs Moran, the head of the Northside Gang. He was in his late thirties, chubby, with side-parted hair, and a drooping, hangdog expression.

Jacob stood back and leaned against a shop doorway, trying to be as inconspicuous as possible. He watched as Moran and the two men walked into the beer hall, and the driver switched off the car's engine. Five minutes later they exited again, got in the Cadillac and drove off, leaving Jacob wondering if Moran had been in there to see Georgiev, and if he had, why he was going to see the friend of a dead Capone stooge.

As he headed back home he mulled it over, wondering if Benny Roebuck had been murdered by Anton Hodiak, or if the dead man had been involved in something that went right to the top of Chicago's gangland hierarchy.

13

After Ida and Michael had been all but thrown off the Van Haren property, they drove downtown to Illinois Central to see if Gwendolyn had actually made it onto the train bound for Montreal. If she had, there was a chance she was still alive, that she was safe from whatever it was she was running away from, that they could make the trip to Montreal themselves and track her down, maybe offer her some protection.

They parked up a couple of blocks from the station, then walked through the shade of its thirteen-story clock tower, through its great arch and into the rush of people moving about the platforms within. Thirty train-line operators ran services out of Chicago's six intercity stations, making Chicago the center of the country's rail network, a waystation, a sorting office for the disenfranchised of the world, and nowhere was this more apparent than at Illinois Central, where the available routes open to someone fleeing the city were countless and entangled.

They consulted the timetables placed in huge bound ledgers across one wall of the station, consulted the route maps, and figured there were only a couple of services Gwendolyn could have taken at that time of night – the *Twilight Limited* and the *Wolverine*. A woman at the Michigan Central Railroad desks told them that someone using the name Florence Smith had indeed booked a cabin on the red-eye *Wolverine* to Detroit, with an onward ticket on the New York Central Railroad to Montreal, but that the woman had never actually boarded the train. Somewhere on the cab ride between her house and the station, Gwendolyn had disappeared.

'I guess we need to speak to the cabdriver,' said Ida as they walked away from the booths.

'I guess we do. Your turn to drive,' said Michael, tossing her the car keys.

A half-hour later they were back in the Gold Coast, pulling up to the garage and filling station that was the home of Gold Coast Cars. They walked through the concrete yard where the company's fleet of Model 06 sedan cabs was parked up, all of them painted in a scheme of yellow and black, making them look like a swarm of bumblebees.

They stepped out of the sun into a space filled with cars undergoing repairs, automotive equipment, spare parts. People were milling about – mechanics, and drivers in the company's porter-like uniform – but no one paid them any attention. They spotted a desk in one corner, covered in documents and telephones, behind which sat a fat man who looked like he was in charge. They walked over and he glanced up at them from his paperwork.

'Destination?' he asked, picking up a pen. He was in his sixties, Ida guessed; his eyes were rheumy and his mustache was tinted mustard yellow from decades of nicotine.

'We're here from the Pinkertons,' said Ida, showing him her ID.

'We don't do corporate discounts,' the man replied, in an odd sort of voice.

'We're here to speak to one your drivers,' she said, ignoring the sarcasm. 'Someone picked up a girl from the Van Haren house on the twenty-seventh, sometime after ten p.m. You keep a record of that kind of thing?'

'Sure I do. Why you asking?'

'That's confidential.'

The man stared at her a moment. He ran his gaze from her face down to her ankles and back up, and Ida could almost feel his eyeballs scraping against her flesh.

'What are you anyway?' the man asked, frowning at Ida's skin, at her hair with its ever-so-slight kink in it. 'A dago or a coon?'

No matter how old she got, she felt a stab of sadness when it happened, a hopeless feeling that some things would never change. The anger always came later.

Michael made a move toward the man, and Ida put her hand up to stop him.

'You going to help us or not?' she asked.

'You here on State's Attorney's business?' the man responded.

The Pinkertons often worked with the SA, and when they did, they were on official business, and people could end up in official trouble if they didn't cooperate. But when they were on a private job, they had no such legal authority, and the man seemed to know all of this.

'No,' said Ida, 'it's a private matter.'

'Well, then, there ain't no reason for me to help you, is there?'

The man grinned, and leaned back in his seat and folded his arms in front of his chest, as if he'd just issued them a challenge.

'No. I don't suppose there is,' Ida sighed. 'Like you said, things'd be different if we were here with the SA, or the Secretary of State's Automobile Division. Isn't that right, Michael?'

'Yes, it is.'

'We do a lot of work for the Automobile Division,' she continued. 'Running checks on missing cars, accident investigation, insurance scams. What was the one we did a few weeks ago?'

'Oh, that was a real peach,' said Michael. 'A garage owner in Calumet City. Caught him leaving tacks on the road coming up from Gary. A half-mile from his repair garage. Did a roaring trade selling new tires to those poor folks whose old ones he'd punctured.'

Ida nodded and turned to look at the man once more.

'Funny thing about our friends in the Automobile Division,' she said. 'Something else they do is check the roadworthiness of business vehicles. Like taxicabs. Now wouldn't it be a coincidence if tomorrow morning a few of our friends from the division came down here and impounded all your cars while they conducted a spot inspection?'

She turned to look at Michael.

'That would be a coincidence,' he said.

Then they both turned back around to look at the man, their faces as blank as oven doors. The man glared at them a moment, then he rose and stalked out into the main floor of the garage.

'Dumb Southern fucks,' he muttered as he passed.

They turned to watch him walk over to a shelf, take down a ledger and consult it. Then he shouted through the gates to the men in the yard.

'Someone get me Weiler!'

Then he returned to Ida and Michael and sat back down at the desk, glaring at them all the while.

A few seconds later a Negro in his forties, tall, solidly built, hair cropped short, walked into the garage. His boss watched him like a hawk as he walked over to them.

'These two wiseguys are from the Pinkertons,' said the boss. 'Tell 'em what they need to know.'

'Sure thing,' said the Negro. He turned to Ida and Michael and smiled.

'Donald Weiler,' he said, holding out a hand for them to shake.

As Michael reached out, Ida looked down and noticed something that made her stop – the skin on the man's hands was a ghostly white, bleached all the way up to the elbow, where there was an inch or so of indeterminate color, then his brown skin resumed, all the way up to where he'd folded up his shirt-sleeves.

'The Stockyards,' said the man, looking at Ida with a smile on his lips. 'I do shifts in a salting pit.'

Ida had heard of the thing before, but never actually seen it – years of working in the Stockyards rubbing salt into pork had bleached the pigment from the man's arms and hands.

'I'm sorry,' she said, 'I didn't mean to stare.'

'It's all right. It's quite something, ain't it?' he said, looking at his own hands, turning them over, as if appraising an antique. 'Maybe if I did the rest of my body I wouldn't have to keep working here,' he said, before bursting into a laugh which caused the boss to look up from his paperwork with a scowl.

'Is there anywhere we can talk that's a little less noisy?' Michael asked.

'Sure,' said Weiler.

He led them out into the yard and around to the side of the building, where a patch of asphalt sloped down to a fence that separated the garage from its neighbor. A few hosepipes lay about, and the asphalt was wet and glittering in the sunshine.

'I guess this is about the Van Haren girl?' said Weiler, leaning against the fence and taking a pack of cigarettes from his trousers.

Michael gave the man a quizzical look and he shrugged.

'Ain't nothing else happened to me that'd make two Pinks wanna come talk,' he said, smiling again, but more guarded this time. He lit his cigarette and inhaled.

'What happened? Someone kill the girl or something?'

'Why d'you say that?' asked Ida.

'Cuz it was damn clear she was in a jam and running away from someone.'

'Why don't you tell us what happened from the start?' said Ida.

'Sure,' the man replied. 'I got the call and drove over to the house and the maid was waiting out on the street. I knew the house. I mean, I knew whose house it was, what family lived there. The maid told me to drive round to the back and keep the engine running low. I got round there and the maid hustles the girl out through the gardens. The girl's got a suitcase in her hand. Looked shook up, you know? I went to put her case in the trunk but she said she wanted it on the seat next to her. That's all right, I said. She got in the back, told me to head for Illinois Central and I did.

'The whole way she's looking over her shoulder, biting her nails, agitated, jumpy. When we were a few blocks north of the station there was a holdup on Clark and she starts getting more nervous, you know. And then she tells me she'll walk the last few blocks, and gets her purse out and throws me a five-spot. Says keep the change. I asked if everything was all right, but she just nodded and jumped out.'

The man finished the story with a shrug and took a drag on his cigarette.

'You remember what time this was?' asked Ida.

Weiler thought a moment. 'Can't say as I do. I picked her up 'bout ten maybe. Ten-thirty. Me and the boys at the cab station were listening to the game on the radio and I got annoyed I had to take the call before it ended. Maybe it was coming up to eleven by the time she paid up and hopped out.'

'You remember exactly where you were when she jumped out?'

Weiler took a puff on his cigarette, rubbing his chin.

'Not sure. Maybe between Ninth Street and Eleventh. I can't say more than that.'

'And after she got out – you see where she went?' Ida asked.

The man shook his head.

'You notice anything else after that?'

'No. I drove on up to the station and got in the rank to catch a return fare.'

'You speak to anyone about this? The cops?'

The man shook his head. 'Why would I?'

'Well, if anyone does come asking questions, you keep your mouth shut and give us a call.'

Michael handed him a card and the man took it in his strange white hands, stared at it a moment and nodded.

'Thanks for your help,' said Ida.

'Pleasure,' he said, grinning back at her.

'You work here and at the Stockyards?' she asked.

'I do night shifts at the Yards when I can, seeing as neither job pays enough.'

A lot of the companies in the Stockyards worked around the clock, having realized from the example of the city's steel plants and forges, which ran like a ring of fire around Chicago, that it was cheaper and more profitable never to switch anything off.

'Must be tough,' said Ida.

'You know how it is, they whistle while you work,' he said, nodding in the direction of the garage. 'Ain't the worst work in the Stockyards. I could be sweeping lard.'

'What's so bad about that?'

'The smell. It never comes off. People been retired ten years and they still stink of it.'

14

The Chicago's Greatest Burlesque was a 'refined' burlesque show on an unlimited run at the State-Congress Theater, a tumbledown venue in the dingier end of the South Loop which showed two-reel movies in between the live acts. Jacob headed down there for the matinee and found the place about half full with patrons who were exclusively male and exclusively drunk. Any pretense that the Chicago's Greatest was a 'refined' burlesque was quickly slashed – Jacob had to sit through a Scottish minstrel brigade, a couple of ancient Keystone comedies and a 'chicken concert' of Irish bagpipes, which the rest of the audience lapped up.

Eventually the Lollipop Girls came on, to cheers, wolf whistles, boisterous obscenities and riotous applause. The Lollipops were eight Negro girls in skimpy, sequin-strewn dresses and feather hats, dancing a jazz variation of the cancan as the pit band played up-tempo ragtime numbers. Jacob scanned the faces of the girls, trying to figure out which one had, until his untimely demise in a Bronzeville alleyway, been dating Benny Roebuck. Not one of them seemed stupid or desperate enough.

Jacob left a little before the girls had finished their second dance routine and headed over the road to a grocery. Out front were three or four rows of shelves containing fruit and vegetables wilting in the summer heat and picking up a dusting of fumes from the cars driving by on State Street. Also on display was a selection of hastily slapped-together bouquets. Jacob bought one of the less dead-looking ones and headed back to the theater, circling the exterior till he found the stage door.

He knocked a couple of times and the door opened to reveal

a sour-looking elderly woman in a grey business suit, makeup pasted onto her face with the consistency and pinkness of cake decorations. Jacob could see she wore her seven decades well, with a certain arrogant dignity. She eyeballed him and the sorry-looking flowers and figured she had his number.

'The girls don't see visitors,' she said, tone sharp, taking a puff on the cork-tipped cigarette in her hand. 'But if you leave your flowers I'll gladly pass them on.'

'They're for Esther.'

'Oh . . .' At his mention of the name the woman stopped short. 'Esther hasn't been in the last few nights,' she said in a different tone, quieter, hesitant.

'Where's she been?'

'None of us know.'

Jacob thought a moment and decided to change tack. He took his press pass out and showed it to the woman. 'Esther's boyfriend was killed a few nights ago and I'm looking into it. I'm worried Esther might be in trouble. Can I talk to you about her?'

The woman stared at him warily, making no move.

'Please,' said Jacob. The word came out of his mouth with more exasperation than he'd expected it to, and he hoped he hadn't made the woman even more suspicious.

'I didn't really know the girl,' she said after a pause. She took another drag on her cigarette, thought some more; then beneath the layer of makeup, her expression softened.

'You're better off speaking to Geneva,' she said. 'Come in. I'll see if she wants to talk.'

The woman swung the door open and led Jacob into the backstage area. They walked down a narrow, wood-paneled passageway made narrower by pieces of scenery and stage equipment propped up against the walls. They turned a corner and the old woman opened a door onto a cramped and dazzlingly lit changing room.

'Wait here,' she said, and stepped inside.

Half a minute later the door opened again and the old woman nodded at him to enter.

'No touching the merchandise,' she said, before turning and hobbling off the way she had come.

Jacob stepped into the room to be greeted by the eight Lollipops in various states of undress, a row of mirrors, hundred-watt light bulbs, cigarette smoke, rails of flimsy clothing and bare brick walls. At the end of the room, next to a Chinese paper screen, a statuesque girl in a silk dressing robe made eye contact with Jacob and raised her hand. He walked over, skirting around the other girls seated in front of the mirrors.

'Geneva? I'm Jacob.'

'Take a seat.'

She motioned to a flimsy-looking wicker chair in the corner behind her. Jacob sat and she studied him a moment, and then she noticed the flowers.

'There's a garbage can over there,' she said, turning back to the mirror. Jacob dumped the bouquet, and looked at her reflection. She was generously curved, with dancer's legs in peach-colored stockings. On either side of her face were streaks of glitter which she was removing with a cotton ball.

'You know what's happened to Esther?' she asked, catching Jacob's eye in the mirror.

'No. All I know is her boyfriend got killed a few days ago. About the time she disappeared, I'm guessing.'

'Benny's dead? What happened?'

'Someone strangled him. You knew him?'

She paused a minute, taking in the news, then she shook her head.

'No. Just what Esther told me.'

'Which was?'

'That he was no good. All she ever did was complain about him, but that's what she's like, complaining there's air to breathe.'

She spoke with practiced terseness, wiping the makeup off her face with quick, strong swipes.

'You mind if I smoke?' asked Jacob.

'Not if you're sharing.'

Jacob took out his Luckies, passed one to Geneva, and leaned over to light it for her. As he did so she met his eye and smiled, and Jacob caught a glimpse of a mouth crowded with too many teeth. He sat back, lit his own cigarette, and Geneva started removing the festoon of pins and barrettes holding her hair in place.

'You think Esther's in trouble?' she asked.

'Maybe. I'd like to find out but I don't know much about her. Can you fill me in on the details?'

'Like?'

'Her second name, her address, what she looks like . . .'

Geneva took a puff on her cigarette, then laid it in the ashtray on the counter, rummaged around in a drawer and pulled out a piece of paper which she passed to Jacob.

'That's her a couple of years ago,' she said. 'She used to work at the Sunset.'

Jacob looked at the menu she'd handed him, on the reverse of which was a photograph of two dancers. The Sunset Café was a Bronzeville Black and Tan, run, indirectly, by Capone's Outfit. Like many of the Black and Tans it had a set regime for its entertainments: professional dancers would get on stage and perform a new dance step, and then the floor was thrown open to the customers, who would try to copy it. To assist, the dance steps and photographs of dancers performing them were printed on the menus.

The photo on this one showed Esther doing the Heebie-Jeebie, the dance popularized by the Louis Armstrong song of the same name a couple of years previously. In the photo Esther was dressed up like a jungle bunny in a straw skirt with fur bands around her ankles and wrists. Her male companion was holding a spear. She was a slight girl, pretty, light-skinned and well-proportioned, a fiery stare under long lashes.

'You got a second name? An address?' Jacob asked.

'Esther Jones,' said Geneva. 'She lives out near Federal Street. Not sure where. Ask the venue manager – that's the woman who brought you in here. Esther would have filled out her address on the employment form.'

'Age?'

'Twenty-five, twenty-six.'

'Anywhere else you know of I could ask after her?'

Geneva thought a moment. 'There's a school out in Hyde Park. A charity kind o' place run by a bunch of rich, old Gold Coasters. I don't know the name. But Esther used to help out with dance classes over there. Give it a try if you want.'

As he jotted down all the details in his notebook, Geneva stood, whisked off the dressing gown and threw it over one of the clothes rails and Jacob caught a glimpse of her statuesque body, a flash of calves that had been well walked in. She slipped into a black evening dress fringed with gold and zipped herself up. Then she turned to look at Jacob and smiled, her eyes sparkling, reflecting the flames of a fire that wasn't in the room, making Jacob think how a ton of mascara and a quart of Spanish blood couldn't have made her look more sultry.

She was about to say something when the door opened and a girl poked her head in and shouted across the room.

'Skip the gutter, Geneva!'

Geneva nodded at the girl, then turned back to Jacob.

'That's my ride,' she said. 'When you track down Esther, tell her to call me. We're all real worried.'

'Will do,' said Jacob with a smile, and Geneva smiled back. She grabbed a cloche hat from the counter, wrapped her hair under it, picked up a purse and headed toward the door in a stride as long as her legs. Jacob pocketed his notebook and headed past the other girls, following Geneva's path to the exit. He walked down the corridor till he found the venue manager, who was standing outside a storeroom discussing something with one of the men from the Scottish minstrel brigade, who was still wearing his kilt and hadn't removed the black shoe polish from his face. She broke off the conversation when she saw Jacob approaching and looked at him expectantly.

'I was hoping to get Esther's address. Geneva said you'd have it.'

The woman eyed him a moment, deciding whether to give it to him or not.

'I just want to talk to her,' he said. 'If I find out she's all right, I'll call to let you know.'

The woman thought some more and eventually looked at the minstrel.

'Wait here,' she said, and she took Jacob into a cramped, messy office and got Esther's employment card from a filing cabinet. She looked at it and puzzlement scraped along the creases of her face.

'Well, I'll be. She's left her address blank.'

The woman passed the card over to Jacob and he looked at it. The name was there, and the date of birth, but nothing else. Jacob passed back the card.

'Much obliged anyway,' he said, and the old woman nodded, still looking perplexed.

When he got back outside, he headed straight to the grocery from which he'd bought the flowers, where he'd seen a pay phone. He checked the time and called Lynott at the station. While he waited to be connected, he took the menu out of his pocket and stared at the photo of Esther once more, wondering why a girl like that would be going out with a man like Roebuck – a middle-aged, low-level thug whose horses were always coming in fourth.

Lynott's voice came down the phone line. 'Yeah?'

'Lynott? It's Jacob. I just found out that Roebuck's girlfriend went missing about the same time he got killed. His *Negro* girlfriend. I think she might be in trouble too.'

'Shit.'

'It's starting to look like Anton Hodiak again. Can you call the Bureau for a search?'

'Sure, let me get a pen . . . okay . . .'

'Esther Jones, date of birth January thirteenth, 1904. Negro, about five eight, I guess, dancer's build. We need to move quick on this, Frank. God knows who else he might have abducted.'

15

Babe Ruth swung his bat through the air and it connected with the ball in a thunderous, piercing crack and then the ball was on the other side of the ballpark, people rushing toward it, a swirl of bodies in the stands, a whirlpool. The scene was watched from the opposite side of the stadium by two figures with the resigned expressions of men who had watched their team get trounced plenty of times in the past, and would probably see them get trounced plenty of times more, at least whilst Ruth, Gehrig and Combs were playing for the opposition.

'This is embarrassing,' said Walker, Michael's friend in the State's Attorney's, who'd telegrammed the previous night to ask him to drop the Van Haren case.

'That it is,' said Michael. 'That it is.'

He cracked a peanut between his thumb and forefinger, let the fibrous scraps of shell fall to the floor and threw the peanuts into his mouth. He hadn't had a chance to eat yet. After the trip to the taxicab company he'd headed downtown to meet Walker, while Ida had gone to meet Gwendolyn's friend who was somehow involved in the plot to steal the girl away to Montreal.

'You remember McCue?' Walker asked, and Michael nodded, conjuring up the image of a lean, wise-cracking Dubliner, an investigator at the SA's.

'He got a job with the Yankees,' said Walker, nodding down at the fat man waddling through the dust far below them. 'Baby-sitting Babe Ruth. They got seven detectives there working shifts, following him around, making sure he doesn't get into trouble. The way McCue tells it, there's a whole wake of chaos following

Ruth around – honeypots, whores, pimps, swindlers, blackmailers, con men, gamblers – all of 'em making a beeline for him as soon as the Yankees arrive in town. And Ruth's too stupid to see the trouble coming on his own.'

Michael nodded and looked out over the field, to the distant, chubby figure heading toward the dugout, looking as much of an athlete as the overweight vendor who'd sold them the peanuts.

'Sounds like quite the gig for McCue,' Michael said. Walker was stalling him with the story about Ruth and his brigade of detectives. He'd been stalling since they'd met outside the game and bought their tickets, and it being Michael's opinion that people only ever stalled when they had bad news, he wanted Walker to get on with it.

'You didn't ask me here to talk about the Yankees,' he said, maybe a little too tersely, and Walker turned and gave him a peculiar sort of half-shrug.

'I've been asked to offer you a job,' said Walker. 'What are you making over at the Pinkertons? Four grand a year?'

'Something like that.'

'We'll pay you six.'

'Six grand a year for an investigator?'

'Chief investigator. You'll have your own team,' said Walker, 'and you'll be doing something useful – actually helping convict criminals. What are you doing over at Pinks? Peeping in keyholes? Busting strikes? You're better than that, Michael. It'll be like working for the police again. You'll have some authority.'

'And what are the strings?'

'The strings are you have to drop the Van Haren case.'

'Just like that? Why?'

'They didn't tell me.'

'And how exactly would I have to do it?'

'Stall her. The mother, I mean. Tell her you're looking into it and let it grow cold. You know how it works, you used to be on the force.'

Michael nodded. If he told Mrs Van Haren he was refusing the case, she'd just go to someone else, and then Walker would be having this chat with another private investigator. They didn't just want him to drop the case, they wanted him to lie to her.

'And if I refuse?' asked Michael.

'Things'll happen I won't be in a position to stop. No matter how much I like you as a friend.'

Walker turned to look at him and gave him that half-shrug again.

'We've known each other years, Walker – tell me what's going on.'

'I said I don't know.'

'Well, tell me what you *do* know.'

'Nothing. Jesus. Yesterday afternoon I was in the office and Senator Deneen came in to see Schmidt.'

Michael nodded. Schmidt was Walker's boss, the head of the Criminal Prosecutions Bureau, and was allied to the Deneen faction of the Republican Party.

'Schmidt closed his office blinds and they had a big, long powwow and a half-hour later, Deneen strides out of the office and Schmidt's secretary says he wants to talk to me. I go in there and he starts asking me about you, making sure the two of us are still friends, and then he tells me I should make you a job offer in return for dropping a case. Said make the offer and if that doesn't work, scare him.'

Michael paused to think. Yesterday afternoon, just a few hours after Mrs Van Haren had visited them. Whoever was informing on her was making speedy work of it. And now she was passed out in the middle of the day, a bottle of sleeping pills on her bed-side table.

'What's the link between the senator and Van Haren?'

'No idea. Van Haren's a financier, ain't he? Probably helped swell the senator's campaign coffers,' said Walker. Then he turned to look at Michael, and when he spoke again, his tone was different, softer. 'I don't like being the messenger here, not by a damned sight, but what can I do?'

'Doesn't look like either of us is in a position to do much at all,' said Michael, his eyes on the game.

'You're in a position to drop the case and take the job.'

Michael stayed silent and cracked a peanut between his fingers and tossed it into his mouth. 'And what happens to Ida? She get to be in my team?'

'You know we can't have someone like that in the State's Attorney's. She can stay on with the Pinks. A girl like that'll do well wherever she is.'

Walker shrugged. There were plenty of females working in the justice system, deputy SAs, lawyers, reporters, doctors, pathologists, but none of them were Ida's race.

He thought about his protégée, about how a couple of hours earlier she had been handling the manager of the cab company, how she hadn't reacted to his jibes, how deftly she had forced him to bring them the driver, without asking for Michael to take over, or even raising her voice.

'You know much about a man named Charles Coulton?' Michael asked.

'Which one?'

'There's more than one?'

'There's Charles Coulton Senior, the banker, and then there's Charles Coulton Junior, the wastrel. Why these rich guys are always giving their sons the same name I'll never know.'

'Beats me,' said Michael. 'One of them's engaged to the missing girl. I'm guessing the son. He's disappeared, too, by the way. You know anything about him?'

'The son? Nothing much,' said Walker. 'A rich boy about town, drinks a lot, socializes a lot, wakes up late a lot.'

'And the father?'

'That he's wealthy and he's shady. A self-made social climber.'

'Where's he from?'

'From the dark side of the far side of the wrong side of the tracks.'

Michael frowned at him and Walker smiled before explaining. 'Washington DC,' he said. 'I heard he was involved in one of those cons down in Florida – you know, selling swampland to people like someone was going to build a hotel on it. Then he got involved in the oil-reserve scandal with all those Harding secretaries.'

Michael nodded. President Harding's administration earlier in the decade had gone down as the most corrupt in American history. The president had appointed only personal friends to the cabinet and in the administration's twenty-nine-month life, they'd managed to embezzle or squander over two billion dollars, either because the president was in on it, or because he was too stupid to notice. The largest of all the corruption scandals centered on the fraudulent awarding of naval oil-reserve leases. Eventually some of the politicians and oilmen who had colluded in the frauds had been put on trial, but mostly they escaped scot-free, with the money still in their pockets and the taxpayer left to pick up the bill.

'Seems like on one side, Michael, you got a world o' trouble,' said Walker. 'And on the other side you got a better job paying a helluva lot more money. Why'd you wanna go up against a senator and a millionaire and the State's Attorney's and whoever the hell else is involved?'

Michael thought about the two paths in front of him, imagined walking down them both. He and Ida had filed the reports of their initial meeting with Mrs Van Haren. And they'd made no mention of her offer of a reward, or a bribe, or hush money, or whatever it was, meaning they'd get sacked if anyone found out. And now it turned out a senator was mixed up in it, and a financier with connections in Washington, and Michael was getting the feeling they'd put their jobs on the line for something they didn't have a hope of seeing through. But despite all that, or maybe because of it, Michael's resolution hardened like a bruise.

'You got kids, Walker?'

'I got two.'

'Then you'll understand my position in not wanting to rail-road a grief-stricken mother by shit-canning the investigation.'

Walker peered at him, surprise chased across his face by a sad sort of acknowledgment. He nodded eventually and they looked out over the game once more, and Michael thought how he'd have to tell Ida and Annette that the circumstances had changed for the worse.

'I didn't think you'd take it,' said Walker. 'You've got the whole dogged routine down pat.'

'Dogged?'

'You're the only man I've ever met who fits the word.'

16

The Illinois Women's Athletic Club was one of the Magnificent Mile's many new and ostentatious buildings, part of a decade-long building spree that had seen skyscrapers sprouting up on either side of the road, like so many bony fingers groping at the sky. A tall thin slice of bright redbrick, it rose seventeen stories into the air, and was dotted all over with tastefully chosen Gothic motifs – bay windows, arches, parapets, stone tracery, finials, and on each of its corners, castle towers topped with crucifixes. The uppermost eight floors were given over to the use of the Athletic Club and it was in the reception there that Ida waited that afternoon, staring through a window eastwards over Tower Court, across the rooftops to the shimmer of the lake beyond.

'Miss?' said a hesitant voice and Ida turned to see a receptionist flitting toward her.

'Miss Marlena is in the solarium. If you'd like to follow me,' she said, holding a hand up to the interior of the club.

'The solarium?' said Ida, as they went through a set of doors.

'It's a room that faces south, to catch the sun.'

Ida nodded again, trying to brush off the condescension. They walked down a corridor with walls of *fleur de rose* marble and a floor of sparklingly bright maple parquetry. They passed by dressing rooms, dining rooms, exercise rooms, reception rooms, then past a library finely paneled in mahogany, up some stairs, and into the solarium. The receptionist opened the door and stood by as Ida entered, then she pointed out Miss Marlena Jansen seated in the far corner, and departed with a smile.

The day before, when Mrs Van Haren was in their office, one

of the details they'd taken from her was the name of Gwendolyn's closest friend, Lena Jansen. They'd called her and arranged an appointment for the following afternoon. Then in the morning Gwen's maid had mentioned that Lena was involved in the plot to spirit Gwendolyn away. So what was supposed to be an interview to get some background information had turned into something more. Ida had to find out what she knew: why Gwen had run away; how she'd spent her last day in the city; what the Negro she'd visited in Bronzeville had to do with it all; and most importantly, what Gwendolyn had seen that had scared her so.

Ida crossed the long, rectangular room, passing by armchairs and sofas in which groups of women were chatting, some of them in sports clothes, others in city wear. On the room's southern side, a huge bank of windows opened out onto the city and through them the afternoon sun cascaded in, rightly earning the room its name. The windows were open and on the impossibly high ceiling, large electric fans whirred away, doing their best to dispel the heat. Ida passed by some plants in great metal pots and stopped at a corner where two bamboo lounge chairs were arranged around a bamboo coffee table. In one of the chairs, with her back to Ida, sat a female figure reading a magazine and Ida noticed that despite the heat, the figure was wearing chamois gloves that went all the way up to her elbows.

'Miss Jansen?' said Ida, and the woman turned around, studied her a moment, and broke out in a sly grin.

'You're the detective?' she said a little incredulously.

Ida stepped forward and passed the woman her business card. The woman took it and stared at it a moment with a smile.

'Please, take a seat,' she said, waving to the chair opposite her. 'And please call me Lena.'

Ida sat and waited as Lena continued to scan the card with a smile on her face that suggested she found the idea of being interviewed by a female detective delightfully bohemian, and Ida could already feel herself becoming an anecdote. She looked about the room once more, taking in the dark green wallpaper of a peacock-tail design.

'You're very good-looking for a detective,' the woman said finally, looking up from the card. 'Would you like a drink? I'm having a lime-juice soda. It's what they drink in India to cool down.'

'I'll have one too, then. Thank you.'

The woman raised her hand, and in a moment a waitress was at her side and she was ordering the drink. As she did so Ida cast her eye over Marlena Jansen. She was in her early twenties and was finely made, with eyes the color of slate, and hair marceled into gleaming flaxen waves that rolled across her forehead and crashed down her neck.

'You're the same Ida Davis that solved the Brandt kidnapping?' Lena asked when the waitress had left. Ida nodded.

'Kudos. I followed the case in the papers. I'm no judge of these things but it seems it was quite the achievement. So, how can I help?'

'Well, Miss Gwendolyn's mother asked us to investigate her disappearance and she gave us your name as her closest friend. And your name also came up when we spoke to Miss Florence, Gwendolyn's maid.'

Ida kept her eyes on Lena's face and noticed a twitch under her skin that momentarily disturbed the surface of her beauty.

'No need to lie to you, then?'

Ida shook her head. 'Florence told us about the arrangements to get Gwendolyn to Canada. You haven't heard anything from her yet?'

'Unfortunately not.'

'She also told us that on the day she disappeared, Gwendolyn was looking for her fiancé, to break off their engagement. She went to see a man in Bronzeville called Randall Taylor who she thought might know Charles Coulton's whereabouts. Then, hours later, she turned up at the Van Haren house in a state of shock.

Between being dropped off at Marshall Field's and her return, her whereabouts are unaccounted for – that's at least half the day and most of the evening. Do you know where she was in those hours?'

'I honestly don't know. Looking for Chuck, I guess – that's Charles Coulton.'

'Why did she lie about going to Marshall Field's?'

'I suppose she didn't want her parents to know she was going to Bronzeville. Whatever happened to her in between, when Gwendolyn returned to the house she was hysterical. Her maid didn't know what to do, so they called me up. Gwendolyn ranted down the phone at me, not making sense, saying she'd seen something awful and she had to get away. I spoke to Florence and we made the arrangements to get her on the train while her parents were out. She was supposed to call when she arrived, but she never did.'

'She didn't say what she'd seen?'

Lena shook her head. 'Something about bloodied hands, and a bloodied face. She used the word "slaughter".'

'You don't know if she ever caught up with Charles Coulton?'

Lena shook her head again.

'And this man that she went to meet, Randall Taylor – do you know him?'

'I know him very well. He's a Negro go-between we employ sometimes, when we go slumming in Bronzeville.'

Ida frowned, surprised that these people went slumming and that they used go-betweens: Negro fixers who organized nights out for rich whites in Bronzeville. The men arranged for booze and narcotics and entry to nightclubs and the best seats in the house and prostitutes in apartments – buffet flats – for after the nightclubs closed.

'Gwendolyn went slumming too?'

Lena nodded. 'There's more life in the Black Belt than in the rest of this city put together, Miss Davis, but I suppose you already know that,' she said, smiling.

'What does he look like?'

'Good-looking. Pleasant. Fair-skinned for a Negro. But not as fair-skinned as you,' she said, with that smile again.

'You know where I can get in contact with him?'

'I'm afraid not. Chuck and Lloyd always dealt with him.'

'Lloyd?'

'Lloyd Severyn – a friend of Chuck's.'

At that moment the waitress returned with Ida's drink. She placed it on the coffee table between them: a tall thin glass on a small dish of embellished metal.

'Why Montreal?'

'She'd been there often, she knew the place well. It's out of the country, too – I suppose that was a factor. And I don't think she had any relatives there, no one to tell her parents where she was hiding out.'

'Why was it so important that her family didn't find out?'

'Because they would have forced her to stay in Chicago, to go through with the wedding.'

Lena took off her gloves, revealing slender fingers topped off with a moon manicure, the base of the nail left unpainted. She reached into her handbag and took a cigarette case from it, a delicate box of Siberian jade. She took a cigarette from the case and lit it and offered the case to Ida. Ida smiled and took one of the cigarettes and when she put it into her mouth she realized it was cork-tipped – no need to worry about swallowing stray flakes.

'What are they like?' she asked, lighting the cigarette.

'The Van Harens?' asked Lena. 'The usual kind of Gold Coast family, rich as the rain and just as sad. The mother is hysterical, the father distant. Gwendolyn had no brothers or sisters. It was just her and them. It's no wonder she ended up confiding in that maid of hers.'

Ida smiled and nodded. She picked up the glass and took a sip, and the citrus and soda fizzed in her mouth, sharp and cool with a metallic tang.

'And the wedding to Charles Coulton? That was arranged?'

'I'm not sure "arranged" is the right word. The Van Harens need Coulton's money. They need it enough to overlook the fact that the engagement was something of an embarrassment to them.'

'In what way?'

Lena smiled ruefully, took a drag on her cigarette.

'Coulton Senior's an arriviste, and he's got a murky past,' she said. 'There's an upper crust to Chicago society, and stupid as it may seem, these people who've only been rich for a couple of generations look down on "new" money. They're snobbish and entitled, and to them, Senior's a joke. For his attempts at fitting in, for his accent, his manners. I've heard him described by them as all manner of things – "an ape in a suit", "as hard as rigor mortis", "rougher than a rent collector". The Van Harens are part of that set, so you can imagine how everyone laughed when it emerged their children were engaged.'

'So Gwendolyn wanted to call it off because she was being forced into it?'

'Well, yes, but there was something else.'

Here Lena trailed off, took a drag on her cigarette and stared at Ida as she pursed her lips and exhaled the smoke. 'Chuck's romantic tastes didn't extend to people like Gwen. There were some incidents with Chuck when he was at college. The father brushed it all under the carpet. He forced Chuck to go into the family business, forced him to marry Gwen. I suppose he'd have gone along with it all for a quiet life, and met up with his boys on the side.'

Ida nodded and thought back to the engagement photos, Gwendolyn's expression.

'When did Gwen find out about Chuck?' she asked.

'I think it just dawned on her. She came to me and we spoke about it, and she wasn't sure what to do. A few months later she asked her mother to call off the wedding and her mother strong-armed her to go through with it. I think her mother was forced into a loveless marriage too and saw it as some kind of duty. I suppose that's why she's so grief-stricken at Gwen running off like that – feels guilty.'

Just then there was a commotion behind them, the sound of a door bursting open, voices, a chorus of laughs. Ida turned around to see a group of four or five girls who had stumbled into the room by accident and were hastily trying to get back out. They were dripping wet, wearing bathing costumes and towels. Ida frowned, thinking she recognized one of the girls. But before she could be sure, they stepped out again and closed the door, and all that was left were the tuts in the air from some of the older women, and a few puddles of water on the floor, which one of the waitresses was already approaching with a towel in her hand and an annoyed expression on her face.

Ida turned back to Lena, still frowning.

'Was one of those girls Clara Bow?' she asked.

'I believe so,' said Lena. 'The town's filling with celebrities for the boxing match in a couple of weeks. Some of the starlets have been here using the pool.'

'There's a swimming pool here?'

Lena nodded. 'Opulent, no? A tank of thousands of gallons of water all the way up here, while in the depths below, the city swelters.' She grinned, as if she understood the decadence involved, and liked it all the more so for it.

'If you'd like to go swimming I can arrange a pass for you,' she continued. 'I'm sure most of the women won't notice your complexion. At least not the older ones, who are the ones you have to watch out for. There's loungers on the roof too, for sunbathing. I think that's where Miss Bow and her companions were heading when they took a wrong turn.'

'Thank you for the offer,' said Ida, returning the condescension with some of her own. 'But . . .'

'But you'd prefer getting back to business. What else is it you'd like to know?'

'Tell me about Gwendolyn's suicide attempt.'

Lena raised her eyebrows. 'You *have* done your detective work,' she said. 'Although it's "attempts", plural. Twice she tried it, though she's had sinking spells ever since we were girls. She took a razor to her arms last Christmas and a few months after that she stole some of her mother's sleeping pills.'

Ida nodded, wondering how bad it had to get to seek the solace of razors and pills. In the silence she listened to the whirring of the fans above, to the glassy fizz of the soda and ice on the table.

'And her parents?'

'What could they do? Put her in an asylum? The family reputation couldn't stretch to that. It was tarnished enough by them having to marry her into new money. I suggested they take her to a psychological doctor, but they dismissed that as far too Jewish. Then I suggested we take her away somewhere on holiday but they wanted her close by, in case she tried to do it again. The girl was their meal ticket to Coulton's money. They ordered the staff at the house to keep an eye on her, after taking away anything that she could harm herself with.'

Ida nodded. Then Lena leaned forward to stub out her cigarette and Ida saw on a chain around her neck a pendant in the shape of a tiny spoon, silver and shining. Ida had seen other young girls around town wearing them; they were used to snort cocaine, the drug of choice among flappers and high-society fashionistas. Ida guessed that beyond their practical use, the tiny spoons were some kind of statement, a membership card for a secret and mischievous fellowship.

Lena finished extinguishing her cigarette and looked up to see Ida staring. She smiled, leaned back in her chair, lifted her hand into the air and ordered herself another drink.

'Tell me about Chuck's friend, Lloyd Severyn.'

'Chuck met him during the war. They served in France together. He's not the type that Chuck would have befriended under any other circumstances, but I suppose war binds people in ways we can't imagine.'

'And a physical description?'

'Oh, tall and thin. Brown hair. Narrow eyes. Has scars on his neck and a burned-out voice. From the mustard gas in the war. It did something to his vocal cords and now he can only speak in, well, I guess you could call it a whisper, but not quite. Somewhere between a whisper and a growl. Like the inside of his throat is coated in rust. It's quite unsettling.'

'Seems like a strange man for Chuck to stay friends with.'

'They're not just friends,' said Lena, arching an eyebrow. 'And you have to understand Chuck to understand why they'd maintain an acquaintance.'

'Meaning?'

'Meaning Chuck's weighed down by his father's expectations. He's been sent to all the best schools so he can fit into the upper crust. I suppose his father wanted him to come out of college as a horse-rider, a yachtsman, a strong-jawed captain of industry, someone to take over the family empire. Instead Chuck's come out of it sensitive and soft and terrified of his father, sees him as some kind of ogre. The two of them can't be in each other's company. Then there's the question mark over how his father came upon his money. I suppose Lloyd's a bridge for Chuck, between the old man's background and the expectations he has for his son.'

Ida frowned, picking her way through Lena's insinuations that Chuck's father was a criminal, and maybe Chuck's lover was too. Lena, seeing her confusion, waved her hand about in the air, implying it was of no consequence, a by-the-by fancy of hers.

'Chuck went missing on the same day as Gwen – according to Gwen's mother,' said Ida, 'but Florence said he'd disappeared before that. And no one's filed a missing person's report. I was wondering why that might be.'

'I think Mrs Van Haren got that wrong. Chuck vanished some time before Gwen. That's why she had to go searching for him.

And as for a missing person's report, I don't suppose his father's pride would stoop to looking for him.'

'What about Chuck's mother?'

'She died giving birth to him. Another reason why the father is less than fatherly to him.'

At this point the waitress returned and took away Lena's empty glass and replaced it with a fresh one As she did so, Ida peered about the room once more and her gaze alighted on the peacock-tail wallpaper. The circles at the center of each tail looked like so many eyes splayed all over the walls, and they gave Ida the feeling of being watched, of standing in the center of a poultry farm.

After a moment, the waitress departed and Ida turned her gaze to Lena once more.

'Thank you, Miss Jansen, you've been very helpful.'

'I'm glad to help. I've been worried sick about Gwendolyn. Anything I can do.' She smiled at Ida and Ida smiled back, thinking how the woman had looked and acted far from worried about her friend.

'And if you'd like to come swimming with me . . .' said Lena, taking a calling card from her purse, 'here are my details.'

She handed over her card and smiled, a gleam in her eye, that same unsettling look Ida normally only saw in men. Lena lit a new cigarette, and Ida watched the smoke from it languidly coil upwards, all the way to the ceiling fan, whose blades chopped it into pieces with the grim efficiency of an executioner. Ida was reminded of the processing machines she had seen in the Stockyards, the precision of their timing, the rhythmic doling out of death.

Five minutes later she was in an elevator heading back down to the city, out of the clouds, positing the following as the most likely explanation for what had happened: Gwen had met the go-between on the day she'd disappeared. He'd given her some way of finding Chuck. She'd found Chuck, told him she wanted to split up from him, and something had gone horribly wrong. She'd gone home, packed her bags and tried to leave town, but Chuck, or Severyn, or the go-between, or maybe all three of them, had caught up with her at the station and abducted her. Coulton's father was trying to cover it up, had leaned on the police to can the investigation, had got the State's Attorney's involved.

The explanation fitted all the evidence. But that's all it was, an explanation, a hypothesis, conjecture. They'd have to look into Gwendolyn's fiancé, but also his father with the murky past. Initially she'd thought the Van Harens were odd, but now the Coulton family seemed even more so, as did the friend, Lloyd Severyn, and the go-between, Randall Taylor. Plenty of leads to be getting on with.

The elevator reached the ground floor, dinged open, and Ida strode through the foyer. Gwendolyn's friends, wayward and wealthy, went slumming in the Black Belt, and they employed a go-between who Gwendolyn had spoken to the day she disappeared. Ida smiled. If go-betweens and Bronzeville jazz clubs were involved, she knew exactly who to call for help.

PART THREE

BRIDGE

'Chicago is the imperial city of the gang world, and New York a remote provincial place governed by a proconsul . . . Beer has lifted the gangster from a local leader of roughs and gunmen to a great executive controlling a big interstate and international organization. Beer, real beer, like the water supply or the telephone, is a natural monopoly.'

ALVA JOHNSTON, *NEW YORKER* MAGAZINE, 1928

'There were many evidences that the Police Department was demoralized; that there were distinct and well-known alliances between the police and under-world celebrities; that gambling and liquor-running were not to be interfered with, and that it was risky for any police official to exercise any initiative on his beat or in his district without specific orders from headquarters. It was demonstrated early in the survey that the office of State's Attorney was being used extensively for political purposes and many habitual offenders and dangerous criminals were being released with little or no punishment.'

THE ILLINOIS ASSOCIATION FOR
CRIMINAL JUSTICE, 1928

17

A rent party was in full swing on the top floor of the Mecca Flats, a block-sized housing complex on 34th and State Street. The Mecca had been built for the World's Fair back in the 1890s, and something of its former grandeur could still be seen in its marble floors and art nouveau ironwork. But like much of the Southside, the Flats had slowly fallen into disrepair, and its middle-class tenants had moved out to be replaced by blue-collar workers, prostitutes and pimps, and a bohemian set of aspiring artists, writers and musicians.

When those same tenants were in arrears and didn't have any money, they'd host a rent party and charge an entry fee to scrape together the cash that'd keep the eviction notices from being pasted to their doors for another few days. Typically, as well as the booze, the hosts laid on the music, which due to the size of the apartments was normally just a Victrola or an upright piano, played boogie-woogie style, so the sound was full enough to dance to. It was a style that was exceptionally hard to play, the hands having to leap great distances across the keyboard with lightning speed. The man at the piano in the rent party that night was doing a good job of it, and the sound boomed through the apartment and echoed around the vastness of the courtyard.

At some point just after midnight, four young men in sharp suits walked through the overspill on the balcony and into the party proper – Louis Armstrong, Earl Hines, Zutty Singleton and Wild Bill Davison – and they found the place stiflingly hot, dangerously overcrowded, and dripping with good times.

Earl Hines was mobbed by the crowd as soon as they recognized him. Chicago's greatest piano player was ushered straight over to the upright, and much to the annoyance of the man already seated at the instrument, Earl was put on the stool, and ordered to play in his trademark 'trumpet style'. The crowd got even more frenetic in their dancing when he broke into his first number, an up-tempo rendition of 'Muskrat Ramble'. A girl who'd been leaning against the piano looking a little worse for wear perked up on hearing the melody, straightened her back and began singing the lyrics, straining to project her voice over Earl's playing. Louis, Zutty and Wild Bill – the only white man at the party – slunk off to the far side of the dance floor and claimed a spot by the windows, where they hoped there might be something of a breeze. Wild Bill sat on the sills and commenced rolling a reefer and Louis squeezed his way back through the crowd to buy them all some drinks.

He pushed past the people dancing and chatting and the couples in corners reaching all over each other and he made it to the kitchen where a crowd was waiting to refill their cups. He got in line and a few people looked his way and recognized him, and nodded hello or clapped him on the back. It had been six years since Louis had left New Orleans and arrived in Chicago. Six years since he'd gotten off that train and stepped into the Lincoln Gardens and been dazzled by what he saw, and in those six years, he'd become something of a star, not only to the people of the Southside, but to jazz fans all over the world.

He reached the front of the line, grabbed some drinks, and returned to the living room. He sat on the windowsill next to Wild Bill and Zutty, handed out the drinks and surveyed the crowd. It was the kind which always flocked to these sorts of parties – blues people that worked six days a week for subsistence wages, ground between the millstones of poverty and race hate, letting loose in the few free hours they had between clocking off on Saturday afternoon and church on Sunday morning.

He felt something scrape along his back and turned around to see what it was. Flypaper. A half-dozen rolls of it had been glued to the top of the window frame and left to dangle. The long brown strips were covered with scores of dead flies, and the thumping of the dancers' feet was shaking the strips of paper, making all those dead flies pulse with the music. Louis stared at it all a moment, the strips jumping in front of the clear night sky.

'Louis, I don't mean to alarm you,' said Wild Bill as he finished rolling the reefer, 'but ain't that Lil that just walked in?'

At the mention of his estranged wife's name, Louis' heart skipped a beat. He sat up and craned his neck to look through the crowd. And there she was, in a slinky dress and pearls, hair combed back into a perfect bob. Louis panicked, his thoughts helter-skelter. He was supposed to be meeting Alpha, his girl-friend, at the party, and he couldn't face dealing with a scene.

'What the hell is she doing here?' he asked, and Wild Bill shrugged.

Lil was an airs-and-graces kind of girl, from a good family, university-educated. She spent her nights at the theater, at the opera, at classical music recitals. A ratty rent party in the heart of the Southside was the very last place he'd expect her to be.

'I don't know,' Bill said, 'but she's seen you and she's heading this way.'

He grinned and together with Zutty, got up off the sill and disappeared into the crowd, leaving Louis alone. As Lil slipped through the crowd toward him, Louis noticed her pass the piano and turn to look at who was playing it. When she saw it was Earl Hines, she tried not to let the sting of it show on her face – Earl was the man who had effectively replaced her as the piano player in Louis' band.

'Hello, Louis,' she said in her hoity-toity tone of voice. 'How are you doing?'

'I'm doing good, Lil. How are you?' he said, hoisting a smile onto his face.

'Fine,' she replied, and both of them looked embarrassed at how awkward they were with each other, as shy as when they had first met, when Lil was the piano player with Joe Oliver's band, and Louis still an awkward greenhorn from down south.

'Quite the party,' she said, and Louis wasn't sure if she was being sarcastic, mocking the blue-collar people there and the low-down form their entertainment took. 'I see your boy Earl has no trouble turning his talents to the house style,' she said, nodding in Earl's direction, and Louis kept silent, not rising to the bait.

He nodded and they watched the man play a moment, letting loose a cascade of melody and rhythm. Hines was a classically trained pianist, just like Lil, but unlike Louis' wife, Earl was supremely talented, as talented as Louis. His timing was so perfect the drummers he played with complained at having to keep up, his chord changes so inventive and startling the rest of the band complained at having to follow his melodic line. It was only Louis that could match him, the two of them spurring each other on. When they played together, with Louis' perfect tone, and Hines's trumpet style punching through the rest of the band, the effect was something like a tornado.

'I heard you got a gig going at the Savoy,' said Lil.

'Sure,' he said. 'Me and Earl and Zutty. We're doing good.' He looked at her and smiled. He wanted to ask her what the hell she was doing there, and a paranoid notion rose up in his mind that she had followed him. He tried to think of something to say to her, figured he should ask after someone, but whom?

'How's your mother?' he said finally, and before the words had even left his mouth his heart was sinking. Lil gave him a look. It was Lil's mother that had given her all those airs and graces, who upon learning her daughter was dating an uneducated jazz player – and one from New Orleans, at that – had done every-thing in her power to stop them being together.

'Okay . . .' said Lil, still a little confused, and the two of them settled into another awkward silence, and they both stared out across the crowd. Earl finished the song he was playing, and the crowd whooped and he slid straight into the opening bars of 'Mecca Flat Blues', Jimmy Blythe's song about the housing project they were currently in. When the crowd recognized the melody they cheered, and began dancing once more, and the girl by the piano began singing the lyrics.

> . . . *Talk about blues but I've got the meanest kind*
> *Blue and disgusted, dissatisfied in mind* . . .

'He's good,' said Lil, nodding at Earl.

'I know.'

'I've been hearing those records you two have been putting out,' she said. 'They're real nice, Louis.'

Something about the way she said it made Louis feel there was a 'but' at the end of the sentence that had been left unsaid. Don't bite, he thought, and then a second later he ignored his own good advice.

'But . . .' he said.

'But what?'

'You were going to say "but", and then you didn't.'

He turned to look at her and she shrugged, her face all innocence.

'Oh, it was nothing,' she said, and the way she pronounced the 'Oh' – so rounded, so enunciated – rankled him.

> . . . *My Mecca flat man, he really don't understand* . . .

'You know, I was in Lyon and Healy's the other day,' she said airily, 'and they had a Victrola set up there, and they were playing a piece by Fletcher Henderson, and one of the customers said it was only after he'd starting buying records that he'd ever really heard jazz, and I thought that was so strange, you know? So I asked him what he meant, and he said that he'd heard it in clubs and parties, played live, but it was only once it was on record, in the peace of his own home, that he'd been able to sit down and really hear it, you know? Been able to study it.'

'What's your point, Lil?' said Louis, annoyed at her mention of Henderson.

'The point is,' Lil explained, 'I think there's an opportunity there. At the moment it's just jazz on records, but sooner or later someone's going to come along and turn it into more than that, turn it into art, into culture, into something that lasts. The only question is, who's that person gonna be? Who's gonna take jazz out of the nightclubs and turn it into art? Something that stands the test of time?'

> . . . *Mecca flat woman must be a jazzing hound*
> *Keep fooling with me and I'll cut you down . . .*

Louis looked at her and she smiled coyly. 'You're better than every other jazz player in this city,' she said, her tone rueful, as if she was talking about something she'd lost. 'It'd be nice if you lived up to your potential.'

She said it so resolutely, so disconsolately, that Louis couldn't even muster up any anger at how patronizing she was being. Beneath the words, he got the feeling that to Lil, Louis Armstrong was something she'd helped construct, something she still had an interest in. And Louis knew there was some truth in her view. He had always been shy, wanting to stay out of the limelight. He was happy playing second cornet, covering up Joe Oliver's mistakes. It was Lil who convinced him that Oliver was short-changing him, financially and artistically. She was the one who persuaded him to strike out on his own, had got him music lessons with the teacher at Kimball Hall, the German who had in turn been taught by Brahms. She had bought him sheet music to perfect his technique, drilled him for months on end so he learned classical fingering styles, pushed him to be as good as he could be, and even though they were now estranged, on the down slope to divorce, she was still pushing him on, goading him, managing him.

> *. . . Mecca flat woman stings like a stingaree*
> *Mecca flat woman take your teeth out of me . . .*

'Lil . . .' He turned to stare at her and saw her expression, a mix of shock and anxiety, and he followed her gaze across the dance floor to the far side of the room, but couldn't make out what had startled her.

'I gotta be going,' she said suddenly. She looked at him and smiled. 'I'll see you round.'

Louis peered once more to the other side of the room. Had she seen Alpha there? Lil stood and whisked herself off into the crowd and Louis lost sight of her, and then she resurfaced on the other side of the room and everything was made plain. She was by the door to the kitchen, talking to a man, trying to convince him of something, trying to convince him to leave. The man was good-looking, tall, light-skinned, and at least a few years younger than Louis. He wrapped his arm around Lil, and the two of them turned and headed for the exit.

'Shit,' said Louis, and his heart sank. That was how she'd ended up in the depths of the Southside: she was on a date with a man who was everything Louis wasn't.

> *. . . I'm going to find my Mecca flat man today*
> *Got the Mecca flat blues and somebody's going to pay . . .*

'I thought she'd never leave,' said a voice, and Louis looked up to see Wild Bill and Zutty standing in front of him, the two of them snickering.

'She put you through the wringer?' asked Zutty, passing Louis a reefer. How was it she could get him so riled up in such a short space of time?

'I don't know,' said Louis, with what must have been a forlorn expression because his two friends burst out laughing.

A few drinks later, Louis was still slumped on the window-sill watching the other people having a good time, the dead flies dancing. He was still feeling put out, still annoyed, still hearing Lil's words looping over and over. Was he not living up to his potential? Was he not producing hit records? Was he not playing to packed houses every night? Had he not become the poster boy for the artistic blossoming that was occurring in the city? What else did she expect from him? He was annoyed he hadn't justified himself to her, but the justifications he had by now perfected had come too late, so what was the point? Should he memorize them for when he next bumped into her? Waste all that energy carrying around arguments in his head?

Then there was the thought that maybe he was annoyed because she was telling the truth. He *was* looking for an artistic breakthrough – a new way to craft solos, to arrange them into a song. He'd been experimenting with Earl, who was likewise attempting to innovate, to elevate the piano beyond being just a rhythmic accompaniment, and they'd been successful, but something was still eluding him, and Lil had chimed right into it, the innovation he knew was there, lurking somewhere in the fledgling art form they'd all had a stake in creating.

Then he wondered about her mention of Fletcher Henderson; if it was supposed to be a dig at him, a reminder of his humiliation in New York. After Louis had been in Chicago a couple of years, Joe Oliver's band had split up and Louis had found work in one of the country's premier orchestras – Fletcher Henderson's band, which was based in New York. But the move out to the east coast turned into a bust. Louis became a joke amongst his colleagues, and a flop with the audiences, and after just a year he'd been kicked out of the band and, humiliated, he'd had to scurry back to Chicago. When he arrived in the city for a second time, he'd discovered Lil had been playing the field in his absence – something that Louis had likewise been doing in the Big Apple.

At some point after one o'clock, he spotted Alpha entering the party. He perked up when he saw her, smiled and waved her over. She looked good in the summer dress she was wearing, dark-skinned, seven years younger than him, bright with youthful expectation. It was only then that Louis realized he had left Lil for her opposite, too; Alpha was homely, unpretentious, uneducated, down-to-earth, non-judgmental. He guessed it wasn't a point of failure, but one of self-awareness. He was a month shy of twenty-eight years old, and he'd already left behind two wives, and if things went well with Alpha he'd have a third before he was thirty.

'What's wrong?' Alpha asked when she reached him and saw his face.

'Oh, nothing,' he said. 'What took you so long?'

'I had to wait for Momma to get home before I could leave Clarence,' she said.

'Everything all right?' he asked, and Alpha nodded.

'Good. What you wanna drink?'

'Bourbon,' she said, and he stood and was turning to head toward the kitchen when she touched him on the arm.

'I almost forgot,' she said. 'Ida called the house.'

'Oh, yeah?' he said, frowning. 'What she want?'

'Business. Said to call her back first thing tomorrow.'

Louis thought a moment, then he headed into the kitchen, casting a look at the dead flies dancing in front of the night sky as he went.

18

It was all on account of a girl, just the wrong side of sixteen. Greek and blonde – how often do you see that? Al had taken her virginity and put her up in a luxury suite at the Metropole, and pretty much kept her under lock and key, and he knew none of his men were stupid enough to touch her, so when she started burning and went to see the doc and took the Wassermann test and the doc diagnosed her with the pox, it meant she could only have gotten it from Al. She moaned and whined and bitched until Al agreed to get himself checked out too, even though he knew what the doc would say.

He found a clinic outside Chicago, in a two-bit town in the middle of nowhere, far enough away that word couldn't get out, and he dropped the Capone and booked in under the name Al Brown. He'd driven out there one afternoon in the emerald-green Rolls-Royce, stripped naked, sallied through an onslaught of tests, and now he'd gone back to get the results. Just him and his driver and Jack and Frank in the Rolls. The convoy he normally traveled in – a flivver in front, a touring car behind – he'd left in Chicago, figuring for these two trips the Rolls would be enough, with its bulletproof windows, steel sides, combination locks and machine gun strapped to the driver's seat.

He'd gone into the clinic and listened to the doctor for twenty minutes, asked a few questions, and walked out again in a daze, stepping onto the front steps and standing there looking at the street, the doctor's words still roaring like motorcycles round the metal drum of his brain.

Tertiary syphilis, mostly likely. That's third stage. It means it's spread. Maybe to the nervous system and the brain. For early stages, there's an arsenic-based drug – Salvarsan. But for late stage, I'm sorry, there's no cure. What exactly do you know about the disease?

There was the green Rolls, parked up on the sidewalk, and there were Jack and Frank, smoking cigarettes, turning to look at him, their faces dropping.

'Boss?' said Frank, hurrying over. 'Jeez, you look like you seen a ghost. What the hell happened in there?'

It took a couple of seconds, but Al snapped out of it. 'Let's get the fuck out of here,' he said, brushing past Frank and into the car.

They pulled into traffic, and Al stared out of the window.

Syphilis is caused by a spirochete, a worm-like bacterium, shaped like a corkscrew. (Here the doctor spiraled his finger through the air.) *First stage happens soon after infection. You get a chancre or boil on your genitals. Then it goes away. Second stage happens a few weeks later, you may get rashes on your hands and feet. Flu-like symptoms. Again, it all goes away, and the disease enters a latent stage. And then, in roughly a third of infected people, about fifteen years after infection, it comes back as tertiary syphilis. Unfortunately, it looks like you're one of them.*

Fifteen years. Flashes of Brooklyn. Borough of Churches. Navy Street in Red Hook, the slum where Al had grown up. It was next to the ocean, flushed with the brackish air of the Atlantic, spattered with seagull shit and the burned-oil smell of shipyards, and whatever businesses trailed in the wake of docks and sailors – saloons, tattoo parlors, gambling houses, brothels. Among the whores on Sands Street was an Irish girl, red-haired, the ocean in her eyes. His brother Ralph had caught something too. But like Ralph's case, Al's had cleared up. He remembered stepping out of her building, onto the street, a smile on his face.

If it develops into neurosyphilis, the spirochete may enter the brain, attack the frontal lobes – your personality may become exaggerated. You may suffer from mood swings, irritability, anxiety, loss of memory, mental impairment. Judging by what you've reported, you've experienced most, if not all of these symptoms. Eventually it erodes the personality completely, and you'll lose your mind. After that, it's just a matter of time.

He ran the doctor's words through his head, as if by repeating them over and over they might take on new meaning; he might discover he had misunderstood them, that it wasn't inevitable he'd go mad and die. He looked up to see his driver giving him a funny look through the rearview. The man's gaze flicked back to the road as soon as they made eye contact.

Al looked out of the window and saw they were driving through the Factory Belt. Soon they'd be in the Bungalow Belt, the ring of middle-class suburbs that encircled the city in a crescent shape, where people who had the means to escape the urban chaos moved. Al had always thought of them as suckers, drones who had to work for a living, but recently he'd started to envy them; he'd realized too late in life that unlike luxury suites and mansions and holidays, you couldn't purchase peace of mind and domestic tranquility with money and violence.

Roughly six percent of Americans have the disease. When the draftees were tested for the Great War, that number went up to ten percent. The vast majority recover from it. I'm sorry to say, for you, Mr Brown, it's a case of managing the disease, rather than curing it.

As they were driving through the slums on the outskirts of Chicago, he realized he didn't want to go back to the Metropole just yet, to face the questions and bantering of the men. He needed to be alone for a little bit longer.

'Take me to the *schvitz*.'

'It's nearly evening, boss. It'll be closing.'

'Then they'll open it.'

They pulled up outside the 14th Street Bath House, near the Maxwell Street ghetto. Al had learned about *schvitzs* from Jack

Guzik, one of the many Jews he was friends with, and employed in the Outfit. Jack had taken them along and they'd all become regulars, though it was years since Al had last visited the place.

They walked into the lobby and Frank and Jack spoke to the owner, and with a nod and a glance at Al, the owner, an old, stooped Yid, locked the door and hung up a sign: *Closed For Boiler Repairs*. Al told his men to wait outside, and he went into the changing rooms alone, hung up his clothes in the rusty metal lockers alone, walked into the *schvitz* itself alone, and sat in the Stygian heat and darkness and steam of the main sauna room alone. He couldn't remember the last time it had happened; being surrounded by sentinels was part of his life. Always bodyguards in front of him and behind, from the moment he woke to when he fell asleep. That was another thing those suckers in the Bungalow Belt had that he didn't – privacy, and the space to think.

But then he realized he wasn't alone, not quite. There was another customer in there who'd yet to leave, a middle-aged man sitting on a bench at the other end of the sauna. He smiled at Al through the gaps in the plumes of steam, and Al wondered if the man was a fairy. He glared at him through the gloom, but the man must not have seen; he continued to sit there, smiling, sweat dripping through the hairs on his chest, black and coarse. Then the steam billowed and the man disappeared and Al was alone once more.

He'd been in gangs in Brooklyn, but then most of the boys had. He'd met Frankie Yale and Johnny Torrio, but even then he'd been mostly legit. After he left school in the sixth grade, he worked three years in a munitions factory and another three as a paper-cutter. He met Mae and married her, and the two of them moved out to Baltimore and Al got a job as a bookkeeper for a construction firm. He wore a suit, learned accounting, spent his free time playing pool and dancing. That was his unremarkable life, and that might have been it – Al Capone the accountant. But then his father had died and it unearthed some deep-buried urges and anxieties. He quit his nine-to-five and called up his old mentor Torrio and asked him for a job. Torrio had told him to head out to Chicago to run one of his brothels. From there came riches and infamy and de-facto control of the world's third-largest city.

If it develops into neurosyphilis, the spirochete may enter the brain, attack the frontal lobes – your personality may become exaggerated.

Al had always thought his decision to go from regular working Joe to gangster had been caused by his father's death, by it triggering some deeper understanding of his own mortality. Now, in the darkness of the *schvitz*, he wondered about the spirochetes. What if it was them gnawing away at his brain that had been responsible for his decision? He imagined them like tiny worms, long and thin, not the spirals the doctor had suggested. Serpents or dragons, like the Chinese ones he saw snaking their way down chopsticks or the sides of chop-suey joints. Thousands of them in his head, eating away at his brain, deciding on his personality and the course of his life.

He thought about all the people he had beaten and tortured and killed, all the lives he had changed – had all that been caused by the spirochetes, too, plotting away in the darkness of his skull? And if all the bad things he'd done were the work of the worms, what did that say for his chance of entering heaven? If they were in charge, what did any of it matter – good or evil?

He couldn't be losing his mind. He couldn't *not* be in charge. Not now he was facing a war on three fronts – with Bugs Moran looking like he might make a move any minute, and the mayor withdrawing his backing, and the possible fight with New York that was looming.

Al rubbed the sweat from his face and looked about the gloom for the metal bowl of cold water. He found it near his feet, pulled the birch branches from it and swatted himself, the iciness trickling down his torso, cooling him, relaxing him.

When Al had originally moved to Chicago years before, the

idea was to set up Chicago as an outpost for the New York Mob. But Torrio and Al had been so successful that Chicago ended up the more powerful of the two cities. Now Al was hearing that New York was going to try and wrestle back control, that Frankie Yale and some up-and-comers – Meyer Lansky and Lucky Luciano – were in on the plan. Al knew the New York mobsters considered him an embarrassment – a man who courted the press, who'd turned himself into a celebrity, who made waves, who got them noticed by all the wrong people in Washington. Was that need to make himself famous the spirochetes too? That grasping after greatness? That grandeur that seemed forever just beyond his reach, in the haze at the top of the mountain?

. . . *your personality may become exaggerated.*

Now in the middle of one possible war with New York and another with Moran, half the Republican Party had been poisoned at the Ritz. Al had called Dante over from New York to investigate, and Dante had come, not suspecting he was being set up. If Dante got to the bottom of the poisoning, so much the better. But Dante was also friends with Lansky and Luciano back in New York. So if they did try to make a move, Al had one of their friends in Chicago, ready to be abducted, made to squeal, held for ransom, killed. And if Dante was in on it, and tried to double-cross him, the men Al had assigned to follow Dante would pick up on it.

It was a win-win situation for Al – inviting the friend of his enemies to his table. It was the kind of knight's move he used to take pride in, the kind of stratagem that had got him to the top and kept him there. But now he was wondering if it wasn't just foolishness; some overly elaborate plan the spirochetes had conjured up. The doctor's diagnosis had shaken his confidence in his wits. How could he tell the difference between smart moves and stupid ones, if he was going mad?

In the gloom, the plumes of steam parted, and Al looked up and saw the man on the bench opposite staring at him once more, smiling, a gleam in his eye. Al glared back at him, and wondered if the man had bad eyesight not to see the look on Al's face. Then the man blew him a kiss, and an unholy rage welled up inside him and he imagined picking up the bronze bowl of cold water at the end of the bench, turning it over, beating the man around the head with it.

You may suffer from mood swings, irritability, anxiety, loss of memory, mental impairment.

Al tried to calm himself, and the steam moved in between the men once more and Al stared down, at his toes resting on the hot tiled floor. As he stared on, the image of Frankie Yale came into his mind, a year and a half ago in New York, when they were making their deal. It was on the same trip that Al had taken his only child, Sonny, to the surgeons in the city to have the mastoid infection in his left ear fixed up. A wave of guilt washed over him and more of the doctor's words circled through his brain, causing the spirochetes to quiver like willows in a breeze.

Congenital syphilis is passed from mother to child. Perhaps you could tell me about your son's symptoms?

Like his mentor, Torrio, Al had picked an Irish girl for his wife. He'd wed Mae when he was nineteen and she was twenty-one, at St Mary Star of the Sea. He remembered signing the marriage license. *I declare I am free from all venereal diseases and infections.* Now it was clear what had happened: Al had infected his wife, and she'd given birth to a child with the disease. That was why Sonny's life had been full of illness. Illness that Al had caused. It also explained why he and Mae had never had any other children – the spirochetes had left them barren.

Now Al wondered what the point was of building an empire, if all it had to rest on were Sonny's sickly shoulders.

He sighed. And something about the idea of an empire tugged at his despondency. He took a long moment to think about it, then out of despair came hope. He'd been looking at it all wrong. He realized that now. If the spirochetes were in charge, he was free to do as he pleased. Not being in control could be a form of freedom, if only he saw it as such. All it took was looking at things in a new way, and the way he looked at it was, paradoxically, something he could control. A great warmth washed over him, and he grinned, elated with the joy of a liberated man.

He rose, suddenly in a rush to get back to his empire, to his men, to the high life and intrigue of *la malavita*. He fixed his towel around his waist and walked toward the shower-room. The fairy watched him go, a look of disappointment on his face.

Al stepped into the bright lights and cold white tiles of the shower-room and froze, suddenly realizing something, something that made the starkness of the shower-room seem even more hellish than the sauna. His mood had swung from despondency to joy in just a few seconds. Was that the spirochetes at work, too? Were they also playing with his feelings? His happiness was replaced with a sense of injustice. After all the work he'd put in to get where he was, would he be left to enjoy none of it?

He turned and stomped back into the heat and gloom of the sauna. He picked up the bronze bowl, and in a burning rage, he beat the fairy to death with it.

PART FOUR

SOLO

'The gangster's defense of his mode of life arises only when he comes in contact with the legitimate outside world. Only then does he become conscious of a conflicting way of living. In his own group, on the contrary, he achieves status by being a gangster, with gangster attitudes, and enhances his reputation through criminal exploits.'

THE ILLINOIS ASSOCIATION FOR
CRIMINAL JUSTICE, 1928

19

The lobby of the Ritz Carlton was so spacious and abuzz with people that it had the feel of a great bazaar or a Continental train station. About halfway through the morning Dante entered through the revolving doors, holding the dog in his arm, letting it hop onto the floor when they were inside the lobby. The dog had stayed in the car the previous night, refusing to budge when Dante had started the engine to head home, so he had taken it back to the Drake with him, washed it down in the bathtub and ordered it a steak tartare from room service. The next morning, when Dante had to leave for his meeting with the house detective at the Ritz, it gave him doe eyes.

Dante sidestepped bellboys and porters and scooted around guests, the dog scuttling behind him all the while. He got to the bar, sat on a stool and called the barman over, a tall man with a hooked nose held high into the air, and macassared hair with a center parting so severely straight Dante imagined the man standing in front of a mirror with a comb and a set square.

'Would sir like something from the special menu?' he asked in a hoity-toity tone of voice.

'Yes, he would,' replied Dante. 'A beer, please. Chicago brew.'

The barman about-turned and got him his drink, which was served in a tall metal cup, a sweat of condensation on the outside, and was accompanied by a porcelain bowl loaded with salted cashews. He laid a few cashews down on the carpet for the dog, then took a sip of his beer.

Chicago was one of the few cities in the country it was easier to get a beer than it was hard liquor. Distilleries were simple enough to hide, but for a city to be as full of breweries as Chicago was, it took a whole army of policemen and politicians to look the other way, to not notice the noises and smoke coming out of buildings that were supposed to have been closed down years before, to not notice the convoys of trucks going in and out all day. Half the neighborhoods in the city, especially the German and Czech ones, were permanently drenched in the sweet aroma of malt, hops and fermented yeast. It took corruption on a truly grand scale to make it so easy to buy a beer, but with beer sales in the city topping thirty million dollars a month, the bootleggers had enough spare cash to keep oiling the machine.

'*Il cavaliere!*' shouted a voice through the din, and Dante looked up to see a man in an off-white suit and a red carnation in his lapel approaching through the hordes. Dante grinned when he saw him, and the two shook hands warmly.

Inigo Vaughn was in his fifties, dark-haired and suave, an immigrant from Cardiff who for over twenty years had been the house detective at the Ritz.

'I didn't believe it when I heard you were back in town,' Inigo said in his sing-song Welsh accent. 'We all thought you were dead.'

'Yeah, I keep hearing that.'

Inigo looked down at Dante's feet, at the dog curled up at the bottom of the stool.

'Well, if you're Dante, who's that?' he said, pointing at the dog. 'Virgil?'

He flashed a smile and Dante smiled back and shrugged, and tossed a couple of cashews into his mouth.

'How've you been?' Dante asked.

'Getting older and no richer.'

Inigo ordered a drink from the bar, and sat on the stool next to Dante. 'I suppose you want to hear about this little poison party we hosted?'

'Sure,' said Dante, and Inigo gave him his take on the same

story Ralph Capone had told him in the funeral parlor the previous day. Inigo filled in a few more of the details, describing how he'd got safe doctors with stomach pumps there in double time, how he'd got the worst cases into a private hospital, managing to wheel them through the hotel without anyone asking any questions. He'd dealt with the Coroner's physicians and the doctors at the hospital by coming up with cover stories and promising everyone involved Ritz-sized kickbacks. Dante listened to it all and at the end he nodded and expressed his respect for what Inigo had done: thirteen members of Chicago's political elite had almost been killed on his watch, and Inigo ran interference so well not a whisper of it had gotten into a single newspaper or police report.

'Any idea who was responsible?' asked Dante.

Inigo shrugged.

'You've got thirteen of the most powerful, most hated men in Chicago, all in one room. Half the city wants them dead. It could be anyone. Even your boy Capone.'

'That doesn't seem likely since he asked me to investigate.'

Inigo frowned at him. 'Finish up your drink and we'll get started,' he said, before peering down at the dog. 'No mutts in the kitchen though. Leave him with the coat-check girl, she's crazy for the things.'

Five minutes later they were walking through a kitchen the size of a football field, with dozens of chefs and kitchen porters and waiters running about the space, the air filled with a roar of gas jets and the smell of fine French food. They reached a corner where there was a staircase descending into the cellar and a rickety-looking wooden door. Inigo knocked and they stepped into a cramped little office, low-ceilinged and windowless.

A man was sitting at a desk there, and Inigo introduced him as Patrick Harris, the kitchen manager. Harris stood and shook Dante's hand. There were no chairs for Dante and Inigo to sit on, so they perched on the edge of a sideboard running down one side of the office.

Dante inspected Harris a moment. He was chubby, red-faced and scared, with an expression Dante recognized from the restaurateurs who came to his boat off Long Island – the look of a man who, thanks to prohibition, had no choice but to deal with the criminal element. Harris had been told a man would be visiting from Capone's organization to investigate the poisoning, so the kitchen manager was wary, pegging Dante as the type of ruthless gangster the Outfit had a reputation for employing.

'Let's start by me apologizing to you on behalf of Mr Capone,' said Dante, trying to put the man at ease. 'We take pride in providing only the best goods to our customers and when something like this happens, we can only say that it upsets us as much as it does you.'

Harris frowned, surprised, then he relaxed a little, realizing that Dante was not the psychopath he had been expecting.

'Why don't you tell me what happened on the day the booze was delivered?'

'It was a few weeks back,' said Harris. 'Our delivery comes once a week. Wednesday afternoon. Two men in a Model T truck. They drop the crates off, I sign the manifest and they leave.'

'Was it the same two guys that normally deliver the stuff?'

Harris nodded.

'All right, so after the crates arrive, they go to the storeroom, right?'

'The cellar, yeah.'

'Who's got access to the cellar?'

'Managers and head waiters.'

'All right, let's go to the night the poisoning happened. How comes it was that party that got the poison booze? Was it just bad luck?'

Harris shook his head. 'We ordered in the booze specially. They have that party every three months or so, it's a kinda club meeting or something. Whenever they book the room, we order in the champagne and put it aside. It was only ever gonna go to them.'

'And who on your staff knew about the arrangement with the champagne?'

'Everyone. It weren't no secret.'

'When'd you take the booking for the party?'

'I dunno, a couple of months ago.'

'All right. So how does the serving work? Talk me through it.'

'The cases get opened up by the kitchen porters in the afternoon and the bottles are put on ice in the cellar, then the waiters take them up to the function room so they're ready for the guests when they arrive.'

'All right,' said Dante. 'I'd like you to get me a list of everyone who was working the function that night – names and addresses. Can you do that?'

'Sure,' said Harris, and the worried look returned. 'Look, you don't think we were involved? The hotel, I mean?'

'At the moment, I don't think so,' Dante said, trying to make it sound convincing, 'but it pays to be sure. One last question – any staff leave the hotel since the poisoning? Anyone not turn up for work? Disappear? Take a sudden holiday?'

'No. No one . . .' said Harris, before trailing off, as if something had just occurred to him. 'Except for Julius. Julius Clay. He went on holiday after the poisoning.'

Dante turned to Inigo, and Inigo gave him a look – this was news to him too.

'Who's Julius?'

'One of our head waiters.'

'Was he working the night of the poisoning?'

Harris nodded.

'You didn't think to say anything?' said Inigo, glaring at Harris.

'He had it booked off months back,' said Harris. 'He takes

three weeks off every summer to go down to Michigan City. That's where he's from. It's just . . .'

'Just what?'

'He was supposed to come back to work yesterday. And he never showed up.'

'Jesus Christ—' said Inigo. Dante saw he was about to lay into Harris, so he put a hand on his arm to calm him, realizing that the two of them had inadvertently stumbled into a good-cop-bad-cop routine.

'It's probably just a coincidence,' said Dante. 'A lot of people go to Michigan City this time of year.'

'He's been a waiter here two decades,' said Harris. 'I wouldn't think he'd be involved in anything like this.'

'I'm sure he's not,' said Dante, smiling, trying to make out that Julius Clay was not suspect number one.

'You normally let your employees take three weeks off?'

'It's shift work. They take weeks off whenever they like.'

'Okay. Inigo told me you've still got some of the bottles here,' said Dante. 'You mind showing them to me?'

Harris nodded and they headed out of the office and down some stairs toward the cellar. As Harris pushed the door open they heard footsteps behind them and they turned to see a bellboy peering down at them through the gloom.

'Mr Vaughn, sir?' said the bellboy. 'There's a man in the bar to see you, sir.'

'I'm busy.'

'He, uh, he seems kinda . . . irate, sir. Says he works for Governor Small.'

Inigo paused a moment, then looked at Dante. 'You mind?'

Dante shook his head and Inigo disappeared up the steps. Then Harris unlocked the door and they stepped inside. Harris switched on a light, and bulbs high up in the ceiling came to life, illuminating a few patches of what Dante could see was an extensive space, brick-walled and filled with shelves and crates of liquor. Harris grabbed a crowbar that was lying underneath the light switch and they walked over to a stack of crates in a corner.

Harris reached behind the stack and dragged out a crate. It had been nailed shut and someone had written *DO NOT OPEN* across each of its sides in black paint. Harris slipped the crowbar under the plank and with much straining, prized it off. He lifted the lid, pulled out a bottle of champagne from an open case and passed it to Dante. When Dante saw it, the world began to spin and he had to grab hold of one of the shelves to stop himself from falling: the bottle was the same as the ones that had killed his wife and family six years earlier.

'You all right, sir? . . . Sir?'

Harris's voice sounded distant, far off, as if it was underwater, engulfed by the million thoughts running through Dante's mind. He focused on the paving slabs that made up the floor of the cellar, the rigid lines between them, then he took a deep breath and nodded in response to Harris's question.

He took a moment, regaining his composure, then he lifted the bottle high into the air, waited a second, and let it drop to the floor. It smashed in a pop of glass and fizzing liquid and Harris took a step back. Dante watched as the alcohol spread across the paving stones, more and more of it becoming exposed to the air. He crouched over the puddle and waited, the tangy smell of the champagne filling his nose. Then, after half a minute or so, a different smell emerged, caustic and sharp, the telltale sign that the alcohol had been chemically altered, the same fragrance that had filled Dante's kitchen six years earlier.

20

Dante strode out of the cellar and up the stairs and through the chaos of the kitchen, the whole time thinking it couldn't be a coincidence, there had to be some order behind it. He returned to the bar, sat on a stool, fumbled a cigarette from his pack and lit it. He called the barman over and ordered a double whiskey, downed it, and ordered another. He rubbed his temples and waited for his heart to slow, for the whirl of images to stop carouseling through his mind – the bottle, his wife, the cellar floor, the bottle, his wife, the cellar floor – each beat of his heart a stab of guilt and remorse. He'd had these mental attacks countless times before; he knew it was just a matter of time till they passed, and he knew that the alcohol and nicotine didn't help, but when the barman returned with his second whiskey, Dante took it off him and stayed hunched over the bar, drinking and smoking.

When he reached the end of the cigarette, the spinning in his head slowly eased, his heart stopped thumping so strongly against his ribs, and he became aware of his surroundings once more. He looked up, and was surprised to see the world carrying on just fine without him – people were ordering drinks, chatting at tables, coming and going. No one was paying any attention to the pale-looking man at the bar with his head in his hands.

Dante's eyes wandered about the place, looking for something to rest on, to take his mind off his thoughts, something to watch that wasn't a dread-inducing memory, and on the other side of the glass partition that ran through the middle of the bar, he found it – Inigo. He was arguing with a hulk of a man in a blue serge suit whom Dante recognized from the old days as an enforcer named

Corrado Abbate. A man who had more muscle than he could ever use, so rented out the leftovers piecemeal to whoever was in need of them. Abbate seemed to be blasting Inigo with anger and indignation, jabbing his finger into the air between them. Dante remembered the bellboy who'd grabbed Inigo from the cellar saying the angry man worked for Governor Small, one of the men who had been hospitalized after the poison party.

Dante watched the scene, slowly regaining his calm. Inigo, ever capable, seemed to be holding his own against the much bigger Abbate. At some point a woman approached Abbate and spoke to him quickly. She was tall, with a statuesque figure, dressed like night in a black dress, black chiffon hose, and a long-brimmed black hat with a veil draped down across her face.

The woman asked Abbate a question, and Abbate, annoyed, gestured in the direction of the bar, barely breaking off his haranguing. The woman took a moment, then walked around the glass partition and all the men in the bar sized her up as she entered. She looked about for somewhere to sit, and her gaze alighted on Dante. She paused, then headed in his direction, setting off an avalanche of broken hearts.

When she got up close, Dante could see her face through the veil and he finally recognized her – Loretta Valenti, Olivia's best friend, part of the group of friends Dante had grown up with. She stared at him for a level minute, not quite believing what she was seeing, then she flashed him a fireworks smile and Dante smiled back, a host of memories swirling into his mind, and the thumping heart and the carousel of images started spinning once more – Olivia as a teen, Loretta as a teen, a long-lost Chicago careening into the past.

'Dante? I can't hardly believe it.'

He stood and they hugged, then disengaged and studied each other. Through the shadow of the veil, he could see that one of her eyes was bruised, purple and yellow and puffy, the makeup and the veil not quite enough to conceal it. She picked up that Dante had noticed and she reddened, stiffening for a moment.

'I guess I'm not fooling anyone with this,' she said, lifting up the veil, pinning it back to the brim of her hat.

'I didn't notice till you got up close,' said Dante, and Loretta smiled.

'You want a drink?' he asked, offering her his stool.

She smiled and sat, and Dante signaled the barman over and she ordered a Martini, and when the barman had gone she turned to look at Dante, and without the veil he could see how beautiful she still was, eyes perfectly green and wide as a lake, hair tucked up underneath her hat except for a single strand, a spiral of red, tumbling down in front of one cheek.

'I thought you were dead, Dante. We all did.'

'So I've been hearing.'

'I walked in and thought I'd seen a ghost. It would have been good to hear from you, you know. A postcard or something. Where were you?'

'I traveled around a bit, then pitched up in New York.'

'When'd you get back to Chicago?'

'Yesterday.'

'Well, welcome back, I suppose.'

'Thanks. You're the first person that's actually said that to me.'

'Where are you staying?' she asked.

'The Lindbergh suite at the Drake.'

'Fancy.'

'What about you?'

'Pilsen.'

He nodded. 'So what've you been doing the last six years?' he asked. 'Aside from moving to Pilsen.'

'Not growing up. What about you?'

'Same.'

They both smiled, and for some reason Dante sensed a feeling of mutual guilt.

'Who died?' he asked, nodding at her outfit.

'No one. I dressed to match my eye. The veil was the only thing I had to hide it, so I put that on and the rest of it kinda followed. I think there's a life lesson in there somewhere.'

He looked at her black eye once more, then gestured toward the glass partition, beyond which Inigo and Abbate were still involved in their heated discussion.

'You and Abbate?' he asked.

'Yeah,' said Loretta, and Dante noticed an undercurrent of disappointment in her voice.

She looked across the bar to watch them too. After a moment, Inigo left, making his way toward the reception, and Abbate turned about, looking for Loretta. He paused when he spotted her and saw she was with Dante. Then he headed toward them.

'Dante,' said Abbate when he arrived.

'How's it going, Corrie?'

'Peachy.'

'Dante and I were just getting reacquainted,' said Loretta.

Abbate gave her a caustic look, and Dante studied the man. He had a boxer's face, lopsided and thick, with a red plum of a nose pummeled across its center.

'I heard you were back,' Abbate said to Dante.

'Good news travels fast. Drink?'

'No. We're going,' Abbate said, grabbing Loretta by the arm.

Loretta yanked her elbow out of his grasp, then she glared at Abbate, and finally she turned to look at Dante and smiled.

'It was real good to see you again,' she said.

'Short but sweet.'

Dante watched as the two figures traversed the buzz of the lobby, and just as they disappeared through the revolving doors, the barman arrived with Loretta's Martini. He looked around for her and then frowned at Dante, and Dante motioned with a finger for him to put the drink on the bar. He paid for it and the barman disappeared and Dante tried to process what had just happened. The booze that killed his wife had reappeared, and ten minutes later, his wife's best friend. He wondered if there was some sense to what had happened, then he thought better of it. This was what he'd signed up to when he'd agreed to make the trip back home: painful memories and ghosts from the past.

He sipped the Martini, lit another cigarette, and was most of the way through them both when a bellboy appeared calling his name. Dante gestured to the boy who crossed to the bar and handed him one of the champagne bottles, placed in a case and wrapped in brown paper, and an envelope containing the list of names from Harris. Dante tipped the boy, downed the Martini and exited the bar.

He crossed the lobby to the coat check and asked the girl there for the dog. She scooped him up off the floor and passed him over to Dante.

'He's gorgeous,' she said. 'What's his name?'

Dante paused. 'I'm not sure. Virgil?'

The girl gave him a funny look. Then he tipped her and returned to the Blackhawk.

He opened up the windows, sat in the driver's seat and went through the list of employees he'd received from Harris. Twenty or so names. He found the address for the missing waiter, lit a cigarette, started the car, and headed over.

Julius Clay's apartment was a small, tidy, two-bedroom affair in Hyde Park. Dante sweet-talked the landlady at the building entrance into letting him in, then he used his picks to gain entry to the apartment itself. In the man's wardrobe Dante found a large gap where a half-dozen suits and shirts should have been hanging, and the man appeared to have taken all his shoes with him as well. Too many missing clothes for a three-week stint on the beach in Michigan City. The man was on the run.

Dante didn't find any clues as to where he might have gone, except for some letters from his daughter with a return address in Detroit. Possibly he could have gone there to hide out, putting his child at risk. Dante memorized the name and address and a few details mentioned in the letter in case he found himself having to spin her a story at some later date about how he was an acquaintance of her father.

On the windowsill he found finger marks in the dust, and some street dirt on the floorboards just below it. Someone must have broken in via the fire escape a couple of weeks after the waiter had gone missing, meaning someone else was on the man's trail.

21

Dante spent the next few days chasing down his leads. He spoke to the missing waiter's colleagues at the Ritz, trying to figure out if any of them were in on it. He kept close to Inigo. He gathered information on the thirteen poisoned men, trying to figure out which one of them might have been the target. He tried to get in contact with the people who had arranged the champagne from six years ago – guessing that maybe the source was the same. But Dante's old partner from back then, Saul Menaker, was awaiting trial on a racketeering charge in the Cook County Jail, and when he paid Menaker a visit, all his old friend could do was tell him the man who had arranged the original batch had been taken for a ride by 'Machine Gun' Jack McGurn four years earlier in the Westside Beer War.

And so it went with everyone else.

All Dante's old connections were either dead, in jail, or missing. The life expectancy of a gangster in Chicago was twenty-seven years, and Dante's friends didn't seem to be averaging much beyond that. Their lives were short, and the city moved at a savage, deadly speed. Whole neighborhoods had changed color. In just six short years a new generation had grown up and replaced the one before it. The place he knew was now a vanished city, existing only in his memories, entombed.

He steered clear of the neighborhoods where he might be recognized. He kept up a correspondence as best he could with the old fisherman who was looking after his boat back in Long Island. He paid visits to the shoeshine man.

None of it helped.

The more Dante got frustrated at his lack of progress, the more he realized how strange it was that he'd been asked by Al to undertake the mission in the first place, which led him to wonder if he'd been called to Chicago for other reasons, and so with the frustration came a jumpy feeling, a sense of impending doom that not even the dope could alleviate.

When he slept, a reel of ghostly images spooled through his mind: Olivia on their wedding day, Loretta in the bar, an endless corridor in the county jail, Loretta's black eye, the coat-check girl, the dog, a vaulted cellar stocked high with champagne, Olivia on the beach as perfect and easily bruised as a petal. Olivia in a pool of blood.

On his fourth night in the city, an insistent ringing dragged him from this netherworld, and he opened his eyes and they darted to the coffee table instinctively: needle, stash, syringe, spoon. The ringing continued and Dante panicked. He threw the splayed pages of a newspaper over it all and ran for the door, and he was halfway there before he realized that it wasn't the door that was ringing, it was the phone. The rooms in the Drake all had their own phones. Dante cursed his dope-addled brain, spun about and picked up the receiver.

'Hello?'

'Mr Sanfelippo, sorry to bother you so late,' said a nasally voiced hotel employee. 'We have a Miss Loretta Valenti on the line?'

'Put her through.'

The line crackled for a moment, then Dante heard Loretta's voice.

'Dante?' She sounded upset, voice croaky. 'I'm so sorry. I didn't know who to call . . .'

'What happened?'

'It's Corrie . . . I came home and there's . . . Oh, God . . . there's blood everywhere.'

She let out a sob and there was silence for a moment, and

Dante guessed she'd put her hand over the receiver; a few seconds later the line came back to life.

'I'm sorry. I didn't know who to call,' she repeated.

Through the opiate fuzz in Dante's brain he tried to make sense of what was going on.

'Are you still in the apartment?' he said.

'No. I ran out of there. I'm at a grocery down the street.'

'Are you alone?' he asked.

'Yeah.'

'Is there somewhere nearby you can go? A diner or cafeteria or something?'

'Yeah, sure. I think so.'

'You think?'

'I mean . . . yeah. I know. There's a cafeteria.'

'All right. What's the address?'

'Blue Island and Twenty-first. On the corner.'

'All right. I'll be there as soon as I can. Hold tight.'

He put the phone down and rubbed his head and checked the clock on the wall. A quarter past one.

Ten minutes later he was driving south through the hard-scrabble neighborhoods that lay west of the Loop. On the streets, the hawkers and shoppers and businessmen had been replaced by the city's skeleton crew of gin soaks, dope heads, down-and-outs and prostitutes, all of them appearing with the darkness, as if materializing out of the texture of the night.

He hadn't driven through that part of the city since his return, and at one point he got lost, disorientated by the gap between his memories and reality. He had to stop and ask directions from a telegraph-company messenger who was walking along an otherwise deserted street. The boy set him on the right way, and Dante noted how he had something of the street hood to him, and he remembered how when he was a boy, kids from his neighborhood would get jobs as nighttime telegraph-company messengers, meaning they had an excuse to be out on the streets all through the night, cover for the thefts and burglaries they committed.

Maybe not everything changed after all.

Eventually he found the intersection Loretta had mentioned. He parked up and stepped into the cafeteria, a worn, dingy all-night greasy spoon that smelled of stale cigarettes and staler food. He looked around, saw Loretta bundled up in the corner of a booth and walked over.

He'd checked in the mirror on the drive over a hundred times to make sure he didn't look doped up, but he was still paranoid when he strode over and gave her a hug. She hugged him back and they both sat and he looked her over. She had a café-au-lait-colored shawl draped over her shoulders, her hair was pulled under a boudoir cap, and her hands were wrapped around a coffee cup. Dante ordered another from the man behind the counter, and asked her if she was all right. She nodded.

'You call the cops?' he asked.

She shook her head, and Dante figured Corrado had schooled her.

'Tell me what happened.'

'I came home and the door was kicked in and there was blood . . . all over the living room.'

'And Corrado was supposed to be home?'

She nodded.

'It's all right. I'll go in there and check things out. Gimme the keys and the address.'

She fumbled about her purse and handed him a set of keys.

'It's a block down Blue Island. Seven twenty-two. Apartment four.'

'Stay here, all right? I'll be back soon.'

He drained his drink, hoping it would perk him up, then he walked around the corner to the Blackhawk, opened the trunk and took out the Colt. He affixed the coupling to the gun and then the

Maxim silencer to the coupling, then he slipped the gun into his belt and headed to Number 722.

He let himself in and climbed up two flights, stepping on the stair risers all the way so as not to make a noise. The door to Apartment 4 was ajar and Dante could see that both the door and the frame around the lock were twisted and buckled. He bent down to look at the damage. Scuff marks, jagged wood, a streak of dirt from the boot that had kicked it in. He stood, took the .45 from his pocket, held it aloft, and listened for a minute or so.

Silence.

He pushed the door gently and it opened with the slight give of a loose tooth. He walked down a short hall, the walls painted a vivid shade of green, and stepped into a living room; he looked at it through the gloom, staying still, scanning the space for movement, listening.

After a few moments of stillness, the noise of insects the only sound disturbing the air, he switched on the light, revealing a spacious room in the middle of which was what looked like the leftovers of a tornado – a smashed coffee table, an upturned armchair, the rug swirled into a mound, broken glass, and the blood making the floor look like it had been painted red. The window was open and troops of insects had arrived to feed on the blood, making the apartment buzz in a detonation of life.

On the far side of the room was the kitchenette, most of it hidden from view by a counter, behind which a gunman or two could easily be hidden. Dante stepped over the broken coffee table to the center of the room, his .45 trained on the counter. When he was underneath the light bulb hanging down from the ceiling, he lifted his free hand to it, grabbed the end of the shade, and swept the light in the direction of the kitchen, fanning it left and right, looking for body-shaped shadows that might be thrown against the back wall.

Nothing.

He let go of the light and it swung back into place, and he

walked over to confirm there was no one there. The kitchenette was empty, but there was a can of peanuts and a bowl on the counter. He checked the rest of the apartment. It was all empty and untouched. He returned to the living room and inspected it once more under the jaundiced light of the sodium bulb.

The blood was in a pool but was also streaked along the floor and on one of the walls toward the front door. He leaned down and peered at the broken glass: a bottle of whiskey and two glasses. He stood and tried to imagine the arrangement of the furniture before the place was half destroyed. Then he returned to the bathroom to check for bloodstains, found none, and went back to the living room.

He lit a cigarette, leaned against the windowsill and tried to reconstruct what had happened. The two glasses and peanuts meant Corrado had been in there with someone, then some other people burst in and attacked them. There was enough blood in the place to suggest more than just a fight – there'd been a stabbing or shooting. But if shots were fired there'd be bulletholes and the smell of cordite and the neighbors might have called the cops. So two men had burst in and there'd been a fight and they'd stabbed him and they'd kept him there long enough for the pool to form and then they'd dragged him out of there.

Dante grabbed a cloth and a bucket and cleaned up the mess as best he could while the insects swirled around him. He grabbed a laundry bag from the kitchen, went into the bedroom and stuffed as many of Loretta's clothes as he could into it. Then he went back into the living room, turned off the lights and was drenched in darkness once more.

He stepped out into the corridor, kneeled in front of the lock and examined the mechanism. He pushed the lock frame back into position with the heel of his hand, and put the key in the lock. Then he closed the door and turned the key. He pulled it out and inspected the door once more. The jagged fault-lines spiderwebbing across the middle panel of the door would be noticed by anyone walking past, but at least the door was no longer ajar, and it wouldn't open unless someone shouldered it.

As he left, he checked the hallway and stairs a little closer. There were dots of blood and a couple of streaks on the wall about half a foot up from the floor. If a body was being dragged along by a couple of men and a stray bloody hand flopped against the wall, it would be at about the height of the streaks.

Dante returned to the car, put the bag of clothes into the trunk and then returned to the cafeteria to find Loretta sitting where he'd left her.

'You sure Corrado was in there tonight?' he asked after he'd sat back down.

'Sure I'm sure,' she said. 'He told me he was staying home to listen to the baseball.'

'Who was with him?'

'He was alone. What happened, Dante?'

There was no way he could tell her the truth, or at least, the truth suggested by the evidence: that her boyfriend was either dead or soon to be so.

'I'm not sure just yet,' he said. 'What was Corrado working on recently?'

'I dunno.'

'He acting strange at all?'

'Yeah. He'd been jittery the last couple weeks, on account of what happened to his boss.'

'Governor Small? He was working for the governor?'

Loretta nodded. Corrado must have been looking into the poison party on behalf of Governor Small. That was why he was at the Ritz the other day trying to strong-arm Inigo. And Corrado had gotten close to something and been taken out, which gave Dante a string of new leads. But as bad as Dante's curiosity was, it didn't feel right to be questioning Loretta just now.

'I don't think it's a good idea for you to stay there,' he said. 'You wanna go stay with your sister or your ma or someone?'

'Ma's passed away. Four years ago. I could go to my sister, but
. . . I can't turn up there in the middle of the night, like this . . .
I'll check into a hotel.'

'You can take my bed at the Drake,' said Dante.

'I couldn't.'

'It's fine. The place's got a couch bigger than your apartment.
I grabbed a few of your things while I was up there.'

She thought this over for a moment and smiled. 'Thank you.'

Dante dropped some change on the table and they headed for
the exit. They stepped out into the warm night air, crossed the
street to the car and got in. Dante went to turn the key and paused
and looked down the street at Loretta's building. He imagined the
car pulling up out front and screeching off down the road, then
he imagined once more the struggle that would have occurred,
the noise of it all.

'What are your neighbors like?' he asked.

'There's an old woman in the apartment opposite. I never met
the others. Why?'

'No reason,' said Dante.

He started up the engine and punched the accelerator and the
Blackhawk roared into life, and he began the journey north. He'd
been in Chicago just a few days, and in that time he'd acquired a
hotel suite, two guns, a sports car and a dog, and now a stack of
leads and a gangster's girl on the run. He wondered if there was
any reason to the way his life worked itself out, and as he drove
up Blue Island Avenue, he mused that a man forever falling on his
feet was still a man forever falling.

22

When they got back to his hotel room, Dante suggested they took the edge off Loretta's nerves with a sip of whiskey, and the sip had turned into an empty bottle, two packs of cigarettes and the pair of them passing out on the sofa around dawn.

As they drank they spoke of old times so as not to talk about what had happened to Abbate. Loretta railed at Dante for quitting town after Olivia died, drunk talk about how he had left her to deal with the mess of it all. Dante in turn told her about his dazed exit from the city, his years living rough and hitting rock bottom in a snow-covered park in the Bronx. He left out nothing except his addiction, which still caused him deep embarrassment.

Loretta told him of how Olivia's death had affected her, how she couldn't really focus much afterward and how she'd got behind with her studies and dropped out of school. Another item to add to Dante's guilt list. She told him how she was working as a waitress in a cafeteria on the beach to save up enough money to go back to school and finish her last semester. That was the bitch of it, she said, she was only one semester shy of graduating. But the money from the job seemed to drain away each month before she could put any in the bank. Then Corrado had turned up and she began seeing him out of a sense that he might offer her some protection, and now that protection was a pool of hastily mopped-up blood on her living-room floor. And so the conversation cycled back to Abbate despite their intentions and she sobbed and went quiet, and so did Dante, and at some point, they both drifted off into sleep.

*

They woke up a few hours later to sunshine and the dog perched on the coffee table, staring at them. Dante offered to drive Loretta over to her sister's, and Loretta accepted, saying she had to stop by her work to explain why it was she was about to take a couple of weeks off. On the drive over, they concocted a story about her having to look after a sick relative and they debated whether or not her boss would buy it.

When they arrived, Loretta went inside to spin her lies to her boss while Dante took a seat on the balcony that overlooked the beach. People were packed tightly on the sand, and amongst them, peddlers and thieves moved about with practiced steps, seemingly unaffected by the burning heat. Children splashed in the shallows, and further out the rich in their yachts were the first to catch what breeze there was coming over the waters. As Dante blearily looked about the crowds, he realized the beach was the last place he wanted to be after a night of much drinking and little sleep, with its heat and burning sunshine and raucous noise.

A waitress in a blue serge outfit flitted onto the balcony and placed a long metal cup on Dante's table, a paper napkin glued to the condensation on the outside.

'Courtesy of Miss Loretta,' said the waitress with a coquettish smile.

Dante frowned at the drink suspiciously. A milky-looking froth was coagulating at the top of the cup, dripping over the rim.

'What is it?' he asked, his voice still croaky from the previous night's whiskey and cigarettes.

'A black cow. Root beer and vanilla ice cream,' said the girl, before adding in a whisper, 'It's great for hangovers.'

'Thanks,' he said, unconvinced, and as the girl headed back inside he pushed the cup away and took another drag on his cigarette.

He looked across the beach, and noticed how at some point far to the south, in a clearly marked boundary past the line of 29th Street, the red bodies turned brown. Chicago's beaches had become segregated over time, not by any official law, but due to some social consensus, making Dante wonder on people's propensity to segregate themselves in the absence of any laws to do it for them.

'Hey, mister, you after a pair o' sunglasses?' asked a voice.

Dante turned to see a hawker standing on the sand in front of him, holding a board lined with tinted glasses.

'Everyone in Hollywood's wearing 'em. Here, I think these'll suit you just grand.'

The man pulled a pair from the board and passed them up to Dante, who leaned down and took them through a gap in the balcony railing. They were round-rimmed, with tortoiseshell frames, and a dark cellulose film glued over the lenses. Dante put them on and was plunged into a world of green. He looked around, up and down, and the blaze of the sun was magically banished. He could feel the muscles in his face and neck relax, and his headache seemed to lessen.

'First time wearing 'em?' asked the man. 'Quite something, ain't they? Here.'

He slid a pocket mirror from one of the straps on the board and passed it up and Dante checked himself out. With the glasses and the straw boater on his head, he looked ridiculous, but he bought the glasses anyway and leaned back in his chair to look at the world anew.

A minute or two later Loretta stepped onto the balcony and he turned to her and she frowned at him.

'What happened?' she said. 'You go blind while you were waiting?'

'They're for my hangover.'

He grinned at her and she slumped down into the seat next to him, took a cigarette from his pack on the table and lit it.

'So what did your boss say?'

'He said he understood my predicament and then he fired me for being unreliable.'

'You want me to go in there and talk to him?' Dante asked, and she cut him down with a sideways glance.

'He give you your pay at least?' he asked and Loretta nodded. She made a grab for the ice-cream float and took a long suck from the straw.

'You haven't had any,' she said, and Dante grimaced.

'It's good for hangovers,' she said, passing him the cup. Dante took it and peered at the drink once more – the froth on the top of it was starting to collapse, the clotted ice cream sinking into the root beer, forming oil-slick swirls on the surface. The thought of all that dairy and sugar made his stomach turn and he passed it back to her.

'How the hell is that good for a hangover?' he asked.

'Because half of it's vodka,' she said, grabbing the cup back and taking another drink of it. They both went quiet and stared out at the view.

'It always so busy on weekdays?' Dante asked.

'Nah. It's the hot spell,' she said. 'People are dying from heat prostration in the city, so they're coming here to get away from it. Except the beach is getting so full now people are drowning from the overcrowding. *C'est la vie.*'

She picked up the float once more and slurped down a mouthful of vodka and ice cream, and she looked further out, to the waters of Lake Michigan and the pleasure boats packed with revelers plowing about along the horizon.

'Must be nice to spend your summer on boats,' she said, and Dante thought of his own boat in the illegal, floating night market, and he guessed a wistful look must have crossed his face because her expression softened.

'You thinking of New York?' she asked, and Dante nodded, and they both fell silent a moment and Loretta took a drag on her cigarette.

'Is it dangerous?' she asked.

'The *Rendezvous?*'

'All of it.'

Dante shook his head.

'Not as dangerous as working for Al,' he said. 'You can see people coming a mile off. And the law doesn't bother us. Frankie Yale's paid off the authorities, and even if he hadn't, the coast-guard's got thirty-five thousand miles of coastline to look after, and only fifty-five boats. Plus if it does go down to a chase, we got a speedboat we strapped an aircraft engine to.'

He turned to look at her and saw she wasn't really paying attention.

'Corrie always said he would take me out on one of those pleasure boats,' she said, nodding at the lake.

She finished her cigarette and took another slurp on the vodka float.

'I guess we better head over to my sister's.'

They drove to Little Italy with Loretta in the passenger seat and the dog on her lap, its head sticking out of the window, its eyes following the rhythm of skyscrapers marching their way down the street, dizzying every perspective.

'You need to think of a name for him,' she said.

'The dog? Why? He ain't mine.'

'Yes, he is.'

'Inigo at the Ritz called him Virgil,' he said. 'Virgil was the other character in the *Inferno*.'

'Yeah, I know,' she said.

'You've read it?' he asked.

'Yeah,' she said. 'I saw it in the bookstore and thought you'd written it, so I picked up a copy.'

She gave him a look and they smiled. Then she turned her gaze back at the dog once more.

'He definitely ain't a Virgil,' she said.

Fifteen minutes later they pulled up outside a modest wooden house on a quiet street off Racine Avenue, just a few blocks from where the two of them had grown up. Dante switched off the engine and turned to look at her.

'Thanks for the lift,' she said, 'and for everything else.'

Dante shrugged.

'You sure you don't know what Corrie was working on?' he asked. 'Nothing's come to mind since last night?'

She shook her head.

'All right. You got a number here I can reach you at?'

'Sure.'

She opened her handbag and scribbled down a number on the back of a receipt. He slipped it into his wallet and then she seemed to blanch.

'He's not coming back, is he?' she said.

'I don't know.'

'You're lying.'

And Dante didn't know what to say, so they sat there in an awkward silence.

'How do you live with it?' she asked, and Dante knew she was talking about Olivia, but he pretended he didn't.

'Live with what?'

'With someone being there one moment and gone the next.'

'If I figure it out, I'll let you know.'

She stared at him briefly, then leaned over and kissed him, a peck on the cheek.

'You're a good man, Dante. Hating yourself's not helping anyone.'

'I don't hate myself.'

'Sure you don't. All this . . . it's not you. You need to accept who you are and what you've done and stop feeling guilty for being alive.'

She got out of the car and Dante watched her all the way inside. Then he lit a cigarette and tried to think, and he caught the gaze of the dog in the rearview and the two of them stared at each other. He thought of what Loretta had said, and he thought of Olivia, lying in a cemetery somewhere whose location he didn't know, and he thought of how they'd planned to have a family together, plans that now glinted with the sharp and jagged beauty of broken glass. What did you do with shattered dreams? Sweep them up, fix them into something new, or leave them broken on the floor and bloody your feet by walking over them?

And then he faced the fact he couldn't hide from – that he was just a few blocks from where he'd grown up, from where they'd all died, from where what remained of his family lived. He could go there now, get it over and done with. See them all and beg forgiveness. He thought about doing it and tears formed in his eyes. Then he made himself a promise – if he got through the investigation alive, he'd go and see them. No point in turning up there now only for him to wind up in the obituary columns a few days later.

He started the Blackhawk and headed back downtown, stopping at a cafeteria on the way to take a hit in the restrooms.

23

In the long and illustrious list of corrupt Illinois politicians, Governor Len Small was without doubt at the top. As State Treasurer, he embezzled over six hundred thousand dollars of state funds, funneling the money into a bank prosecutors later discovered didn't actually exist.

As governor he ran a cash-for-pardons scheme. In the eight years he had been in the position, he'd sold hundreds of gubernatorial pardons and paroles, even to the city's most hardened felons – Harry Guzik, Fur Sammons, Spike O'Donnell, Bugs Moran had all bought their way out of prison, along with countless other gangsters, killers and rapists.

At his trial for embezzlement he had his lawyers argue that as governor he was above the law, that he could invoke the Divine Right of Kings. When that tactic didn't work, he paid off the jury. He was acquitted, and within a year government jobs were awarded to eight of the jurors. Despite the *Tribune* declaring him to be the worst governor the state ever had, he was re-elected for a second term, with support from Capone, and the Ku Klux Klan, who endorsed all his election campaigns.

Although his official residence was the Illinois Executive Mansion in Springfield, the governor spent as much of his time as he could in Chicago, where the trade in finance, corruption and wealth occurred. So it only took three phone calls for Dante to track him down; he was in the Loop, eating lunch at the St Hubert English Chop House on the top floor of the Majestic Hotel.

Dante headed over there and entered the place to find it was a dim affair; the ceilings were low and the furniture and wainscoting made of somberly dark wood. He had to squint through the gloom to find the table where Small was sitting, in one of the private alcoves at the back. He had positioned himself gangster style, with his back to a wall, a view over the whole of the restaurant, and easy access to the rear exit.

Dante approached across the black-and-white tiled floor and saw Small sitting with a bodyguard who had the physique of a bag of cement. When Dante neared them the two men looked up from their meal and Small gave him the once-over.

'Dante the Gent, I presume?' he said.

Dante nodded and Small gestured with a fork for him to sit. As Dante did so Small gave the bodyguard a look and the man rose and took up a position at the back of the alcove, hands crossed in front of his belly.

'You eaten?'

'Yeah,' said Dante looking at the serving dishes arrayed across the linen: porterhouse steaks, broiled cod, wheat cakes, devilled eggs, macaroni cheese, a basket of French bread, an untouched garden salad.

'You're skinny, boy. You should eat. A man needs heft.'

The governor picked up one of the steaks with a fork and slid it onto a plate and passed it over to Dante.

'Thanks.'

The governor grinned at him, then turned back down to his food, loading up a fork with a piece of steak, a piece of fish and some wheat cake. Then he used his knife to smear it all with macaroni cheese like it was a sealing paste and he popped the whole lot into his mouth.

Dante watched him as he chewed. Small was in his sixties, overweight, bald and mustachioed, and dressed in a well-fitting suit of bureaucrat grey. The man had a great double chin which sagged down over his collar. As he ate, the chin moved up and down, and with each swing, it hid, then revealed the bright red knot of his tie. An effect so bizarre that it momentarily threw Dante off.

'What did you want to see me about?' the governor asked.

'You had your bodyguard, Corrado Abbate, investigate the poisoning a few weeks back at the Ritz?'

'You're damned right I did. I nearly died that night. Had to have my stomach pumped. You ever had your stomach pumped, boy?' the governor asked, shoveling another forkful of food into his mouth. 'It is not a pleasant experience.'

The man started chewing again and Dante watched as the red knot of his tie disappeared and reappeared in flashes behind his chin.

'Last night someone took Corrie for a ride,' Dante said.

Small stopped eating and looked up at him, his great jaw hanging open, a mush of food visible on his tongue.

'What happened?'

'I got a call last night from Corrie's squeeze. She's an old friend of my wife. She said she'd got home late and found the apartment broken into and a pool of blood on the floor. I went round there and cleaned up for her. I know Corrie was looking into the poisoning for you – I saw him strong-arming Vaughn at the Ritz a few days ago. I figured you'd want the heads-up on what happened to him, and since we're both looking into the same thing, maybe we could talk.'

'You're looking into it too?' Small asked. 'For Capone?'

Dante nodded and Small took a moment to think, and Dante could see the alarm on his face. The man had been the victim of a poisoning a few weeks ago and now his main bodyguard had been sent down the river. Dante could guess at how embattled the man must feel. On top of recent events, the governor had lost out to Senator Deneen's candidate in the Pineapple Primary that spring and would be out of office within the year. The most corrupt governor in Illinois history would be politically redundant by January, and someone was taking potshots at him.

'You got any idea who did it?' Small asked.

'I came here to ask you the same question.'

Small stared at him levelly for a good few seconds, then he refilled his wine glass.

'I'm guessing by your coming here, you're not aware of recent events,' said Small.

'Enlighten me.'

'Capone and I no longer see eye to eye. You coming here as his employee means you're either not well-informed, or you've got some balls.'

'Or maybe both,' said Dante.

Small looked at him a moment, then burst out laughing.

'I like that,' said Small. 'I like that indeed.'

'What happened between the two of you?' Dante asked.

'You mean aside from me getting poisoned by his booze? Lots of things. Let's just say while you've been away, the tide has turned against your boss.'

'Even so,' said Dante, 'we're both after the same thing – finding out whoever was behind the poison party. We might as well share our information.' Dante shrugged, leaned back in his seat and took his cigarettes out of his pocket.

'Don't smoke while I'm eating, boy,' said Small. 'And I don't appreciate you calling it a poison *party*. I nearly died.'

Dante nodded, trying to look sufficiently chastened.

'I tell you what Corrie found out and then what?' asked Small.

'I go and find the poisoner.'

'And then you deliver him to Capone,' said Small, picking up his fork once more. 'But where does that leave me? And more pertinent to you, where does that leave Dante the Gent?'

Dante frowned. 'I don't follow.'

Small stared at him and Dante gathered that Small knew something important that he wasn't letting on, some great secret he wasn't sure he should reveal to Dante.

'At first I thought it was someone from Illinois,' Small said. 'I've been getting death threats for years now on account of the pardons.'

Dante nodded. He could see the logic in Small's thinking: some vigilante who'd suffered at the hands of one of the men Small had released as part of his cash-for-pardons scheme had decided to take revenge on the governor.

'You think the poisoning was aimed at you?' asked Dante.

Small nodded. 'I did. Bill Thompson thought it was aimed at him. Capone thought it was aimed at him. I guess that speaks to our vanity. That's why I asked Corrie to look into it.'

'And what did Corrie find?'

'What Corrie found out might upset you, boy,' said Small, a knowing look on his face.

'Go on,' said Dante, dread beginning to make his heart race.

'Two days after the poisoning, a trigger turned up in Chicago from out of town, booked into a hotel. Corrie figured out this trigger had been hired by whoever it was that arranged the attack. The poisoning had gone wrong and now these people hired the trigger to come in and clean up loose ends. Last time I saw Corrie he was going to stake out the hotel, try to find this trigger.'

'Why would that upset me?' asked Dante.

'Corrie figured the trigger was from New York. He figured this whole poisoning wasn't aimed at me or the mayor or anyone else. It was an attempt to destabilize Capone. Now ask yourself who in New York would want to do that?'

'I don't know.'

'Your old pal, Frankie Yale.'

Dante frowned. He worked closely with Yale back in New York. If Capone and Yale did go to war, Dante would be caught right between the two.

'Why would Yale go to war with Capone?' Dante asked.

'About a year and a half ago, Capone visited New York,' said Small. 'He went there so that retard kid of his could have an operation on his head. But he also went there to sign an agreement with Yale.'

Dante nodded. He knew about the agreement the two boot-leggers had signed. Al had enough breweries in Chicago to provide him with beer, and there were enough alky cooks in the city to produce the gut-rot he sold for cheap in his brothels and gambling houses. There was the liquor that came in from Minne-apolis and Milwaukee, too, and at night, the mosquito boats that carried whiskey from Canada to the US across the Detroit River, a narrow stretch of water only a mile wide. But the high-end liquor – the Scotch and Irish whiskey, the British gin, the Carib-bean rum – that Capone sold to restaurants and hotels had to be imported, and that meant bringing it in from New York.

Out east, Frankie Yale's bribery of the coastguard meant boats full of liquor were making their way down the coast each week from Canada, filling the city with premium alcohol, so much so that Yale's warehouse in Brooklyn was over-stocked with the stuff. The agreement the two men had made was for Capone to buy any of Yale's excess booze, and have his men drive it cross-country to Chicago, a six-day trip across the back roads.

'The last six months, more and more of Capone's vans are getting hijacked on the way back from New York,' explained Small. 'And Capone thinks Yale's behind the hijackings. A few months ago he sent Jimmy "Files" D'Amato out to New York to look into things. You hear what happened to him?'

Dante nodded. 'He was shot dead in the street outside a Coney Island crap game.'

Small shrugged. 'So you can understand that the situation between the two cities is a little tense. And in the middle of all that, the poisoning happens. And if Capone suspects New York's behind it, then he didn't ask you to Chicago to investigate the poisoning—'

'He asked me here to keep me hostage in case a war gets declared between him and my friends back east,' said Dante, finishing the governor's statement for him.

The governor nodded. 'You asked me why the news might

upset you, boy, and there it is – your position in Chicago looks precarious at best.'

Dante nodded again, his head spinning. He knew Yale and Capone had struck the agreement, and he knew D'Amato had been shot dead in New York earlier that year, but he hadn't connected the two events, and he knew nothing of the hijackings that were supposedly plaguing the New-York-to-Chicago route. If all that the governor was saying was true, then Dante had been stabbed in the back not only by Capone, but by his colleagues in New York, too.

It suddenly made sense why Capone had called him out west – there wasn't any irony in the job he'd been tasked with, and certainly no coincidence. Capone had planned it all, and Dante's friends in New York had let him go. He rubbed his temples a moment, wishing he could smoke a cigarette.

'You got the details of the hotel the trigger was staying in?' he asked.

'And why should I give those to you?' asked Small.

'Because you still don't really know who's behind it all. And even if it was New York, you were one of the men poisoned, and last night they killed your bodyguard. So I'd say it's personal now for the both of us.'

'And in return, you'll give me any information you find?'

'Sure.'

'Before you give it to Capone?'

'If it turns out I've been double-crossed, sure.'

Small stared at him, and as Dante waited for a reply, he noticed he was drenched with sweat.

'Very well,' said Small eventually. He took a receipt from his wallet and wrote down the name and address of the hotel, then he passed it to Dante, who looked at it and frowned. The hotel was in the Northside.

'Moran territory,' said Small, reading Dante's thoughts. 'Where can I reach you?'

'I'm staying in the Lindbergh suite at the Drake.'

Small nodded and Dante rose and Small looked at his plate.

'You didn't eat your steak, boy.'

'I'll take it with me.'

When Dante returned to the street, he put the steak on the sidewalk outside the Blackhawk and the dog bounded out of the open window and tucked into it.

Dante watched a moment, then lit a cigarette and tried to arrange his thoughts. Was it his friends in New York who were behind the poisoning? Had Capone called Dante back to Chicago to be held hostage, maybe tortured to reveal information on a plot he knew nothing about, maybe killed and dumped in a hole somewhere in the endless plains?

Then there was the trigger, in town to tie up loose ends. He'd killed Corrado, who'd been investigating the poisoning too, which meant he'd probably be coming after Dante next.

And then there was the fact he'd just agreed with the governor to double-cross Capone.

He took another drag on his cigarette and thought about leaving town, getting in the Blackhawk then and there and driving off. But if he did, he'd have Capone hunting him for the rest of his life, and maybe his 'friends' in New York on his tail as well.

As the dog tore into the steak, Dante stood in the sunshine and glare of the street, wondering what the hell his next move should be. The feeling of dread that had hung over him since he'd arrived in the city got worse, making his heart beat faster, sapping his strength, making him wonder if he wasn't already a dead man.

PART FIVE

SECOND CHORUS

'You can kid about Chicago and its crooks, but they have the smart-est way of handling their crooks of any city. They get the rival gangs to kill off each other and all the police have to do is just referee and count up the bodies. They won't have a crook in Chicago unless he will agree to shoot at another crook. So, viva Chicago.'

WILL ROGERS, LETTER TO THE
NEW YORK TIMES, 1928

Chicago Herald Tribune

THE WORLD'S GREATEST NEWSPAPER

TWO NEW BOMBS RIP THROUGH CITY

Total number of bombings in the city this year up to 65

(Picture on back page)

BY JAMES O'DONNELL BENNETT

A bomb was detonated just after midnight in the West Side last night at the Druggists' Co-operative Photo Service, 2641 Congress Street. The bomb tore away the frontage of the store and broke windows in buildings a half a block either side of it, though fortunately the building itself was empty and no one was injured in the blast. Warren Avenue police were inclined to believe the bombing to be caused by labor disputes. The damage was estimated at $1,500.

Following that, at nearly 2 a.m., a second black powder-bomb blast took place at the ice-cream plant of A. Giancane at 1510 Taylor Street. Retaliation for the slaying of Edward Divis, West Side gangster, was thought to be the motive this time, according to Maxwell Street police. The blast was loud enough to be heard in the Loop.

These new blasts bring the total number of bombings in the city this year to 65, with total damage estimated at over $50,000, dashing citizens' hopes that the city had seen an end to the spate of bombings that marred the run-up to the so-called 'Pineapple Primary' Republican election in March –

which saw over 60 bombs going off in the six-month lead-up to the election, including blasts at the houses of the City Comptroller, the Commissioner of Public Services, the Secretary to the State's Attorney, Judges Swanson and Sbarbaro, and most notably, Senator Deneen.

G. L. Hostetter, executive secretary of the Employers' Association, which has been tracking the numbers, said in a statement that half of the bombs were directed at businesses, suggesting labor and union unrest as the main cause, the other half being caused by personal or gang vendettas, protection rackets, and racial turf wars. The use of bombs for terrorization by anarchists – a phenomenon which has plagued recently, among others, New York, Baltimore and Philadelphia – was not cited as a reason in any of the Chicago bombings.

'Bomb making and throwing has become a professional occupation, carried on by a syndicate whose services are for hire,' said Hostetter in the statement issued by the association last week. 'Bombs may be bought and "serviced" – that is, thrown – wherever directed.'

Of all the areas in the city, Halstead Street, between Irving Park Boulevard and 63rd Street, saw the most violence, with 12 bombings already this year, leading the association to name it 'Gunpowder Row'.

24

Jacob awoke to the noise of the phone, its dull metal ring penetrating his sleep with a knife-like sharpness. He got up, rubbed his eyes and rushed into the living room to pick it up.

'Hello?'

'Jacob? This is Pete Geary down at the Twenty-second station. Frank Lynott said you were on the lookout for female shines, mid-twenties?'

'Yeah?' said Jacob.

'One just popped up in Bridgeport.'

'Alive?'

'Nope. Deader than a pharaoh. She's causing a blockage in the Sanitary and Sewage Canal. The assignment's hot. You want it?'

'I want it. Where on the canal?'

'Just past South Fork, keep going and you'll see it.'

'Thanks, Pete.'

Jacob slammed down the phone and rushed to get ready for another long and blood-painted night. He was on the street in less than four minutes, jumping into a cab at the rank a couple of blocks from his apartment in less than seven. It was only when he settled into the back of the taxi that he thought to check the time on his Hamilton – three forty-two a.m. Jacob sighed and leaned his head back and watched the city flash by, night-lights streaking into the darkness behind him. The taxi made good time as the streets were empty, save for a few vagrants and drunks and clutches of lonely souls waiting at the tram stops to catch owl cars back to the suburbs.

When Lynott had searched the Bureau of Identification for Roebuck's missing cabaret-dancer girlfriend and come up blank, he'd put a note in the daily bulletins to the stations for people to be on the lookout for anyone turning up, dead or alive, who matched the description. It had been a couple of weeks since then and Jacob had heard nothing on the missing girl or the dead stooge and despite his best efforts to pursue other avenues, his investigation had stalled. Until now.

After a quarter of an hour he was passing through Bridgeport and by the time he was crossing the river at South Fork, Jacob could see arc lights shining along the southern bank of the canal, police cars, a crowd of cops. He told the cabbie to head for the commotion, and when they got close, the cabbie stopped at the top of the bank and Jacob paid him and walked down toward the lights, making swift progress along the mud, which had been dried hard as macadam in the summer heat.

By the time he reached the crowd of people at the bottom of the bank, Jacob's clothes were drenched in sweat, as if the moonbeams themselves were sending down heat. He looked for brass and saw a detective he knew from the division who he guessed was in charge. Jacob walked over and greeted him. The detective eyeballed Jacob a moment before nodding and walking off to confer with two patrolmen who were standing behind an arc light they'd set up on the roof of one of the cars, sending out a beam across the waters.

Both the men were holding handkerchiefs to their faces against the smell coming off the water. The canal had been built in the previous century, partly to provide a shipping link between the Mississippi and the Great Lakes Waterway, mainly to whisk away the city's industrial waste, sewage and abattoir run-off, causing the waters to run thick with animal blood, offal, entrails, excrement, and dregs from the city's forges.

Between the edge of the bank and the canal itself were yards of swampy, dangerous-looking ground, studded with refuse and high weeds. The beam of the arc light, lemon yellow in the gloom, darted across this wasteland to a spot in the middle of the canal where a tiny island of mud rose up from the rushing water, and the naked body of a Negro girl was half submerged.

Jacob studied what he could see of the corpse a moment, then turned to see a young man standing nearby, maybe an assistant Coroner's physician, who was also staring out across the hellish landscape. The young man noticed him looking and turned his way.

'Who made the call?' asked Jacob, wondering how she'd been spotted in the middle of the night in the middle of the canal.

'Anonymous tip-off,' said the young man. 'The dam controllers in Lockport opened up the causeways in the afternoon and the water level's been dropping all night. Enough to reveal her. We're just waiting for the men from the Sanitary District to come and get her out.'

Jacob nodded and the man turned back to look westwards, away from the city. Jacob followed his gaze into the darkness on the horizon, where every now and again, far in the distance, the sky was lit up by balls of flaming methane bursting into the night from the tower-like chimneys of the forges outside the city, forges that produced steel twenty-four hours a day. The effect was unsettling – the quiet and darkness, then the fiery flash, impossibly high and far away, as if a dragon was laying waste to the land.

A few minutes passed and then there was the sound of an engine, and Jacob and the man turned to see a van arriving with *Sanitary District of Chicago* painted onto its side. Two men got out, spoke briefly to the police, then dressed themselves in boots, overalls and face masks. One of the men strapped a harness to himself, and the other man connected it to the towbar of the van, and with a weariness and efficiency born of having repeated the procedure hundreds of times, the man with the harness waded out into the filthy swamp, placed a rope around the body and dragged it back.

When the body was eventually schlepped onto the bank, the whole crowd of onlookers came by to inspect it. Patches of the girl's skin had been bleached by the industrial chemicals dumped into the canal. The parts of her exposed to the air – one side of the face, one arm, one breast, one thigh – were a light-toned brown, the rest a sickly shade of pallid white, the two different colors swirling around each other in a bizarre marbling effect. One of the Coroner's men retrieved a bucket of water from somewhere and when he poured it over the body, washing away the brown sludge from the canal, the effect was even more pronounced, and everyone, even the battle-hardened men from the Detective Division, stood staring silently at it.

Aside from the swirls of bleaching, other marks of damage were strewn all over the girl's naked body; bruises and cuts from where she had tumbled along the canal; sodden, flaking skin; the bites of insects, fish and gulls; the neck, cleanly broken with the head pushed back at a sickening angle; rope marks from where a weight had been tied to her to keep her body underwater; and lastly, two holes where her eyes should have been, both clogged with canal water, either plucked by a bird, or ripped out by a rat, or gouged out like her boyfriend's, by Anton Hodiak.

Jacob stepped back from the crowd, unsure if this was the dead man's girlfriend or not. He took the menu from the Sunset Café out of his pocket, comparing the healthy-looking dancer to the crooked-limbed, bloated body in front of him. It was her, much transformed. From the feature bill at the Sunset, to the chorus line at the Chicago's Greatest, to a lamentable death in a sewerage canal.

Jacob returned the menu to his pocket before anyone spotted it, and then the team got to work. The Coroner's men conducted a quick examination, after which Jacob took photos. He'd packed his Leica into his messenger bag, a portable 35-millimetre camera that didn't need film plates or a hefty tripod or a flash lamp since, as he'd hoped, the patrolmen had turned their arc light onto the body for him.

As he worked he stayed close to the detectives so as to over-hear what was being said. The consensus was that the girl had been dumped further upstream, somewhere near the mouth of Bubbly Creek, where the Chicago River turned south and joined with the start of the canal. She'd been dumped tied to a weight, hence the ropes around her ankles and wrists. But after a few days in the water, her body had somehow slipped free, and began its journey west. The detectives discussed sending patrolmen up to the creek to canvass for witnesses at first light, and they bemoaned the fact that the killer had chosen such a desolate dump site.

Bubbly Creek was closer to the city, but it was an area of factories, populated at night by vagrants and the desperately poor, who lived by the side of the waterway in crumbling brick buildings, lean-tos and shacks. The place had gained its name decades earlier, when firms in the Stockyards dumped waste into it at such a rate that all the blood, offal and entrails in it combusted and let off carbonic gas, causing the surface to bubble and steam like some pit of hell.

Jacob thought a moment, and looked again at the corpse, at the nicks and bruises and the broken neck the Coroners' men said were caused by its trip down the canal. As fast as the canal rushed, there was no way it was powerful enough to break her neck like that, so cleanly, so forcefully. Jacob thought a moment, something registering on the edge of his consciousness, a memory of a similar injury he had photographed once.

An hour later, as they were all finishing up, the memory finally materialized. Another murder victim, another woman, dumped off the Adams Street Bridge the previous year. The killer had dropped her body head first off the bridge and her neck had broken in the exact same way when it hit the water. Jacob tried to think of bridges upstream from where they were. And then it

came to him – the Ashland Avenue Bridge. It passed right over
the canal, between where they were and the creek. The police
would be looking for witnesses in the wrong place. If he was
quick, he could steal a march on them.

25

Michael and Ida's investigation into the disappearance of Gwendolyn Van Haren continued with them canvassing around the train station where she'd gone missing. They'd made a map of the blocks Gwendolyn could have run down based on the route the cab had taken, then they'd been up and down them in the sweltering heat, hour after hour, going into shops and kiosks, showing the photo, asking if anyone remembered the beautiful heiress who'd gone on the run. They'd gone back in the nighttime too, but still no one had seen a thing.

In the daytime, they continued to check the hospitals, jails and morgues, but she hadn't turned up there. Her fiancé and his friend, Lloyd Severyn, were also still missing. None of their known associates could be found for questioning. And as far as they could tell, the girl's father was still out of town. They'd run background checks on everyone who worked at the house and they'd all come up clean. They called their colleagues in Montreal, figuring maybe she'd got to her destination via a different route, but their colleagues north of the border had no trace of her being in the city.

So they turned their attention to Senator Deneen. Michael had been offered a job in the State's Attorney's office to drop the Van Haren case, and if what Michael's friend Walker had said was correct, the State's Attorney had made the offer because Senator Deneen had pressured them into it. Michael called a contact in the Republican Party, asked for a list of donors to Senator Deneen's election campaign, and there was Charles Coulton Senior's name right near the top. The father of Gwendolyn's fiancé, the man whose son had gone missing without a missing person's report, must have been the one who was behind it. From Coulton to the State's Attorney's to Michael, the power had been exerted down the links. Chicago was like that, a city of lines and force.

It turned out the man's business address was just a couple of blocks from Pinkerton HQ, at the bottom of the La Salle Street Canyon, so Michael had gone down there early the next morning, and now he stood outside, watching the cars coming and going in front of the building. Coulton owned it outright, had built it himself, all twenty-five floors, renting out twenty-three of them to other businesses and keeping the top two for himself.

Michael took a puff on his cigarette and craned his neck to look up at the building. It was clad in Connecticut limestone and like so many other buildings constructed in the years since Carter and Carnarvon had discovered King Tut's tomb, it was decorated in the Egyptian Revival style, with art deco lines running along its stonework depicting Nile reeds, Papyrus leaves, lotuses, scarabs, suns and jackal-headed gods, making it look like a new temple to an ancient religion.

At the building's very pinnacle was some kind of golden statue Michael couldn't make out. He put his hand up to his brow, to dim the glare and get a better view, but the light streaming down from the sky was too strong; it bounced off the asphalt underneath and rebounded off the walls in a billion haphazard zigzags that stung and dried his eyes. More lines of force pressing down from above, needling him, obscuring the bigger picture.

Outside the foyer of the building, a succession of Rolls-Royces and Cadillacs and Isotta Fraschinis were pulling up to disgorge captains of industry at the building's entrance. Doors were flung open by porters in pristine white gloves, and men stepped out onto the red carpet and were whisked up in elevators to their new Mount Olympus at the top of the building. After a few moments a Bentley saloon pulled up and two men stepped out. Michael flicked his cigarette onto the asphalt and trotted across the street.

'Mr Coulton?' he said, and the two men stopped and turned to look at him. Despite the heat both were dressed in somber black business suits. Coulton was tall and well-built, and if it wasn't for the surroundings, and the suit, Michael would have taken the man for an aging street thug.

'My name's Michael Talbot. I'm a detective at the Pinkerton Detective Agency.'

'Ah, the man who rescued the Brandts' baby from those kidnappers.'

Michael paused. The accent, the intonation, the choice of words, they all seemed wrong. They were coarser than those he was expecting, more inflected with the street, with the east coast, with the slums of Washington, Philadelphia, Baltimore. The man was trying to conceal his true accent, and Michael looked at him again, and once more had the impression of a gangster in a well-cut suit.

'Yes, sir,' said Michael.

'The Brandts are fine people. We were all so relieved. Well, what can I help you with?'

'I just wanted to thank you for my new job at the State's Attorney's office, and I was wondering if we could discuss the details.'

Michael watched intently as the muscles of Coulton's face pinched in confusion. The man must have heard by now from his informers at the State's Attorney's that Michael had turned down the job offer, yet here he was, offering his thanks, pulling the rug from under the man's feet. Coulton was wondering if there had been a miscommunication, and Michael was hoping the man's curiosity might gain him an audience.

As Coulton stared at Michael, deciding what to do, the man who had exited the car with him stepped forward and smiled.

'Mr Talbot. My name is Mr Smith, I'm Mr Coulton's personal secretary. We're very busy at the moment, but if you'd like to arrange a meeting, please call me on this number.' He held out a business card and looked him in the eye. The delivery was smooth, and Michael smiled at the irony; Coulton's lackey had the sophistication, the well-heeled manner, the accent, that Coulton himself was striving so hard to ape.

Michael returned Smith's gaze and saw that one of the man's eyes was glass, an expensive replica of his good eye, perfect enough to be almost unnoticeable.

As Michael took the card, one of the building's doormen approached.

'Is everything all right, Mr Coulton?' he asked, stretching out his back and shoulders. Behind them a couple of cars had pulled up to the entrance, were waiting to discharge more men into the building, and the stoppage was holding them up.

Coulton stared at Michael for a moment longer, then he lifted a shaking, stubby finger into the air.

'It's fine,' he said to the doorman. And then to Michael, 'You've got five minutes.'

They turned and walked into the foyer of the building, a foyer which was vaulted and tall enough to fit a greystone in, but which was filled instead with an ice-cold draft from an air-cooling system which bit through Michael's sweat-drenched clothes and into his skin.

They crossed to an elevator bank underneath a mural of the eye of Horus, stepped into a private elevator and travelled all the way up to the twenty-fourth floor in silence. Then they walked down a pristine corridor, through a glass door into an office the size of Michael's apartment. Unlike the Egyptian-themed foyer, the decor here was aristocratic country house: dark polished wood, damask chairs, velvet drapes, all of it trying to add a touch of the ancien régime. Far from making Coulton look like what-ever it was he was aspiring to be, the decor highlighted how far short of it he was, making him seem even more like a street hustler.

And in that moment it occurred to Michael why there was not much to be found on Coulton's beginnings: the man had changed his name. It was exactly the kind of name the man would have chosen if he'd had the choice, a name that fitted in with the furniture and the accent and the business suit and the car. Michael scrabbled together a cliché of a life, a boy from the streets making some money, moving out west, laundering the money and changing his name, getting wealthier, building skyscrapers, marrying his son into what, by Chicago standards, was old money. Except his son didn't like girls, was more interested in slumming it in jazz clubs, and all the plans for a respectable legacy had crumbled. And now both the boy and his would-be wife had disappeared, and the man was having to entertain a Pinkerton detective in his office.

'What are you doing here, Mr Talbot?' Coulton asked once they were seated at his desk, the secretary hovering behind Michael, near the door.

'I wanted to know why you didn't file a missing person's report when your son went missing. As far as I can tell, he's your only immediate family, and it's been weeks since anyone saw him.'

'My son makes a habit of disappearing. He's a good-for-nothing. He disappears, only to reappear a few weeks later in a police cell or a drunk tank, or worse. While you're asking where he is, he's probably drinking cocktails in a Mexican brothel. He'll turn up eventually, and when he does there'll no doubt be a bill attached. A bail note, a blackmail note, a gambling debt, a fee to pay to a journalist to keep his mouth shut. If I called the police every time the boy disappeared there'd be no officers left on the street. Why didn't I report him missing, you ask? I've been on the verge of disinheriting him for the last decade is why.'

'But this time his fiancée has disappeared too . . .'

'His fiancée is as stupid and flighty as he is. In that, they're an excellent match. I take it by your questions that you've not taken up the job offer with the State's Attorney's office?'

'No.'

'You lied to me earlier?'

'You wouldn't have talked to me otherwise.'

At this Coulton paused a moment, then nodded.

'You've chosen a dangerous path, Mr Talbot. And all for what? An air-headed bleeding heart who's chosen to run away, and a wayward boy who's drunk in a hole somewhere. Why are you so interested in all this?'

Michael shrugged. 'I'm interested in doing right by the girl, and by her mother.'

Coulton laughed, a scoffing, belittling laugh.

'You fooled me with that face of yours. I didn't take you for a do-gooder. Look out of the window, Mr Talbot. We're in Chicago. There's no room for do-gooders here. We've got almost double the murder rate of New York and more bombings than any other city in the country. We've got a jail that inmates can walk out of, a lunatic asylum one in four patients escape from, we've got a governor who'll pardon you if you pay him enough, a senator who's so corrupt he wasn't allowed to take his seat in the Senate, and we just had an election dubbed the Pineapple Primary because of the number of hand grenades used in it. If you think this city has any time for do-gooders you're a damned fool.'

Michael looked at the man as he finished his rant. It was the kind of pre-prepared speech people thought up in their spare time and looked to unleash whenever they found the opportunity, and Michael had walked right into it.

'Now unless you have any actual business here, I'd like to get on with mine.'

'I just had one question, before I go. You built this place?'

'I did.'

'It's mighty impressive. Outside, right at the top, there's a gold statue. I couldn't tell what it was from the street. The building's real tall, and with the sun shining down . . .' Michael shrugged and wondered if he was laying on the slow-witted Southerner act a little too thick. Coulton frowned, not sure if he was being made fun of. Then he pressed his fingers together in a steeple.

'It's Plutus, the god of wealth. The Board of Trade Building will have its sculpture of Ceres, and I have my Plutus.'

'I see,' said Michael, wondering why the man had put an ancient Greek god atop an ancient Egyptian building. Michael guessed he must have said it sourly, because Coulton glared at him.

'You have something against wealth, Mr Talbot? Are you one of those Bible-reading fools who think money is the root of all evil?'

It was the second time Coulton had suggested Michael was a fool, and the man probably hadn't even realized he'd done it. Michael had always been of the impression that it was possible to get through life on a shortage of manners, or of money, but never both. Michael, not having much money, opted to be well-mannered. Coulton, it seemed, was his reverse.

'I wouldn't say that,' Michael replied.

'Yet you refused to take a job that would have seen you much wealthier than you are now. The money could have moved you and that half-bred family of yours into somewhere respectable.'

'Oh, the Southside's respectable enough for me.'

'I don't doubt it,' Coulton said. 'You look the picture of contentment. A playwright in ancient Greece wrote a play about Plutus. The god was blind and distributed wealth randomly. Then his sight was restored and he began distributing it according to who deserved it, and you know what happened? Chaos. Society collapsed.'

Michael nodded, getting the point. 'If you don't mind my asking, how did *you* come by your money? When I was reading up about you, the papers didn't have much to say on the subject.'

Michael saw a flash of anger in Coulton's eyes.

'I don't much like your attitude, Mr Talbot.'

'I don't much like it either.'

Coulton glared at him a moment longer, then as if he'd realized something – maybe that Michael was trying to rile him – he paused, and smiled.

'I made a little money in my youth,' he said, 'through hard work. I invested the little money, and it attracted more money. That's the way these things work.'

'Money attracts money,' said Michael.

'Exactly. Like gravity.'

'Or voodou,' Michael muttered, wanting to rile the man further, to see what he was like when angry. But Coulton didn't take the bait.

'You're from New Orleans, aren't you, Mr Talbot?' he said, raising his eyebrows.

'That's right.'

'I went to your city once. Saw a witch doctor. Had my fortune told. For fun. I suppose there is a voodou to money, a magic, a force. You want to know what the similarity between voodou and money is?'

'Sure.'

'They only work if people believe in them.' Coulton grinned, and Michael thought for a moment and grinned back.

'I suppose you've got a point there,' he said.

'I do indeed. Money is life, Mr Talbot. Without it, who knows what terrors lie in store?'

Michael studied him a moment, running the brim of his hat through his fingers. He didn't need any more time with this man. Clearly he was involved in it all. The only question was how.

'Well, I better be going. Thanks for your time.'

Michael smiled and Coulton eyed him as he stood and headed for the exit. The secretary with the glass eye moved toward the glass door and opened it, but just as Michael was reaching it, he remembered something.

'I almost forgot,' he said, stopping, and Coulton looked up at him. 'You got your scripture wrong. Money isn't the root of all evil. *Love of money* is the root of all evil. Big difference, I'm sure you'll agree.'

Michael smiled and Coulton glared at him. Michael popped his hat onto his head and walked out through the glass door, back into the corridor, to the elevator, to the eye of Horus, to the turmoil and roar of LaSalle Street roasting in the heat below.

26

As Jacob walked along the canal, dawn came on, ruby and white, promising another day of heat and hazy weather, the light giving shape to the colossal gas storage tanks, factories and refineries that lined the wasteland either side of the waterway. Beyond them was the bridge. It had been raised to let a steamboat pass through, so on either bank, opposite halves of it were pointing up into the dawn like two great iron fingers.

On Jacob's side, just before the bridge, stood a collection of old huts and shacks running along the water's edge, in front of a makeshift wharf where a few rafts were tied up. The rafts were jerry-rigged and flimsy, made of scrap wood and twine, operated by vagrants who salvaged the effluent poured into the water by the abattoirs, skimming animal fat and hair off the surface to sell on to lard-makers and packagers.

Jacob figured if the cabaret dancer's body was dumped into the canal, then it was dumped at night, so the only people who would have been abroad to witness it were the tramps living in the shacks at the bottom of the bridge. He trotted down the bank to the shacks, and began looking about for people to question.

Those he came across were either drunk or half asleep or crazed, and Jacob soon figured that any of that shantytown's inhabitants who had their wits about them were probably already out on the waterways scavenging for food.

Midday came and went, and the afternoon wound on, and still Jacob hadn't found anyone with any useful information. He left the canal bank and in amongst the factories found a cafeteria, where he had an early dinner. As he walked along the bridge on his return to the shantytown, he paused a moment to look down at the canal, straight as a road as it ploughed its way to meet the Des Plaines River, twenty-eight miles southwest. The canal was just one part of the network of railways, waterways and roads the city cast across the hinterland, using it to pull in people and goods with the grim determination of a fishing-boat captain, rearranging the landscape so that Chicago was at its center, the organizing principle.

A familiar feeling came over him, one he'd often experienced when contemplating the city's mammoth industrial power; that being in Chicago meant being a cog in some colossal, unfathomable machine which was endlessly manufacturing, building, forging, transporting, on such a vast scale that it was impossible for any one man to fully understand the extent of what the city had planned. It was a disorientating sensation, a feeling of powerlessness, insignificance, detachment.

He looked again at the great forges blasting jets of fire into the air, leaving behind them thin trails of purple smoke, sliced by the rust-colored rays of the sun. The clouds of soot and smoke would hover over the canal and the city, and make the humidity even worse, only dispersing if the wind decided to blow the right way and push the clouds out over the lake. He wiped the sweat from his face, looked at the shantytown below him, and went down onto the bank once more.

A little after sunset, a raft pulled up at the wharf and an old bearded man tied it up, then heaved a sack over his shoulder and made his way across the planks laid down in the mud at the canal's edge. Despite the heat, the man was wearing a thick winter jacket and a woolen hat, and grime and soot were smeared so thickly across his face that in the darkness Jacob couldn't even discern his skin color. Jacob thought of the girl, burned white by the canal, and this vagrant, grimed black by it.

He walked over to the man and fell in step with him.

'Sorry to bother you,' said Jacob.

'No, ye ain't,' said the man, keeping his gaze on the path ahead.

Jacob, flummoxed, took his press card from his pocket.

'I'm a journalist,' he said. 'I wanted to ask you some questions and maybe there's some money in it for you.'

'Oh, yeah?'

Jacob looked at the man. The sack he had over his shoulder was foul-smelling and canal water was dripping out of it, splattering onto the hard-caked mud of the bank.

'I was wondering if you were around here one night a few weeks ago. Maybe saw a body thrown into the canal off the bridge?'

'And if I did?'

'Then, like I said, there's some money in it for you.'

The man stopped in front of one of the shacks, a large, half-collapsed building without a door, sitting at a slant among the reeds and grasses.

'Then ye better come in.'

Jacob followed him into the shack. It was dim and close inside, with the fetid air of a sickroom. The man laid down the sack and opened it up. Then he sat, drew a bottle of whiskey from his coat pocket, took a sip from it, and stared at Jacob. His look reminded Jacob of a drawing he'd seen once in a magazine, an illustration of a voodou witch doctor that accompanied a horror story set out in the bayous of Louisiana. The artist had drawn lines emanating from the character's eyes, implying some kind of power in the man's gaze, a mesmerism.

'What do you want to know?' the man asked, grabbing the sack and pulling it toward him.

'I want to know what you saw,' said Jacob, sitting on the ground.

'Two men in a Cadillac throwing a naked girl off the bridge is what I saw.' He started scooping handfuls of something out of the sack, and it took Jacob a moment to realize what it was in the gloom – sodden hair and lumps of lard.

'Dead o' night. Three, four weeks ago. Real big splash. How much ye paying?' he asked, not looking up, laying the hair out in strips on the mud to dry.

Jacob got his wallet, peeled off two fives and held them out in the gloom. The old man looked up at the notes, then at Jacob's face, the line of his voodou glare as sharp as the policemen's arc light cutting through the darkness over the canal.

'I'm poor and I'm drunk,' said the old man, his look infected with derision, 'but I ain't stupid.'

Jacob peeled off another two fives and the old man nodded, a single judder of his chin. He reached over and took the cash.

'You sure it was a Cadillac?' asked Jacob.

'I know one when I see one,' said the man, folding the notes over and slipping them into an inside pocket. As he did so, his coat moved a little and Jacob caught a glimpse of rotting old news-papers, padded into the lining.

'Ain't like we get too many Caddies round here,' the man continued. 'A black one, it was. One of the new ones with the orange license plates. I didn't get the number, before ye ask.'

Jacob thought – orange plates had only been issued once, in the previous year, 1927. How many black Cadillacs were there in Chicago with '27 plates?

'What time?'

'I don't know, just before dawn. Sun was coming up.'

'What were you doing out at that time?' asked Jacob.

'Getting ready for work,' the old man said, holding up a hand-ful of salvaged hair by way of explanation.

'I was walking across the mud there when I saw the Cadillac stopped in the middle of the bridge, lights off, engine off, and ain't that strange, so I stopped to watch a little while, and two men get out, and they get a body out the trunk, coon girl, nice-lookin'. Naked except for some rope they had her trussed up with and some kind o' paving stone or something tied to her. They heave her off the side, and then they watch her a moment and then they get back in the Caddy and drive off. Whole thing took no longer than a minute.'

Jacob rummaged around his pockets for the photo he had of Anton Hodiak. He held it up and the tramp stared at it in the gloom. Jacob clicked his lighter on, and held it next to the photo.

'Is that one of the men?' he asked.

The tramp stared at the photo a while, then shook his head.

'Nah. That ain't him.'

'Look again.'

'I'm telling you that ain't him. I'd remember a face like that,' he said, raising his voice, jabbing his finger at the photo of Hodiak, 'with that goddamn smile carved into one side of it.'

Jacob put down the photo of Hodiak, sighed, and switched the lighter off. He ran his hand through his hair and tried to think.

'Okay,' he said, a little exasperated, his theory about Hodiak being the killer not fitting at all with what the man was saying. 'What did the men look like?'

'One was tall and thin. The other was shorter, just a kid. Looked like a Mex maybe. And the tall one had scars all over his neck. Used to know a man in the boxcars like that. Caught the poison gas in his lungs back in the war and had the scars from where the doctors tried to fix him up. Maybe the same thing happened to the one I saw on the bridge.'

Jacob thought a moment, not quite buying it.

'How far away from him were you that you could see his scars?'

The man glared at him again, annoyed that Jacob was questioning his account.

'I told you I was on the mud,' he said in an irritated tone. 'Where it rises up to meet the bridge. They was on top of the bridge. Ten, fifteen yards.'

Jacob nodded, took out his pack of Luckies, lit one, and

offered another to the old man as a way to placate him. The old man thought a moment, then accepted, and Jacob passed him his lighter. As its flame approached the man's face, Jacob saw he was much younger than he'd originally guessed. There were missing teeth, some wrinkles around his eyes, and that thick paste of grime scraped into all the crevices of his face as if with a trowel, but he was actually not much older than Jacob.

'How old were the men?' Jacob asked.

'The one in charge was about your age, I guess. The Mexican one was in his teens, early twenties.'

'And how were they dressed?'

'What do you mean?'

'Fancy? Rough? Work clothes? Uniforms?'

'Oh, fancy. Fancy, for sure. And not gangster fancy. Rich boy, prep-school fancy.'

27

The hotel was located in a skid-row neighborhood somewhere off Mohawk Street, an area too run-down to take the Blackhawk and remain inconspicuous, so Dante left the car at the Drake and took the dog for a walk. He headed downtown, zigzagging along the blocks, hoping to lose any tails, then he boarded an uptown tram. He journeyed all the way to the car barn near Little Hell, the oval-shaped piece of land in the middle of the Chicago River where Death Corner was located, an intersection so called because it averaged about a murder a week.

From there, walking east down Chicago Avenue, he skirted around the manure piles lying uncollected on the sidewalk, then turned north up one of the smaller streets that led off the avenue. Dante walked past an open lot of land, and then a scrap-metal dealer's, outside of which stood a line of emaciated, hollow-eyed men waiting to sell to the dealer pieces of metal they had stolen or collected and piled up in trolleys and crates in front of them. The men looked homeless, ragged, dirty, and Dante recognized them as junkies – heroin addicts who funded their habit by collecting scrap metal and selling it to junkyards.

The phenomenon had started in New York, and Dante was surprised to see it had spread all the way to Chicago. The drug was making inroads all across the country, and with a gangster's cynical eye, he wondered who the junkies' suppliers were. As he watched them shivering in the heat, he thought how there was really only one difference between himself and them: wealth. Without money, he would be as desperate, dirty and hopeless as they were.

He turned a corner, and saw a fleapit hotel further up the block. He stopped and checked the address the governor had given him and confirmed it was the place where the trigger was staying, the man the traitors had brought to the city to clear up after the failed poisoning, the man who had probably killed Corrado Abbate.

Dante was one step closer to figuring out what was going on, and who was double-crossing him.

A few doors down, on the opposite sidewalk, was another hotel, just as decrepit-looking. Dante went inside and ordered a room with a view of the street, and he sat in the window, watching the entrance to the trigger's hotel for anyone coming and going that he recognized or could pin as a hitman.

The first few hours drifted past in a daze. The sun dragged the day westwards, to another part of the world, and then it was night, and Dante was drenched in a hot cold opiate sweat: he was starting to get the itch. He made himself a needle right there in the window, and when he plunged it in, the dog started barking at him, with what to Dante felt like angry disappointment.

Then he pulled the needle out and the dog calmed down and Dante stared a moment at the aftermath, the pin of blood on his skin, the raised vein. He took the belt from his upper arm and noticed his sweat had dried onto the fabric of his shirt, tidemarks in rings of white across the blue cotton, like foam-crested waves rolling across an ocean. Looking down on it, he imagined he was floating over the waters of Long Island. He felt the salt breath of the sea, the relaxing sound of the waves. There was his boat, peacefully anchored up by the stitching of his cuff. He watched it a while, then his mind came back to the present. This was why he shouldn't do dope on the job.

For the next fourteen hours he carried on sitting in the window, chain-smoking his way through till morning, taking more hits, till at gone midday, his persistence paid off: a man walked out of the hotel and off toward the tram stop, and Dante saw four things about him that all said he was a triggerman on a job; a bow tie on, rather than a necktie, which could be used against him in a fight; a newly grown beard, ready to be shaved off once the job was done; a suit cut baggy around the midriff to conceal any weapons; and on his feet a set of heavy-tread, steel-capped boots.

Dante quickly tidied himself up, left his room, and crossed the street to the other hotel; he passed by it, looking in as he went. Through the window he could see a hallway and a reception desk with pigeonholes behind it. Manning the desk was an acne-strewn kid who was simultaneously reading a copy of *Moby-Dick* and giving himself a manicure with his teeth.

Dante walked back around, took a five-dollar bill from his wallet and entered the hotel.

'Hello. How can I help?' said the kid in a chirpy tone.

'A man just exited here and jumped on a tram and he dropped this five-dollar bill on the street. At least, I think he did.'

Dante passed over the five-spot. The boy took it and smiled at Dante.

'What did he look like?' he asked.

'Tall. Beard. Brown hair.'

'Okay. He's one of our guests. I'll see he gets it,' and the boy folded up the bill and slipped it into an envelope and as he did so Dante ran his eye around the place – an old-fashioned lobby, a staircase, a corridor leading to the rear. He turned his attention back to the boy as he popped the envelope into a pigeonhole. Room 414.

Dante found the rear entrance to the hotel on a quiet, narrow alleyway, lined with garbage cans. The door was safely bolted from the inside so he scanned the building for a way to break in. From every floor above him, clotheslines were stretched across the alley, heavy with washing, brilliant white shirts criss-crossing the blue sky, like so many souls floating to heaven. He wondered a moment how it was possible for all that fabric to shine so white in a city swirling thick with pollution, then he looked across from the clotheslines to the metal fire escapes that zigzagged across the brickwork all the way up to the roof.

He checked the rest of the block. Three buildings down, someone had left a back door propped open with a battered wooden chair. Dante slipped through it, went up a flight of stairs till he got to a window, then climbed up the fire escape all the way to the roof of the block.

He walked back along it, passing by the things people had left up there among the chimneys and clotheslines – plants in tin cans, tables and chairs, a camp-bed, an alarm clock next to a mattress, pigeon cages stacked one on top of the other, abandoned and rusting.

When he reached the roof of the hotel, he lowered himself onto the fire escape and walked down it till he found an open window, swung through it into a corridor, and made his way to Room 414.

He took a moment to get his breath back, then he put his ear against the door and listened. Silence. He bent down and inspected the lock. Cheap hotel issue, bought in bulk and a cinch to pick. He pulled the case from his pocket, got to work and a minute later he stepped inside.

It was a small room, clean and tidy, with a window giving out onto the alley at the rear. Dante made a start on searching the place. He didn't have much time for triggermen; they were the village idiots of the underworld, thugs who could find no other work except killing people. They were often twisted and malicious too, the kind of men who ensured that gunshot wounds were made wider by chewing the tips of their bullets, or who rubbed them with garlic or onion water so the victim's wounds got infected. But every now and again Dante came across one who was intelligent, thoughtful, professional, dangerous. The fact that

Dante couldn't find a single piece of evidence in the hotel room revealing the man's identity showed he belonged very firmly in this second camp.

The break he was looking for came when he opened up the man's suitcase, where he found a shoebox filled with odds and ends. He sat on the bed and went through it, and within a couple of seconds he realized what it was – a horde of items owned by the missing waiter.

It was the triggerman who'd gone over to the waiter's house before Dante, who had left those marks in the dust. And this is what the trigger had come back with; a photo Dante guessed must be of the waiter, books of matches from different bars and restaurants, a letter from the waiter's daughter in Detroit, a bank statement, a receipt from a garage, and a betting slip with a phone number scrawled across the rear of it.

The triggerman hadn't dumped the trinkets he'd stolen, which meant he was still looking for the waiter. Dante went through the horde once more, slowly, turning each item over. Then he came back to the betting slip with the phone number on one side. He looked at the number, memorized it, then he flipped the slip over and looked at the bet, the name of a horse scribbled down in a hand so crabby Dante could only just make it out: Ganymede. Odds of twenty to one, twenty dollars down. The time and date of the race and the name of the racecourse, and the date the bet was made. And on top of all that information, a rubber stamp. Bookies all stamped their slips with their own stylized logo to keep the slips from being copied. This stamp was in red ink and had a design of a horse's head in profile, with a ring of stars around it. Dante recognized it as belonging to Michigan Red, a narcotics dealer and bookie operating out of a pool hall in Cottage Grove.

Dante returned everything to the shoebox and replaced the box in the suitcase. Then he went back to the wardrobe and checked the man's suits. Every one was bespoke and the tailor's tags stitched into the lining all showed addresses in Lower Manhattan, Little Italy. He checked the boots lined up at the bottom of the wardrobe and it was the same story. The trigger was from New York.

Just like Dante had feared he might be. A distant sense of panic rose up in him, claustrophobia, a worry that the trigger might come back at any minute.

He returned everything to how he'd found it, and went back to the alley via the roof, glad to be outside again. On his way back across the street, he passed the front of the trigger's hotel slowly, and peered into the lobby. The gangly kid was still there, still reading *Moby-Dick*, but the pigeonhole for Room 414 was empty. As Dante had hoped, the temptation to steal the money had proved too much, and the trigger would be none the wiser.

GENERAL CASE REPORT

C.P.D. GENERAL
CHICAGO POLICE DEPARTMENT

1. OFFENSE	2. DIST	3. BEAT
Murder	9	907

4. LOCATION
Pullman Ice Works, Lake Calumet

5. DATE & TIME OCCURRED	6. DATE AND TIME POLICE ARRIVED
Unkn.	21 Jun. 28 0230

7. VICTIM'S NAME (FIRM NAME IF BUSINESS)
Abbate, Corrado. M/W/1888

8. RESIDENCE ADDRESS	9. RES. PHONE
Unkn.	Unkn.

10. PERSON REPORTING CRIME TO POLICE
Wilson, Leonard M/C/1878

11. RESIDENCE ADDRESS	12. RES. PHONE
Apt. 9, 340 E. 55th Street	dna

13. PERSON WHO DISCOVERED CRIME
Wilson, Leonard M/C/1878

14. RESIDENCE ADDRESS	15. RES. PHONE
Apt. 9, 340 E. 55th Street	dna

16. WITNESS NAME (A)
None

17. RESIDENCE ADDRESS	18. RES. PHONE
dna	dna

19. VICTIM'S OCCUPATION
Private security / bodyguard

SEX	RACE	D/O/B
M	W	'88

20.A. TYPE OF PREMISES WHERE OCCURRED

Ice Works

20.B. EXACT LOCATION

Hut #43 ext.

21. TOOL, WEAPON OR MEANS USED

Knife

22. METHOD USED TO COMMIT CRIME

see narrative

23. OBJECT OF ATTACK OR PROPERTY TAKEN

dna

24. VALUE OF PROPERTY TAKEN

dna

25. TRADE MARK OR UNUSUAL EVENT

dna

26. VEHICLE USED BY OFFENDER/S

Unkn.

YEAR   MAKE   BODY STYLE

COLOR   LICENSE

Dark

OTHER IDENTIFYING MARKS

27. NARRATIVE

Patrol 907 sent to the above location by CC after report of a disturbance. On arrival met Wilson M/C/1878, a nightwatchman at the former Pullman Ice Works.

Wilson stated that during his rounds at 0200 he noticed a section of fencing had been pulled down,

and two men escaping through the fencing into a
waiting car, which it was too dark to identify. He
called in the report then discovered the body in a
ditch surrounding one of the ice-huts. He led us to
the ice-hut in question (#43). Found the body in
the 'moat' of the ice-hut, lying on back. Numerous
stab wounds across shirt / torso and slice across
neck. No blood at scene.

Officer #601 called central 0215 for assistance and
for Coroner's physician and for officers from the
Detective Division to attend the scene. Search of
body discovered wallet, necktie, cigarette packet.

Items in wallet:
1) Business cards identifying man as Corrado Abbate,
Private hire bodyguard
2) Photograph unkn. woman (White)
3) Small change
4) Card from the Gaynes Club, Bar / Restaurant

Assisted Coroner's physician, removal of body,
awaited detectives till 0330 on site.

Time completed 21 Jun. 28 at 0630 hrs.

REPORTING OFFICER	STAR	REPORTING OFFICER 2	STAR
Hunter, F.	433	Kirby, B.	601

SUPERVISOR APPROVING	
Sullivan, M.	

28

Sick of being stuck in traffic, Jacob descended from the electric and stepped into the chaos of Michigan Avenue. He shimmied through six lanes of speedsters, roadsters, runabouts and sedans that were crawling along, nose to tail, and when he reached the sidewalk, he merged into the mad swirl of pedestrians and continued southwards till he reached Trib Tower, the recently completed neo-Gothic skyscraper that was the home of the *Chicago Tribune*. It was thirty-six floors of stone and glass shooting arrow straight into the clouds, topped with a *tour de beurre* roof that was modeled on Rouen Cathedral, and garnished in so much stonework it was as if some careless chef had sprinkled sculptures across its facade.

Jacob stepped out of the glaring sun and into the building's foyer, and it took a moment for his eyes to adjust and then the lobby came into view: high-vaulted, spacious and glittering. The lobby was the paper's public face and was designed to provoke awe. Chicago had a lot of newspapers, but it was the *Tribune* that mattered, with the third-largest circulation in the world, and the only major daily in the city not owned by Randolph Hearst.

Jacob trotted down the steps into the lobby proper, past the lines of people queuing at the pinewood desks, and crossed to the rear. He caught the elevator to the fourth floor and came out into the newsroom, the roaring epicenter of the paper, a chaos of men and machinery and rushing noise.

If there was anywhere that could be called the heart of the city, the newsroom of the *Tribune* was it, the place where all the information Chicago generated was ordered and made sense of, condensed every twenty-four hours into forty pages of three thousand words each. The vastness of the effort and the break-neck speed at which it happened left most of the people working there broken; the journalists and editors, legmen, rewriters, copy boys and cutters, all of them getting by on a steady diet of alcohol, cigarettes and cynicism, fourteen-hour work days and non-existent marriages.

Jacob walked through the mess of it all, passing by the steam tables and the rows of journalists' desks, each one abuzz with men and women, jackets off, shouting into telephones or typing away at noisy Remington Model 12s; passing by pneumatic tubes shooting parcels between floors, basket conveyors rattling along overhead. The noise was deafening and people had to shout to make themselves heard, which only made it worse.

He headed to the picture editor's office and picked up his pay-check for the last few sets of photos he'd delivered. Then he crossed to the other end of the newsroom and got in the service elevator at the back and pressed the button for the basement. The doors closed and the roar of the newsroom disappeared. Jacob closed his eyes, and he realized how tired and sleepy he was.

He guessed he must have nodded off for a few seconds, because the thump of the elevator reaching the basement jolted him awake. He stepped out into a long cement corridor, cool and quiet, damp and lined with great metal pipes. At a line of lockers, he opened one up and took out a bottle of development fluid he'd left there. He slipped it into his messenger bag, and then carried on going, toward the furthest depths of the basement, where a quiet, dank office housed the most knowledgeable and intelligent man in the building.

Jacob knocked on the door and stepped into a cavernous space full of filing cabinets and reference books, in the middle of which was a desk and fifteen-foot-long blackboard where Oscar Lowenthal was working. He was tall, and a little stooped on account of his age, with grey hair clumped around his ears. He was scruffy in a professorial way, an effect amplified by his bow tie and brown cardigan, worn as there was a pleasant, subterranean chill in the office.

Lowenthal turned to smile at Jacob, revealing behind him a grid of black-and-white squares he'd drawn on the blackboard, and next to it, a scrawl of clues and answers and letter counts, a babelism of words broken down by dashes and parentheses into their syllables.

'And how is the inquiring photographer?' asked Lowenthal.

'Good,' said Jacob, slumping into one of the chairs at the desk and tossing his hat onto the paperwork. He closed his eyes for a moment, enjoying the coolness of the basement.

'I don't know how they can work up there,' said Jacob. 'In this heat.'

'The newsroom?' asked Lowenthal, putting down the chalk in his hand, and heading over to the desk. 'It's not so bad. I used to know an editor at one of the Hearst papers downtown, firmly believed that alcohol produced better copy, so he encouraged his workers to drink on the job. The newsroom was infamous for its reek of vomit.'

He sat on the other side of the desk and Jacob opened his eyes and they looked at each other across the battlefield of Lowenthal's desktop. They were friends by chance. Jacob was one of the few employees to use the lockers in the basement, and his happened to be on the route to Lowenthal's office. The friendship had progressed somehow from the two of them passing the time of day to drinking sessions in which Jacob would listen to Lowenthal's war stories from the newsrooms of the previous century, tales of Old Chicago, the million pieces of trivia the man had stored in his head.

'Something's troubling you,' said Lowenthal.

Jacob thought a moment, and nodded in the direction of the drinks cabinet, where Lowenthal's green celluloid visor of days gone past was hanging from a hook. Lowenthal poured him a

Hennessy and Jacob told him about the investigation. When he had finished, Lowenthal mulled over it all.

'A dead Capone stooge in an alley,' Lowenthal said, 'and his Negress cabaret-dancer girlfriend dead, too. Both of them with their eyes plucked out. And maybe Bugs Moran is involved, and maybe Capone is involved, and since it's being covered up, some-one in the Police Department is definitely involved. But I don't think this killer, Anton Hodiak, is involved.'

'Come on. The eyes, Lowenthal. And the stooge had a black girlfriend.'

Lowenthal shook his head. 'The stooge maybe. But I've seen plenty of bodies dragged out of canals or left to rot in fields with the eyes plucked out by some bird or rodent. You said the stooge had glass in his hand. Maybe he smashed a bottle into someone's eyes and the gouging was revenge. And as for the black girlfriend – half the city's going down to Bronzeville on sex safaris. Plus, there's the two rich kids dumping the girl's body off the bridge. Hodiak's a killing-floor worker – the lowest of the low.'

'Well, he's got rich friends somewhere, seeing as he paid off the governor for a pardon.'

Lowenthal dismissed the suggestion with a wave. 'He prob-ably got that pardon because the Ku Klux Klan raised a collection, or appealed to the governor – he's their man after all. No, it doesn't fit.'

Lowenthal steepled his hands together in front of his face and continued slowly. 'The only thing you know for sure – as long as the tramp on the wharf isn't lying – is that two rich kids in a Cadillac dumped the girl's body off the Ashland Avenue Bridge. Which means they're the only ones you know for certain are involved. You ask me, the thing's veering toward money.'

'How's that?' asked Jacob.

'Cover-ups cost money. So do Cadillacs. And certainly so do rich kids. Things in Chicago only happen because of money. Look at what this city's given birth to – skyscrapers, private detectives, assembly lines, financial derivatives, mail order, meat-packing . . . all of them invented here and concerned, in one way or another, with efficiency and its green-backed child. We even name our neighborhoods after commodities – the rich whites live in the Gold Coast, and the poor Negroes in Bronzeville. Money's the magic that turns the wheels. In Chicago it's never *cherchez la femme*, Jacob, it's *cherchez la loot*. You need to ask yourself who's got money to make by killing the stooge and his girlfriend, or more likely, who's got money to lose if they stay alive.'

Jacob nodded. He'd been certain that the killer was Hodiak, but Lowenthal made a convincing case that he wasn't, and now Jacob was losing confidence in his hypothesis, and by extension, his own skills of deduction. He rubbed his temples and looked at the crossword, half composed on the blackboard, and studied the answers that had been filled out – Queensbury, slugger, turn-buckle, Schmeling. A boxing theme. Lowenthal liked to keep the crossword topical.

'Is that in aid of the match?' asked Jacob, waggling his finger at the blackboard. The bout for the heavyweight championship of the world was to be staged in Chicago at the start of July.

Lowenthal nodded. 'The fight should be good for you,' he said. 'Word is, every famous person in the world's going to be descending on Chicago to watch it. You could be out snapping celebrities in hotels instead of corpses in alleyways.'

'Not really my kind of thing.'

'No, I don't suppose it is.'

They settled into a comfortable silence, and Jacob closed his eyes, his mind swirling about the plughole of sleep.

'You look tired,' said Lowenthal after a moment.

'I feel it,' said Jacob, opening his eyes. 'Can I use the phone quickly before I go?'

Lowenthal nodded and returned to the blackboard, and Jacob put a call through to the Detective Division.

'It's me,' he said when Lynott picked up at the other end. 'There's been developments.'

He told him about the stooge's dead girlfriend in the canal and the two rich kids with a '27 Cadillac.

'I'll put a call through to the Automobile Division,' said Lynott. 'Should have a list of them in a day or so. What's the description of the two kids?'

'One Hispanic, early twenties, average height. Second one was in his thirties maybe. Tall and thin, scars across his neck. Maybe a veteran.'

'All right, I'll get in touch with the Bureau and the Automobile Division. I'll call you when I know something.'

It took Jacob an hour to get home, and when he did, he spent the rest of the morning studying the photos of the dead girl in the canal he'd developed the night before, looking for details, lying on his couch in the heat with a beer he'd gotten from the super's daughter. It was a recipe for falling asleep on the job, which he did, and at some point in the evening, he was awoken by the sound of the phone ringing.

'Jacob? It's Frank. I got something for you. First up, I got a call from our liaison in Florida. Anton Hodiak was picked up in Jacksonville four weeks ago for assaulting a Negro outside a brothel. He's been in lock-up there ever since, awaiting bail. There's no way he could have been involved.'

Jacob paused to let the news sink in, feeling foolish and put out.

'All right,' he said, trying to keep his voice steady.

'Sorry, bud,' said Lynott. 'We all got pet theories that don't work out.'

'Yeah, yeah. What's the other news?'

'Nothing on the Cadillac yet, but I got something on your veteran with the neck scars. Turns out you're not the only one looking for him. Seems a dick at the Pinkertons is looking for the same man – a tall thin veteran with a broken voice and scars on his neck. The Pink made an inquiry earlier this week. She had a name for him too – Lloyd Severyn. Know anything about it?'

'First I've heard of it.'

'Well, the Pink goes by the name of Ida Davis. Quite the spellbinder by all accounts. Works with that freak with the small-pox scars. They're the ones that solved the Brandt kidnapping a couple of years ago. Remember?'

'Sure, I remember. The *Trib* had us on shift round the clock.'

'Maybe you should give her a call. Might be you two are investigating the same case. You want her number?'

29

Ida met Louis late that afternoon on a bustling corner of the Loop and they took a turn down Michigan Avenue. They caught up on things, and Ida told Louis about her investigation into Gwendolyn's disappearance, the fact that on the day she disappeared, the girl had met a go-between in Bronzeville by the name of Randall Taylor.

In the years since the two of them had moved from New Orleans to Chicago, every now and again Ida asked Louis for help in an investigation. Louis was by no means an underworld figure, but the jazz clubs he worked in served booze, and booze was bought from criminals, and so the worlds of nightlife and crime had become ever more intertwined over the prohibition years, meaning, more often than not, Louis knew someone who knew someone who could help Ida find what it was she was searching for.

'And you think this go-between might be involved?' Louis asked.

Ida shrugged. 'She went to meet him the day she disappeared to find out where her fiancé was. Then a few hours later she went back home scared witless.'

Louis nodded. 'I ain't heard of a Randall Taylor,' he said, 'but I'll ask around.'

'Thanks,' said Ida, and they walked on a little bit more.

'How's things with you and Alpha?' she asked.

'Good. I've moved Clarence in with them and he's doing good. Got his smile back after all these months.'

Clarence was Louis' adopted son. The boy was the product of

Louis' cousin being raped by the white man she worked for as a maid. The father refused to acknowledge the boy, and when the cousin died a few years after the birth, Louis had adopted him to save him from the orphanage, even though, at the time, Louis was still only a teenager himself. A few years into his guardianship, the boy had fallen from a balcony at Louis' home back in New Orleans and hit his head while Louis was supposed to have been looking after him, and the fall had left the boy slow. Louis had forever felt guilty about what had happened, had spent most of his money on doctors to care for the boy, and when he'd settled down in Chicago, he had brought him up to the city, and Alpha and her mother helped take care of him.

Ida remembered Louis telling her Clarence hadn't much liked it when they were living with Lil and her ma – Louis' wife and mother-in-law had tried to force Clarence to live by the house rules, had made no concessions to the fact that he had a brain injury. Alpha's family, by contrast, treated him with warmth and affection, like one of their own.

'You seen much of Lil since you split?' Ida asked.

'Yeah,' said Louis, an odd expression on his face. 'Maybe a little too much.'

Ida nodded and had the sense not to push the subject. She liked Lil and was sorry to hear things had gone badly for the two of them. Lil had been good for Louis, had pushed him to start his own band, to train, to be a star. When Louis' mother was ill back in New Orleans the previous year, it was Lil who went down south to get her, braving the worst floods ever to hit the country. When they'd buried her, it was Lil who took care of the arrangements.

They turned onto Lake Street and found themselves under the elevated railroad. The sun shining through the tracks above cast everything below into alternating oblongs of light and shade, which slid over the contours of the street as they walked, warping over cars and fire hydrants and awnings like bands of oil.

'What about you?' he asked.

'What about me?'

'What's happening romance-wise?' he said, raising an eyebrow. Ida felt the same embarrassment she always felt when asked the question. Nothing was happening apart from her work. It never did. No loves or flings, no crushes or infatuations or one-night stands. It was nothing that she minded, but she felt other people expected more, and that expectation meant she couldn't ever answer the question without squirming, without feeling that maybe there was an emptiness there, that maybe she was floating through life in danger of becoming a cautionary tale in a lonely hearts column.

'Nothing much,' she said. 'I'm kinda busy work-wise.'

'Oh, sure,' said Louis, nodding sarcastically and grinning, and she smiled and slapped him on the arm and they walked on in silence for a little, contemplating the rush of people, the buildings, the illuminated signs which flickered in the artificial dusk of the elevated's shadows.

When they reached the L station they turned onto State Street and found themselves in front of the Balaban & Katz Movie Palace, and Louis stopped to read the sign above the entrance: *Buster Keaton in Sherlock Jr. – Screenings Every Hour on the Hour.*

'You seen it?' asked Louis, and Ida shook her head.

'A Sherlock Holmes you haven't seen?' he said sarcastically, poking fun at her love of the detective. 'Let's go in,' he said. 'Place is air-cooled, we can chill for a bit.'

'I dunno, Louis,' she heard herself saying. Louis caught on to her apprehension and gave her a stern look. And in the silence between them, an elevated train roared past on the tracks above, a thunderstorm of iron rolling through the sky.

'Let's risk it,' he said, once the train had pulled into the station. 'Plus it's a Sherlock Holmes, it might give you an idea for your case.'

They bought two tickets and stepped inside the foyer, feeling instantly frozen by the air-cooling. Louis went to the concession to buy a box of popcorn and Ida looked about the place. The building was seven stories high, and the lobby took up five of them, containing mezzanines, balconies, chandeliers and a staircase which, a sign informed her, was modeled on one in the Paris Opera House.

The building craze that had swept through the country over the decade had included the construction of an endless series of opulent cinemas. In Chicago alone there was the Renaissance-style Congress, the rococo-style Norshore, the baroque-style Tivoli, and as if in response to all this European influence, the Oriental, built to look like it was the home of an Indian prince. Each of them had an auditorium with more than three and a half thousand seats.

Louis returned from the concession, already munching on the popcorn, and they went over to the ushers, who directed them to the balcony, where another usher directed them to the aisle seats of the section in the extreme far corner of the space, where the few other black souls who'd had the temerity to enter a downtown theater had all been lumped together.

'Well, look at this,' said Louis, sitting down. 'They made us our own little ghetto. Ain't that nice.' And he burst out laughing, and some of the people sitting around them laughed too, while a few others turned around to give him disapproving looks. He shrugged and swept his hand in front of him, indicating the other few thousand seats in the place, half of which were empty. Both Ida and Louis were used to such things having grown up in New Orleans, but the cinemas in Chicago were supposed to be desegregated. And they had paid for tickets in the stalls, front and center.

They settled down and watched the screen as the shorts flicked past. Then Louis leaned over and nodded at a pair of great black boxes on either side of the stage far below.

'Speaker system,' he said. 'It plays back recorded sound so you don't need musicians to accompany the film. Cinemas are sacking orchestras all over town. Loew's aren't hiring organists anymore. The union's in uproar.'

'What about you at the Vendome?' Ida asked. Louis had a gig in the orchestra pit at the Vendome cinema in the Black Belt, playing there each evening before heading off to the nightclubs.

'We're safe for the moment, I guess. But with the sound systems and the speakies and the clampdown on the nightclubs, cats are getting jittery about where their next paycheck's coming from. All everyone's talking about is moving to New York.'

Ida nodded. She knew New York was somewhere Louis was hesitant to return to after his brief stint there a few years earlier.

They watched the last of the shorts and then the Buster Keaton feature came on. In a film-within-a-film structure, the movie showed Keaton as a cinema projectionist who falls asleep whilst screening a Sherlock Holmes film and dreams that he is Sherlock Holmes, going on a bizarre, mystery adventure.

Ida and Louis wiped tears from their eyes as Keaton dodged freight trains, jumped off buildings, went on a ride through Los Angeles perched atop the handlebars of a motorcycle. Toward the end of the first reel, Louis took a reefer from his pocket and lit it up, and they passed it between them and laughed all the more for it, and when the lights went up and they wandered back out into the opulence of the foyer, they were red-eyed and spent from so much laughter.

They stepped out onto the street and the heat hit them and it took them a moment to adjust their senses to the glare of sunlight and the rush of people and noise on State Street. The gage she'd smoked wasn't helping, leaving her with a speeded-up heart and a slowed-down head. They said goodbye to each other, and Louis tipped his homburg onto his head, and she watched him disappear into the torrent of people cascading through the shafts of sunlight. Then she turned and headed up the stairs to the elevated station and waited for her train.

She had met Louis through her father. When Louis was

twelve years old he had been sentenced to an indefinite stay at the Colored Waifs Home – a Victorian correctional institution just outside New Orleans – for firing off a pistol in a New Year's Day celebration. Ida's father was the music teacher at the home and he'd taken Louis under his wing, coached him, brought him home to duet with Ida on the piano, and the two lonely children had become friends. They'd stayed friends through their teenage years in New Orleans, and through their twenties in Chicago.

Whenever she spent time with him, it brought to her attention how their characters had changed in the years since they had moved north; Louis had lost his country-boy air and settled into a contentment with who he was. Ida, however, was still haunted by the insecurities she'd felt as a youngster. She'd always thought that at some point her self-doubt would fall away and she'd be like the adults she saw breezing through life, competent and self-assured. But here she was, approaching thirty and the realization was dawning on her that she'd never shed her sense that she didn't quite fit in; that experience, unfortunately, did not equal confidence. All those things that she'd prayed she'd grow out of had turned out to be part of who she was – daunted, alone, at an angle to the world.

Meeting up with Louis, who was on such good terms with life, who jumped into everything whole-hog and wholehearted, reminded her of her shortcomings, but also helped soothe her too. Alone, she felt the good times were always going on elsewhere; with Louis, she felt at the heart of things, invited to the party.

The train arrived and she boarded and stared out of the window as it traversed the South Loop. The sun set, and by the time the elevated was snaking through the rooftops of Bronzeville, the sky was dusky and dim. She got off at Garfield Boulevard, and trudged down the stairs to the street.

It had gotten dark and the road was buzzing with people. Music was blaring out of bars and clubs, loud enough to scramble her thoughts. The smell of Chinese food and barbecue floated in the heat. Revelers with eyes half lidded from dope and booze stumbled along the sidewalks, swaying in and out of the neon spill that colored the streets like electric stained glass.

Ida headed away from the commotion, as always. She crossed a few blocks to her small, one-bedroom apartment on the fifth floor of a greystone in Washington Park, a quiet, mostly Negro neighborhood.

When she got inside, she opened up all the windows and switched on the electric fan and tried to figure out what to do with the night. CBS wouldn't be broadcasting *Live from the Cotton Club* till much later on, so she contented herself with flicking through the stations, seeing what was on, the buzz of the reefer still in her head, making her easily pleased.

Anyone could set up a radio station so the airwaves were jammed with all sorts of broadcasters – newspapers, churches, shops, gas companies. Over thirty different languages were spoken in Chicago and Ida was sure every one of them was represented at least somewhere on the dial. She stopped to listen to a warm male voice speaking in a strange, Slavic-sounding language. It had a harsh sort of musicality to it, this unknown language floating into her apartment on a sea of a static. She tried to guess at what it was, putting a name to the swarm of syllables whose consonants rubbed together and sparked – Czech, Polish, Russian?

She eventually stopped at a station playing light dance music. The performer was singing in the crooning style, the new, softer sound designed for the radio, that wasn't so loud it blew out the vacuum tubes of the device, as did the voices of the opera and cabaret singers who were quickly falling out of favor. It would do till Duke Ellington woke up over in Harlem.

She closed her eyes and tried to think about the case, to let the clues and leads and possibilities swirl about her mind, bump into each other, make connections, break, realign, like so many molecules of information. Time passed, and at some point, the Duke was up and playing some nocturne or fantasia, and she looked out of her window and saw the skyscrapers in the distance, towering over the city, lit by a million night-lights. The electric pointillism pricked her skin and a horde of feelings stepped out of the shadows. Each speck of light outside her window was a life carrying on without her, a life that she'd never touch, and the emptiness of that, the loss implicit in it, made her cry. That was the thing about the city: living amongst an ocean of strangers made the loneliness starker, sadder somehow.

The feeling didn't last too long. It never did. It washed over her and passed and she dried her eyes and eventually drifted off into a strange half-sleep. She dreamed of Chicago as a fairy-tale city, under the shadow of a scar-ridden king, a city of twinkling castles rising into the clouds, lakes in the sky, merchant princes, monsters, peasants, princesses trapped in golden palaces: poor, lonely damsels awaiting their fate.

She awoke to the phone ringing. She rubbed her eyes and picked it up.

'Hello?'

'Hello, is that Miss Davis?'

'Yes.'

'Hello, Miss Davis. My name's Jacob Russo. I'm a photographer with the *Tribune* and the Detective Division. I, uh, I'm sorry for calling so late, but I have a feeling we might be looking for the same person.'

He had a deep voice, and he spoke quickly, nervous and uncertain.

'And what person would that be?'

'Lloyd Severyn.'

Ida paused and thought a moment, wishing she wasn't still half asleep, that she hadn't drunk so much bourbon or smoked the gage. She ran through a list of people who knew she was looking for information on Severyn, and which ones had access to her home telephone number.

'Why do you think I'm looking for a Lloyd Severyn?'

'Let's just say we know the same people at the Bureau of Investigation.'

'And why are you looking for him?'

'I wanted to ask you the same question. Perhaps we could meet?'

30

When Dante got back to the Drake from the stakeout, he peeled off the sweat-soaked clothes he'd been wearing for the last two days, took a long cold shower, and took a hit. Then he ordered some food for him and the dog, ate and passed out.

He woke in the morning and ordered more food, and as he drank a coffee he browsed through the complimentary copy of the *Tribune* that had arrived with room service, and came across the report of Corrado Abbate's body turning up at the old Pullman Ice Works. He put the paper down and thought a moment.

He needed to head over to Bronzeville to replenish his stash and follow up the betting-slip lead, but just as he was planning it, the phone rang. It was Frank Nitti, informing him that Al wanted an update, that Al would be playing a round that morning down in Burnham, and Dante was expected on the course.

Dante agreed to go over there and put down the phone. He thought about the timing of it all and what the hell he could tell Al. Since his chat with the governor, Dante had realized that Al was probably having him followed, hence Al's gift of such a conspicuous car. Whoever was tailing him had probably told Al that Dante had spent the last two days in a hotel in Moran territory. Hence the timing of the phone call. Al wanted to know what the hell Dante was up to. Dante couldn't tell him about the New York connection because he might incriminate himself, and he couldn't tell him he hadn't come up with anything either.

He looked again at the diminished lump of dope on the table, then at his jittery hands, and wondered if he should go to the meeting shaking or doped up. The dog looked at him sternly, and Dante decided to wait.

It took them over an hour getting to Burnham, a suburb far to the south of the city, where the mayor was a friend of Al's, and the Outfit owned a nine-hole golf course, and Al's caddie's sister worked as a waitress in the clubhouse and gave Al special favors.

Dante parked up in front of the clubhouse and ambled through the greens to the fourth hole, where Al, 'Machine Gun' Jack McGurn, Frank Nitti and Johnny Patton, the Mayor of Burnham, were just teeing off. They were all dressed in luridly colored golfing gear, Al's get-up a particularly striking shade of lime. The four of them were surrounded by a small army of caddies and bull-necked bodyguards. As Dante approached, he noticed one of the hangers-on eyeing him, a man about his own age, with a bushy black mustache, wearing a brown suit with a matching bowler hat. Dante caught the man's gaze, smiled at him, and the man gave him a surly look back.

Dante reached the group just in time to see Al take a swing, and they all watched as his ball arced into the air before disappearing into a clump of trees to the side of the fairway.

'I think you killed another squirrel,' said Jack, and they all burst into howls of laughter, and Al shook his head, and handed his club to his caddie, and only then did he notice Dante standing at the edge of the group.

'What's with the mutt?' asked Al, nodding to the dog at Dante's feet. 'They let you in the Drake with that thing?'

Dante shrugged. Then they watched as 'Machine Gun' Jack teed up and took a swing and his ball traced an elegant curve in the air and landed slap in the middle of the green. Jack was one of the best golfers in Chicago. He gave lessons at the Evergreen Golf Course, might have made a fist of going pro if he didn't make more money as a hitman for Al. After him, the mayor teed off, landing on the fairway, and the group went off in search of their balls, Al and his caddie and Dante heading toward the tree line.

DEAD MAN'S BLUES

'So?' Al asked, when they'd split off from the others.

'So,' said Dante. 'It turns out a waiter at the Ritz called Julius Clay was involved. He skipped town the day after the poisoning and when I went round to his apartment the place had been searched. Professional job.'

'I never heard of him. You ask about?'

'That's all I've been doing. There's something else. Governor Small got agitated about the whole thing – figured it was a hit aimed at him – so he got his bodyguard, Corrado Abbate, to look into it. Abbate found something out, then someone took him for a ride, then his body turned up at the Pullman Ice Works the other day. So I went to see the governor and he told me Abbate had found some connection to a hotel uptown. I've been staking it out the past couple of days, but I didn't find anything, so I'm guessing Abbate got it all wrong.'

Dante turned to look at Al, trying to see if he'd buy the story. But Al stayed silent, gave nothing away, just kept his gaze on the scenery in front of him. They reached the tree line and stepped into the shadows and searched about for Al's ball, and as they did so, Al lit a cigar.

'So if Abbate got it all wrong,' said Al, 'how comes he ended up in the Ice Works?'

'Beats me,' said Dante.

Al thought a moment, then began swiping his club against the undergrowth, trying to uncover his ball.

'So what's the next move?' he asked.

'The waiter,' said Dante. 'We find the waiter, we find out who was behind this. I've got an idea where I can track him down.'

Al stopped to think a moment, rolling the cigar between his fingers, then taking a puff. Dante wiped the cold sweat from his forehead, noticing that his hand was trembling. And in that moment he realized, if Al was having him followed, he would know about Dante's trips to the shoeshine man. He looked up to see Al eyeing him.

'You don't look too good, Dante.'

'I've been living in a shithouse hotel room the last two days on a stakeout eating canned beans. How d'you want me to look?'

Al continued to eye him, and Dante noticed there was something changed in his old friend, that there was a vacancy in his expression, that he was distracted by something. Then Al turned to look at the caddie.

'You find it?'

'Naw,' said the caddie, a gangly teen who looked like he'd done a month's worth of shaving in the last five minutes.

'Nix it.'

The caddie nodded, took a new ball out from the golf bag and put it down on a stretch of ground near the edge of the tree line, where Al had a clear view to the green. Dante looked at Al and Al shrugged.

'I'm playing five hundred dollars a hole,' he said, 'and I'm already two grand down.'

Dante nodded. He knew that all the men cheated at their golf, not just Al, and on more than one occasion they'd pulled guns on each other in the middle of a game.

Al selected a club, swung, and the ball landed some way off the green. Al was as bad a golfer as he was a gambler. As they walked toward the rest of the group, Dante noticed that the man with the bushy mustache was staring at him once more.

'Who's that with the brown suit and bowler hat and the dead rat on his lip?' asked Dante.

Al smiled. 'Sacco. Why?'

'No reason,' said Dante, memorizing the name.

They eventually made it to the green, where the other men continued to needle Al over his lack of golfing prowess. The more they ribbed him, the more Dante could see Al was getting annoyed by it, ready to burst at any moment. Dante needed to get out of there, get to the car, take a hit before his shakes got even worse.

'Al, I might head back to town,' he said.

'What's the rush?'

'I got leads to chase.'

'We're leaving soon, too. Stick around. Play a game.'

'I don't know how to play.'

'Neither does Al,' said the mayor, and the men burst into laughter once more, and Dante checked Al's face, and could see the annoyance that had been building up had reached boiling point and Al could no longer hold it in.

'Next hole we play robin,' said Al softly, before stalking off alone toward the next hole. 'Stick around, Dante.'

Dante frowned and turned to the others, noted how the good humor had now been drained from the group, replaced by a mutual dread. He looked to the others to get a sense of what Al was referring to, but got nothing back. They all followed in silence, stealing nervous glances, till they got to the start of the next hole.

'Whose turn is it to play tee?' asked Al when they'd arrived. No one said anything for a moment, then Frank spoke up.

'Johnny,' he said.

They all turned to the mayor, and a look of worry crossed the man's face.

'Come on, Al, what's this shit? Always with the fucking robin,' he said. 'Give it a rest for once.'

'You know the rules,' said Al. 'It's your turn to play tee.'

The mayor looked from Al to the rest of the group, who refused to meet his gaze; they were hanging him out to dry.

'Come on, Al.' The mayor was pleading now, but Al didn't respond, didn't even look at him, just stared down the fairway, planning his shot.

The mayor looked again at the other men, hoping for some sort of response this time round, but again none of them met his gaze except for Dante, who, not understanding what was going on, held up his hands and shrugged.

Then after a moment, the mayor accepted his fate. He kneeled down on the grass, and lay flat on his back.

'I guess I'm first,' said Al, nodding at his caddie.

The caddie walked over and placed a ball on the mayor's chin, taking a moment to make sure it was balanced. Then he stepped back, selected a club and passed it to Al.

Al lined up his shot. He swung his club down a few times, practicing his shot, stopping just short of the mayor's face, causing the man to flinch each time, making him stifle a sob, making the ball wobble.

'Let's see how many squirrels I kill with this one,' said Al.

A look of grim determination crossed Al's face. He tensed, and with what seemed like all his strength, he swung his club down in the direction of the mayor's face.

He hit the ball and it thwacked across the fairway, and the mayor let out a yelp as the club missed his face by a hair, a yelp that seemed to contain all the fear and dread that had built up in him over the last few minutes, and the relief that Al hadn't caved his head in.

Dante looked at the mayor's face, saw the fear and powerlessness on it; then he looked up and saw Al staring at him, wild-eyed, and Dante wondered if the show was just because Al had gotten annoyed at his friends, or if it was a message for Dante, too, a demonstration of who was in charge. Or maybe it was something else, maybe Al was losing it, going steadily mad, and Dante felt a chill as he wondered what that meant for him, and for the rest of Chicago.

'Who's next?' said Al.

Jack stepped up, and his caddie laid down a ball on the mayor's chin, and Dante realized the show wasn't over quite yet, that they were going to play a full round like that, and on the next hole, someone else would be the tee. And all Dante could think about was how soon he could be in Bronzeville, picking up some small brown slabs of nothingness.

BUREAU OF IDENTIFICATION
DEPARTMENT OF POLICE
CITY OF CHICAGO

Name: **Severyn, Lloyd**   Reg no.: **98282**
Alias: Color: **White**
Residence: **Apt. 1, 4702, S. Halsted Str.**   Occupation: **Coal dealer**
Previous known residence/s: D.O.B.: **2/3/1894**

BERTILLION STATISTICS – DESCRIPTIVE

Height: **1m. 85**	Head length: **18.7**	L. Foot: **27.0**	Col. of eye, circle: **Greenish**
Age: **22**	Eng. Height: **6' 1"**	Head width: **16.4**	L. Mid. F.: **12**
Col. of eye: **Brown**	Apparent age: **22**	Outside A.: **88.5**	Cheeks width: **14.4**
L. Lit. F.: **9.2**	Trunk: **91.7**	R. Ear: **6.6**	L. Fore A.: **48.8**
Forehead ad incl.:	Nose projection:	Ears:	Hair: **Dk. ch**
Forehead height:	Nose length:	Teeth:	Complexion: **Sal.**
Forehead width:	Nose breadth:	Chin:	Weight: **173**
Forehead pecul.:	Nose pecul.:	Beard: **None**	Build: **Med.**

Marks, scars, moles, other peculiarities:

Date description taken: **4/20/1916**

KNOWN ASSOCIATES

Name: **Brandel, Adam**   Name: **Malloy, Shaun**
Alias: Alias:
Address: **1542 Sedgwick Street** Address: **780 Division Street**
Occupation: **Unkn.**   Occupation: **Florist**
D/O/B: **6/15/1888**   D/O/B: **Unkn.**
Reg no.: **97284**   Reg no.: **87712**
Nature of association: Nature of association:
Crim., ref CHC-29763   **Crim., ref CHC-29763**
Reg no.: **97761**   Reg no.: **89734**

RAY CELESTIN

ARREST AND PROSECUTION RECORD

Date	Charge & descr.	Disposition of case	Ref.
Feb. 13, 1908	Assault. (Street brawl)	Sentenced to 6 weeks in Pontiac Reformatory.	23-JoP-2892a
Aug. 8, 1910	Assault. (Street brawl)	D.W.P.	—
Sep. 5, 1912	Theft. (Robbing telephone coin boxes)	Sentenced to 6 months in the House of Correction and fined $50 and costs.	CHC-29763
Jul. 17, 1914	Malicious mischief.	Unkn.	SAA-987346-01
Apr. 20, 1916	Fraud. (Baggage check scam)	D.W.P.	CPD-14-899

31

The photographer sat at the desk in Michael and Ida's office and told them his story in the same warm and jittery voice Ida had heard over the phone. In person the jitteriness was accompanied by an animated physicality – hand movements and shrugs and shakes of the head that made him an engaging presence. He was a little older than Ida, with a wiry build, and eyes of pale green that were ringed red through lack of sleep.

He told them about the murder of a Capone stooge called Benjamin Roebuck in an alleyway three weeks earlier, and the death of Roebuck's girlfriend, a cabaret dancer, and how two rich-looking kids, one with neck scars, were seen throwing her body off the Ashland Avenue Bridge. He told them how he'd investigated it all, and when he'd finished speaking, Michael voiced the question both he and Ida wanted to know the answer to.

'You said the first murder happened three weeks ago? What was the exact date?'

'The twenty-seventh.'

Michael turned to look at Ida – the night Gwen had gone missing.

'And what time was the murder?'

The photographer shrugged. 'The body was discovered in the morning, but it had been there hours. Any time between midnight and four or five.'

Ida tried to put the timeline into some kind of order, and after a few moments she looked up to see the photographer staring at her.

'I've told you my side of the story,' he said. 'Perhaps you could tell me yours?'

Ida turned to look at Michael, and Michael nodded, and Ida told him about Gwendolyn's disappearance on the same night, and Coulton and Severyn's likely involvement, and the photographer smiled as she spoke.

'They're connected then,' he said when Ida had finished. 'Coulton and Severyn killed Roebuck and then your missing girl stumbled on them while they were cleaning up.'

Ida shook her head. 'The dates match, but the timings don't,' she said. 'Our men were at the Illinois Central station after eleven. They couldn't have gone from there to the Southside with Gwendolyn already in the car, killed Roebuck and driven back downtown. Plus Gwendolyn said she stumbled on them with bloody hands earlier that evening. That was hours before Roebuck was killed.'

'They could have split up,' said the photographer. 'I can't believe that there's two different men, tall and thin, with neck scars, committing separate crimes on the same night. If the list of owners of black Cadillacs comes back from the Automobile Division with Coulton or Severyn's name on it, then that proves the link.'

'I suppose it does,' said Michael. 'How long till you get the list?'

'I don't know. Later today, tomorrow.'

'We've got a missing heiress,' said Michael, 'and a dead Capone stooge, and the two of them are probably linked by Coulton and Severyn. The question is how.'

'You've got Severyn's file, don't you?' asked the photographer.

Michael nodded. They'd picked it up the day before and spent much of the intervening period going through it. He grabbed the file from the desktop and tossed it to the photographer.

'There's nothing much in it,' said Ida, who'd run the leads.

'The address is years out of date and the KAs are dead. None of the other detectives in the division know much about him beyond that.'

Jacob quickly scanned through the pages in the folder. Then he looked up at them again in turn when he'd finished.

'What is it you want, Mr Russo?' asked Ida.

'Please, call me Jacob. Or Jake. I'd like you to send me any information you come across on the dead stooge and on Severyn. In return, if I uncover anything while I'm looking into my end of things, I'll let you know. If you're worried about divulging information to someone not directly in law enforcement, then send it to my friend in the Detective Division, Lieutenant Lynott.'

He rummaged around his pockets, found a business card and passed it to Ida. She took it and inspected it and saw it was for the man in the division he'd already mentioned as a friend.

'You can ask around the division. They'll vouch for me, but I get the feeling you've already asked.'

'We have,' said Ida.

'And what did you hear?'

'Some people said you make a nuisance of yourself trying to solve unsolvable cases. Other people said you're the best detective the division never had.'

'I've heard people say the same about you two.'

He looked at them and smiled in a slightly embarrassed way.

'May I ask what your interest in this is, Jacob?' Ida asked, sounding sharper than she intended. 'Why are you so interested in tracking down Roebuck's killer? He was just a low-level gangster.'

'Every day I go to work and see lazy, incompetent cops not doing their job,' he said. 'And innocent people are dying because of it. I'm just trying to make a difference.'

He smiled ruefully at the two of them, and Michael and Ida shared a look. He may have made a good detective, and looked every bit the earnest young man, but his response was too scripted, too self-righteous. There was another reason he was investigating it all, which he didn't want to disclose.

'All right,' said Michael, 'if we come across anything related to the killings, we'll let you know, and if we get anything concrete on Coulton and Severyn, we'll pass it along to Lynott at the Detective Division.'

Jacob smiled. 'Thank you,' he said. He stood and put Severyn's file back on the desk. When he stepped forward Ida noticed his slight limp, as if his leg had gone dead while he was talking to them. They shook hands and after he left Michael turned to look at her.

'What do you think?' he asked.

'There was something off about him,' she said, displaying her constitutional skepticism. 'I don't buy the concerned-citizen routine.'

'What about the frustrated-amateur-detective act?'

'That one I buy. I was one myself. I get him and his pal Lynott working cases on the side, but why's he so interested in this one?'

'Professional curiosity?' said Michael. 'It's an interesting case. Eyes gouged out. Dead cabaret dancers.'

'Maybe,' said Ida. 'His whole story brings it back to Bronzeville. Gwendolyn was meeting a go-between there, the stooge died there, and the stooge's girlfriend was a dancer at the Sunset Café.'

'Which is owned by Capone.'

'Who the stooge worked for,' said Ida. 'This is all cycling back to that club, and to Capone. You think Capone's involved with Gwendolyn going missing? Someone pretty high up's trying to cover all this up.'

'Maybe,' said Michael. 'How about we give the dancer's name to your pal. See if he can come up with anything.'

32

Dante returned to the Drake from the golf course in Burnham via the shoeshine man in Bronzeville. He shot up, took a moment to let the jitters melt from his body, then set about chasing down the only lead he had in finding the missing waiter – the betting slip he'd found in the hotel room. He called around some bookies he knew, asking them to check the odds on the betting slip, discovering in the process that the twenty-to-one shot the waiter had backed had never gone further out than sixteen to one on anyone else's books. Dante thanked the men and headed straight over to Cottage Grove, driving through the city as the sun was setting, the color of it washing over the buildings, coating them in waves of red.

As he drove he made a few loops and checked the rearview, trying to see if anyone from the Outfit was tailing him. But he couldn't spot anything at all, and he began to wonder if Al really had set him up, if maybe instead the stress of being back in his hometown was sparking his paranoia. Then he realized how absurd it was that the fact that no one seemed to be following him was making him feel edgy.

He parked up opposite the pool hall, which was located in the basement of a building just off 64th Street and was marked out by a large green neon sign, shaped like an arrow, pointing down the side of the building to the basement entrance.

He headed down the steps and through the door underneath the arrow's point. The place was spacious and quiet and so dimly lit it was impossible to make out anything except a bar to one side and beyond that a grid of pool tables, dozens of them, descending into the depths, each one illuminated by an overhead lamp hanging low over the green baize, like a lattice of emerald squares, floating on a sea of blackness.

Dante headed over to the bar, catching glares from the pool players he walked past, all of them colored and pegging him for a cop until they saw the scruffy dog trailing in his wake. The barman glared at him. He was a six-footer, bald-headed, wearing a white vest that strained over his bulk. Dante smiled and took his hat off.

'I'm looking for Red.'

'He ain't here.'

'Tell him it's his old pal Dante.'

'He ain't here.'

'You always so quick with your answers?'

'You want me to stutter?'

Dante kept the smile fixed to his face as he slumped onto a stool and dropped his hat on the bar.

'Well, I guess I'll wait then. Fix me up a whiskey, will ya?'

The barman glared at him for a few seconds more, then he sighed and slunk over to a phone lying on the counter. He picked it up and exchanged whispers with someone down the line, then he hung up, turned to Dante, and nodded his head toward the depths. Dante swiped his hat off the bar and turned toward the rear of the place, straining his eyes against the darkness, not able to make out how far back it extended.

He walked down one of the rows, and after a few seconds he could finally see the rear wall, along which stood a row of booths, each upholstered in red velvet with its own overhead light. In one of the booths Dante could see Michigan Red, sitting in a swirl of smoke either side of a couple of knucklemen and a boy in a white shirt who looked simultaneously high as a kite and bored as hell.

When Red saw Dante approaching a broad smile crossed his face.

'Dante the Gent,' said Red. 'Back from the dead and you brought a dog.'

'The dog's not from the afterlife, Red, he's from Chicago.'

'And the difference is?' Red grinned. 'Take a seat.'

He nodded to the two knucklemen and they stood and headed toward a door where the row of booths ended. The boy stayed where he was, sitting on the inside, slumped against the wall, eyelids at half-mast, his shirt open three or four buttons at the neck, revealing fresh skin and lithe muscles. Dante sat opposite Red and Red took a toke on the reefer he was smoking. Then he offered it to Dante, who shook his head.

'Makes me jumpy,' he said.

'Yeah? Makes me the opposite,' said Red, and once again he grinned. He was a thin man, his face long and skeletal, and when he smiled the skin stretched across his high cheekbones in a way that made him look delicate and gentle, feminine almost. He wasn't quite light-skinned enough to pass for white, but his face was covered with freckles, and what was left of the red hair that gave him his name was slicked back with pomade. He was wearing a burgundy-colored three-piece suit, and a gold tie pin and diamond collar studs which glittered and flashed in the beam from the lamp.

There was a sudden flood of bright white light and noise and Dante turned to see the two knucklemen had opened the door they'd been approaching and had stepped into a busy office beyond. Dante caught a glimpse of dozens of workers; a bank of phones, race lists pinned onto the wall; a blackboard full of calculations in spidery chalk; an annotated map of the neighborhood. And then the door shut, muting the sound and light, and they were flooded by darkness once more.

'So? To what do I owe the honor?' Red asked.

'You heard of a waiter called Julius Clay?' said Dante, and before he could stop himself, something twitched in Red's face.

'Sure. Why you asking?'

'He served a few city bigwigs poison booze at the Ritz a few weeks ago and then he skipped town. I need to talk to him before some other people catch ahold of him and shut him up permanently.'

'And you're talking to me why?'

'Because you're from Michigan and he's from Michigan and I found a betting slip of his with your stamp on it with the most goddamn generous odds on them I ever saw. Twenty to one on a horse every other bookie in town didn't push past sixteen. Which made me wonder why you're giving outsized odds on a sucker bet to a runaway waiter from the Ritz.'

Red paused. He took a long drag on the reefer, held in the smoke for a few seconds, then blew it out into the light beaming down from the overhead.

'Who you working for, Dante?' Red asked, leaning forward and passing the reefer to the boy.

'I work for Al.'

'And that's where I start wondering if the heat's gone to your head. From what I've heard, Al probably wants to kill this waiter too. So I don't see how I'm helping the man out by helping you . . .'

Dante frowned, surprised at Red's position. Almost all the city's Negro gangsters had good relations with Capone – he let them run their own affairs as they wished, so long as they bought their booze from him. He made sure the police didn't bother them, helped streamline their operations, and increased their profits. Red's refusal to help with an Outfit request suggested something had happened between the two of them.

'Al doesn't know about this lead,' said Dante. 'Not yet. You gimme his address, I guarantee I won't touch him and he'll have a few days head start before I slip.'

Red eyed him.

'You ride into town on your own, Dante?'

'Sure.'

'And it's really Al you're working for? Not anyone else?'

Dante paused at the question, at the insinuation. 'What's that supposed to mean?'

Red shrugged. 'There's been a few folks coming out here from the Big Apple these last few months. Stirring things up. I'm just wondering if you're one of them.'

'I came here at Al's request,' said Dante. 'But if you want to tell me a bit more about the others, I'm all ears.'

'Oh, it ain't nothing,' said Red, suddenly coy, and Dante guessed the worry had shown on his face, because Red's tone had become full of faux reassurance. 'It's just I see things in my line o' work. See how the city's changing, how the people change. Chicago's always changing, except in one respect.'

'Which is?'

'The fact it's always hungry enough to bite you in the ass.'

Red smiled and raised his eyebrows, then turned to reclaim the reefer from the boy.

'Your boss is setting the city on fire,' he said. 'The worst thing that ever happened to this town was Torrio stepping down.'

Dante had heard similar sentiments expressed by many of the old-timers. When the city was run by Johnny Torrio, Capone's predecessor and boss, it ran on a live-and-let-live policy. There was enough money for every gang to profit, if every gang stayed within the mutually agreed boundaries of its bootleg domain. But when Torrio stepped down, Capone started a process of ruthless consolidation, kicking off the series of inter-gang conflicts that became known as the Beer Wars, taking out one gang after the other, subsuming each little kingdom into his own. And now, out of all those little kingdoms, there were only two outfits left in the city, Capone's and Moran's.

That was the narrative peddled about the underworld, but it wasn't quite true. Torrio never handed his empire to Al Capone, he handed it to the Capone brothers. All of them. Al just happened to be the one who courted the limelight. If Al's brother Frank hadn't been killed years earlier in an election-day shoot-out, chances are it would have been him in charge of the Outfit. And the Torrio days, too, had had their fair share of violence and gang war, something else that got lost in the history.

'You know what I've realized in the years since I moved to Chicago?' said Red. 'This city runs on one man trying to get the better of another man. Feeds on it. All that competition, all those men trying to grab a dollar before the next man. That's the voodou that gets a million workers outta bed in the morning, builds the buildings, turns the world.

'But you take that shit to the extreme like Capone has? Then all you get is war. Which is what we've had since he decided to make himself king. And you know what's funny? People love him for it. They stand and cheer when he sits down at baseball games, you know that? There was a magazine poll the other day asking Harvard students who they respected the most. Your boy Capone was on the list. Up there in the top ten with Gandhi and Ford. I mean, I get why he does it – making himself famous, giving out turkeys at Christmas, setting up soup kitchens – so he can get the people on his side. He even got the niggers thinking the sun shines outta his ass. But all that publicity, for a gangster? It can't last. What I'm saying is this ship you on is sinking. And if I give you information on this runaway waiter, it's like I'm stepping on board, too.'

Dante thought a moment and nodded. Then he leaned in to speak to Red softly. 'Here's the situation,' he said. 'Whoever's behind this poisoning, they've sent a trigger after your pal Julius. A trigger he doesn't stand a chance against. If I can talk to the man, I might be able to hold off the trigger and Capone. If not, he's as good as dead. And this isn't Capone asking – it's me. I'm in over my head on this and I need some answers, and I need your help.'

Even as Dante spoke he could hear the emotion breaking into his own voice and was surprised by it – the undercurrent of stress.

Red eyed him, seemingly just as surprised, then he deliberated, running the options through his head.

Years earlier, Red had set up a telegram switchboard in a room above a train station that sent race results to his offices in Chicago six or seven minutes before all the other bookies in the city got the news. He'd hired an army of men to place hundreds of tiny last-minute bets on the races, a scam which wrung the rest of the city's bookies dry. If Dante could trust any of the city's gangsters to evaluate the situation and make a rational decision, it was Red.

He leaned forward, staring levelly at Dante, tapping his fingers against the tabletop. 'Dante the Gent . . .' he said, almost to himself. 'A man whose word you can trust. Ain't that how you got the name?'

'I don't know how I got the name. And truth be told, I don't much like it. But I've never gone back on my word.'

'Okay,' said Red eventually. 'I'll speak to my man, and if he wants to talk to you, I'll arrange a meet. But if you do go back on your word, I'll find you, and I'll slice you. Whether you've got Al's backing or not. Understand?'

Dante nodded. 'How comes you and this waiter are so tight anyway?' he asked. And Red grinned, leaning back in his seat, relaxing.

'We came here from Michigan together. On the train up we got jumped by a bunch o' white kids coon-hunting. He saved my life. Got a broken hand stopping me from catching a hammer blow to the head.'

Red lifted his hand up in front of his face, acting out what the man had done all those years ago. 'I give him good odds on his bets as a thank-you. Don't mean much to me on account of the shit-for-legs horses he's always backing, but . . .' Red finished off with a shrug – *What can you do?*

Dante nodded. 'And he came to you for money before he skipped town because the people behind the poisoning never paid him?' And as he watched Red for a reaction, he saw a tiny jerk of a muscle somewhere.

'Stay sharp, Dante,' said Red, playing it off good-naturedly. 'I did a friend a favor, let's not call it a sin.'

Dante nodded, thought a moment.

'What is it?' asked Red.

'You reminded me of an old Jewish saying of Menaker's – *If on the Day of Atonement, you have no sins, look at your good deeds.*'

Red considered this, then said, 'Ain't that the truth. How is the old man?'

'He's in Cook County looking at twenty to life. Thanks again for all your help.' Dante held out a hand and Red shook it and winked at him, then he looked at the dog.

'You know, as sidekicks go, he fits you just right,' said Red.

'Yeah?'

'Yeah. He a shaky dog, jus' like you.'

33

Of everything he was exposed to in 1920s Chicago, nothing puzzled Louis more than the slumming. Negro Southerners like Louis had arrived in the North and found the place cold and lonely and unwelcoming, so had helped create a new culture in its cities, a culture that looked back to the South and forward into the future, a culture that was vibrant, modern, sophisticated and, most of all, black. It was all so new and exciting that white people flocked to Bronzeville to experience it.

The first whites to arrive in the Black Belt were jazz aficionados, music students, young, male and awkward, willing to brave the dangers of the slum to hear the music of tomorrow: a white teenage rebellion, set to a soundtrack of urban, black songs.

Many of these whites began taking the music they heard in the Southside and playing it in the hotels and cabarets in the center of town, where black bands were barred by the racist Musicians' Union. They played the music on the radio and got to sell their records in the main parts of record stores, not in the 'race records' sections. They were getting rich off the music Negroes had invented, and for all their enthusiasm, the financial exploitation of someone else's culture left many of the original jazz musicians feeling short-changed, and they came up with a name for the whites that stole their music – *alligators*. The appropriation of jazz was so complete that people across the country who'd spent the last few years dancing to the music, assumed it had been invented by white people.

The spread of the music's popularity inevitably led to a change in the types of people pitching up in Bronzeville, from jazz zealots to tourists, from poor whites to idle rich. The trickle turned into a torrent, and then it seemed like the whole city was shunning the Loop to come and dance in the Southside, much to the annoyance of the Musicians' Union.

Eventually even Gold Coasters started flocking there too, the children of the men who owned the factories and corporations that so ruthlessly exploited the Black Belt workers, turning up in Bronzeville and treating it like an amusement park. And so the people who had been there from the beginning complained bitterly that these newcomers were not only ruining the neighborhood, they were destroying the culture, too.

It was the influx of these rich whites that led to the rise of the go-betweens, the Negro fixers who arranged nights out for them in Bronzeville. Many of Louis' colleagues found it distasteful, and looked upon the go-betweens as something like guides, the type of friendly natives you might hire if you were going on safari in Africa. But if the Southside was the jungle, and the go-betweens were the guides, what did that make the people who lived there?

There was a sad inevitability, it seemed to Louis, that the whole thing would end up with missing rich girls, grieving mothers, criminal investigations. And this was what soured his thoughts as he got ready that evening, a rare night off from his gig at the Vendome, standing in front of the mirror in the bathroom at the Ranch – the apartment he rented with Earl and Zutty, the two other members of the 'unholy three'.

Louis had been there all day, smoking gage and working on some new arrangements with Earl for the recording sessions they had booked in for the next week. Then they'd eaten and he'd washed and now he was ready to step out into the night.

He headed north up Calumet Avenue, into the heart of Bronzeville, to 35th Street and the Sunset Café. The strip was pulsing with music and people; queues outside the clubs; 'hipsters' taking sips from hip-flasks they'd secreted in purses, pockets, garter-belts; dealers selling bonded bourbon at eight dollars a pop, hustling through the neon rain cast onto the sidewalks by the illuminated adverts high above. Louis passed through it all, nodding hello to the people he knew – the bouncers, fans, jack-rollers and pimps, the old-timers sitting on kitchen chairs slamming dominoes onto shaky tables.

When he reached the Sunset he walked to the front of the queue, and the bouncers nodded at him, and the rope was lifted and he stepped inside. He walked through the foyer and into the main hall and was assaulted by a wall of noise, from the band playing on the stage, and the hundreds of dancers throwing themselves around the floor, and the people seated at the tables behind.

He headed for the bar and ordered a drink, and while he waited, he looked out over the dance floor and the frenzied people there. He could never quite get used to it. In New Orleans people danced slow to the blues, the music was made that way. But in Chicago the music was much too fast for that; the people threw their bodies about with abandon, with no thought or time for romance.

Louis' drink arrived, and he paid, took a sip of it and lit a cigarette. He watched the stage where a chorus line made up of twenty-four girls light-skinned enough to almost pass for white came to the end of their dance number, and a young emcee – Cab Calloway – came on and introduced the next act. As he reached the end of his patter, Cab spotted Louis at the back, and when the next act was safely underway, he made his way through the crowd to greet him.

'Hey, Cab,' said Louis, 'how's the second-best jazz player in Chicago?'

'I don't know, Louis, you tell me.'

They laughed and hugged each other. When Louis had worked at the Sunset the previous year, he'd given Cab his big break, and now that Louis had moved to the Savoy, the younger man had gone on to be the star attraction at the place.

'How's the Sunset keeping you?' Louis asked.

'It's all good 'cept the raids. Half the band's talking about upping sticks and heading out east.'

'Yeah, so's everyone else. You think we're all gonna end up in New York?' asked Louis, who thought back to his time in that city with something approaching dread.

'We all ended up in Chicago, didn't we?'

Cab tapped a cigarette out of a case and lit it up and they looked around and spotted a group of rich young Gold Coasters walking in, already drunk and boisterous. They both watched as the group were given prime seats at a table near the front, from where they could request songs and throw tips onto the stage more easily – a big deal for the performers since tips often amounted to more than their actual pay.

'This go-between you're looking for, he's gone on the lam,' said Cab, and Louis turned to look at him. Louis had called his friend that afternoon, knowing he still worked at the Café, and had asked him for information.

'Yeah? How so?' asked Louis.

Cab shrugged. 'No one's seen him for weeks. Disappeared into thin air. None too soon neither, the man's bad news.'

'Why'd he run away?' asked Louis.

'He was pimping out a few of the girls that worked here, without telling Capone about it. You can imagine how that went down.'

Louis nodded. Although Capone wasn't legally the owner of the Sunset Café – Capone was legally the owner of nothing except a modest family home in the Chicago suburbs whose mortgage was yet to be paid off – the Sunset Café was an Outfit venture, with Capone having a personal stake in it. When Louis and Earl had played there, Capone had been their boss in a round-about way, had visited the club often, and they'd got to know him more as a patron of the establishment and a jazz fan than as the nightclub's owner.

Capone also ran most of the prostitution in the city, and if

Randall Taylor was pimping out girls who worked in one of Capone's clubs without cutting Capone in, then he had every reason to go into hiding.

'So the Outfit found out?' asked Louis.

'I don't know,' said Cab. 'I figure a man stupid enough to run girls from an Outfit joint is probably stupid enough to be doing a dozen other things he'd wanna run away from. There's rumors about this cat.'

'Such as?'

'Such as he weren't your average go-between. He ended up working exclusively for this gang o' rich kids. I mean real rich, even for the Gold Coast. Rumors say he'd arrange parties for 'em in buffet flats. Paid for girls, and sometimes boys too, to go along and keep 'em happy, and afterwards, so it goes, some of those girls and boys never made it back home. Like I said, they're just rumors. But all the chorus girls backstage, they all say they know someone who knows someone who went to one o' these parties and disappeared. One of these girls was even talking 'bout voodou.'

Louis frowned at him and a heavy silence descended on them. Cab took a drag on his cigarette, and they watched as a pair of waiters rushed over to the Gold Coasters' table to set up champagne buckets and ice.

'What about this girl? Esther Jones?'

'She was one of the dancers here. She was also one of the girls Randall Taylor was pimping out.'

Louis nodded. Ida had called him earlier with the name, asking him to dig around. Now it turned out the dead dancer was linked to the go-between, and the go-between was linked to the missing heiress.

'You know anyone that might know where this go-between's gone?'

'Yeah. He got a lil' brother, Stanley. He's an alky cook, makes moonshine in the basement of a cathouse where Randall got a few of his girls holed up. Might be worth looking at.'

'Yeah, I guess it might.'

Cab gave him the address, then they leaned against the bar and watched the show for a while longer.

'I better get back. They're almost done,' said Cab.

The two men hugged.

'Hey,' said Cab, just as he was about to leave. 'I got some comp tickets to the Whiteman gig next week. You wanna come?'

'Whiteman's coming to town?'

Cab nodded. 'Playing the Chicago Theater. He's bringing Bix Beiderbecke. Maybe you should come along and check out the competition,' he said, grinning at Louis mischievously.

'Maybe I will.'

Cab grinned again, then turned and disappeared into the crowd, and Louis leaned back to survey the scene once more. On the dance floor, he spotted a few Negroes dancing in amongst the whites. Although it was Chicago's most famous Black and Tan, the Sunset's high prices – a dollar entry at weekends, and more on drinks – kept most colored people out. Louis watched them all as he mulled things over, nursing his drink. For the Orleanais musicians like Louis who provided the soundtrack to Chicago's racial intermingling – musicians who had grown up in a culture of violent segregation – to walk into a nightclub and see whites and Negroes dancing together was a sight that evoked an unsettling mix of emotions.

In the clubs blacks and whites might dance together, laugh together, maybe go to one of the hotels close by and spend the night together. But in the morning they would most likely wake up and head back to their own segregated worlds. The Musicians' Union would continue to stop Negroes from playing in the hotels and ballrooms of the Loop; housing covenants would continue to stop Negroes from moving to the suburbs; beaches and cinemas and fairgrounds would continue to be segregated; and when bands like Whiteman's came to town, Louis wouldn't be allowed to play with them: much like boxers and baseball players, black men and white men were barred from sharing a stage as equals.

Not that it made much difference to people like Louis. To circumvent the laws, jazz bands of different colors met up after hours, when the clubs were supposed to have closed; the bouncers locked the doors and the musicians got on stage together and jammed till dawn to an audience in the know. If Louis and Whiteman's cornetist, Bix Beiderbecke, really were the two greatest horn players in the world, and they were both going to be in Chicago that summer, it only made sense, race line or not, for the two of them to jam.

Louis finished his drink and stepped outside, nodded goodbye to the doormen and walked back down Calumet toward the Savoy, passing by the revelers and the couples on tiptoes at the curb, trying to hail down cabs. Above it all shone a gibbous moon, looking swollen and greasy in a night sky that was larded with heat.

On the corner, Louis passed a pair of cops and Cab's words about police raids buzzed inside his head. New laws enacted the previous year, so-called 'hip-flask' laws, made it easier for federal agents to raid anywhere they suspected people were drinking alcohol, and they'd used the laws to clamp down zealously on jazz venues, as if jazz music was somehow the cause of all Chicago's problems.

And maybe it was, for the people in authority. Chicago ran on segregation, on the friction of it, and what was jazz but an oasis from that, balm for a wounded city, the ointment that dissolved the boundaries. It was only natural that it would be seen as a threat to those in charge, those who profited from how Chicago was sliced up.

So it made sense that the city was trying to clean its hands of them, the jazz musicians who for ten years had helped make it the most vibrant place in the country. The recent events were prompting many to wonder if the great era of Chicago jazz was coming to an end.

There was a saying among jazz musicians that jazz was born in New Orleans, and grew up in Chicago. Now Louis was wondering if it was going to go to New York to be middle-aged. A place where the jazz clubs were steeped in racism. In Harlem nightspots like the Cotton Club, the only black people allowed to enter were the ones who worked there. It was like taking a trip back to the slavery era. Even the name had echoes of it.

And up on Broadway things were no better. They'd all heard from the players returning from stints in musicals like *Shuffle Along* about how the musicians in the orchestras had to memorize all their parts and not use sheet music, so the white people in the audience could have their prejudice confirmed that blacks were unable to read music, that their musicianship was primitive and unrefined, and not the product of years of discipline and cultivation.

Louis knew his view of it all was prejudiced by the bad time he'd had in New York with Fletcher Henderson. The band leader and his men had looked down on Louis, considered him a country boy, not sophisticated enough for the Big Apple, despite the fact that Louis' music was more modern and avant-garde than theirs. Louis had had to endure them laughing at his clothes and his manners, his dark skin, even though it was his band-mates who arrived to gigs late or drunk, who dressed and played sloppily, who tailored their sound for mass appeal.

When Louis stepped up to perform his first-ever solo at the Roseland on Broadway, he had played so loud crowds gathered on the street outside, and the whole auditorium stopped dancing and just stared at him, uncomprehending. Louis was trying out new ways to build a solo, new ways to construct phrases, taking the sounds that normally only appeared in breaks and stringing them together into complete passages. But people didn't understand what they were hearing – it was too revolutionary for them. The same sound that was lauded in Chicago as groundbreaking went over people's heads in New York. Over the months things had spiraled downwards, with Henderson trying to limit his solos and tone his performances down, and Louis feeling more and more humiliated, until in the end he handed in his resignation and headed back to Chicago.

Looking back on it three years later, with every trumpet player in the country copying his style, Louis knew he'd been right. The months he spent in New York hadn't been a total bust; he'd made some friends, made some money, had gotten to record some sides he was proud of, as a backing musician for Bessie Smith and Ma Rainey. But the final humiliation was left for the end – at his farewell party he had gotten so drunk he had caused a scene and before passing out, had vomited on Henderson's shoes.

Better to stay in Chicago, where the clubs were free, and the attitude was modern and despite the limits to it, there was actually some intermingling. He prayed that the authorities, in their rush to run the gangsters out of town, didn't accidentally destroy this beautiful thing the city had created. Especially when Louis had a personal stake in it. He felt he was on the cusp of something important, some crystallization of all the innovations and strides into the future he had made over the last few years. He prayed things didn't tumble away underneath him before he managed to reach the peak he sensed was somewhere in the mist above him.

34

Jacob went to Trib Tower to drop off a set of photos and pay a visit to Lowenthal in the basement, where he found the old man working at the blackboard.

'How's the investigation?' he asked when he saw Jacob enter.

The two of them sat and Jacob told Lowenthal about his meeting at the Pinkertons, and how earlier that morning, Lynott had called him to say the Automobile Division had Charles Coulton Junior on record as the owner of a black Cadillac sports sedan, Series 314, registered the previous year. At the mention of Coulton's name, Lowenthal frowned, and after Jacob had finished talking, Lowenthal paused to think about it all.

'I met the boy's lawyers once,' he said eventually. 'Six, maybe seven years ago, when I was still an editor, working the grave-yard shift. The police had busted a fruit bar out in Hyde Park, arrested a few dozen men, some of them dressed as women. They dragged them back to processing where one of our photographers snapped them all on their way in. Later that morning some law-yers turned up with an order from a judge commanding us to turn over all the photos our man had taken. We handed them over, secretly kept some copies, and tried to work out what was going on, figuring someone with pull was involved to be getting a judge out of bed at that time in the morning.'

'And?' Jacob asked.

'Eventually someone recognized the Coulton boy in the photos, and we guessed it was all on account of him. I saw the photos. The boy and his friend with the scars on his neck. I remember thinking what an odd couple they made. And a third boy, much younger.

Mexican-looking and dressed up like a female gypsy. Just out of curiosity we checked the police reports on the incident a few days later. All mention of Coulton had been erased from the records, along with the name of his friend. It stuck in my mind, how swiftly they moved, how powerfully. That and the teenage boy dressed up like a chorus girl out of *Carmen*.'

Lowenthal grinned and Jacob grinned back, and after a moment, a solemn look descended onto the old man's face.

'These people have pull, Jacob. They can mobilize judges and whole police departments if they have to. You tread carefully.'

An hour later, as Jacob was walking up the stairs to his apartment, he heard his phone ringing. He hobbled up the last few steps, and managed to grab the receiver before it rang off.

'Hello?'

'Jacob? This is Ida Davis over at the Pinkertons. We met the other day.'

'Yes, I remember. How are you, Miss Davis?'

The image of the girl came back into his mind. Beautiful and intense and overly formal.

'I'm well. I was calling because something came up. A friend of mine happened upon some information. The dead man's girlfriend, Esther Jones, turns out she was a prostitute working for the go-between that features in my missing person's case, the go-between that Gwendolyn Van Haren was with just before she disappeared. We got an address for a cathouse in Bronzeville where some of the go-between's girls work. I was planning to go down there and, as per the terms of our agreement, I thought I'd let you know.'

'When were you planning on going?'

'Today. Now. Is that a bother for you?'

She had a silky voice made soft and warm by her Louisianan

accent, and there was a certain primness in the way she expressed herself, in her choice of antiquated words.

'Not at all. What did you have in mind?'

'Apparently in the basement there's a still where the go-between's brother cooks alky. I figured I'd chat to the brother, ask him to put us in contact with the go-between. The go-between's the key to all this. Once we get ahold of him, I think both our investigations'll pretty much wrap up. What do you think?'

'The brother's on the run,' said Jacob. 'How are you going to get him to talk?'

'Come along and find out.'

Jacob caught an electric down to Bronzeville and waited where they'd agreed, and then he saw her come round the corner looking a little flustered, dressed in a blue business suit and a matching beret. She smiled when she saw him, and he smiled back, and they walked the last few blocks to the address together.

'Where's your boss?' Jacob asked.

'Canvassing around the station where Gwendolyn disappeared. We still haven't found anyone that witnessed her abduction.'

Jacob nodded.

'By the way, I got that list from the Automobile Division this morning,' said Jacob. 'Coulton Junior owns a black Cadillac that matches the one the tramp at the canal saw on the bridge. I also heard an interesting story about Coulton Junior from a few years ago.'

Jacob told her Lowenthal's anecdote about the boy and the fruit bar and the order from the judge. Ida nodded, and looked like she was going to make some comment on the story, but before she could they came upon a car parked up on the sidewalk, in which two men in rumpled suits sat, smoking cigarettes, looking overheated and grumpy.

Ida approached the car and nodded at the men in it, and the men nodded back.

'Gentlemen,' she said.

The two men got out of the car and Ida turned to Jacob and introduced them. 'These are Agents Eriksson and Dressner of the Prohibition Bureau. They owe me a favor. Agents, this is Jacob Russo, he's attached to the Detective Division.'

'Attached?' said Eriksson.

'He's a crime-scene photographer,' Ida explained, and the two prohibition agents looked at each other a moment.

'All right,' said Eriksson, leaning against the car and putting his hands in his pockets. 'We had a look about the place. There's girls on all the upper stories. Round the back there's an alleyway running parallel to the railroad. There's a trapdoor there gives onto the basement and a smell of alky coming out of it.'

'Okay,' said Ida, 'Jacob and I'll go round the front. You two stay in the alley.'

The two men nodded and they all walked the last block to the address.

Ida and Jacob stopped when they reached the front steps, and waited for Eriksson and Dressner to get into position on the other side of the house.

'Did you bring a gun?' she asked.

'No. Did you?'

'Yeah, I brought two.'

She opened her handbag and passed him a .38 Derringer.

'You know how to shoot?' she asked.

'I was in the war,' said Jacob, slipping the gun into his belt.

She nodded at him and they walked up the front steps, and Jacob rang the bell.

After a few seconds a colored girl in a negligee opened up, bare-footed, hair tied back into a bun, a puffiness to her eyes.

'Hello,' said Ida. 'I'm sorry to bother you. We're here to talk to Stanley Taylor.'

'Ain't no one called that lives here,' said the girl.

'Yes, there is. He cooks liquor in the basement. Some men are after him and his brother Randall. The police are, too. In fact, they're probably already on their way. I'm here to offer you all some protection.'

'And who the hell are you?'

'Ida Davis. I work for the Pinkertons.'

Jacob watched as Ida took out a card and tried to hand it over.

'Then you ain't the police?' asked the girl, making no move to take the card.

'No.'

'Then I ain't gotta talk to you. High-yella bitch.'

And with that the girl slammed the door in Ida's face.

Ida waited a moment, her hand holding the card still hovering in the air.

'I guess the girl's thinking about things,' she said, returning the card to her purse. 'I give it a few seconds before she runs into the basement to tell Stan Taylor there's detectives at the door, and maybe police on the way.'

'And then Taylor'll make a dash for the alleyway?'

'Most likely.'

They made their way to the rear of the building, where they found agents Eriksson and Dressner standing in front of the open trapdoor. At their feet, sitting on the ground, was a third man, drenched in sweat, with his hands cuffed behind his back. Stanley Taylor was an obese Negro in his early twenties, with close-cropped hair and a screw-faced expression. He'd managed to throw a jacket on over a string vest and a pair of trousers before attempting to flee, giving him the air of a hobo. He looked up when Ida and Jacob approached and the screw of muscles in his forehead tightened.

'The fuck are you?' he asked.

'I'm Ida Davis, from the Pinkertons. This is Jacob Russo — he's attached to the Detective Division.'

'Attached?' Taylor asked, but Ida ignored the question and kneeled down in front of him, and Jacob stayed back, intrigued to see how the girl would handle the man.

'We're not after you, Stanley,' she said. 'May I call you Stanley?'

'You may,' he said sarcastically, mocking Ida's Southern manner of speech.

'We're after your brother Randall. We need to talk to him about a friend of his that's gone missing.'

'Randall? I don't know where in the hell Randall is. I ain't seen him for weeks.'

'Sure. We know he's gone to ground and we need to speak to him. Before Capone does, and the police do, and maybe whoever else is after him. You're cooking out of his basement, so chances are you know how to get hold of him. Are you going to help us?'

'What do you think?' the man replied sarcastically.

'All right, then,' she said. 'Let me explain your choices. One, you tell us what we want to know and we'll let you go, free to get straight back into the basement and carry on your cook. Two, you refuse to cooperate and the agents here arrest you and take you into federal custody. They charge you with running the still and running all the girls working out of the upstairs rooms. That's a felony offense.'

'I don't have nothing to do with those girls,' Stanley protested.

'And then after you're booked, the agents might put you in a holding cell together with an inmate who works for Capone – cuz we all know there ain't a holding cell in Chicago that doesn't have at least someone from the Outfit locked up in it – and as the agents are talking they might get careless and let slip your name and whose brother you are. Meanwhile, the federal agents here will have to return to your basement and seize all your cooking equipment as evidence, and what they don't seize, they'll have to destroy. So all things considered, I'd say it's in everyone's interests for you to talk to us. Especially yours. What do you say?'

He glared at her a moment, trying to play it hard-boiled, but Jacob could see his resolution already flickering like a dying bulb.

'Have a think on it while we go look round your basement,' Ida said.

She rose and turned to look at Jacob, and Jacob, impressed, nodded at her. They walked through the trapdoor, which was still flung open, and into a basement that was thick with the caustic scent of alcohol. Guns raised, they scanned the space, but there was no one in there, just the tubes and drips and other paraphernalia of a home distillery.

Alcohol vapor was seeping out of the pipes, thick enough for the click of a cigarette lighter or the bullet from a gun to blow the whole basement sky high.

'Still's got a leak,' said Jacob.

He slipped his gun back into his belt and looked about the apparatus; found the boiler and the gas jets underneath it and switched them off.

They checked the other rooms in the basement, but found no sign of the missing go-between. Then they climbed the stairs to the first floor, where they saw the girl who'd answered the front door standing in the hallway, glaring at them.

'Stanley's under arrest out back,' said Ida. 'Show us the parlor or you'll be, too.'

The girl thought about it a moment, then slunk off down the hallway and they followed her into a living room which was occupied by four girls, young and Negro, half undressed and scared-looking. Red sheets had been hung in front of the windows, bathing everything in a warm, rose-pink tint, and rolls of taffeta had likewise been hung from the walls, softening the angles, the effect of it all making Jacob think of marshmallows and cotton candy.

'Keep an eye on them,' said Ida. 'I'll check the rest of the rooms.'

She left and Jacob lit a cigarette while he waited, looking over the girls. They all had the sunken eyes and skeletal physiques of heroin addicts, and they stared at him, frightened and wary. Jacob, not wanting to look at them too long, stared instead about the room, noticing how the red light coming in from the windows helped conceal the shabbiness of the furniture and the layer of dirt which covered the walls and floor.

Eventually Ida returned and looked at him and shook her head – the go-between wasn't hiding out in the building.

'Let's get out of here,' she said. 'Feels like we're standing in a womb.'

They walked back through the basement to the alley, where the two agents were smoking cigarettes and Taylor was still sitting on the ground, handcuffed and cantankerous.

'He said he'd cooperate,' Eriksson said. 'But he needs to make some phone calls. We'll take him back to HQ, hold him there till the brother shows. What do you want to do about the meet?'

'Let the brother arrange the details,' she said. 'I want him comfortable when he talks. Call me at the office when you know more.'

Eriksson tipped his hat at her, turned and signaled to Dressner, who hauled Taylor up to his feet. They all walked around to the front of the building, and the agents put Taylor in a car and drove off with him, leaving Ida and Jacob on the street alone.

'What are you doing now?' Ida asked.

'Heading home, I guess. You?'

'Back to the office. I need to have a talk with Michael. You want a lift?' she asked as they reached a green Chevrolet touring car, parked up on the sidewalk.

'You own a car?' Jacob asked, surprised.

'No, I couldn't afford a car. I signed it out of the Pinkerton car pool.'

They drove through midday traffic all the way back to Jacob's. At first he felt a little embarrassed to be sitting in the passenger seat while a girl did all the work of driving, but after a while he got used to it, mostly.

'You handled Taylor well,' Jacob said. 'And the two agents.'

'It's my job,' she replied.

'How long have you been a Pink?'

'Oh, coming up to ten years now,' she said.

'You like it?'

'Less and less.'

They talked a bit more about the case, and then about the hot weather, and then about other slight things that are classed as small talk. As they chatted she seemed to relax a little, the formality he'd noticed in her earlier dissolving, and he wondered if at the root of it there wasn't some trauma in her past, and he thought about his own traumas and wondered if she, like him, had learned to put distance between her inner self and the outside world.

Sooner than Jacob expected they were on his street. Ida pulled up outside a speak-easy a couple of doors down from Jacob's building, and let the car idle, the engine turning over uncertainly with a rattle like a chain-smoker's cough.

'Thanks for the lift.'

'You're welcome. I'll let you know what happens with Taylor.'

'Sure. I'd appreciate that.'

They smiled at each other and then there was a commotion in front of them – two men burst out of the door of the speak and ran across the street to a waiting car. Jacob saw the determined looks on the men's faces, saw the car screech off as soon as they'd jumped into it. Ida and Jacob both realized what was going on a second too late.

When the bomb went off they were parked right in the path of the blast, outside the windows of the speak. The shockwave sent glass and burning metal and shrapnel out onto the street, cutting through the air, the roar of it making their ears ring and bleed.

PART SIX

THIRD CHORUS

'Bombing, combined with window smashing, slugging and shooting, has become a profession practiced by specialized crews or gangs. The apprehension of bombers is made difficult by the quick get-away provided by the automobile. Their conviction is very difficult because of terrorization of witnesses; the disappearance of witnesses after indictment; and the fact that gangsters are able to raise defense funds, often enormous, as the sinews of war against constituted authority.'

THE ILLINOIS ASSOCIATION FOR
CRIMINAL JUSTICE, 1928

35

The next morning Dante still hadn't heard from Red about whether or not the missing waiter wanted to meet. The waiting around made him anxious, as did the feeling that he was slowly being encircled, that in the murky depths, a net was being slowly drawn around him.

He needed something to take his mind off it all, and he also needed to pay his condolences to Loretta, so he hopped into the Blackhawk and drove over to her sister's house in Little Italy. The dog stuck its head out of the window for the journey, letting the world lash itself against its tongue. The sun was up, gilding the streets, and Dante took in the speed and pulse of a city on a summer's morning sailing confidently into the future.

In the heart of the Loop, the sidewalks and shops were whirring with people and wealth and opulent commerce. The country was on a decade-long spending spree, tumbling in and out of love with whatever new and exciting thing it could grasp ahold of, but beneath the rush of it all there was anxiety, and Dante could feel it even here, a sense that for all its glamour and speed, modern living was crushing spirits and increasing loneliness with ever quickening and frenzied power.

After twenty minutes, he arrived in Little Italy, parked up and rang the bell of the run-down house where he had dropped off Loretta. When they were kids, it was Mary – Loretta's sister – that was the pretty one, and Loretta the gangly, bookish sister, and as Dante peered at the house on the nondescript Little Italy street, he wondered how comes it was the sister with all the options that had played it so close to home.

He heard a racket of children from inside, then a harried-looking woman opened the door. There were only a couple of years separating the two sisters, but Mary looked so much older – face lined, shoulders slumped, hair thin and pulled back under a gingham bandanna. She looked Dante up and down and grinned.

'Well, I'll be,' she said, leaning her hip against the door jamb. 'How's tricks, Dante?'

'Tricks are good, Mary. How's things with you?'

'Oh, I'm fine. Just waiting for the rain, and boiling like a lobster while I do. Come in . . .'

She pushed her hip off the door jamb and opened the door wide and Dante stepped into a living room crammed with furniture and strewn with children's toys. All of the windows were open and an electric fan was trying its best to keep the place cool.

'Lorrie! *Il cavaliere*'s here!' she shouted up the stairs, before turning to give Dante a knowing grin. Dante smiled back at her awkwardly, then turned to look about the place. Three children were lying on the floorboards by the fireplace, in front of a Serenader radio on a table broadcasting a Western serial, the noise of gunshots and horses' hooves on dusty plains filling the air.

'Nice place you got.'

'You should have seen it before the sprouts destroyed it,' she said, nodding at the children. There was a noise of feet trotting down the stairs, and they both looked up to see Loretta, wearing head-to-foot black.

'My condolences,' said Dante, figuring from the get-up she'd heard Abbate's death had been confirmed.

'Good riddance to bad rubbish,' Mary said, and Loretta shot her a look. Then Mary shrugged and turned to walk into the kitchen.

'Nice seeing you, Dante,' she said, looking at him over her shoulder.

'You okay?' Dante asked Loretta.

She nodded listlessly.

'How you finding it here?'

'It's good,' she said. 'Nice to be around the kids but a little cramped, you know?'

Dante nodded. On the radio gunshots rang out, and the children squealed.

'You wanna go somewhere?' he asked and she nodded again.

'Wait a sec. I'll just get my purse.'

She turned and went back upstairs, and Dante leaned against the post of the staircase and looked over the living room, at the scuffed furniture strewn with doilies, the three children lying on their bellies, their feet wheeling through the air as they listened to the serial. Then Loretta came down again. She'd put on a pair of pumps, and had pushed her hair back under a cap, and in her hand she had a purse.

'Remember when I met you in the Ritz,' she said, smiling awkwardly. 'I was dressed in mourning, too.'

'Sure I remember.'

She turned to the kids.

'Tell your ma I went out,' she said, and one of them turned around and nodded.

Dante opened the door and they stepped out into the muggy day.

'What do you want to do?' he asked.

'I don't know. Let's just drive.'

'Out of the city?'

'Yeah.'

They got in the Blackhawk, and the dog bounded into Loretta's lap and she stroked its neck. Dante started up the car and thought a moment about whether or not anyone would be following them, or if it was just his anxiety, or if it mattered either way.

Then he put the car into gear and with the windows wound down, they sailed west out of the city on the land breeze, looking for the consolation of wide open spaces and unhindered skies.

36

In her years at the Pinkertons Ida had been shot at, strangled, and attacked with a knife, an iron bar, a hammer, a paint tin full of acid; but she had never been caught up in an explosion before. As the blast wave passed she found herself in a mist of smoke and brick dust, sitting in the car covered in glass shards, with a piercing ringing in her ears that was making her skull shake.

She looked up to where the blast had come from: the ragged front of the speak-easy. The windows had been blown out, and choking black smoke was pouring from the frames, and in between the billows she caught glimpses of the charred hell inside.

As she tried to gather a wire of thoughts to cut through the chaos, she saw Jacob was next to her, his hands cradling her face. He was saying something she couldn't hear over the ringing in her ears, and then he turned away from her and got out of the car. She watched him walk into the plumes of smoke to look for survivors, and it was only then that she saw there was blood on his hands and she checked her face, and realized there was a cut on her temple.

She got out of the car and tried to stand and the world swerved away beneath her and she caught hold of the car's door handle to steady herself. She breathed slowly and tried to tense the muscles in her legs, and it was then she noticed the dents in the side of the Chevrolet from the blast and the shrapnel. She looked away from the car and saw there was a line of people running into the bar, some running out, carrying the wounded. Then Jacob was next to her again.

You okay? he was mouthing. She looked down to check herself. Two arms, two legs, no blood pouring from anywhere except that cut on her temple. She nodded and Jacob said something else she couldn't hear, and he passed her a handkerchief and she put it to her head and he put his arm around her and led her away.

Then they were going up some stairs and she realized they were going to his apartment. Was that what she'd agreed to? They were in a hallway, then at a door, then in a living room. He led her to the sofa and she sat and then he was sitting on the coffee table in front of her with a medical kit, tending to the cut on her head. She could hear the scraping of the cotton wool on her skin, and then she could hear his voice.

'How are you feeling? Can you hear yet?'

She nodded. 'It's coming back,' she said, and her voice sounded distant, muffled, not her own. She felt the sting of iodine on the wound, and then he tied some padding into place with a bandage.

'Thank you,' she said. 'How are you?'

'I'm fine. If you want, we can go back down? Talk to the police?'

She shook her head and the padding felt strange as she moved, unbalancing her skull.

'Maybe some whiskey?' he said. 'For the shock.'

She nodded again and he came back with two glasses filled with clear liquid – moonshine whiskey. They drank, she on the sofa, he on the coffee table. She was surprised to find she was sitting with her legs tucked under her knees. He stood and crossed to the windows and opened them up, and it was only then she heard the shouts and commotion outside.

'I'm just going out to see what's happening,' he said.

She didn't reply and he climbed out onto the fire escape and stood there with his drink, looking down on the chaos. It was then she remembered he'd been in the war. Maybe he'd seen dozens of such scenes and become used to them and that was why he was so calm. And then she realized that she too was acting calmly and she wondered why that was. Maybe she was so shaken by the bombing that it would take some time for the emotions to come, for the aftershocks of terror to pump through her body.

She stared at the Persian rug below her, at its pattern fading out of the weave where it had been left threadbare and thin as a beggar. She found its geometry hard and rigid and unsettling, and a harrowing sense of loneliness gripped her and she looked up at the windows once more and saw Jacob drain his drink, and step back inside.

'Police are there now. Medics too. You wanna go and let a professional help you out?'

She shook her head, worried she might start crying.

'What do you want to do? You can use the phone to call someone?'

'I want to go home,' she said.

'You want me to go with you?' he asked, and before she'd even thought about it, she nodded. She wanted to be somewhere she felt safe, but she didn't want to be there alone, not when the shock wore off.

They left the apartment a few minutes later and hurried past the scene on the street. Medics were tending to the injured and the police were holding back a crowd. In the middle of the debris was Ida's green Chevrolet, pockmarked and dented, looking like a tin can someone had squeezed in their fist. They made it to an intersection and Jacob hailed down a cab and they rode back to hers. They stayed silent for the most part, trying to process what had happened in their own ways.

When they got to Ida's they sat on the sofa, drinking bourbon, chain-smoking Luckies tip to tip, burning the smell of death out of their nostrils. When the drink started working, they started talking.

She asked him how he'd ended up a photographer, and he told her he wanted to be a policeman but he wasn't allowed on account of his leg; and she told him she wanted to be a policewoman but she wasn't allowed on account of her skin; and she laughed for the first time since the bombing, and after a moment he laughed too.

Then she asked him what had happened to his leg, and he told her the whole sorry tale, and about going off to fight in the war in France, about coming back and struggling to adjust, about all the hours he put into exercising his damaged ankle, trying to regain as much strength and control as possible, and how that still wasn't enough to get him into the police. Then they talked about the case, and why they were so invested in it. He told her about the violence and brutality he saw in his work every day and all the other traumas that he'd been through in his life.

'How do you deal with it?' she asked. 'Seeing all that horror? All the crime scenes and battlefields?'

He paused and thought a moment, his face flushed from the bourbon.

'You have to look at it. The hell. If you close your eyes, you'll always be scared. But if you stare it down, at least you can draw strength from the fact that you had the courage not to look away. The only danger is, maybe it'll warp you, you know? Maybe looking at it leaves you empty inside.'

'Is that what happened to you?'

He shook his head, then went quiet a moment as he mulled it over.

'Maybe. At first,' he said. 'But the emptiness is the starting point. Maybe it's meaningless so you've got the space to build your own meaning. At least, that's what I tell myself.'

He turned to her and smiled awkwardly, and she sensed he was embarrassed by what he'd said, but she wasn't sure why. The fact that he was willing to be so open with her, so honest, made her feel comfortable about doing the same, and she told him about New Orleans, about the hatred and the poverty, and all the other things that had led her to swap brutal hurricanes for brutal winters.

Time crawled by, and the sun made its scorching way across

the sky, skipping in and out of the gaps between the buildings, until eventually it dipped into the dusk of the prairie to the west and night came on. She switched on the light and the radio and it was still tuned to CBS and she kept it there, and at some point when they were silent and listening to the music, they looked at each other and they kissed. And when they got up the world spun around them, and they realized how drunk they were.

They managed to make it into the bedroom, stumbling and grabbing at each other's clothes, and they made love in a needy sort of way, clawing at each other, reaffirming their own existence and their hold on life.

And afterward they lay on the cotton sheets and listened to the Duke Ellington Orchestra on the radio. Around midnight Jacob rose and went back into the living room to get the bourbon and cigarettes, and Ida wondered why she had let it happen, and she guessed it was because they were still so close to the death that had stalked them that afternoon.

He came back in and she watched his body through the moonlight, athletic and lithe. He lay down next to her, poured two glasses of bourbon, passed one to her and lit them a couple of cigarettes, and they smoked and drank in silence for a while, peering through the gloom.

The Duke played a blues, mournful and wordless, so plaintive it seemed to Ida to be a blues about death. It set her mind drifting back through her life, past the burned bodies she had seen that afternoon, to all the killings that had surrounded her.

'I murdered a man once in New Orleans,' she said. She didn't look at Jacob, but from the corner of her eye she could see that he had taken the revelation calmly.

'Why?' he asked.

'He was trying to kill me.'

'Then it wasn't murder.'

'Suppose not . . . But it sure feels like it.'

Then they put their cigarettes in the ashtray and wrapped

their arms around each other and listened to the Duke play 'Creole Love Call' and 'Black and Tan Fantasy' and all the while the cigarettes burned in the ashtray, releasing lines of smoke that curled upwards and around each other in a ghostly double helix, and they held onto each other, floating on an undercurrent of loneliness.

37

The audience at the Vendome on State Street at 31st was almost exclusively Negro, and it whooped and clapped as the compere announced it was time for the feature piece of the evening's entertainment – a solo from Louis Armstrong. Louis stood and smiled at the crowd, then made his way through the pit where he sat with the rest of the orchestra.

He climbed the steps to the stage, and stood alone in front of the closed curtain, in the circular burn of the spotlight. He looked out over the expectant faces arrayed before him and tried to make a decision about what he would play that night.

Sometimes for his feature act he would sing a song, often a tune called 'Little Ida', but that particular night he didn't feel like singing, so instead he raised his trumpet to his lips and blew out the opening bars of the music he'd become famous for playing, a piece from the Mascagni opera *Cavalleria Rusticana*. When the crowd recognized the melody, roars and clapping rolled around the one-and-a-half-thousand-seat auditorium.

As Louis found his way into the piece and it began to flow out of him, he noticed two men enter through the doors at the rear and approach the only pair of empty seats in the front row. The first was a hulk of a man in a jacket that seemed indifferent to his shape; the second was thin and dark, and was dressed in a lime-colored suit. Louis knew them both; they were night undertakers, men whom criminals paid to dispose of bodies. They also worked for Capone, two of the numerous Negro gangsters the Italian employed and, by all accounts, treated well.

As Louis played, the two men took their seats and then they

started staring at him, so relentlessly that even though there were another one and a half thousand faces there to cast his gaze over, Louis' eyes kept on returning to those two men against his will, like a tongue to an ulcer. He wondered if their appearance was related to the visit Louis had paid to the Sunset Café. Maybe someone had talked to Joe Glaser, the Sunset's manager, and Glaser had talked to Capone. And now Capone had sent local toughs down to the Vendome. Or maybe it was to do with something else entirely. He prayed it was.

He did his best to continue with the solo, feeling exposed and jittery and unsure of himself. And eventually he reached the end of it, and the crowd stood and cheered, even though it wasn't one of his best.

He took a bow, and returned to the pit, arranged his sheet music and looked up to see the two thugs still glaring at him, their stares boring a path through the forest of flutes, clarinets, trombones and music stands poking into the air. Then the curtain on the stage rose and revealed the venue's cinema screen – the Vendome was both a live music venue and a cinema, with its twenty-strong orchestra providing musical accompaniment to movies and newsreels as well as giving recitals in between the films.

On the stage, the screen filled with the silver image of the Pathé newsreel logo, and as the logo was replaced by a shot of a dusty Indian reservation in Oklahoma, Erskine Tate, the band leader, swooped his baton into the air and down again, and the orchestra launched into one of Brahms's 'Hungarian Dance's. Through the sea of moving hands and elbows and heads in the orchestra pit, Louis made eye contact with the two thugs, and one of them raised a finger into the air and made a twirling motion with it, and Louis got his meaning and nodded back at him, and the arrangements agreed upon, Louis relaxed a touch. Whatever they wanted, he'd find out at the end of the performance.

When the newsreel came to an end, the orchestra performed

another classical piece and then the feature film started, *Street Angel*, a German production about a girl on the run from the police. Louis managed to make it through the whole film without missing his cues, despite the presence of the two men in the front row.

Eventually the feature finished, and there was a final, short recital, and then eleven o'clock rolled around and the show was over, and the musicians all filed out of the pit to their room backstage. Louis smoked a quick cigarette and left by the stage door, opening it up to see the two thugs waiting for him in the alleyway there. He smiled at them, tipped his hat, and addressed each of them in turn.

'Eubie. Johnson. Enjoy the show?'

'It was superb, Louis,' said Eubie, the wider of the two.

'Terrif',' chimed in the other. 'Those krauts really know how to shoot a flick.'

'What did you want to see me about?' he asked.

'Capone's calling you in,' said Eubie. 'Tomorrow at the Metropole. Room four-oh-six. You got that clear?'

'Clear as gin. He say what it was about?'

Eubie gave him a look, then he tipped his hat at Louis, and the two of them turned and strolled off down the alleyway. Louis watched them as they walked through the trash littering the ground, turned onto State Street, and disappeared in the glare of its bright lights.

He shook his head, ruing his luck, and trudged down the alley toward State Street too, on to his gig at the Savoy. He was being called in, and the prospect filled him with dread, even though he and Al had been on good terms when Louis had worked at the Sunset. Like most of the young men in the city, Al was a jazz fan. When the man and his entourage turned up in the clubs, they mixed with the musicians as if they were equals, for the most part.

When trumpeter Doc Cheatham needed a job, Louis asked Al, and Al got him one. When Earl was going on a trip and was worried about security, Al sent two bodyguards to keep him safe. When the bassist Milt Hinton was in hospital after a car crash, Al made sure the doctors treated him well. There was even a rumor that for Al's birthday a few years previously, some of Al's friends kidnapped the pianist Fats Waller, and forced him to play at the three-day-long birthday party at the Hawthorne Inn, sending him on his way at the end of the debauch with a sackful of dollar bills.

There was still, however, an undercurrent of racism to it all. Louis remembered an occasion when Al asked Louis' old band-mate Johnny Dodds to play him a number and Dodds had told Al he didn't know it, causing Al to tear a hundred-dollar bill in two and give one half to Dodds with the words, 'Nigger, you better learn it for next time.' Dodds had smarted over that for days, and still harbored a grudge against Al for it. But what could you do with a grudge against a man like Capone? About as much as you could when he called you in.

38

The previous day Dante had driven with Loretta through the skyscraper maze out into the countryside west of the city. They'd found a meadow somewhere, pulled the car over, and sat on the grass, drinking from a bottle of Canadian Club. They stayed there all afternoon. Loretta slept a little, and Dante left her for a bit and risked a shot. And maybe it was the peaceful setting, or the whiskey, or the dope, but over the hours, Dante finally relaxed.

Then she woke and they watched the sunset and then the ocean of stars above them, the night sky entangled in the trees, the furrows of the fields smudged with moonlight. Loretta had cried and Dante had comforted her and when they were both worn out they slept, and drove back to the city in the dead of night.

Loretta had said she didn't want to go to her sister's, so he'd taken her to the hotel, and as the sun was coming up, eliminating the last thin wisps of night from the sky, they parked up outside the Drake and went inside. She lay down in the bed to sleep, and Dante saw that a bellboy had left a message for him – a phone number. Dante called the number despite the early hour, and the call connected to Red's pool hall in Hyde Park. Someone there gave him a place and a time and hung up.

Relief ran through Dante. He washed, ate breakfast, and headed out sleepless to the station to catch the morning train to Michigan City. He walked around the station a few times, making sure no one was following him, then he hopped onto the train.

Two hours and a fifty-mile train trip later, he was sitting on the benches outside Hagenbeck's Freak Show Deluxe in the blazing heat, wishing the missing waiter had picked a better spot to meet. The promenade ran along the lake front and was packed with the usual attractions – burlesque shows, tattoo parlors, candy stores, souvenir shops – all of them thronging with people, mostly day-trippers from Chicago and Gary and South Bend.

Dante thanked God he could view it all from behind the protective green film of his sunglasses, saving his eyes from the solar glare bouncing off the white beach, and the parched planks of the boardwalk.

After a few minutes, a man approached, a Negro in his fifties, slight of build and well-dressed, with grey hair cropped close and tidy. Dante recognized him from the photograph he'd seen in the trigger's hotel room. The man made eye contact with Dante and they nodded at each other before he walked over.

'You Red's friend?' the man asked.

'Yeah. You're Julius?'

The man nodded. 'Let's walk,' he said, and he held up his hand to the promenade. Dante stood and they proceeded along it. He took out a cigarette and Dante saw a great scar down the man's hand, a groove in-between the middle bones, and Dante guessed it was a memento from the hammer attack Red had mentioned.

After they had gone a few yards, they reached a lookout point where the boardwalk bulged out in a semicircle over the beach, and there was a row of benches with penny telescopes lined up along the railings for looking out over the waves. The man found an empty bench and sat on one end of it, and Dante sat on the other.

'Red said you were a man who could be trusted.'

'I'll stick by what I told Red,' said Dante. 'You tell me everything that happened and I'll help you out. The men who killed the delivery drivers are after you, and they'll be here soon enough. I've no doubt of that. And when the Outfit finds out – and they will – then you'll have two lots of killers on your tail. I can stall the Outfit for a while, but these other men, no dice.'

Julius nodded solemnly. 'What do you want to know?' he asked.

'Start at the beginning. How'd you get roped into it?'

'That was down to Dorsey and Pete. The two deliverymen. One day they hung about after a delivery and asked me if I wanted to make some money. I didn't know 'em so well. They'd drop off the booze at the kitchen and I'd oversee sometimes. That was it. But I said sure, and we went to a bar together.'

'When was this?' Dante asked.

Julius shrugged his shoulders.

'Must be a couple o' months back,' he said. 'I can't remember.'

Dante nodded, and gestured for him to continue.

'So, we went to a speak and got some drinks and they told me they'd had an offer to drop off some booze in the kitchen with the usual batch, and to make sure that batch made it to a party in a few weeks' time. They'd handle the delivery part of it. All I had to do was make sure it was their crate of booze that got served up. I asked them what party it was, and they told me it was that Republican shindig.'

'Did they ask you to serve a particular person at the party?' Dante asked. 'Like, make sure Governor Small or the mayor or someone gets a glass?'

'No. They never said nothing about that. Just said make sure it gets served is all. I knew straightaway it was a hit. I guess they saw it on my face because they said it wasn't like that, that no one was gonna die. The idea was to make 'em all end up in hospital, get the story in the papers, make 'em all lose face. I didn't believe 'em but . . . They made out like these orders were from Capone himself. How's a darkie waiter with no juice gonna say no to a man like Capone? I didn't realize till I spoke to Red these two had switched.'

Dante nodded. Plenty of hustlers around town pretended they worked for Capone, using the name to coerce people into doing what they wanted them to do. It was a dangerous game for the

hustlers to play – if they got caught, they were as good as dead
– but it showed how even Al's name alone had power, like a magic
word, a voodou spell that could summon up a demon. Such was
the length of the shadow Al cast over the city, and the minds of
the people who lived in it.

'They didn't say anything about who was employing them?'
Dante asked.

Julius shook his head. 'Just that it was an Outfit job,' he said.
He took a last drag on his cigarette, then he flicked the butt onto
the boardwalk and wiped it out with his shoe.

'The deal was I was going to get fifty upfront and fifty afterwards. That was the first time I figured they were out to gyp me.
I figured I'd book my holiday for the day after, so I could hightail
it if it all went wrong. Damn glad I did. When I saw those bodies
being wheeled out of the hotel I knew I'd been right first time,
and then I was really on my heels.

'Next day I was supposed to go round to this address to collect
the other fifty. Guess I've had too many dealings with those kinds
o' people before, so I figured I'd go round there on the sly. See
what was what.'

'And the address?'

'Thirty-three thirty South Morgan Street. I ain't ever gonna
forget that shit. It was one of those streets where the basement
steps are in front of the houses, you know? So I went down
the steps of one of the houses opposite and just watched the
place for a bit. I didn't see Dorsey or Pete, but about a half-hour
before I was supposed to be there, a car pulled up, and three men
got out and headed into the building, all of 'em carrying big heavy
bags. That's when I knew for sure the fix I was in.'

The man shook his head, and Dante could see he was still
shook up, still pulsing with the nervous energy of someone who'd
managed to escape death by a slip. And as much as he was telling
his story in return for Dante's help, Dante could also see that the

man wanted to unburden his secrets, find some relief in reliving it all at a safe distance.

'I got the hell out of there. I went to see Red. Me and him go back. It's on account of saving his life I got this.'

He held up his hand, and this time Dante saw the wound from the palm-side, where he guessed the hammer had hit. The man watched Dante stare at the wound, then he put his hand down and continued talking.

'Red gave me some cash and I caught the train out here and waited, and then a couple of days later I found out in the paper that Dorsey and Pete were dead, and since then I've been trying to figure out what the hell to do, and then Red called and told me there was a man looking for me, a man from the Outfit, but that he could be trusted.'

He turned to look at Dante with an inquisitive look, and Dante recalled the man's earlier comment about being suspicious of those types of people, and Dante wondered if he meant gangsters or Italians or white people in general. Dante nodded, reassuring him once more that he'd keep his secret.

'All right,' said Dante. 'I need to ask you a couple more questions.'

'Shoot.'

'They ever say anything about who they got the booze from?'

'Nah,' Julius said, shaking his head. 'They never said who. But they did say where. Said they had to go on up to the Millersville Roadhouse before they paid me. You know it?'

Dante shook his head.

'Drive north up the Milwaukee Road. You hit Millersville after two or three hours, depending on how fast you're going.'

'You've been there?'

'Nah. I've passed through once or twice. Man like me ain't got no business stopping though.'

'Okay. The men with the bags you saw going into the house, what did they look like?'

'I don't know. I was a way away and my eyesight ain't that good no more. Three big guys. Scary-looking. Outfit types.'

'And the car?'

'Black Cadillac sedan.'

Dante nodded and thanked the man. They went quiet and Dante's mind raced and he lit a cigarette for something to do. If there was no single target for the poisoning, then it was an attack on Capone. The waiter's information opened up new avenues of possibility, and now Dante felt he was not far from solving the mystery. Just a step or two more and he'd have it wrapped up, and maybe then he could get the hell out of Chicago.

'So?' Julius said. 'The deal was I tell you what happened and you helped me out. I'm still waiting for the help.'

Dante paused, and sighed. How to tell the man the rest of it, that his life might well be over, all for fifty bucks?

'I'm in charge of the Outfit's investigation into all this,' Dante said. 'I'm the one standing between you and Capone putting a hit out on you. I'm not gonna say anything. I promised Red. You're free to go on your way and I'll keep what you said quiet for as long as possible. Enough time for you to get away. But eventually, someone in the Outfit's going to come look for you – I can only stall them for so long. The worse news is some other people are going to come looking for you, too. The people that killed the drivers, the same men you saw at the house that day. I've seen one of them and I know that if it's between you and them, you don't stand a chance.'

Dante paused, and took a puff on his cigarette.

'If I were you,' he continued, 'I'd move somewhere a lot further away from Chicago than Michigan City, maybe keep going till you hit a coast. And I'd move today, right now. I'd change my name. Lay low. And maybe in a few years' time, you might be able to leave the house without looking over your shoulder. This life you got now, it's over. I'm sorry . . .'

Dante looked at the man and saw him staring at his hands,

which were folded over each other in his lap. He could sense the fear, the realization that this was only the beginning, that he'd been lucky so far, but if he wanted to survive it'd take years more of being lucky.

'I'd also tell your daughter to go to the police. The men searched your apartment, found her address on an envelope. They'll go looking for her. They'll try and use her to find you.'

Dante looked over again and saw there were tears in the man's eyes, holding the reflection of the sunshine glinting on the lake. Dante stood, reached over and squeezed the man's shoulder, hoping the gesture wouldn't come off as patronizing, hoping it would provide him with some comfort at least. Then he took his wallet out of his pocket and peeled off five twenties and held them out to the man.

'It's from Red,' Dante lied, not wanting to offend him. 'Said I was to give it to you as a gift. Use it to get somewhere safe.'

39

Michael took the stairs to Linnemann's office with a faint sense of trepidation; he was being called up to see the boss, and that only ever happened when something had gone seriously wrong.

'Hello, Michael. Go right in,' said Linnemann's secretary, and there was something pitying in her voice, confirming Michael's suspicion that he was about to hear some bad news. He knocked and stepped inside and saw Linnemann at his desk, sitting opposite a pair of elderly men, who turned to look at Michael as he walked in. Linnemann smiled and gestured at an empty chair and Michael sat, feeling hemmed in by them all.

'I'd like to introduce you to Mr Jennings and Mr Edelhart, both of whom sit on the board of directors,' said Linnemann.

Michael nodded at the men. Both the directors were in their seventies, patrician-like, with unreadable expressions on their heavily lined faces.

'I brought you in here to get an update on the Van Haren case,' said Linnemann.

'I see,' replied Michael. 'And what's Mr Jennings' and Mr Edelhart's concern in this?'

'As I said, they're both on the company's board of directors, and they're also both friends with Mr Coulton, to whom you paid a visit recently. Mr Coulton was upset by your behavior, and he requested that we all sit down for a discussion.'

'I see.'

'Would you like to explain your actions?'

'I thought Mr Coulton might have some useful information with regards to the disappearance of his future daughter-in-law, so I went by his offices to ask him some questions. He's not a suspect and as it turned out, he didn't have any useful information, but it was a lead worth pursuing. I don't believe I acted in an improper manner. At least, not in a manner that would upset Mr Coulton, and his non-executive director friends.'

Linnemann paused and gave Michael a look.

'What suspects do you have?' he asked.

'None as yet. Certainly not Mr Coulton,' Michael replied, and even as he said it he realized he was slapping on the fake politesse a little too thickly.

'Well, we can't have you harassing prominent members of Chicago society. You and Miss Davis will be put on probation while an investigation is conducted.'

'Probation?'

'During which the Van Haren case will be reassigned.'

Michael's heart jumped, and he thought for a moment about protesting, banging his fist on the desk and shouting at the man. But just as quickly as his indignation rose up, so did his sense of pragmatism, and he gritted his teeth and stayed in his seat.

'Reassigned to whom?'

'To whomever's free. I believe Clancy and Becker have a light workload at the moment.'

Michael nodded. Clancy and Becker had a light workload because they were all but incompetent. Mrs Van Haren was being railroaded, her case shunted off to two men who were incapable of finding her daughter. 'Any further participation by either you or Miss Davis in this case will result in both your contracts being terminated. Immediately. Please let Miss Davis know of the decision. And send her my wishes for a fast recovery. I heard about the bombing.'

'I'm sure you did,' said Michael petulantly, and Linnemann gave him that look again.

'Speak to Mankowski about getting yourselves some new cases. Thank you, Michael. You're dismissed.'

Michael nodded and rose, cast a look at the two directors, and returned to his own office in an angry daze. When he stepped inside, Ida looked up at him from the car-pool paperwork she had on her desk.

'Well?' she asked.

Her eyes were still puffy, a scab mark marring the skin around her temple. When she'd arrived at work that morning she'd told him about the explosion, and said that she was fine. But to Michael's eyes she'd looked sleepless and faintly traumatized, and the fact she didn't want to talk about it worried him. And now he was about to add to her troubles.

'We're being put on probation and they're taking us off the case.'

'Why?'

'My visit to Coulton. Two of the directors were in there with Linnemann, friends of his.'

He sat in the chair opposite her and they looked at each other across the desk, and up close, Michael could see just how weary she looked.

'Did he say we aren't to contact Mrs Van Haren again?' she asked.

'No.'

'Then how about we pay her a visit? To let her know we're off the case. And we have every faith in Clancy and Becker's ability to continue our good work?'

She looked at him and smiled and he smiled back, wondering why he hadn't thought of it first.

40

Louis parked up in the shade of 23rd Street, switched off the engine, and stared over the road at the Metropole Hotel. It was seven stories tall, with bay windows that bulged out of its walls and ran the height of the building, looking strangely like turrets half embedded in the brickwork, as if the place was midway through metamorphosing into a castle. He frowned and breathed deeply against the sense of dread creeping over him. Regardless of the fact that Al and Louis had been friends, a meeting with Al Capone was still a meeting with Al Capone.

Louis sighed, got out of the car and walked over to the hotel's canopied entrance, up the front steps and into the lobby. There were knucklemen all over the place – lounging about in armchairs and sofas – and they eyed Louis as he made his way to the concierge's desk. The hotel had been overrun completely by Capone, who rented fifty rooms on the top floors and had even built a gym there for his men to train in. On Sundays politicians and judges waited in the hotel's lobby to be granted an audience, like suppliants to a king.

'I'm here to see Mr Capone,' Louis said.

'Mr Capone doesn't live here,' said one of the men.

'Room four-oh-six. I'm expected.'

The concierge stared at him a moment, considering.

'Name?' he said eventually.

'Louis Armstrong.'

He picked up the phone and dialed a number and as Louis waited he looked about the place, once more taking in the men in suits. They all looked tense, like an army waiting for the order to march, and Louis thought once more of castles, of fortresses under siege.

The concierge put the phone down and nodded at the elevators a little further on. Louis walked over to them, and the elevator boy grinned and Louis stepped inside.

'Here to see Mr Capone?' the boy asked, and Louis nodded. The boy pulled a lever and turned a switch and they were whisked up to the fourth floor. The doors opened and Louis stepped out into a long, windowless hallway, red-carpeted and wainscoted, at the end of which were two great wooden doors decorated with elaborate carvings, flanked on either side by knucklemen in suits, each of them with the build and bearing of a military guard.

'That way?' Louis asked, pointing at the men. The elevator boy nodded.

'Good luck,' he said, as the elevator closed and began its clunking descent.

Louis walked down the corridor, and with each step, his sense of trepidation increased. He reached the friskers and they patted him down and opened the doors and he stepped into Al's office – a vast room in one of the corner turrets that was filled with high-ticket furniture. The floor was covered in a wall-to-wall carpet and the place was cold, blissfully chilled by an air-cooling system humming away somewhere unseen. At the far end was a mahogany desk where Al was sitting, chatting with a few men.

Al looked up and saw Louis at the door and gestured him over and Louis crossed the room, the carpet so high-piled it felt like he was sinking with every step. He reached the desk, and took a moment to frown at the bullet-ridden wall behind it, on which had been pinned a giant American flag.

Al motioned for Louis to sit, and he did, and as he waited for Al to finish his conversation he looked about the place – at the flag, and the bulletholes, and the giant turret windows; and the desktop littered with ashtrays, and whiskey tumblers, and newspapers, and documents, and a box of Cuban cigars, and a mound of cocaine and a rolled-up banknote resting on a silver tray; and, bizarrely, elephant sculptures, dozens of them, in all shapes and sizes on the desk, but also on the windowsills, on the coffee tables, on the carpet by the walls, standing on plinths either side of the doorways, elephants resting and walking, alone or in groups, most of them with upturned trunks.

'Good-luck symbols,' said a soft voice, and Louis turned to see that Al was staring at him, and the men had risen and were heading to other parts of the room. Louis nodded and grinned and studied his erstwhile boss. Although they were both the same age, Al looked like he was past forty. It was possibly the first time Louis had seen him outside of a nightclub and the harsh daylight streaming in from the windows was accentuating the makeup pasted to one side of the man's face, making Louis struggle not to keep flicking his eyes to the ugly bumps of his scars.

Al stared at him, took a puff on his cigar, and thought for a moment. 'Cuban?' he asked, gesturing to the cigar box on the desk.

'Sure, boss. Thanks,' said Louis. He leaned over and took a cigar, figuring if he was going to be whacked for what he'd done, he might as well go out smoking a Romeo y Julieta. He cut the end off the cigar with a gold cutter that was on Al's desk, and lit it with a match.

'You like it?' asked Al, continuing to stare at him, a peculiar smile on his face, his features unsettlingly placid.

'Sure. It's real nice,' said Louis, after taking a pull.

'I guess you smoke a lot, that gravelly voice o' yours.'

'Funny story, boss. It weren't the smokes that did it. I got a cold a while back, a sore throat. A few days later the cold left but the voice stayed. Been like this ever since. Had the clearest damn voice before that cold, too.'

Louis took another puff on the cigar, which did indeed taste good, and he gave Al his biggest smile, pretending they were just two friends having a chat, that he wasn't becoming increasingly anxious with all the aimless small talk.

'Is that so?' said Al, pretending to mull things over. In the quiet, Louis could hear the hum of Michigan Avenue floating in through the windows, the noise of the traffic, and the people milling about outside the showrooms that made up Automobile Row.

Al leaned forward suddenly, and Louis wasn't sure if it was the quickness of the action, or his own inflamed nerves, but the move almost made him flinch.

'I hear you've been asking about the Sunset.'

'Yeah. Yeah, I have,' said Louis, starting to panic. 'On account of a go-between I been looking for.'

'Randall Taylor? Why're you looking for him?'

'He owes a friend o' mine money. Skipped out on him. My friend knows Taylor worked the Sunset and I did, too, so he asked me if I could ask about. I didn't mean to put anyone out by it.'

'You don't remember Taylor from when you worked there?'

'Can't say I do.'

Al eyed him a moment.

'So, you find him yet?' he asked.

'Nah, boss. He's still missing in action.'

'And this friend o' yours. He still looking for him?'

'Yeah.'

'Well, if either of you find him. I wanna know. Me and that go-between got unfinished business, and I don't want him getting away on account of your friend. This Taylor's bad news, Louis.'

'I wouldn't be looking for him if he weren't.'

'You tell your friend that it don't pay to spend time with a man like that. Sleep with the dogs and you end up with fleas.'

'Sure thing, boss,' said Louis. 'I'll pass the message on.'

He wondered what was behind it all, whether Al was after the go-between purely because the man had been running girls out of one of his establishments, or if there was another element to it, something much more serious. Whatever it was, Louis knew he was now in hock to Al, his name entered into the favors list in indelible ink.

Al continued to eye him with that same eerie calmness, giving off a sense that he might explode at any minute, and Louis noticed how he was a little wilder around the eyes than he remembered. He'd heard rumors that Al was becoming increasingly unstable and he wondered if maybe it was true, or if it was just his inflamed imagination. If Al was losing it, Louis didn't want to be around to witness the consequences. He'd seen it in New Orleans, years before, how one man's madness could cast a shadow over a city, a darkness that spread like fire, taking hold of first one person's mind and then another's, filling them with fear, voodou-like. But the man in New Orleans had turned out to be a nobody. This man, on the other hand, was the king of Chicago.

Louis thought again about how different he looked, how much older, and all their other differences and similarities ran through his mind. They were the same age; they had both been born in poverty; they had both faced racial prejudice; they had moved to Chicago within a few years of each other, seeking their fortunes, attempting to leave behind the slums they'd grown up in; they were both fathers to lone disabled sons; they had both achieved great success; they both lived under the shadow of New York; and their paths had finally crossed the previous year when Louis had taken the job at Al's Sunset Café. But they also had fundamental differences too, in temperament, personality and outlook, and that was what worried Louis.

Eventually Al leaned back in his seat and his face softened, and Louis got the sense that Al had had a change of heart about something, that his mood had swung. Louis relaxed a little, and as they both took puffs on their cigars, he hoped Al wouldn't spot his hand shaking.

'I heard the Paul Whiteman Band's coming to town,' said Al out of nowhere. 'Playing a few nights in the Loop.'

'Yeah,' said Louis, 'so I hear.'

'I heard,' Al continued, a gleam in his eye, rolling the cigar through his fingers, 'Whiteman's got a cornet player there by the name of Beiderbecke. I heard people are saying he's the greatest cornet player in the world.'

Al paused a moment and grinned mischievously and Louis thought about how to take the bait.

'Well, that's only cuz I switched to the trumpet last year,' Louis said, and there was a long moment as the two men stared at each other, and then they burst out laughing.

'Maybe I'll catch you at the concert, Mr Capone.'

'Yeah, maybe you will. And if you and Whiteman decide to have any "jam sessions" late one night, let one of the boys know.'

'Will do, boss,' said Louis.

'And if your friend finds Taylor, I wanna be the first to know.'

Al took a bankroll out of his pocket, slid off two hundred-dollar bills and held them for Louis to take. But Louis, despite wanting to, knew he couldn't accept the money, that taking it would only underline his position as someone in debt to Al Capone.

'Nah, I'm cool, boss. I don't need it.'

Al shrugged.

'I don't need it either,' he said.

Then they looked at each other and burst out laughing once more.

As Louis walked back to his car, a great sense of relief rushed through him. He wasn't out of the woods just yet, but he was glad to be out of the meeting, out in the open. The feelings of anxiety and claustrophobia he'd felt in the room poured from him, evaporating, leaving room for some strength to return to his muscles.

He passed a group of people turning the corner onto Michigan Avenue, walking down the middle of the road, holding up traffic. Cars driving by on the cross-street were honking their horns, and shouting and yelling, and after a moment Louis realized what it was – a repeal march. Men and women holding up banners – *Beer for the Nation, Beer for Taxation – Prohibition's Failed. Do Something About It.*

As Louis got closer, a woman stepped out of the crowd and handed him a leaflet. He took it, smiled and said thank you and went on his way. As he left the crowd behind, he heard them start up a chant of *We Want Beer, We Want Beer*, and he was reminded of the rallies he had seen in New Orleans ten years earlier, where men and women had walked down streets, and chanted, and handed out fliers for the exact opposite law, for prohibition to be enacted.

A decade later, the tide had swung the other way; public sentiment, moral outrage and crime statistics were all on the side of the wets, leaving Louis wondering what the point had been. All prohibition had done was put millions of businesses and everyday citizens in contact with the criminal element. Sleep with the dogs, indeed. Louis wondered how repeal would work out for Capone, if he'd turn himself into a legitimate booze dealer, or go back to exclusively running brothels and casinos. Then he wondered how the rest of the country's gangsters would fare, too, if they weren't already figuring out what their next moves would be.

Louis folded up the flier, slipped it into his pocket and reached his car. He opened up the windows and doors and got back out, leaning against the side of the car while he waited for the inside to cool down, and the protest march to clear from the road ahead. He took a puff on the cigar and saw a poster a few yards down the street:

GENE TUNNEY VS JACK DEMPSEY FOR THE
HEAVYWEIGHT CHAMPIONSHIP OF THE WORLD.
HERE IN CHICAGO.
SOLDIER FIELD.
TICKETS ON SALE NOW.

Louis ambled over and looked at the cutout photographs of the two boxers underneath the writing. Neither of them looked a patch on Jack Johnson or Harry Wills. He stared at the two white men a little longer and thought about the way Chicago thrived on setting people against each other: Tunney versus Dempsey, Al versus Moran, Louis versus Bix. The whole city ran on the energy of one human battling another, as if that was what made the world turn.

Louis had caught his fair share of it in the past: trumpet players came from all over the country to battle him in onstage cutting contests, and Louis knocked them all out with ease, usually by playing the complicated trumpet pieces he had learned with Lil, or with Brahms's student at Kimball Hall, or with Tate at the Vendome. So he knew how Al and Tunney felt, having to deal with so many challengers to the throne.

Louis sensed they all shared the same longing – the tantalizing feeling that there was always something greater just out of sight, waiting to be realized. But it was the way they sought to alleviate that longing that was their biggest difference; Louis didn't share the others' ruthless individualism, even though it was Louis who was teaching the world how to solo. Things didn't have to move forward via the clash and jostle of opposites; progress also occurred through texture. It was the decade of the self, of building your own melodic line to cut through the noise, and it was Louis who was teaching the world how to do it, but even he knew that solos were nothing without chorus.

41

An hour after their chat in the Pinkerton office, Michael and Ida were seated across from Mrs Van Haren in a conservatory at the back of her mansion. Michael could tell she had been heavily sedated at some point in the last twenty-four hours. The jitteriness she'd exhibited when they had met her in their office had dimmed to a fearful sort of listlessness. As they told her the details of their investigation, she listened to them slumped back in her chair, taking long drags on her cigarette, staring fixedly at the potted shrubs and flowers dotted about the place.

They told her that Gwendolyn had attempted to run away to Montreal, but had been abducted on her way to the station. They didn't say that Coulton or Severyn were probably the ones who had abducted her, or that Gwendolyn had witnessed some kind of blood-soaked crime. They did tell her, however, that people were trying to stop their investigation – Coulton Senior for one – and that judging by the speed at which Michael had been offered the job at the State's Attorney's, someone was probably spying on Mrs Van Haren.

On hearing the last she finally came to life.

'Oh God,' she muttered. She rubbed her temples, then took another long drag on her cigarette before finally looking up at them, frightened.

'My husband's been trying to talk me out of it the whole time. Said the Pinkertons couldn't be trusted. He was furious when he found out I'd gone behind his back and hired you.'

Michael frowned and turned to look at Ida, who looked back at him with an equally perplexed expression.

'You're saying it's your husband?' Ida asked. 'He's trying to obstruct the investigation?'

But Mrs Van Haren had seemingly not heard the question, had returned to her fear-soaked daze, to whatever mental hell it was she had built for herself.

'Mrs Van Haren?' Ida pressed.

But the woman carried on staring at some invisible terror in the middle distance, near the terracotta pots by the French doors.

'Mrs Van Haren? Why would your husband obstruct our investigation?'

Then she finally turned to look at them and frowned. 'Because he's in it with Coulton, of course,' she said, as if she was baffled that Ida had to ask the question. She looked at them for a moment, then resignation suffused her voice. 'I just need her back. I need to tell her I'm sorry,' she said.

And with that she started to cry, and oddly Michael felt relieved at the display, by the fact that the woman's emotions hadn't been completely burned out of her by sodium thiopental.

'I've had dreams,' she continued through her tears. 'Of Gwendolyn, dead. In a white shroud. I pray they aren't true. I pray this city hasn't killed her. It's sharp and dangerous and she's lost out there and I need to tell her I'm sorry.'

She raised her handkerchief to her face and sobbed into it, and Michael and Ida shared a look.

'Mrs Van Haren,' said Ida soothingly. 'What is it your husband and Coulton are in together?'

'You need to find her.'

'Mrs Van Haren. We've been taken off the case,' said Ida. 'That's what we came here to tell you.'

And somehow the words got through and she looked up at them, suddenly alert.

'Why?'

'Mr Coulton complained about my behavior when I interviewed him,' said Michael. 'That's the official reason. Our replacements, however, were chosen in the expectation that they wouldn't make progress with the case.'

'No,' she said, her voice surprisingly firm. 'You have to continue. Can you work it in your spare time? I'll pay you more if needs be. I have to find Gwendolyn. I have to make it up to her.'

'Where's your husband, Mrs Van Haren?' Michael asked.

'He's here in Chicago. He'll probably be home any minute,' she said, shaken by yet another tumult of fear. 'You'll have to leave. I can't face another argument with him. Not just yet.'

She leaned forward suddenly, grasping Michael's hand.

'But please,' she said. 'I'm pleading with you, carry on looking for Gwendolyn. Don't leave it with these other men. There's so much I need to tell her. I'll give you all the reward money. Don't worry about my husband. The money is my own. In my own personal account. It's all yours if I can just know where she is.'

Michael nodded at her, making a conscious effort not to shrink back from her touch: despite the sweltering heat, her fingers were icy cold, and it was then that Michael noticed something else strange about Mrs Van Haren. She wasn't sweating. Sunlight was pouring in through the conservatory's glass ceiling, causing both Michael and Ida to roast in the heat. But Mrs Van Haren, sitting in her wicker chair, in a white cotton dress, had not a single bead of sweat on her.

Five minutes later Ida and Michael were sitting in their car on the road a few yards down from the mansion, staring at the quiet elm-lined street ahead of them.

'When I saw those Pentothal pills on her bedside table the other time,' said Michael, 'I just assumed someone was drugging her to keep her out of the way.'

'They covered up the daughter's mental issues,' said Ida. 'Looks like they're doing the same with her mother.'

Michael took his cigarette case from his pocket and they shared out a couple of smokes.

'The thing that gets me is she knows something,' said Ida. 'And she's too scared to tell us. She knows her husband is involved, and Coulton, but she won't say why.'

Michael nodded, took a handkerchief from his pocket and mopped his brow. The sun was beating down relentlessly and he was feeling it in a torrent of sweat. He thought of the woman sitting in the heat of the conservatory, cold and clammy to the touch, her head filled with the demons of dread and guilt and sodium thiopental and God knew what other torments.

He returned the handkerchief to his pocket, and as he did so he spotted a Duesenberg limousine turn onto the street in the distance, warping in and out of the haze rising up from the asphalt. It slowed when it reached the Van Haren house, and turned up the drive.

Ida opened up the glovebox and took out the viewing glasses they had there, passed a pair to Michael and raised another to her own eyes. Michael took them and looked through them and caught focus on the Duesenberg as it stopped outside the front steps. A man in a black suit and fedora got out of the back. Adolphus Van Haren was of medium build and would have been tall once, but now his posture had been broken by age and he was so stooped over, Michael was surprised he was managing to walk without a cane. He must have been in his mid-seventies at least, and it made Michael wonder on the age difference between the man and his much younger wife.

When Van Haren got to the front doors they opened and the butler stepped out and the two of them conferred about something there on the porch and Van Haren became irate, throwing his arms about, his face reddening.

'I guess he just found out we paid a visit,' said Ida.

'I guess he did.'

The two men stepped inside the house, and Ida and Michael lowered the glasses from their eyes.

'So, what do we do?' asked Michael, turning to look at Ida. He already knew where his path lay, but he didn't want to jeopardize his protégée's career on it, too.

'We carry on looking for Gwendolyn,' said Ida, not missing a beat. 'Whether or not the father's involved. Whether or not the mother knows more than she's telling us – grief's gotten the better of the woman.'

'We get caught, that's it,' said Michael.

'I'm willing to run the risk.'

'For the money she offered? The more the woman talks about it, the more I reckon that money's never gonna materialize.'

'Even if she doesn't pay us, I want to help the woman,' Ida said. 'And I want to know what those men have done to Gwendolyn. And I want to get back at whoever it is that's trying to ruin us. Plus, we're almost there.' She turned to look at him, all earnestness and gritty determination. 'We've almost got the go-between. He's the key to all this and we've almost got him. Let's go and see what he's got to say.'

'We do that and there's no going back,' said Michael. 'It's all or nothing.'

'I'm in,' said Ida. 'But I don't have a wife and kids.'

'She already gave me the go-ahead,' said Michael.

They looked at each other a moment and smiled ruefully. Then he started up the car and they headed for LaSalle Street, downtown, the sweltering heart of the city.

42

Dante stood at the bar of the Drake drinking a Martini, waiting for Loretta to come down from the suite. When he'd gotten back from Michigan that afternoon he'd been surprised to find her still in his rooms, lying on the sofa, reading a book, the dog nestled under her arm.

'If I'm going to be cooped up,' she'd said, 'it might as well be in a luxury suite.'

Dante couldn't fault the logic. He didn't have time to prepare for a trip to Millersville that night – he wanted to make a few calls first, visit some people and make some discreet inquiries, see if anyone in Chicago knew anything about the roadhouse. So he decided to spend the evening with Loretta, having dinner, pretending to be a normal, civilized person, hoping that the pretense might actually make him so.

He took a shower and dressed and left her in the suite to get ready alone, arranging to meet her in the bar whenever she was done. He'd ordered the drinks and stood around looking at the crowd – the moneyed elite and the people that trailed in their wake.

As he was taking a sip of his drink there was a commotion in the lobby and he turned to look through the great arch that connected the bar to the hotel's reception to see what was going on. He saw a troop of people entering from the street – a debonair man in a sharp black suit at the front of the group, accompanied by a slight, pretty girl, then some clerks, then a gaggle of bellboys and porters rolling their luggage in on overloaded trolleys. Dante recognized the man, but couldn't place him.

'Charlie Chaplin,' said a voice next to him, and Dante turned to see a short man on a barstool to his side, dressed in a pinstripe suit, with a Cosmopolitan in one hand and a cigarette holder in the other. The man smiled at Dante, revealing unnaturally white teeth made to seem more so by an unnaturally brown tan.

'The whole town's filling with celebrities,' he continued, 'for the boxing match, you know. Yesterday morning Al Jolson checked in, and I was in the gift shop this afternoon and saw Douglas Fairbanks browsing the paperweights.'

Dante nodded and smiled, and they watched Chaplin a moment as his entourage headed to the reception desk to check in. He was even shorter than Dante had imagined, but much better-looking than his films portrayed. The man on the stool next to Dante took a sip on his drink and a puff on his smoke, and the way he held the cigarette holder so horizontal, and took a puff by somehow pecking at it, made Dante think of a bird at a feeder.

'You know, I came to Chicago from Hollywood thinking I'd get away from all the stars, and I'm bumping into more of them here than I do back home.' The man grinned, stuffed the cigarette holder into his mouth and held out a hand.

'Sam Halpert,' he said.

'Dante Sanfelippo,' Dante said as they shook hands. 'So what brings you to Chicago, Mr Halpert?'

'Sam, please. Business. I'm a movie producer.'

'You're shooting a film here?'

'No. There's a young writer in town I've come here to meet. He's writing a book about Capone and we're thinking of purchasing the rights to turn it into a film. I had to meet the boy, read the draft, decide whether we should make an offer.'

'A film about Capone sounds like a dangerous enterprise.'

'Oh, we'll change the names,' said the man with a shrug, taking another peck at the cigarette holder.

'I see.'

In the lobby, Chaplin and the girl were being led away from the reception desk toward the elevators.

'I didn't realize people made films about gangsters,' said Dante.

'It's a new trend,' said Halpert, sighing. 'We'll see how long it lasts. I'm also here looking for actors, or rather, gangsters that want to turn their hand to acting.'

Dante gave him a look.

'People want authenticity, the real deal. You know Al Jennings? The train robber? He's got a job working in the pictures. And Spike O'Donnell's been approached by a British studio to star in a series they've got coming up.'

'O'Donnell the bootlegger?' Dante asked, bemused, and Halpert nodded. O'Donnell owned breweries in Chicago and Wisconsin, had been implicated in bombings and election-day beatings, had killed people in the Second Beer War, and he'd still be doing time in Joliet for armed robbery if it wasn't for Governor Small's cash-for-pardons operation.

'O'Donnell in the movies . . .' muttered Dante.

'Maybe he got sick and tired of being shot at,' said Halpert.

'I suppose,' said Dante. 'Must be strange, though, going from being a real gangster to a fake one.'

'Oh, he won't be a fake gangster, he'll be the real Spike,' said Halpert, taking another sip from his drink and another peck from his cigarette. He peered at Dante, intrigued that he seemed to know something of Spike O'Donnell.

'So what do you do?' he asked, his eyes trained on Dante as if he was appraising a starlet.

'I work in restaurants in New York.'

'And what brings you out west?'

'I grew up here. I'm just in town catching up with old friends.'

'You know, you look familiar. Have you ever done any acting?'

'No, Mr Halpert. At least not any that wound up on the silver screen.'

Dante smiled and the man smiled back, then Dante spotted Loretta stepping into the bar through the great arch, passing by the cigar stand, looking for him. She was wearing a pale green dress he'd never seen before and he wondered where the hell she'd got it from if she'd been in the hotel all day. He raised a hand and she saw him and headed toward them.

'Your date?' Halpert asked.

'A friend.'

'She's a fine-looking friend. I'll leave you to it Mr . . . Why, I've forgotten your name already.'

'Sanfelippo. Dante Sanfelippo.'

The man frowned again, then nodded and hopped off the stool and wandered off into the crowd.

'Who was that?' asked Loretta when she arrived.

'A film producer from Hollywood. And you just missed Charlie Chaplin, too.'

The hotel's dining room looked like something out of a fairy tale, with chandeliers like blooms of glass, and great pillars stretching to a ceiling as ornately painted as a Russian church. They ate coquilles St Jacques and mushroom bisque, and grilled langoustines with lemon butter, and they spoke of Olivia, and Loretta's sister, and people from their neighborhood, and New York and Chicago, and what they were planning on doing with their lives, as if either of them knew. They spoke of nothing much at all and got steadily drunk on white wine.

'Why did you change your name?' Loretta asked when they were halfway through their entrees, and the candlelight and wine fuzz were starting to make them feel like they were in their own little world, intimate and warm.

'How did you know I changed my name?' he asked.

'That first night I called the hotel, they didn't know who you were till I mentioned you were staying in the Lindbergh suite.'

Dante shrugged. 'I felt like a fresh start.'

'Why Sanfelippo?'

'It's the name of the church in the Bronx where the priest saved me from hypothermia – St Phillip's. You don't like it?'

'It doesn't suit you,' she said, shaking her head. 'I preferred your old one.'

'Maybe I'll change it back someday.'

'Good. Names are important. You know you're the only person that doesn't shorten my name to Lorrie?'

'Really?'

She nodded. 'I always liked that about you.'

When they'd finished he asked the waiters to put the bill on his tab and Loretta went to use the restroom and Dante waited for her by the doors to the lobby. He watched the couples heading into the ballroom and he poked his head in to have a look around. The people on the parquet floor were dancing to watered-down jazz, the staid kind played in high-end hotels like this one, white jazz, near-beer jazz, a pale imitation of the pieces they'd stolen from the black musicians in Bronzeville.

When Dante and Loretta stepped through the lobby and out onto the hotel entrance they breathed in the fresh air, and the freshness made the alcohol they'd drunk hit them with even greater force, and their heads spun and they both knew they weren't going anywhere that night.

'We could wait it out back in the suite?' he said.

Five minutes later they were on the bed, kissing and undressing. Loretta tugged at Dante's shirt and he took it off, not thinking, and she ran her hands over his arms, and stopped, and frowned, and Dante realized she was staring at the needle marks, at the self-hate stenciled all over his arms.

'Oh,' she said, upset, disappointed, and there was nothing he could say to stop himself feeling wretched. She ran her fingers down the roll of scars tenderly, looked up at him, kissed him, and they carried on again, slower this time, different.

Afterwards, when they were lying in each other's arms, he told her all about it; falling in with the needle fiends. She listened with her head on his chest and afterward, he felt like some great burden had been lifted, and he realized it was the first time he'd ever told anyone his story, all of it. And when he'd finished she'd said nothing, just turned her head and kissed him and they'd fallen silent.

As he lay with his arm around her, he suddenly thought of Olivia, and waves of guilt rushed through him so forcefully he flinched. He'd slept with plenty of women since his wife had died, had even gotten close to some of them. But Loretta was Olivia's best friend and suddenly a sense that he had tainted all their shared memories ran through him, a sense of betrayal, of pollution.

'What is it?' Loretta asked, turning to look at him.

'Nothing,' he said, knowing not to bring up the subject.

'You're thinking about Olivia,' she said flatly, and Dante saw the tears in her eyes.

'Yeah,' he said.

'Me too.'

She turned away from him again, and they lay there, each staring at nothing.

'Maybe it ain't too bad,' she said, after a while. 'She'd want us to be happy.'

'Sure,' he said listlessly.

'You got a girl back in New York?'

Dante stayed silent for a moment, trying to think of a way to lighten the mood.

'Sure. I got lots of girls. Safety in numbers.'

He smiled and she rolled her eyes.

'Nah, I ain't got any girls back in New York,' he said more solemnly. 'I ain't got nothing much at all back in New York.'

'And I ain't got much here in Chicago neither,' she said, and Dante didn't reply, and they stayed like that, seeking refuge in each other, and the dark hours collapsed.

43

In the golden light of dawn, a group of men in rumpled suits, carrying musical instruments in cases, looking tired and a little the worse for wear, stumbled into Okeh Records' Chicago studio to begin a day-long recording session. The men recorded under the moniker Louis Armstrong's Hot Five, even though there were six of them. They had all played in Carol Dickerson's Orchestra at the Savoy the previous night, and had gone for Chinese food and drinks after the nightclub had closed, and had come straight from the restaurant to the studio without having slept, leaving them fuzzy-headed and contemplative, none more so than Louis, who had been mulling over recent events more than he knew he should have.

As the recording room was being readied, and the others in the band joked about, Louis sat on a chair in a corner, took his trumpet from its case and assembled it, and as he did so, he thought about the death of his mother the previous year, the death of his first wife, the death of his marriage to Lil.

He remembered the hope he'd had in him when he'd first arrived in the city, when he'd gotten off the train from New Orleans and turned up at the Lincoln Gardens and felt he was witnessing the dawn of a new day. He wondered how all that hope had ended up in slumming parties and buffet flats and go-betweens and exploitation and the people in charge of the city trying their best to destroy the jazz clubs and the musicians who worked in them.

'Be ready in a bit,' said one of the technicians as he dashed past Louis on his way to the recording booth carrying a cardboard box full of equipment.

'Sure thing, boss,' said Louis, not really bothered by the wait. He looked at the trumpet in his hand, then at the studio as it bustled with his band-mates setting up music stands and arranging sheets, and tuning their instruments, and his mind drifted back to the first time he'd ever entered a recording studio, a year after he'd arrived in Chicago, when he was still playing second cornet for Joe Oliver.

His old mentor had arranged for the band to go on a whistle-stop tour of dance halls across Illinois, Indiana and Ohio. The endeavor was a dangerous one considering the hatred there was festering in the dusty old towns that were on their route. If they passed through a settlement and didn't see a black face, they carried on going, knowing from bitter experience that to stop and ask where they might buy some food in a whites-only burg could well lead to them getting run out of town, or beaten, or lynched. So much of the journey was spent on the hop, hungry, looking for black people and food.

Louis whiled away most of the trip staring out of the windows of trains and buses and vans, watching the vast inland ocean of the prairies crawl past. The landscapes were mostly empty, fields with an occasional silo or barn perched here or there, stooping lines of telegraph poles limping their way forlornly across the hinterland, as if they knew their attempt to cross such an endless expanse was inevitably doomed.

It was boring, especially for a twenty-two-year-old, even if Lil – on whom Louis had developed a crush – was traveling with them. But when they got to Indiana, with its quarter of a million Klansmen and its blanket of racial hate, and they made it to Richmond, they stopped off at the home of the Gennett brothers' recording company, and Louis entered a studio for the very first time.

It was a low-rent affair, situated on the grounds of a piano factory, where the brothers signed up whichever musicians happened to be passing through and recorded them then and there. The studio was jerry-built, with rugs and draperies and sawdust shoved into the walls to keep the place soundproofed, mostly; recording sessions still had to be halted whenever a train rattled past on the tracks outside.

The recording equipment itself consisted of a great conical horn that was connected via tubes to a needle in another room that etched sound vibrations onto a wax cylinder. It was such a primitive and sensitive set-up that any instrument with punch made the needle skip and ruined the recording. So Baby Dodds had to swap his drums for woodblocks, and Bill Johnson had to swap his double bass for a banjo, and Louis was exiled all the way to the very back of the room as his cornet so overpowered Joe's. And on top of all that the room had to be kept at a steady eighty-five degrees to keep the wax soft and so they had to sweat it out, hour after hour, on the verge of fainting from the heat.

The recording sessions proved to be the undoing of the band: Joe Oliver stiffed them on their royalty checks, and the Dodds brothers threatened to attack Oliver if he didn't pay up, and Oliver bought a gun to keep them at bay. The band split, and Lil convinced Louis to go it alone, and five years on, Louis had his own band and they were all getting paid a packet to record in a state-of-the-art studio, equipped with Bell's Western Electric recording technology. There were no Klansmen outside, no trains rattling past, no boiling heat to contend with, no band leader stealing their money, and blessedly, they'd be recording into a microphone, rather than an inverted megaphone.

Still, he missed those early days, even though he knew nostalgia was foolish, it being nothing more than homesickness for a place you couldn't revisit.

'Louis, you all right?' asked Earl from where he was sitting behind the piano. Louis looked up at him and smiled.

Even though the rest of them looked like they'd been dragged through a hedge, Earl didn't have a thread loose. He was perched on his stool with his suit immaculate and his trademark bowler hat and walking cane propped up against the wall to his side. Earl was always the best-dressed musician in Chicago. He'd come up in Pittsburgh, where employers picked up musicians off the street, so looking well-dressed and respectable often meant the difference between paying the rent or not.

'I'm all good,' said Louis.

They settled down and spent the morning laying down sides of 'Don't Jive Me', then after lunch they went to the back of the building to smoke some reefers, and then they returned to the studio and set about recording a song called 'West End Blues'. It was a Joe Oliver number, Louis' mentor having first recorded it earlier that month in New York with the Dixie Syncopators. Earl and Louis had been practicing their own version of it round at the Ranch all week. The lyrics, which they weren't recording that day, told the story of a woman angered by a cheating man, drunk on gin, grabbing a gun and heading to New Orleans's pleasure district, the West End, to find her man and his side woman and shoot them down. Louis had wondered on those lyrics, whether the woman ever did get hold of her man, really did shoot him down; whether the song, as well as being the wail of a wronged woman, was also a dead man's blues.

They ran through the arrangement until they all had it fresh in their heads and were ready to record, then Louis opened the spit valve on his trumpet and cleared the condensation from it. He looked at each player in turn and they nodded they were set, so he turned to the technician who got the wax going, and when he got the signal back, Louis turned to the mic, lifted his trumpet to his lips, and then, for a moment, there was silence.

He blasted out a flourish to start the tune, a cadenza, a quick, chromatic fanfare that spun and vaulted through the air, and after twelve seconds of rhythmic elasticity, the rest of the band were tumbling along in his wake, at ninety beats a minute, slow by their

standards, but fitting to the song and its hazy, shifting arrangement, making it feel like a rhapsody rather than the blues suggested
by its title and lyrics. The wistfulness of it was carried in Louis'
trumpet and wordless vocals, in Fred Robinson's trombone, in
Zutty's shuffle beat, in the tremolos on the piano courtesy of Earl.

After the cadenza and the first chorus came a duet, then a solo,
then a second and a third chorus, then a gap for improvisation,
and then a final chorus and then there was the coda, rounding it
all off.

Three minutes after they'd started, they were looking at each
other, grinning and high, washed in the song's beautiful calm,
knowing they'd recorded something worthy of their talents,
something that would stand the test of time.

Until Zutty mistimed the cymbal clop that was supposed
to bring the song to an end and the whole recording was ruined,
bringing everything to a crashing halt, sucking the energy out
of the room. Everyone looked up in silence, as if they'd all been
shaken from a trance, some sultry dream the song had hypnotized
them with.

As they realized what had happened, one by one they turned
to glare at Zutty, and Zutty shrugged. Then they turned to look
at each other, wondering wordlessly what the hell had just happened, how close they'd come to capturing that perfect thing they
all knew was out there.

Then it was Earl of all people who started laughing and
shaking his head, and the rest of them sighed and Louis rubbed
his temples and everyone cursed Zutty and called him a fool in an
outpouring of exasperation and Zutty grinned embarrassedly.

In the room adjoining, the technician loaded up a new piece
of wax, and they all set themselves up once more, ready to record
again, to try and recapture the perfection they'd almost caught
just a few minutes before.

'Okay, let's try it again,' said Louis, trying to sound bright,
and he nodded at the technician and they all started again. And on

the second attempt they were halfway through the tune when Zutty messed up once more.

'These things happen,' he said, in response to the curses being hurled his way. 'All the time.'

So they set up again, and tried to compose themselves, knowing they were on the verge of something great, something timeless, and they had to get it right.

And on the third attempt, they did.

44

Stanley Taylor, the go-between's brother, was still in semi-official custody in the Federal Building on Adams Street, but he had managed to get through to his runaway sibling and they had arranged a meeting – Ida and Michael were to go to a chop-suey joint near Cottage Grove, where they'd meet with the missing go-between, and if he told Ida and Michael all they wanted to know, Stanley would be released from the holding cell he was in.

When Ida and Michael received the details, they put the other cases they'd been assigned on hold, booked out a car from the pool and headed south for the meeting. As they drove through mid-afternoon traffic, Ida got the sense they were being followed and, not sure if the bombing was still rattling her nerves or not, she kept checking the rearview and side mirrors, catching glimpses of a grey sedan a half a block behind them.

'What is it?' asked Michael.

'The grey sedan in the left lane about five cars back.'

Michael looked in the rearview. 'Should we make a loop?'

'No, let's pull over after the next intersection, get a look at them.'

Michael nodded and drove through the next junction and waited till the sedan had passed through it, too, so there was nowhere for it to turn off, and then he pulled over to the sidewalk. The sedan drove past them and they caught a glimpse of two men inside it – one in his thirties, mustachioed, with a brown bowler hat on, and another, the driver, younger and clean-shaven, wearing a shirt and waistcoat.

'Recognize them?' asked Michael after they'd driven past, and Ida shook her head.

'You get the license plate?' he asked.

Ida nodded.

They continued their journey, parked up off 63rd Street, and crossed a block to a crumbling old building with a neon sign outside it: *Chu Gow Noodle Parlor – Authentic Mandarinic Cuisine.*

The place had dozens of tables positioned in a neat grid, and dim lighting, and red velvet coverings all over the walls, making it feel furtive somehow, mysterious. They picked a table with a view to the door and waited. Ida lit a cigarette and peered at the paintings on the walls; Chinese gods and wise men and beautiful women in flowing gowns, and dragons curling through banks of clouds.

Then the front door opened and a man stepped in off the street, tall, young, good-looking, light-skinned. He scanned the faces of the people at all the tables, looking for someone.

'I think that's our man,' Ida said, and Michael nodded.

He spotted them and Michael raised a hand, and the man wandered over.

'You the two Pinks?' he asked, and they nodded. He glared at them, and sat.

'I'm Randall Taylor. Y'all got my brother arrested?'

'He hasn't been charged with anything,' said Michael. 'And he won't be if you tell us what we want to know.'

The man stared at them a moment longer, taking them in, and Ida looked him over and could see how he would make a good go-between; with his light skin and straightened hair, he was the good-looking, non-threatening type of Negro who would be trusted by Gold Coasters going on safari in the Southside.

The waitress brought them over the bill of fare and Ida and Michael waved it away, but Randall took a copy and scanned the dishes.

'This on you?' he asked, and Michael nodded, and Randall

ordered barbecued pork and rice, and a side of greens in oyster sauce, and beers for all of them. Ida could tell the food order wasn't just for show – the man was hungry, looked like he hadn't eaten in days.

'Where you from?' he said to Michael, picking up on the accent.

'We're both from New Orleans.'

'Is that right?' he said, staring from Michael to Ida. 'So what you wanna know that's so important you done locked up Stanley?'

'We're looking for Gwendolyn,' said Ida softly. 'We've been hired by her mother. We heard you saw her on the day she disappeared.'

'Gwen's disappeared? When?'

'The twenty-seventh. The day she came to Bronzeville to meet you, looking for Coulton. No one's seen her since.'

Ida filled Randall in on the events that had happened that evening, culminating in Gwen's probable abduction from outside the train station. Randall listened to it all, and his anger seemed to dim, and Ida could see that he cared for Gwendolyn and was upset by what had happened to her.

'She called me up the day before,' he said, when Ida had finished speaking. 'Said she was looking for Chuck, that she needed to speak to him, said she wanted to meet me to find out where he was.'

'Why did she think you'd know?'

'No idea. I didn't have a clue where he was.'

'But you met with her anyway?'

'I liked the girl,' Randall said. 'I wanted to help her out. Chuck had told me about her. You know she tried to kill herself a few times, right? I was worried she might try again, that's why I came to meet her. She was telling me she was finally going to break it off with Chuck. That she didn't care what her parents thought anymore.'

'Okay,' said Ida. 'Then what happened?'

'So we talked a bit and I calmed her down, and then she went on her way.'

'Went on her way where?'

Here Randall let out an exasperated sigh, as if Ida had asked the one question he didn't want to answer. Then the waitress arrived with their drinks. She put down a blue-and-white china teapot and three tiny matching cups and headed back to the bar. Michael picked up the teapot and Ida watched as he poured beer from it into the cups.

'She asked me if I knew where Chuck might be,' Randall continued. 'See, Chuck and Lloyd had a buffet flat they rented in Bronzeville, a crash-pad, but a few months ago they let the lease slide on the place, and then they rented a new one they didn't tell anyone about, except me. They didn't want their names on no leases so they paid me to use mine. Gwen had been down to the old flat, found out they weren't renting it no more, and figured I'd know where the new flat might be. So I gave her the address of the new place and let her get on her way.'

Randall took a sip from his beer, and Ida eyed him. She knew he was telling the truth, but still his story didn't make sense.

'So you gave Gwen the address, she went there, saw them involved in some blood-soaked crime and they abducted her. And now she's missing. You know what it was they were doing there?' asked Ida.

'No.'

'You know where the flat is?'

'Sure. Back o' Yards.'

Ida frowned and turned to look at Michael; the Back of Yards was not the neighborhood for the crash-pad of a man about town.

'Why there and not Bronzeville?'

'Chuck and Lloyd said they wanted somewhere a little more private.' He smiled as he said it, and there was something twisted to his expression, as if a screw had been turned in his cheek, and his lips had lifted into place with a sinister automation.

Ida looked at him once more – the approachable-looking man who made money selling the urban black experience to privileged whites – and something about him seemed off, and she wasn't sure if it was just the man who was making her feel that way or if the bombing was still making her jump at shadows.

'Why did they need somewhere private?' she asked, but Randall didn't answer, stared instead at the teapot on the table, at its inky pattern of blue mountains and clouds and seas.

'We've heard rumors about the two of them,' said Ida. 'About what they got up to in those buffet flats you arranged for them. That people went missing. Is that true?'

'True as rent day,' he said, smiling again, that same mechanical turn of a screw. The casual way he'd said it, and the expression on his face, sent an icicle of a shiver down Ida's spine.

'Is that what they were using this flat for?' she asked.

'How much d'you know about Chuck and Lloyd?'

'Why don't you enlighten us?'

Randall paused before speaking again. 'There's something dark about those boys. You know how they met, right? In the war. Lloyd saved Chuck's life. Then Lloyd got caught by the mustard gas and it destroyed his throat, and that's how he ended up with those scars on his neck and that voice of his. Anyway, I don't know what it was they saw out there, or maybe it wasn't even out there, maybe they always had it in them, but those two . . . They'd goad each other on till they started looking for things to do that weren't right. If you go through life collecting experiences, and you've already collected all the ones that're normal – where d'you go from there? When the only experiences left to collect are the dark ones? I saw it. They'd bring back boys and girls to that apartment and do stuff just for the hell of it. Cuz they were bored with life and they had the money to cover it up. I grew up around hustlers and killers, people that'd slit your throat for a dime, but they didn't have nothing on those boys. If something bad's happened to Gwen, those two're behind it.'

He looked at them, from one to the other, and the glint in his eye said to her that he'd been warped by hedonism just as much as Severyn and Coulton, that on those nights of debauchery, Randall was more than just a bystander, that whatever it was they got up to, he was involved in it all as well.

Ida felt a chill of revulsion and turned to look at Michael and saw he'd had the same reaction to what Randall had said. Then the waitress arrived with Randall's food. She put down a bowl of greens, and a plate of sticky steamed rice and barbecued pork, and Randall listlessly picked up his fork, his appetite seemingly gone.

'I don't get it,' Ida said. 'You must have known Chuck and Lloyd would be mad as hell at you for giving Gwen that address, but you still gave it to her?'

'I know,' said Randall. 'But I liked the girl. I mean, really liked her. And she liked me. And I couldn't see her upset like that. And there's something else. The last few months, Chuck and Lloyd told me they were working on something, something big, and they didn't have time for playing around no more. I didn't see them much, and then one day, just like that, they gave me the gate.' Randall lifted up a hand and snapped his fingers. 'They told me I was fired. They didn't want to see me no more. And that was the last I ever heard from them.'

'So you gave Gwen the address to get back at them?'

'I figured she'd go round there, see what they were up to and then she'd come running back to me. They'd be put out, and I'd get the girl. Two birds with one stone. I didn't know they'd abduct her.'

He shrugged and Ida stared at him, saddened by the fact that this man, too, had used Gwendolyn for his own ends.

'When did they fire you?' she asked.

'A couple of months ago. And I ain't seen either of them since.'

'And what about Esther Jones?'

At the mention of the name, Randall twitched – surprised,

then annoyed. 'Who?' he asked, pretending he'd never heard of the girl.

'She was a dancer at the Sunset Café. She turned up dead in the Sanitary and Sewage Canal a while back. You were pimping her out to a Capone stooge named Benny Roebuck. He ended up dead as well, in an alleyway off State Street. The same night Gwendolyn disappeared.'

'That shit was all on account of Lloyd and Chuck, too,' he said eventually, after he'd realized there was no point in lying about it. 'They came to see me three or four months back, saying they needed to set someone up for some long game they were working on. Knew this white man that liked it dark. Wanted me to find a girl to fake being with him for a few months while they set up whatever this hustle they had planned was. I knew Esther from when I worked out of the Sunset. I told her there was good money if she faked a meet with this Roebuck character and pretended to be sweet on him, and she did it.'

'They tell you why they wanted her to do it?' Ida asked.

He shook his head. 'Nah. But I know it was linked to this big thing they were working on.'

'Tell us more about that.'

'Ain't nothing to tell, they kept real quiet about it. All except one morning, after we'd been up a few days and they were both drunk and high, and they were bragging, talking about doing something that was gonna change the city, that was gonna set the place on fire. That's what they said. It was after that they sacked me. I figured it was all related. Whatever it is they got planned, they didn't want me knowing about it. Now Esther's dead, and this Roebuck character's dead, and Gwen's missing. Seems to me like they're tying up loose ends, and what the hell else am I if I ain't a loose end? So I'm staying on the low till all this fades away.'

Ida nodded, taking it in. She looked at Randall, then past him to the paintings on the wall, just visible in the gloom, the dragons curling about in the mist.

'You know where we can find Chuck and Lloyd?' she asked.

'No. But I figure if you're looking for clues there'll be plenty at that apartment in Back o' Yards.'

'Give us the address, Randall.'

He shook his head. 'Not till my brother's released. I hear from him that he's safe, and I'll send you the address. Let him go today, and you'll have the address tomorrow morning.'

Ida turned to look at Michael. He shrugged.

'All right,' Michael said. 'We'll tell the agents to let your brother go, but if we don't get that address tomorrow, we'll re-arrest him, and charge him, and we'll get warrants out for you, too. Understand?'

'Sure,' said Randall, before downing another cup of beer.

'By the way,' he said, 'you got something wrong. Benny Roe-buck. He wasn't a Capone stooge. He was working for Moran.'

Ida frowned, eyed Randall closely, trying to see if he was lying.

'You sure about that?' she asked. 'We heard different.'

'You bet I'm sure. Whatever it is they're up to, it didn't have to do with no Capone stooge. The man worked for Moran, that's why they targeted him. Now, thanks for the food. I'll be waiting to hear from my brother.'

And with that he wiped his mouth, and left the restaurant.

'What do you think?' Ida asked Michael when they were back outside.

Michael shrugged and took his Virginia Slims from his pocket and lit one. 'He's quite the storyteller,' he said, passing the cigarette case to Ida.

'You buy the thing about Roebuck working for Moran and not Capone?'

'Sure. He was muscle for hire. He lived in the Northside. Who told us he worked for Capone?'

'Jacob. The photographer from the *Tribune*,' she said, lighting up and passing him back the case.

'And where'd he hear it from?'

'I dunno. Maybe someone at the station?'

'Maybe you should ask him,' Michael suggested as they headed back to the car. 'You did well in there,' he said, when they were walking along the sidewalk. 'Conducted the whole interview on your own.'

'Did I?'

'Sure. I didn't say a word. Difficult interview too. Hostile witness. I thought you'd lost him for a moment at the start but you reeled him back. You did good, kid.' He said the last in a mock-patronizing tone of voice and they both smiled.

'You think he'll come through with the address?' Ida asked.

'That I ain't so sure about. But even if he doesn't we can trawl through the housing records in the Back o' Yards, see if we can dig something up.'

They reached the car and as Ida waited for Michael to unlock it, she looked up into the sky and for the first time in weeks she saw clouds gathering overhead, wispy and bedraggled.

'It's fixing to rain,' said Michael, who'd followed her gaze. Ida nodded and Randall's words about a plan to set the city on fire came into her head.

Michael got into the car and let her in, and as they settled themselves inside, they saw, further up the block, a sedan pull out from the curb in front and head off downtown. They turned to look at each other.

'Was that the same one?' asked Ida.

'I'm not sure. I couldn't see the license plate.'

'Me neither.'

They both sat in silence a moment. Then Michael started the engine, and pulled out into the road, and they drove and smoked wordlessly for a few minutes, watching the city as it prepared to launch itself into another evening.

'What I don't get in all of this is Chuck,' said Ida after she'd been mulling things over. 'I mean, Lloyd Severyn I get. He's from the wrong side of the tracks. He goes to the war and meets Chuck, who's some rich boy he'd never meet anywhere else, and the two of them get along and Severyn thinks he's found his meal ticket and the two of them come back to Chicago and the good times roll. But Chuck . . . everyone we speak to's got a different character description. Randall's making out he's some kind of rich-kid sadist, his father makes out he's a clueless drunk, Lena made out he was a soft, pampered college kid, and then there's what Gwen said, that she saw him doing something so awful she had to leave town. I mean, who the hell is he?'

Michael shrugged. 'I don't know. Maybe all of the above. But I figure we find out who he is, and where he is, and we find out what happened to Gwen.'

They carried on driving and at some point Michael turned to look at her. 'What are you doing now?' he asked. 'You want me to drop you home?'

'No, I'm meeting a friend.'

45

Ida met Jacob at a restaurant in Little Italy. They ordered tagliatelle in tomato sauce, which arrived in huge portions, accompanied by a bowl of parmesan, and a green salad, and black olives, and white bread, and a bottle of dago red. They were awkward with each other at first, but as they ate and drank, the doubts that normally swirled about Ida melted away, and the two of them found a match in their misfit personalities; both of them sensitive people with brutal jobs, working amongst the horrors of the city, the gruesome reality that underpinned everyday living.

They finished the bottle of wine, but not the mound of tagliatelle, and they stumbled out of the restaurant and looked up at the sky and saw the storm nestled in the clouds. Then they went back to Jacob's, passing by the bombed-out speak. Its front had been boarded up, and a sign said it would be open again soon.

They sat on Jacob's sofa and drank moonshine once more, and an hour or so after nightfall the rainstorm started, torrential and electrical, clattering against the buildings and the sidewalks.

They got up to close the windows, but instead heard the noises from outside and stepped out onto the fire escape. The whole neighborhood was alive with rain, lit up by lightning flashes, and everything was cool and refreshing for the first time in weeks – as if someone had turned on a giant air-cooler in the sky.

They let the rain splash against them and basked in the coolness of the storm and watched as the streets below filled with children, splashing each other and playing beneath the bruised undersides of the clouds. When Ida and Jacob were thoroughly drenched they went into Jacob's bedroom, peeled off their clothes and slept with each other once more, this time without the shadow of the bombing hanging over them, and so it was different, more familiar, more certain.

Afterwards they lay in bed and listened to the tumult of the storm, the occasional boom of thunder and watched the rain run down the windows, daubing the city lights outside into a glistening blue wash.

'I don't think I'm going to be able to sleep,' he said.

'Me neither,' she replied. 'Wanna go out?'

When they stepped into the auditorium of the Savoy they were hit by a roar of horns and drums, as hot as the blast of a furnace. Louis was on stage with a white man, and the first thing Ida thought was how odd: a black man and a white man sharing a stage. She recognized a few of the players in the band as friends of Louis, but then there were white men up there, too, sitting in, two bands merged together. Jacob had stopped, too, and was also staring at the stage. She turned to him and smiled, and they pushed through the crowd to the bar, where the people waiting were in rows five deep. She listened to the music and recognized the tune, Noël Coward's 'Poor Little Rich Girl', a favorite with both Louis and Chicago's jazz crowds. Even with her back to the stage she could tell it was Louis freewheeling over the top of its chorus – no one else on earth could hit that many high Cs in a row.

They eventually got their drinks and turned to watch the band. Louis was in the midst of his solo, and the crowd were either dancing crazily or standing spellbound, listening in awe as each note came along, perfect in its clarity, its tone, its timing, its relation to the notes around it. And as she listened to the solo flitting across the rhythm like a skimming stone, Ida noticed the phrases were getting faster and more complex, each one leaping further than the one before, until they reached a crescendo that exploded with the power of a storm.

The crowd roared and pulsed with energy, and Louis grinned and bowed and took a step back, and the white man stepped forward, raised a cornet to his lips, and Ida felt sorry for him – how the hell did you follow one of Louis' solos?

'Who's that up there?' she asked a boy standing next to her, his eyes fixed on the stage.

'That's Bix,' he said, 'Bix Beiderbecke.' And he smiled at her, and she smiled back and turned to look at the stage and finally recognized the white band – the Paul Whiteman Orchestra. Then Beiderbecke began his solo, starting out slow, coasting against the rhythm, then moving back into it, and as Ida listened she realized he wasn't trying to outdo Louis, he was simply finding his own way, and as he got into it, the crowd did, too, and the notes came faster, bounding out of the cornet, punchy and clear, rolling on to a finale in an unflappable cascade of precision.

The audience roared once more and the horns clambered over each other and crashed into a chorus, and the song came to an end in a sheet of sound. A great energy coursed around the place, and Ida thought of something that Louis had told her once, that jazz was born in the hurricanes of New Orleans, and that groups of ragged Southerners had brought those hurricanes north, concealed in the valves of trumpets and the hollows of double basses, and when they played, they let those storms loose into the world once more, releasing all that energy with just the touch of lips on a mouthpiece, the brush of fingers on keys, the pluck of a string.

And maybe that was why Louis ran the risk of playing with these musicians; they were teaching each other the techniques – the pedal tones, hand stops, lip trills – that summoned up the energy she could see rushing about the place, in people's smiles and the movement of their bodies, and that energy was more important to them than social norms, than race, than divisions, than getting arrested.

On stage Louis and Bix took their bows, and Bix went to get a drink and Louis lit a reefer and passed it around his bandmates. Then Whiteman conferred with Earl at the piano, and they nodded at each other and launched into a rendition of 'Basin Street Blues', a slow, rumbling New Orleans blues. It was only in these after-hours shows that bands played Southern style, rough-edged and slow enough for them to make their instruments moan and growl, to slide and bump in melismatic slurs.

The crowd started dancing once more, slower now, couples hugging, torsos locked and getting lower to the ground. Louis stepped to the front of the stage and sang the lyrics, and as he did so, he spotted Ida and a grin broke out on his face.

We'll take a trip to the land of dreams
Blowing down the river, down to New Orleans

The mass of bodies parted for an instant, and Ida caught a glimpse of the tables by the dance floor, the prime seats, where a group of men she recognized were sitting – Al Capone, Frank Nitti, 'Machine Gun' Jack McGurn, and a dozen other hangers-on and skimpily dressed girlfriends and mistresses, all at a table strewn with liquor bottles and ashtrays erupting with cigar ends. They were watching the stage and cracking jokes with each other, arms slung over chairs, ties askew. And among them was a man with a bushy mustache – the man who'd followed her and Michael that afternoon in the grey sedan.

The band is there to meet us
Old friends to greet us

Ida stared at him, shocked, hoping she was seeing things wrong.

'What is it?' asked Jacob, noticing she'd become distracted by something.

'That man at the table with Capone,' she said. 'He was the one that was following us this afternoon.'

'Which man?'

She pointed him out to Jacob, and he turned to look at the man.

'I know him. His name's Sacco. I was in the Second District station a few months back when he was getting hauled through it, kicking up a fuss.'

'What do you know about him?'

'Not much. Just that he's in charge of one of the Outfit's liquor runs.'

As he said the last, a gap in the crowd appeared once more, and through the gap, Sacco turned and saw them, and for an instant he and Ida stared at each other and time seemed to slow.

> *That's where the line and the dark folks meet*
> *A heaven on earth, they call it Basin Street*

Then the gap closed again, and Ida and Jacob looked at each other and when the crowd parted once more, Sacco was standing, saying his goodbyes to his friends, and heading for the exit. They watched him flit in and out of the crowd and then he stepped through the front doors and was gone.

> *Now, you're glad you came with me*
> *Down the Mississippi*

Jacob turned to look at Ida with a concerned expression on his face.

'You okay?' he asked.

'Sure, I'm fine.'

'You maybe want to head back home?'

> *We took a trip in a land of dreams*
> *And floated down the river down to New Orleans*

'No. I'm fine,' she said, shaking her head. She thought once more about hurricanes and storms, and realized she was a daughter of all that, and she had nothing to fear. She smiled and led him to the dance floor and they swayed along to the music and the energy that was washing about the place like so much rain.

46

Dante dressed in dark, inconspicuous clothes and together with the dog, left the hotel and jumped into the Blackhawk. It was pouring with rain outside, just the kind of weather he didn't want for his trip up to the Millersville Roadhouse. He drove around the empty, rain-washed streets of the Gold Coast for a quarter of an hour, hoping to shake off any tails who might be following him, then he headed north out of the city, through the Bungalow Belt of Bennett pre-cut houses, and the ring of forges and steel plants, out into the hinterland beyond.

About three hours into the drive he arrived at Millersville, an insignificant lakefront place where the only sign of life was the gas station at the end of town. Dante pulled in and filled up and asked the attendant if there was anywhere he could get a drink round there and the attendant sighed and said there was the roadhouse a couple of miles along and he explained how to get there.

Dante carried on driving and after a few minutes he turned right onto a gravel track which sloped down toward the lake and afforded him a bird's-eye view of the water down below, stretching all the way to the horizon. Either side of the track was a wood thick with pine trees and dripping with rain, through which he could see lights shining. He turned a bend and the road-house came into view – a long, single-storied building, squat and wooden, crowned with a shingle roof. There was an open space in front of it where dozens of cars had been parked, illuminated by spotlights on posts. Among the sedans and coupes, there were trucks and vans, the odd tractor, and speedsters with jacked-up suspensions – the super-powered cars bootleggers used to run cat-roads and county-line blockades.

Dante parked up as near to the track as he could, reversing the car into a spot so that it was ready to accelerate out of there if he had to leave in a hurry. He pocketed his Colt and the silencer, then stepped out into the rain, and his foot sank into the mud of the parking lot. As he pulled his foot out of the mire, the dog bounded across the seats and out into the darkness, and Dante cursed his luck. Despite the rain he left one of the windows half open so the dog could get back in if it needed to, then he set off toward the roadhouse.

As he approached he could hear the dull thud of music emanating from the building over the sound of the downpour. There was a man standing in front of the entrance, a huge man with a five-day stubble, wearing blue jeans and a red lumberjack shirt. He gave Dante the once-over, then swung open the door, and the roar of good times spilled out into the night. Dante nodded, wiped his feet on the canvas sacking laid out in front of the door, and stepped into a brightly lit, spacious room.

There were people everywhere, men, kids from the local farms, old-timers huddled together in booths, sporting girls looking for marks. There was a band on the stage, playing jug music, and a dance floor in front of the stage where drunk couples were swinging around.

Dante walked through the crowd scanning the faces, looking for anyone familiar. He got to the bar and ordered a beer and as he sipped it, he inspected the surroundings as subtly as possible, trying to figure out if there was anything there that could possibly be connected to the poisoning back in Chicago. He'd spent the day making phone calls and paying visits, trying to gauge what anyone knew about the place. But no one knew anything at all, and now Dante was here, the place seemed too far away and provincial to be associated with a sophisticated hit on Chicago's politicians, and he began to wonder if the waiter had got things wrong, had misheard the delivery drivers when they mentioned the roadhouse as the source of the poison booze.

Dante drank his beer and ordered another, and midnight came and went and more people arrived and the place got rowdier, the music faster, the dancing more frenetic. He finished his drink and headed for the outhouses in the yard at the rear of the building. He stepped into the night air and trotted through the rain, across a stretch of mud to a row of four stalls lined up over a cesspit. He entered one, relieved himself, then waited for the men in the stalls next to him to leave. Then he stepped back out, checked the coast was clear, and looked around. Just behind the stalls was a fence that ran parallel to the roadhouse itself, cutting off the view of whatever was hidden in the rest of the yard. Dante walked along the fence and heard barking. He guessed there were guard dogs on the other side of the fence and wondered what might be there for them to protect.

He scrambled onto the fence, which was slippery with rainwater, and hoisted himself to the top, and looked about. On the other side was a clearing as large and as muddy as a football field, which stretched all the way to the tree line in the distance, where the hill descended toward the lakeshore. He couldn't see the guard dogs, but near the middle of the field was a low wooden shed where he guessed they must be locked up.

He hauled himself over the top of the fence, and dropped down as quietly as he could into the clearing.

To one side was a track that led back around to the front of the building, and to the side of that track three vans were parked up. Dante walked over and inspected them. They were the same kind of vans the Outfit used for deliveries to Chicago. Inconspicuous enough, till you looked inside and saw them full of crates that were strangely free of any markings or stamps. Dante thought about the Outfit's whiskey routes. Most of the organization's liquor came from New York, courtesy of Frankie Yale, and there was the other route through Detroit, the mosquito boats that crossed the river there. But there was also the third, much smaller route that delivered bonded liquor from the warehouses and distilleries of Minneapolis and Milwaukee to Chicago. These vans had to be from that route, diverted to stop at this roadhouse. Whoever was in charge of that route must know the roadhouse, must somehow be involved.

Dante checked the vans more carefully, and that was when he noticed where they were parked – at the end of a path that led down the hill to the lakeshore. Maybe whatever it was the vans were picking up was coming in via the lake. He hunched over by the side of the van while he took the Colt from his pocket and affixed the silencer to it. The silencer wouldn't do much to stop any gunshots from being heard, but it dampened down the muzzle flash, meaning he could shoot the gun in the darkness of the woods without it so obviously giving away his location.

When the Colt was ready, he slipped it into his belt, and set off toward the lake, making a huge circle through the woods. After a few minutes, he came out at the other end of the field, where the forest sloped down toward the lake. From where he was standing he could see a track winding through the trees to a secluded bay below him where, half hidden among the beach grass, a speedboat was pulled up onto the pebbles. It was as good a place as any to bring in shipments. A boat from Canada could anchor a mile or so out, and the speedboat could make trips out to the larger vessel to bring a load to shore. But the speedboat was tiny; a large shipment of alcohol would have meant it going back and forth to the larger boat all night.

So what the hell were they moving through the place if not booze? What was less bulky than booze but just as valuable?

And in an instant everything fell into place, as if every clue and piece of information he'd come across since he'd arrived in

Chicago had been tossed into the air and had fallen to the floor in perfect alignment. He thought about the ease with which he could pick up his dope from the man in Bronzeville; the fact that it was the same stuff he got in New York; the line of bedraggled junkies waiting outside the scrapyard; the fact that the city was starting to flood with the drug despite Capone's distaste for it. He thought about what Red had told him in the pool hall, about the city changing, and people arriving from New York, and now he realized what he'd meant. Red was a heroin dealer, would know first-hand what was going on.

Dante thought back to his connections in New York, the routes they had set up for getting the stuff into the country, Turkey to Marseilles to Canada to New York. But now someone had started to move it from Canada into Chicago, too. Against Capone's wishes. It was sailed down and dropped off at the roadhouse and driven a few hours into the city and distributed there through a network that was already well established. And that was the great irony – they were doing it in Capone's own trucks, trucks the police knew not to interfere with.

It explained the poisoning. Someone was trying to get Capone out of the way. He was the biggest block to consolidating a heroin line into the city. Whoever was in charge of Al's northern whiskey run was the traitor. Dante just needed to get back to Chicago and make a phone call and he would have solved it all. Simple except for the fact that it put Dante in danger. It was the same French-Turkish dope he got back home and the same route through Canada – which meant the people behind it were the men he associated with back in New York.

His friends.

A chilling hollowness filled him, a sense of loneliness rather than betrayal. He didn't feel anxious at the revelation that he had fewer friends than he'd supposed, and more enemies. He felt foolish. But he supposed anxiety would come soon enough.

As he was heading back to his car, he heard a noise, saw a flashlight cutting through the forest. He ducked down low, and scanned the surroundings. He saw the man in the lumberjack shirt who'd been standing by the entrance, side by side with another man, checking the vans in the yard, looking at the footsteps in the mud there. Dante cursed himself for being sloppy, and he crept backwards through the trees. Then he heard a noise in front of him. Barking. They'd set the dogs on him, and from the sound of it, the dogs had picked up his scent.

He turned and ran, looking behind him, seeing the beam of the flashlight, black shapes bounding toward him. The incline made his knees and thighs burst with pain, left him out of breath, and the men were getting closer, the barking louder, and he turned around to check where they were, and he tripped on a tree root and a searing pain ripped through his ankle, and the next thing he knew he was on the ground, the muddy earth smacking into the side of his face.

He spun about to see the two men step through the tree line and come to a stop. The one in the lumberjack shirt was holding two leashes, at the ends of which strained two Dobermans, black and lean, all muscles, claws and teeth. The other man was older, wearing a Stetson and a light grey summer suit; he had a shotgun in one hand, and a flashlight in the other. He stared coolly at Dante a moment through the gloom, then he turned the beam onto Dante's face, blinding him.

'Settle!' the man in the lumberjack shirt shouted. 'Settle!'

And the two dogs stopped their foamy barking and sat on their hind legs and panted. And the two men stared at Dante, and in the silhouette world he could hear the rain, and the distant jug-band music bleeding out into the night.

'Drop your gun or we'll loose the dogs,' said the older man.

Dante frowned and turned to see his Colt still in his hand. He couldn't remember taking it from his belt. If he relinquished the gun, he was as good as dead. Tortured to tell them what he knew and then shot and buried in the forest, or fed to the dogs. But if he didn't relinquish it, the dogs would rip him apart, and so would the shotgun. He certainly couldn't outrun them with his now injured ankle.

'We ain't gonna tell you twice,' said the man.

Dante didn't move and the man sighed, turned to his companion and nodded, and the companion reached down to unleash the chain from the Dobermans and as he did so, the dogs began to bark and snarl and strain against their leashes, almost pulling the man over with their strength. Dante stared at the dogs, two bullets of muscle.

And then there was a noise from the tree line and the man with the flashlight turned and a shape bounded out of the trees. His dog, but changed somehow; it was vicious, a stray, all teeth and claws, the fighting dog that he'd seen that first night at the beach. It jumped and sank its teeth into the lumberjack's fist. Dante fired off a shot at the suited man, and there was a flashing in front of him, and the man spun about and fell, and the beam of the flashlight pirouetted through the darkness and thumped into the undergrowth.

Dante fired again, caught the second man, and then the Dobermans were free. He aimed at them and emptied the chamber. But it was too late. In the stretch of ground illuminated by the dropped flashlight he saw that the two Dobermans had already torn his dog apart. With a sickening feeling, knowing there was nothing he could do, he stumbled to his feet, put his weight on his ankle, and ran as best he could through the last of the muddy woods.

He reached the roadhouse, ran around its side, and prayed they hadn't slashed the tires of the Blackhawk or disabled it in some other way. He reached it, fumbled the keys from his pocket, got in, gunned the accelerator, barreled onto the approach road and got the hell out of there.

As he swerved the car onto the main road back to Chicago, a

jittery feeling washed over him, a sense of safety mixed with aftershocks of fear. And it was only then that he noticed the steering wheel was slick with blood. And he looked at his hands and his arm, and his sleeve was dripping with the stuff, gushing out of a hole in his upper arm.

He pulled over to the side of the road and eased his jacket off, the pain suddenly excruciating. He rolled up his sleeve and inspected his arm, but he couldn't see much of the shotgun wound for the blood and gore. He tried to think what he could use to make a tourniquet. He took off his shirt and ripped off a sleeve, and after folding it over a few times, he managed to tie it up above the injury and the pump of blood slowed. Then he looked through his jacket for the tin box with his needle and dope, and he managed to make up a spike despite his shaking hands, and he injected himself and within a few moments the thudding pain in his arm had faded into nothingness and he took a moment just to breathe.

The junk mixed with his adrenaline, the cocktail of it all surging through him, and with it came a flood of emotion, and he hunched over the steering wheel and for the first time in years he cried, and felt ashamed of himself for doing so.

He wasn't sure how much time passed, if it was moving quick or slow; he seemed to enter some timeless state, the sadness and panic and relief all flowing through him, making his heart race, each sob more painful than the dull throbbing in his arm and ankle. He knew he had to move or he'd bleed to death, but despite knowing this, his body didn't act. Maybe he wanted to stay where he was and pass out and never feel anything again.

But eventually, through no effort of his own, the tears dried, and his chest stopped heaving, and he opened his eyes and it was as if he'd woken from a dream. The rain had stopped, the air was fresh and clean, scented with the smell of the pine forest. He looked up at the lonely, rain-washed road in front of him and saw that above the earth a new day was beginning, sunlight sprinkled across the sky as soft and yellow as sawdust.

And the beauty made him start sobbing all over again. But he wound down the window, rested his damaged arm on it, and tried to focus on the pain, knowing it would keep him in the here and now.

Then he started the car and wondered if he'd make it back to Chicago before passing out.

47

Ida and Jacob awoke in the cool of morning, soothed, refreshed, emptied of their dreams. They ate breakfast at the kitchen table and when they'd finished Ida called the office and found out a message had been left for them by the go-between, with the address of Coulton's apartment.

She took down the details on a scrap of paper and stared at the address. There it was, the bloodstained apartment Gwendolyn had been to before she disappeared. She knew roughly where it was, one of the desolate streets between West 47th and the Grand Trunk Railroad, part of the slash of slums that ran down the edge of the Stockyards like a scar.

Ida felt a sense of relief as she looked at it, sure they would get their break there, that the solution to the mystery was in that apartment, that they were just a step away from finding out what had happened to Gwendolyn.

She called Michael and arranged the details, then they headed out. They walked along streets that had been washed cool by the rain, the fire escapes and street signs still dripping with it, the sweetness still hanging in the air. They sidestepped puddles muddy with weeks of summer dust, and reached the tram stop and waited, looking up at the sky, which was still laden with clouds, appraising the chance of another storm.

The tram dropped them off near the corner of 47th and South Loomis, a block from Coulton's address. Michael arrived in a Pinkerton car, parked up, and they walked over to the apartment, passing the industrial buildings and factories that lined the outer edge of the Stockyards. A lucrative industry in slaughterhouse by-products had emerged in the shadow of the abattoirs – businesses that used the leftovers to produce leather and soap, shoe polish, glue, violin strings and perfume – and it was these factories that littered the area.

As they walked toward the address, around the puddles and ruts that blotched the street, Ida could see why Coulton had picked it; the whole area felt abandoned, suffused with vacancy, and the desolation must only have increased after dark. She imagined what it must have been like for Gwen to go there on the night she disappeared.

When they reached the address, they saw it was on a run-down, low-rent kind of street, nothing much more than a mud track, that dwindled out into a hinterland of warehouses and machine-shops. Despite the night's rain, the air was heavy with the smell of the slaughter yards just beyond.

They reached the building and checked the front doors: locked. Ida bent down and peered through the keyhole – an empty hallway, dusty and neglected. They checked the labels by the buzzer but all the names had faded. They buzzed the apartments but no one answered. Then Michael looked up and down the deserted street and shrugged.

'No one around,' he said. 'Ida?'

She kneeled in front of the keyhole, took the picks from her pocket and got to work on the door. After a few minutes the lock clicked open and Michael and Ida stepped inside. They had agreed that the two of them would go in and search, while Jacob kept watch. They checked the mailboxes in the lobby: all of them empty and caked in a layer of dust weeks in the making.

Then they took the stairs to a lightless corridor, came to the apartment and Ida got to work with the picks once more. When she got through the door they saw the rooms inside were large and sparsely furnished, with the eerie emptiness of a theater set. They went through every room, checking no one was home and the place was free of traps, and while Michael made a last sweep in one of the bedrooms, Ida stood guard at the living-room windows.

She saw Jacob in the street below, smoking a cigarette in the drizzle that had started up. On the opposite side of the street stood a row of factories, and beyond them the Stockyards. Ida had never looked down on them from a height before, and from this new angle she could really take in their immensity: the endless abattoirs, the canals and railroads, the sidings where the animals were unloaded; and closest of all, on the very edge of the Yards, the pens where the animals were held before being taken off to the killing floors.

Each pen was constructed of wooden fences arranged into a perfect square, and made up part of a grid that covered hundreds of acres of ground. The geometry of it all was so structured and planned that Ida was reminded of city blocks.

Michael returned to the living room and nodded at her and they got to work turning the place over. They did it systematically, sifting through rooms and corridors, wardrobes and closets. They ran their hands along the tops of lamps, the undersides of sinks, the backs of sofas, the box-springs of beds, the seams of the suits hanging in wardrobes. Like blind men they groped every surface, sculpted every void.

Ida had expected to find something useful in the apartment, something to help her figure out Coulton's whereabouts, or Severyn's, or some clue as to what they'd done with Gwendolyn, or discover details of their plan to set the city on fire.

Instead, nothing.

They finished and looked at each other in exasperation.

'It's a bust,' she said.

Michael nodded, looking equally frustrated by this latest dead end.

They returned to the front door and Ida went into the bathroom quickly to wash the grime from her hands. As she was about to turn on the faucet, she noticed something in the sink, a thin line of residue creeping toward the plughole. She called Michael and he came in to look at it, too – a sticky tar of dried black particles.

'Mud?' he said, frowning, and Ida thought of the morning's rain. Had someone been in there just now? Had they, by a fraction, missed someone come in off the streets, washing the mud from his hands or boots? Michael peered at her, and they made their way back to the front door, pressed an ear against it, waited.

Silence, except for the rain outside.

They left the apartment to see the drizzle had turned into a rain shower which had sent Jacob off to the awning of a building on the opposite side of the street.

'What did you find?' he asked when they'd joined him.

But before they could answer, a man sauntered round the corner, an Hispanic in his early twenties, and Ida thought of the tramp's description of the two men that had dumped the girl off the bridge. The man looked up and saw the three of them huddling under the awning, and a surprised look crossed his face, and he slowed to a stop, turned and ran.

'You two follow him,' said Michael. 'I'll get the car.'

Ida and Jacob sprinted after the boy. As they ran, she heard a car behind her, too quick to be Michael. Her pulse skittered and she turned to see a coupe screeching toward them, its wheels splaying mud. She caught a glimpse of the men inside raising tommy guns to the windows and realized they'd been caught in an ambush.

Just as the sound of gunfire split the air behind them, they ducked down an alleyway on the Stockyards side of the street. But they'd turned into a dead end, a chain-link fence stretching across the alley's other end. Beyond the fence, Ida could see the grid of wooden animal pens.

'Come on,' said Jacob. And they ran down the alley and climbed the fence, which was slick with the rain, praying they could get over it in time. Ida heard the coupe screech to a halt behind them and turned to see three men enter the alley. She and Jacob clambered over the top of the fence and dropped into the animal pens on the other side. They landed in a mire of mud and manure, and Jacob winced as pain coursed through his bad leg. Then the guns roared, setting the animals off squealing and jostling.

She nodded to Jacob, and they burst into a run, keeping low, hopping out of the pen and running along the mud track beside it. Behind them, the men were still spraying the space with bullets and as Ida and Jacob ran through the haze of machine-gun fire and rain mist, she caught glimpses of blood, of trapped animals ripped apart, sending a horrific squealing into the air.

They reached the last of the pens, dropped down behind it and took a moment to get their breath back. Ahead of them was an empty space, the muddy no man's land between the pens and the dozens of railroad tracks and telegraph wires running all the way to the slaughterhouses beyond. On the other side of the tracks were some sidings, packed with boxcars and cargo containers, then further on the station, where there were people, and public spaces, and safety.

Behind them the shooting stopped and they turned to see that the three men had shouldered their guns and were climbing the chain-link fence. One of them was tall and thin, with black hair slicked back, but from that distance, Ida couldn't tell if he had scars on his neck or not.

'How's your leg?' she asked Jacob.

'Hurting like hell, but I can run on it if I have to.'

'Except we don't have time to run,' she said.

'I know.'

Either they stayed where they were and engaged the men in a gunfight, which they were sure to lose, or they ran across the open space and got mowed down.

Then one of the cows inside the pen they were leaning against kicked a post and it rocked violently, causing Jacob to frown.

'Shoot your gun a couple of times at the men,' he said.

'I can't waste bullets.'

'Trust me.'

She frowned, got her Colt out, got it steady in her hands, then jumped up, spun about, sighted the three men through the rain, and let off two shots. The men saw her and the place erupted with the roar of gunfire once more and at the sound of it the cattle became even more overwrought.

Ida ducked back down behind the fence and Jacob ran along the edge of the pens, opening up their latches as he went. Cattle burst from them in all directions. He'd started a stampede. A rampage. Cover.

He ran back, grabbed her hand and they sprinted out into the wasteland, running for the railroad tracks on its far side. And then they were hopping over the tracks, heading toward the siding. They reached the first of the boxcars, and got onto its far side.

Safety. For now.

They got their breath back and looked at each other, then peered through the space in the boxcar back to the carnage on the other side of the tracks. The cattle must have smashed into other pens and freed more animals because now there were dozens of cows and pigs running about the space, and there were dozens of others lying prostrate on the ground. And through the shifting bodies they could see the men approaching, the fire spitting from their guns, all the more orange for the heavy blue rain. Soon they would be in range, and the bullets would be pinging against the iron of the boxcars.

Then the shooting stopped, and there was just the distant bleat and whine of the animals, the sharp violin of the wind across the telegraph wires, the raindrops hitting the mud.

They heard the sound of someone running, scurrying along the far side of the boxcars. Then they made their way down the track, peering into each boxcar they passed, each one delineating a perfect cube of emptiness. Until the fourth one, where they found the source of the noise, a cadre of hobos, homeless men who had made the rolling tenements of the trains their home, disturbed by the chaos as they waited for the boxcars to be linked to locomotives and whisked across the continent. The men looked up at them through the gloom, cowering in the darkness.

Then the world behind them exploded in a salvo of bullets and the air was filled with the rapid anger of the guns pinging off the boxcar walls. They crouched and ran, rolled under one of the boxcars, stayed there in the darkness as shots bloomed in the mud around them, clanking off the rails.

Eventually the gunshots stopped, and Ida heard footsteps, and she turned to look at Jacob. But Jacob wasn't there. She was alone under the boxcar. Her heart pounded, pulsing with dread. She had felt his hand in hers as they ran. Now he was alone without a gun, and someone was approaching.

Then she realized she had made tracks in the mud. Tracks anyone with a brain could follow. She got onto her elbows and crawled along the underneath of the car. And then she saw a pair of muddy boots approach, stop, kneel down to inspect the tracks. She looked at the puddles of water in the mud. On the surfaces of the puddles were reflected the last of the clouds in the sky, and the face of the man just a few feet away from her. A long face, thin and drawn, and underneath it, scars all across the man's neck.

Severyn.

All he had to do was look under the boxcar and he'd find her. Then, bizarrely, Severyn looked up and smiled, a smile as hard as white marble. He stood and turned in the other direction, and Ida couldn't see what was going on.

'Out,' he said, issuing a command in that whisper she'd heard so much about, gravelly and cut up, as if filtered through broken glass. Then there were footsteps and a single burst of gunfire and someone collapsed into the mud in front of her, just inches from her face, and she realized with a sickening sensation it was Jacob.

Reality unspooled and Ida's heart whirred and she wanted to scream. Jacob turned to look at her, and he smiled, but she could see he was already delirious, blood pouring from a hole in his chest. He coughed up blood and shuddered and then a second round of gunfire burst through the air right next to her and she closed her eyes. And when she opened them she knew Jacob would never move again.

Her world cleaved away and pins of fear avalanched down her spine, and then an unholy anger took hold of her. She scurried out from the other side of the car, walked back around to its corner, raised her gun, took a breath, and wheeled about, ready to shoot Severyn dead.

But he wasn't there; the space was empty save for Jacob's body. Her heart sank and she had to force herself not to look down at him. But she couldn't help herself, and the rage sparked her spirits once more. She looked around and saw a dozen or so boxcars being shunted along toward the station, moaning and creaking, moving as slowly as a herd of elephants. She walked along them, her hands tense as they held her Colt, arms straight, muscles straining, like she was stretching to keep the gun as far away from her heart as she could.

As each boxcar passed, a half a second gap appeared between its end and the start of the next car, a gap through which she could see what was on the other side of the tracks. After the fifth car passed, she caught a glimpse of one of the men through the shuttering gap. His back was to her, but she knew it wasn't Severyn.

She had a couple of seconds till the next gap appeared. She eased back the hammer. The gap appeared. The man was facing her now. She shot him on instinct – twice in the forehead. The gap closed. A boxcar went past. The gap reappeared. Empty sky. Then another boxcar. Then the herd of rusting mammoths was gone, moving off toward the station, and there was the dead man lying on the other side of the rails.

She stepped over to him and pulled the tommy gun from his grip. It felt heavy in her hand after her own much smaller .45. She checked that the gun was working, had rounds in it, was ready to fire. She holstered her Colt, and for a moment inspected the man she had killed.

Then she walked over to the cargo stacks, put her back against one of them and looked about for any signs of movement. She heard the sound of sirens in the distance, the animals close by, the rain. And then footsteps.

She followed the sound with her gaze, and saw Severyn, halfway across the no man's land, heading back toward the pens. She grimaced and squeezed the trigger and the tommy burst into life, and the force of it smacked her back against the crates, the bullets spraying crazily. She eased her finger off the trigger and was about to run after him when she heard a voice.

'Put the gun down.'

Ida turned to see him, the third man, in amongst the maze of cargo stacks behind her. He'd found her by the sound of the gun going off, by her stupidly giving away her location. He was a tall man, with a close-cropped brown beard, wearing a suit and bow tie and heavy boots.

'Put the gun down,' he repeated flatly.

Her spirits sank and she tossed the tommy to the ground, leaving it to the suction of the mud. He grinned at her, revealing yellow teeth, one of them snapped in half, a rough edge where it had cracked away, the grooves clotted with nicotine tar. He raised his tommy to his shoulder and closed one eye and a delta of wrinkles rose up on the side of his face. Ida's heart thumped out of her chest and in the distance she heard the low of a cow.

Then two red flowers bloomed on the man's forehead, and there was the crack of gunshots, and with a surprised expression, the man fell backwards, squeezed the trigger, and a spray of bullets arced through the air, and clanged against the cargo stack to Ida's side. Then the bullets ran out, and as the rain landed on the gun's burning-hot nozzle, the raindrops turned instantly to vapor, and wisps of steam sashayed into the air.

Ida turned to see Michael standing behind her, frozen, battered by the rain, his arms still raised, his Colt still pointed at the man he'd shot. Michael looked at her, then she looked at the dead man, lying in a puddle, blood streaming from his forehead into his open mouth, over those yellow teeth. Then she was crying into Michael's chest, and he drew her in and hugged her, and they stayed like that till the police arrived. And when she eventually opened her eyes, her view was of the space over Michael's shoulder, the space where Severyn had disappeared, the muddy field where animal corpses lay, steam rising from their spilled insides, the emptied pens, the great city beyond them, the buildings pale in the haze of rain.

She tried her hardest to stare at the view, and not the image in her head of Jacob lying dead in the mud. But she couldn't do it, and her sense of loss increased, and she sobbed all the more.

PART SEVEN

IMPROVISATION

'For the first time, instruction on the Thompson Sub-Machine Gun was given to a number of Detective Division Squads. This instruction embraced the nomenclature of the weapon; dismounting and assembling; carrying and handling the weapon, as well as firing same.'

CITY OF CHICAGO POLICE DEPARTMENT
ANNUAL REPORT, 1928

48

Michael sat in the holding room in the 18th District station, picked up the phone and dialed.

'Hello, Provident Hospital.'

'Hello, ma'am, I'd like to speak to Annette Talbot, please. She's a nurse on the burns ward.'

'Who's calling, please?'

'It's her husband.'

'One moment, I'll put you through to the ward phone.'

As Michael waited, the silence was disturbed only by the ticking of the clock on the wall. He turned to look at it: five seventeen p.m. Only a few hours since the shoot-out, but it felt like a lifetime.

'Hello. Burns ward.'

'Hello, ma'am. My name's Michael Talbot. I'd like to speak to my wife Annette, please. She's a nurse on the ward.'

'I'm sorry, sir, this line's not for personal staff calls.'

'I understand that, ma'am, but there's been a family emergency. I need to speak to her urgently.'

There was silence on the other end of the line as the woman decided.

'One moment, please,' she said eventually. 'She's out on the ward. I'll need to go fetch her.'

He heard the phone at the other end being put down and footsteps against a floor, receding into the distance, and then a few seconds later more footsteps, getting louder.

'Michael,' said Annette, her voice rustling down the line. 'What's happened?'

'Nothing. Everything's okay . . . I'm really sorry, but . . . you're going to have to leave.'

'Leave town?'

'Yeah.'

There was silence. She knew what it meant. They'd already had to do it once before, three years earlier. Ever since then they'd been prepared: there were money stashes in the house, and in the bank; there were bags of clothes at one of Annette's friends; there was another friend in Detroit who ran a guest-house; there were excuses already prepared for their absence. Annette had the sense not to ask Michael what the danger was, but he knew when they saw each other next they would have the argument, and he already felt terrible about it.

'Is this to do with the rich girl?'

'Yeah.'

'I see,' she said. 'Detroit?'

'Yeah. Get the kids out of school now.'

'Is it safe to go home before we leave?'

'Better not.'

Silence.

'Better not?' she repeated.

'I'm sorry to have to put you through this,' he said weakly, asking himself what kind of man put his own family under siege. More than once.

'I'll call you tonight when you're settled in,' he said.

'All right.'

'Annette, this is the last time. I promise you that.'

But she put down the phone and cut the connection.

He rubbed his temples and took a moment. He imagined Annette going home and telling the children they had to leave, imagined them rushing down a platform to catch a train. Then Ida's image rose into his mind. After the firefight he had led her through the lines of police, sat with her through the initial questioning and the drive back to the station. The whole time she was quiet, withdrawn, shocked, the blanket they'd given her wrapped tight around her shoulders. They gave their statements separately, then Michael had asked to use a phone, and had been directed to the room he was in now.

He listened to the ticking of the clock once more and made another call, this one to the Pinkertons. He explained what had happened, where he was, and the need for a car and a safe house. Once it was arranged, he turned and stepped into the corridor and was surprised to see Walker, his friend from the State's Attorney's, standing there. Michael hadn't seen him since the baseball game and for some reason he found his reappearance at the station unsettling. Walker was talking to two detectives, and he must have sensed Michael staring at him, because he turned Michael's way, then cut the conversation short and headed over.

'I just read your witness statement, and Ida's,' he said, motioning to the files he had in his hands. 'I'm sorry, Michael.'

'Can I have a look at Ida's?'

Walker passed one of the files to Michael and he scanned through it, and it was only then he realized the full horror of what had happened in the Stockyards. Severyn had gunned down Jacob right in front of Ida, just a few inches from her face. No wonder she was wrapped up so tight.

He read it back once more. She might have been shook up but she'd kept everything in the statement as vague as possible: the address, the descriptions of the people involved, the reason they were there, those she suspected. The detectives must have known they were railroading them, but they'd probably hold off till they spoke to Pinkerton brass and figured out what the hell was going on. And when Michael's bosses did find out they'd been investigating the Van Haren case against orders, they'd be suspended, then sacked.

'Have the two dead shooters been identified?' he asked.

'One of 'em,' said Walker.

'Can I get a look at his sheets?'

Walker nodded. 'Not here, though. There's an interview room upstairs. Forty-seven. Gimme five minutes.'

Michael nodded and headed for the stairs, stopping by the washrooms on the way. He walked in, and splashed water on his face. He looked at himself in the mirror, staring past the scars and the wrinkles and the bags under his bloodshot eyes, past the black voids in his pupils, staring past everything till he was staring at nothing, and a chilling emptiness filled him. And in that emptiness materialized the image of the man he had sent into the abyss a few hours earlier, and he wondered if it was the fifth or sixth man he had killed, and a gut-churning self-disgust filled him that he didn't have the decency to remember them all.

Then another, stronger feeling: guilt at having put his family in danger. He should have seen it coming, he should have seen the risk. But he hadn't. He made a vow to himself, that whatever happened, he'd be resigning from the Pinkertons. He'd put this case to bed, and that would be it. He'd look for less dangerous ways to make a living.

Walker was already in Room 47 when Michael arrived. He had the reports on the table and two paper cups of terrible coffee and a look of concern on his face.

'Before I give you these, I want you to tell me what happened,' Walker said. 'Not what you put in the statement – the real deal, all of it.'

Michael decided to put his trust in the man and told him everything, not just as a means to get the files, but because he needed to talk to someone about it. He talked and Walker listened and nodded, and at the end he blew air through his teeth.

'This is quite the mess.'

'Yes, it is.'

'And maybe more messy than you think. The guns the shooters had – they were police issue. That's going to complicate things.'

Michael thought a moment and nodded.

'Best get started then,' said Walker. 'One of the shooters we haven't identified yet. The detectives are sending his details down to the Bureau of Investigation in case he's an out-of-towner.'

Walker picked up one of the files and opened it. 'The other one was Abraham Roth,' he said, passing the file to Michael. Michael inspected the mugshot pinned to the top sheet. It was the man Ida had shot.

'A low-level enforcer. Petty raps all through his teens till he got busted in a fruit bar a few years ago, and after that he went silent.'

Michael frowned, flicked through the pages of the report, looked again at the photo. He was young, early twenties, with a sinister twist to his mouth. And something stranger: makeup, mascara, most of it wiped off before the mugshot was taken, but enough still there to make him look oddly androgynous. Michael checked the date stamp on the photo against the date the man got arrested in the fruit bar and saw they were the same.

He thought back to the ambush. The Hispanic kid walking down one end of the street, the car coming from the other. Then he remembered the story Ida had told him about Coulton Junior getting busted in a sweep on a fruit bar a few years back. Maybe it was a coincidence too that one of the shooters had a similar conviction or maybe it was what connected them all.

'This bust in the bar sweep a few years ago,' said Michael. 'Can you get me a list of all the people arrested there? I reckon the Hispanic kid might have been one of them. We can get the kid's name from that and maybe an address and some KAs.'

'Sure,' said Walker. 'Gimme an hour.'

They both left the room and Michael went looking for Ida. He found her in a holding pen still looking traumatized, sitting with a female police-worker. Michael hated to see his protégée like this: shook up, pulling the blanket tight. There was something childish to the gesture, something so unlike Ida.

'How are you feeling?' he asked, sitting next to her.

She shrugged.

'I arranged for a safe house.'

'Thanks.'

'I looked through the files of one of the shooters. I think I got an angle on the Mexican kid.'

She nodded, uninterested. 'You get Annette and the kids safe?' she asked, and Michael nodded. At some point he'd have to tell Ida the details of the promise he'd made to Annette, of his decision that even if they managed to make it through it all without losing their jobs, he'd be resigning anyway.

The door opened and a beat-cop stepped in, young and bright and smiling – everything they didn't want to be around.

'There's a car outside,' he said. 'A driver from the Pinkertons.'

They drove over to the safe house in a heavy silence, the two of them staring absently out of the windows. When they arrived, Michael saw it was decent enough by Pinkerton standards: a two-room walk-up on the third floor of a greystone. Two men were stationed in the apartment, two men outside.

Ida perched herself on the sofa and said nothing.

'You want me to call anyone to be with you?' Michael asked.

Ida shook her head.

'I'm going to head off and chase down those leads,' he said, and she nodded, and Michael left her there, feeling guilty about what had happened to her, guilty about leaving her, guilty about the fact she wasn't up to carrying on the investigation just yet, and worried she might never be.

He stepped out into the street and nodded to the two Pinks parked up out front. Ida was safe, Michael's wife and children were heading out of the city. It was time to get to work.

*

He found a bar and made a call to an armorer he knew, then he drove back to the station, hustled through the place till he found Walker and the two of them found a room to talk in. Walker held up the file of a Mexican man called Arturo Vargas.

'I went through all the names from that bust. This was the only one that matched,' he said, passing Michael the file. Michael took it and opened it up and recognized the face of Arturo Vargas as the shifty-looking boy from the ambush, probably the boy who had helped Severyn throw the dancer's body off the bridge. He checked the file. A rent boy with a history of soliciting offenses and getting rousted in bars and brothels. Michael noted down his home address, his known associates. The address would have been abandoned long ago, but it was a good enough starting point.

'Can you get me info on these KAs?' said Michael.

'Already did,' said Walker, and he handed him a list of names and addresses.

'Thanks. Are the police onto any of this?'

Walker shook his head. 'Not while I've got the files. Plus they're busy doing damage control on the police-issue guns, trying to figure out who they can pin it all on.'

'How long can you keep these leads hidden?'

'How long do you want?'

Michael thought. 'Twenty-four hours?'

Walker smiled. 'I'll see what I can do.'

Michael's house was dark when he got in: dark, empty and soulless with his family on the *Wolverine* to Detroit. He walked into the kitchen, found the stash spot under the sink and took out the wad of money hidden there. Then he went into the living room and sat on the sofa and didn't bother switching on any lights. He lit a cigarette and waited, looking about the place. It was strange being there alone; he couldn't remember the last time it had happened. What good a house, he thought, without a family to live in it?

He finished his cigarette and lit a second, and rolled his head from left to right, loosening up the muscles in his neck, easing the knots he sensed there. He could feel the fatigue in his muscles and bones, like he'd been exhausted for decades.

Then there was a buzzing at the door. He rose and turned on the lights and the brightness stung his eyes, and he let in the armorer. The man shuffled into the room with a great duffle bag weighing down his shoulder. He was a slight man, Chinese, clean-shaven and balding, dressed in a seersucker suit with a blue bow tie and a yellow carnation in his lapel. He'd always struck Michael as the kind of man who looked like he should be working in the theater, or as a roper in front of some vaudeville on the Michigan City boardwalk, trying to entice customers inside.

'Nice place,' the man said, putting the bag on the floor.

Michael forced a smile and nodded. The man opened the bag and laid his wares out in front of him.

'A bulletproof vest, a twenty-gauge Chesterfield pump-action, a tommy with a Cutts compensator, two cartons of shot, and four fifty-round magazines for the tommy.'

'How much?'

'All in, let's call it four hundred.'

Michael handed over the money.

'Thanks. Now, you don't happen to be in the market for any hand grenades, nitroglycerin, marijuana or cocaine?' he asked, and Michael shook his head.

'Fair enough,' said the man. 'Rental rate's seventy per subsequent week.'

'All right,' said Michael. 'Say, you deal anyone any police-issue tommies recently?'

The man shook his head. 'I stay away from police-issue anything. Too many questions.'

When the man had gone, Michael loaded the weaponry into a bag. Then he locked up the apartment and stepped out into the Chicago sunset.

He had a car, and a bag full of guns, and a list of people to see.

49

Dante hobbled into the lobby of the Drake at some point around noon. His jacket had a gunshot hole in it and was covered in blood, and his trousers and shirt were smeared with mud, and his hair was plastered to his face from the rain, and he was limping badly. All of which caused the concierges and bellboys, and customers in the bar having their teas and coffees, to stop and stare at him as he crossed the space.

'Morning, Pete,' he said to the elevator boy. The boy gawped at him, then set the elevator going and after a minute or so Dante was unlocking the door to his room and stepping inside. He took off his jacket and went over to the phone and called the direct line for the Metropole and a gruff voice he didn't recognize picked up.

'Yeah?'

'It's Dante. Who's that?'

'It's Tony. You sound rough. You all right?'

'I need a safe doctor. Now.'

'What happened?'

'I got shot. I need him here now.'

'"Here" being the Drake?'

'Yeah.'

'I'm on it. Gimme fifteen minutes. Twenty, tops.'

Dante put the phone down and his head swirled. He saw a pack of cigarettes lying next to the phone, took one out and lit it. He peeled off his shirt gingerly. Then he rummaged through his jacket for his things, made up a needle and spiked himself and while he waited for the pain to go away, and the help to arrive, he smoked the cigarette and stared at the dust swirling through the room in the sunlight.

He must have passed out because he heard a ringing at the door and he came to and shouted that the door was open. A small, pudgy man entered, holding a black leather Gladstone bag, wearing a stern expression and a dark grey business suit.

'You Dante?'

'Yeah, you the doc?'

'That I am,' said the safe doctor. 'Name's Herschel.'

The Outfit employed dozens of safe doctors, mostly men with legitimate practices, who, for a fee, would provide emergency medical services with no questions asked. The man crossed the room to where Dante was slumped on the sofa, and sat in front of him on the coffee table. He popped a pair of silver-rimmed spectacles onto his nose, and inspected Dante's arm.

'Just the arm, is it?'

'The ankle, too.'

The doctor peered at his leg a moment.

'Let's take care of the gunshot first,' he said, smiling. He went into the bathroom and returned with a bowl of steaming-hot water. He spread a towel across the coffee table, placed the bowl on it, and took his things out of the bag, setting them on the towel one by one. Then he lifted up Dante's arm once more and inspected it all over.

'Ordinarily I'd suggest a shot of morphine before we got started but I see you're already self-medicating,' he said.

The doctor cleaned the wound with padding and iodine, then he took a pair of forceps, sterilized them, and inserted them into the largest wound. Dante winced from the sheer pain of it and after a moment, the doctor pulled out a piece of shot, and then another, and then another. Each time he removed the forceps from the wound he opened them wide and a piece of metal clunked onto the glass of the coffee table.

'Well, that's the easy one done,' the doctor said, referring to the larger hole. 'These smaller ones are going to be a lot more painful.'

After the most excruciating twenty minutes of Dante's life, the doctor inspected the wounds and judged all the shot to be out of them. He cleaned them all again with iodine, took some padding and wrapped it into place with bandages.

'You're all right for now,' he said, 'but there's still a strong risk of infection. Change the bandages every few hours so they're dry and clean, and if you see any signs of infection – increased discharge from the wound, a color change, a bad smell, swelling, red streaks on your arm, a temperature, you give me a call straightaway.'

He pulled a business card from his inside pocket and placed it on the coffee table.

'And if I don't answer,' he continued, 'get straight down to the hospital. I'd hate for you to lose your arm because I was out making a house call.'

Dante nodded.

'Now let me look at that ankle.'

The doctor confirmed what Dante already suspected – a serious sprain, but no break. He prescribed rest and a raised foot for a few days and ice packs to reduce the swelling, then with another smile and a nod he went on his way, leaving behind some spare bandages and padding and a bottle of iodine.

As soon as he'd gone, Dante turned himself around on the sofa so his bad leg was propped up on the armrest and he rested his wounded arm on top of his chest and he drifted into a deep and feverish sleep where he dreamed he was being chased through some endless, primordial woods by a pack of hell-hounds, and no matter where he ran, he always came to some ravine and had to face the choice of jumping into an abyss, or being ripped apart by the dogs.

A ringing noise awoke him hours later and he opened his eyes to see the room had been plunged into a raw darkness, illuminated only by the moonlight streaming in from the windows. He wondered if he should bother getting up to answer, but the ringing continued, on and on, piercing and shrill. He eased his legs off the armrest and as he did so the blood rushed into his mangled ankle and it pulsed with pain and he thought of calling room service and asking for some ice to be brought up. Then he stood, tested his leg to see if it could take his weight, and as he did so the wounds in his arm began to throb, and he wished he had made a sling for his arm before he had fallen asleep.

He stumbled across the room, but just as he reached the phone, it stopped ringing, and he cursed his luck, and slumped down in the chair next to it and peered out of the window. He could see from the clock on the building opposite that it had just gone eleven. He called down to reception and ordered ice and some food – a cheese burger and fries and a couple of bottles of beer – and the man at the other end asked if he wanted to order anything for the dog. Dante choked out a no and put the phone down, overwhelmed by a rush of loneliness.

He switched the lights on and the place suddenly seemed strange to him, as if he was seeing it for the first time, as if it was someone else's room, and he thought again of his dream and at that moment he couldn't quite figure out who he was, what he was doing there, what calamitous series of events had led to him being half naked and bloody, in a gilded hotel room floating over a dark city. He knew the meaning of the word 'epiphany' from childhood, from having to go to Sunday School classes at his mother's insistence – a moment of realization, a sudden knowledge of self – and he wondered if the word had an opposite, if there was a word for a sudden loss of knowledge, the realization that you were bewildered and had lost your way, lost any sense of who the hell you were.

And as he was struggling to deal with the feeling, the phone recommenced its shrill ringing, and he reached over and picked it up.

'Hello?' he mumbled.

'Dante, it's Loretta. Oh, God. Where've you been? Did you hear?'

'I was out of town. Hear what?'

'Oh, God. It was in the paper. Jacob died.'

Dante's heart froze at the mention of his brother's name, and the pit of despair loomed larger.

'Jacob?' he repeated.

'It was in the paper,' said Loretta again. 'A shooting at the Stockyards. Oh, God, I'm so sorry.'

PART EIGHT

FINAL CHORUS

'There has been for a long time in this city of Chicago a colony of unnaturalized persons, hostile to our institutions and laws, who have formed a supergovernment of their own, who levy tribute upon citizens and enforce collections by terrorizing, kidnapping and assassinations. Evidence multiplies daily that many public officials are in secret alliance with underworld assassins, gunmen, rum-runners, bootleggers, thugs, ballot-box stuffers and repeaters, that a ring of politicians and public officials are conducting a number of breweries and are selling beer under police protection.'

PETITION TO CONGRESS,
BETTER GOVERNMENT ASSOCIATION IN
CHICAGO AND COOK COUNTY, 1926

Chicago Herald Tribune

THE WORLD'S GREATEST NEWSPAPER

GENERAL NEWS

FIGHT PILGRIMS ARRIVE BY AIR, LAND AND WATER
LOOP HOTELS FILLED TO CAPACITY

*Details of fight news-stories from the Dempsey and Tunney
training camps, etc. – in sporting section*

BY KATHLEEN McLAUGHLIN
(*Chicago Tribune* press service)
(Picture on back page)

Jack Dempsey, who lost the heavyweight championship of the world in a downpour of rain in Philadelphia
last year, tries tomorrow night to take it back from
Gene Tunney at Soldier Field, and it is safe to say the
sporting event is the greatest Chicago, and America,
has ever seen. The estimated audience for the bout
is 150,000 with an estimated gate of $2,500,000, the
largest in history. Trains, boats, planes and fleets of
automobiles have been mobilized by sports fans to
bring them to the fistic battle, with numerous groups
from around the country chartering their own trains
– up to one hundred extra – and existing locomotives
to the city running at double and sometimes triple
their length (tonight's *20th Century Limited* is set to
leave New York with three times the usual carriages).
And fight fans are not the only ones to be chartering
their own transportation. The *Tribune* has chartered
a speedboat so reporters and photographers can

bypass the crowds via the lake and get you the latest news first.

Meanwhile men around the country have been congregating in cigar stores, bars, hotel lobbies, street corners and trains to discuss the fight, and police have reported seeing a sharp rise in street brawls as discussions over each fighter's merits turn ugly. In the Loop, thousands of visitors are registering at the hotels, with one housing over 5,000 tonight. Taxi drivers have been complaining the pilgrims are slowing down traffic.

Among the people descending on Chicago for the fight are numerous dignitaries. Spotted so far in town at various hotels and restaurants by our reporters and informers have been: Charlie Chaplin and Douglas Fairbanks, Al Jolson, Gloria Swanson, Clara Bow, Harold Lloyd, Damon Runyon, Walter Chrysler, Ty Cobb, Somerset Maugham, nine senators, ten state governors, the Mayors of Minneapolis, St Paul, San Francisco, New Orleans, Memphis and Kansas City, Dukes and Earls from England, Princes from Africa, and even an Indian Maharaja.

While the influx continues, fight promoter Tex Rickard has revealed Chicago is awash with counterfeit tickets, with three federal secret service agents seizing over 1,000 bogus tickets from cigar stores and pool rooms in the Loop. He urged fans to buy legitimate tickets from the box office in the Palmer House Arcade, and from the ten extra ticket booths that have been opened on Michigan Boulevard between 10th and 11th Street today.

Counterfeits or not, if the gate receipt estimates are reached, Tunney is set to receive a million-dollar purse for the fight, the largest ever, with challenger

Dempsey set to receive half that. The two pugilists left their respective camps in Fox Lake and Lincolns Fields yesterday afternoon for a press conference at the Illinois Athletic Club on Michigan Avenue, causing thousands to flock there and block traffic. Below is a brief round-up of the tidbits of information revealed in the press conference. For a fuller report, please turn to the sporting section:

1) Former marine Tunney has pledged to provide every disabled marine in Chicago tickets and free transportation to the fight.

2) Dempsey revealed more on his adoption by the Blackfoot Indian tribe at his training camp earlier this month. Dempsey, who claims to have Utah Cherokee blood, was christened 'Thunder Chief' by the twenty-seven braves and a chief who came all the way from their Glacier Park reservation for the ceremony.

3) When asked how they would spend the day of the fight, champ Tunney of Greenwich Village, N.Y., known for carrying with him at all times a copy of *The Rubaiyat* – a book of ancient Persian poetry – answered that he would be going for a five-mile run, then spending the afternoon reading rare manuscripts in the library of the Fred Lundin home with the British novelist Somerset Maugham. On the other hand, people's favorite Jack Dempsey revealed that after doing a similar five miles' roadwork, he would spend the afternoon playing cards with members of the press and well-wishers.

4) The *Tribune* has installed 100 special telephone trunk lines to answer calls from fight fans requesting updates on the night. An estimated 20,000 calls are expected, and we're hoping to be able to keep up with demand.

50

Ida sat on the edge of the wicker chair in the safe-house bathroom and stared up at the mourning dress hooked to the shower rail. From where she was sitting it felt like the dress was floating above her, swaying in the breeze coming in from the window, black as a flock of crows, blacker still for the grid of white tiles glowing in the sunlight behind it.

She couldn't face putting on the dress just yet, so she lit a cigarette instead, stared at her toes, at the frayed hem of her chemise, at the window above the bathtub, a rectangle of glowing sunlight, a hint of blue skies. Jacob's funeral should have been on a rainy day, a grey day of cold and wind. Instead the weather looked good: hot, sunny, not a cloud in all the heavens. There was something sad about it, that the elements refused to grieve with her.

There being no family left the police had made the arrangements. Maybe that was why it had all been done so quickly. With the autopsy out of the way, the funeral had been arranged for that afternoon, just a few days after Jacob's death. In the intervening time, Ida hadn't left the safe house at all and the day and the hour had somehow crawled up on her.

That morning a girl from the Pinkertons' personnel department had arrived with the dress and a hat to go with it. Ida could tell the dress wouldn't fit her, but it was still a nice gesture. She looked at it again, floating above her, echoing death. She took a last drag on her cigarette, ran water from the faucet over it and tossed it into the garbage. Then she stood, pulled off her chemise, reached a hand up and took death off its hanger and slipped it on.

She found the zip at the back, pulled it up, and looked at herself in the mirror over the sink. How she'd aged in just a few days. Eyes baggy, face puffy. You'd think the face would get smaller once all those tears had left it.

She didn't bother with makeup; the hat the girl from personnel had brought had a veil pinned to it. Ida sat on the edge of the chair and pulled on her stockings, slipped on her shoes. She took a moment, then stepped into the hallway.

In the two nights since Jacob had died she'd been taken with insomnia, had slept in total for maybe a couple of hours. The images and sounds of what had happened kept tumbling into her mind, making her sob, tumbling on into the vast blackness whence they came. She wondered if she could have saved him somehow. She made lists of all the things she could have done differently, cursing herself for every one of the thousand million steps that led to his death.

Most of all she cursed herself for her decision to close her eyes at the fatal moment. She had seen the gun being raised and she had closed her eyes. She heard the shots, and saw the aftermath, but the moment of death was a blank, a darkness. What if he had turned to her in that moment, looking for support, and her eyes were closed? Even though she knew it was impossible, it would still be a weight on her soul for the rest of her life. She *had* closed her eyes, and now she had to imagine the moment it happened, what it looked like, and maybe the imagining, the gap into which she was falling, was worse than the memory that would have formed if she'd allowed it to.

She remembered what Jacob had said that night after the bombing, about having the courage to not look away, and the fact she'd failed so miserably in his last moments made her anguish all the sharper.

On the few occasions she had fallen asleep, she'd woken up seconds later to wonder where she was, and then she'd remembered where and why and the fact of Jacob's dying, and the remembering was like learning of his death all over again, and she'd had to deal with the shock of it all over again, had to start mourning all over again, not only for Jacob, but for the time, just a few seconds earlier, when she was still ignorant of everything that had occurred. Best not to sleep at all than go through a trauma every time she awoke.

In the living room there were two Pinks – one of the bodyguards sitting on the sofa, and the girl from personnel, staring out of the window, a hand to her chin. They turned to look at Ida as she entered, and the girl smiled at her, comforting, patronizing. Ida had noticed she had the clarity and focus that comes sometimes from sleep deprivation, but also the irritability. She forced herself to smile back at the girl, and the girl walked over to the table, picked up Ida's hat and passed it to her. Ida put on the hat, pulled the pin from the veil, let it drop in front of her face, and the girl helped her put the pin back in. Ida thanked her and then there was movement in the hallway and Ida turned to see Michael stepping in from the corridor.

He looked rough, like he hadn't slept in years, like he was weary and sick of it all, like he was on his way to lower realms. He looked how Ida felt. He came over to her and she saw that he'd shaved hastily, and had bags under his eyes to match her own, and his knuckles were scuffed and cut, his hands bruised. She guessed he'd been chasing down leads since she'd last seen him, his hands a clue as to the form the chase had taken. After a moment he took her arm and without saying a word they stepped out of the apartment.

Four Pinks were milling about on the street by the car that was waiting for them. They got in and the driver took them to the cemetery.

'How's the case going?' she asked once they were on their way, not because she really cared, but because she couldn't think of anything else to say.

'I've been working with Walker – we've managed to track

down the boy from the attack. He's at a hide-out in Pilsen. Walker's keeping an eye on him.'

'You haven't talked to him?'

Michael shook his head. 'We caught him this morning. I came here first. To see you.'

'I'm not much to look at.'

She leaned her head against his shoulder and they stayed quiet for a while.

'If you want to talk about it . . .' said Michael, and his voice had a warm concern to it, a softness that she guessed he used when he spoke to his children.

'No,' said Ida. 'What's there to say? He was just there and I couldn't save him. Just an arm's length away. And I closed my eyes . . .'

And even as she said it she started crying, and Michael squeezed her tight.

'It wasn't your fault,' he said.

She nodded but said nothing, and they stayed like that for the rest of the journey. Slowly, as the city spun past, the tears stopped and she no longer had to dab at her eyes, and at some point she propped her head up, and realized they had arrived at the cemetery.

The afternoon sun was shining down on the flower beds and lawns and chapels, making it all look picture perfect, which made Ida want to sob once more – as did the fact that the place was crawling with police and Pinks.

While the people milled about waiting for the ceremony to begin, Ida watched Severyn shoot Jacob for the millionth time, and her heart jumped and she felt like she was going to swoon, and she thought, selfishly, of how this all must be aging her and she wished she could burn her memories to ashes. Then one of the workers at the chapel asked them all to come inside, and there was Jacob in his coffin at the front. Closed casket.

The priest made his way through the prayers for the dead, the

Mass for the dead, the absolution – and then they were shuffling out again, into the cemetery, to the grave, to the void.

The coffin arrived and the priest said the Lord's Prayer and another shorter prayer and a final petition for Jacob to rest in peace and they all lined up to throw soil on the coffin. As they waited, Ida noticed a man standing at a distance to the other mourners, near a family tomb, watching the ceremony. He wasn't one of the Pinkerton men and he didn't look like a cop. He had one arm in a sling, and he was wearing a hat and an odd pair of green sunglasses. A journalist maybe? She wondered how he'd gotten through the security cordon.

Despite the hat and the glasses obscuring his face, there was something vaguely familiar about him, and through the fuzz in her head she realized what it was: he reminded her of Jacob. She turned her attention back to the graveside and wondered with trepidation if this would be some new feature of her life, that she would forever be recognizing Jacob in people she encountered, the disparate fragments never adding up to a whole human being, leaving her with countless painful reminders, a jagged emptiness.

Soon enough they were all done at the graveside and there was more milling about and Michael told her there was to be a wake back at the 2nd District station. She told him that she wanted to stay at the graveside a bit more and he nodded and slowly the other mourners melted away, and it was just Ida standing there next to the grave, looking down at the simple bouquets.

She thought of the funerals in New Orleans, grand and beautiful and filled with music, and the gangster funerals in Chicago, pageants of flowers, and her feeling of emptiness increased. This was no send-off. And it made her angry and sad and hopeless all at the same time.

And then she heard a noise behind her and turned to see the man in the hat and the sunglasses approaching the grave, alone, a bouquet of white chrysanthemums in his hand. As he approached he nodded at her and through the fog in her head she again got the feeling that he was familiar. He put the flowers down on the grave, took off his hat and glasses, mumbled a prayer and crossed himself, then he turned around to leave and when he did so Ida caught sight of his face and saw the resemblance to Jacob – the dark hair, the green eyes, the delicate features – and it made the world slide off into a dewdrop, and she was falling, swooning, spinning, and everything went black.

51

Dante saw the girl swoon and reached out to grab her, but before he could, the place was alive with men running toward him, barreling out of the tree line, screaming, pulling service revolvers from holsters. He raised his hands, ignoring the pain in his arm, and tried to explain that she had fainted, but the men carried on coming, and soon he found himself in the center of a circle of police and Pinks pointing Colts at him.

They held him in their sights as a tall man with smallpox scars all across his face approached, looking like he was in charge of things. He gave Dante a quick look, then kneeled to see how the girl was doing. She was already coming to, looking woozy and flustered.

'Anyone got any whiskey?' he asked in a Southern accent, and one of the men in the circle pulled a hip-flask from his pocket and passed it to the tall man, who held it to the girl's lips.

'Who are you?' asked the tall man. 'How'd you get in here?'

'I'm a mourner,' said Dante. 'He was my brother.'

The tall man turned to one of the cops in the gun-circle, who nodded, confirming Dante's identity.

'Frisk him,' said the tall man, and another of the cops holstered his gun, patted Dante down and confirmed he didn't have a weapon on him.

Then the girl sat up and raised a hand to her temples. 'I'm fine,' she said. 'I guess I blacked out.'

On hearing it the tall man gestured to the others to lower their weapons, and as they did so, Dante lowered his hands.

The girl stood, shakily, leaning against the tall man, and when she was upright, she wiped some mud from the side of her dress with the flat of her palm.

'You're Jacob's brother?' she asked, and Dante nodded.

'He told me about you,' she said, in a wistful tone of voice, and Dante guessed she was troubled by his resemblance to Jacob.

'I'm sorry to have shocked you,' he said.

The girl shook her head. 'He said you'd disappeared.'

'I came back. Not long ago.'

She eyed him again, exchanged a guarded look with the tall man, and Dante studied her face, saw it was a strange mix of delicate and hard-edged, exactly the kind of girl Dante imagined Jacob would have gone for.

'The newspaper said Jacob was in the company of Pinkerton detectives when he died. I'm guessing that's you?' said Dante, turning to look at the tall man.

'Both of us,' said the girl. There was a wire of loneliness strung through her words, and Dante wasn't sure if she was Jacob's girlfriend, as he'd first imagined, or just someone he was working with.

'I'd like to talk to you then,' he said. 'To know what happened.'

The girl and the tall man exchanged looks again.

'I'll talk to him,' she said, and the tall man thought a moment, then stepped back. The girl straightened her dress and peered about her.

'Maybe a walk might clear my head,' she said, gesturing to a path snaking through the graves. Dante smiled and they stepped over to it, their shoes crunching on the gravel as they went.

'My name's Ida.'

'Dante.'

'I know. Jacob told me about you.'

'What did he say?'

'That you accidentally poisoned your family, caused Jacob's ankle to wither, then ran away.'

She said it so flatly Dante didn't know if she was deriding him or not. He shrugged.

'Yeah, that's about the size of it,' he said.

She looked at him, but said nothing, and Dante wondered if this was her personality – quiet and intense – or if the shock of Jacob's death had stained her character.

They walked past rows of gravestones, their granite sparkling in the sun, and Dante took in his surroundings, noting the Pinkerton men and cops dotted about the perfectly clipped hedges and lawns, all of them keeping Dante and the girl in their sights, guns at the ready.

'I can't believe I fainted,' she said. 'I thought you were Jacob. For a moment . . .' And she trailed off and turned away.

'I was older than him by fourteen months,' said Dante, trying to explain the similarity, but she didn't seem to hear him, so he switched subject. 'You were with him when he was killed?' he said, and the girl nodded.

'You mind telling me what happened?' he asked.

She peered down at her feet, as if her memories were down there amongst the grass. Then she looked up at him, and told him her story, how she'd been investigating a missing-persons case, and the case had led her to Jacob. She spoke in that same flat tone, businesslike, as if it had all happened to someone else, as if she was in a courtroom, relating the details to a lawyer. She didn't get ahead of herself, or miss out facts, or stumble over her words, and Dante wondered how it was that she could seem so distanced from it all. As she spoke, he learned how Jacob had spent his last few weeks, looking into a murder in Bronzeville, and how it was somehow linked to the disappearance of the heiress that the girl was seeking.

'Why was Jacob so interested in it?' Dante asked, and the girl tilted her head to the side.

'I wasn't sure of that at first, either,' she said. 'But he explained it to me before he died. It was on account of Roebuck. The Moran stooge who was killed in the alleyway. He'd broken a champagne bottle into someone's face the night he died, and when Jacob inspected his body he saw the glass shards on his hands and smelled the alcohol. He realized from the smell it was the same chemically altered stuff that had killed your family. He told me about it. How you brought some champagne round for your sister's graduation party, and how it . . . well, I guess you know better than anyone what happened. Jacob vowed if he ever came across similar booze he'd track it down.'

She carried on speaking but Dante couldn't hear; his thoughts were shrieking, his heart thumping against his chest.

'Poison booze?' he said. 'Jacob was investigating poison booze?' and he could hear the emotión in his voice, and the girl turned to look at him.

'Yeah,' she said, frowning.

'What night did the stooge die?' he asked.

'The twenty-seventh.'

The night of the poison party. Ideas began shooting through his mind like fireworks. A Moran stooge had died with poison booze on him the night of the poisoning. Moran was behind it. Moran had hooked up with some out-of-towners and a traitor in the Outfit. Jacob had stumbled onto it via his police work and had chased it down for the same reason Dante had – the poison booze that killed their family. They were investigating the same case, for the same reasons. After all these years it was still obsessing them both, and that was when it hit him – Jacob had died investigating poison booze; Jacob had died, inadvertently, because of what Dante had done all those years ago. The last member of his family had gone to the grave because of Dante, too.

He shook his head, instinctively, as if maybe by doing so he could dislodge the thought. He knew he couldn't dwell on it, he had to keep his mind on something else lest he fall into the pit once more.

'Tell me again about Roebuck's murder,' he said, his voice strained.

'Why?'

For a split second he thought about telling her the truth, because revenge was the only thing he could think of that would keep him from drowning in his guilt.

'Because I think you, me and Jacob were all looking into the same crime,' he said.

She frowned at this. 'You're investigating a crime? For who?'

'Capone.'

She paused a moment, then shook her head. 'I think maybe you should tell me first what it is you're doing in Chicago.'

As she said it, Dante looked up and saw they were reaching the end of the path, where it met the cemetery gates, and on the other side of them, a little further down the road, was a cafeteria.

Five minutes later the two of them were sitting across from each other in a booth at the back. The girl clutched her coffee mug with one hand, and raised her cigarette to her lips with the other, in an almost mechanical motion. Dante took a drag on his own cigarette and looked about the place: it was bright, airy and high-ceilinged, with large windows that caught the blast of the sun. Two Pinkertons were by the door, and another two by a car parked outside. A waitress was standing on tiptoes behind the counter, in front of an electric fan, trying to cool herself down.

Dante took a sip of his coffee, then told Ida about the poison party, how it was the same booze, the same night, how it pointed to an out-of-towner and a traitor, and now Moran. The girl asked him some questions and they got onto the subject of the two men, Coulton and Severyn, and their involvement with the disappearance and a plan they supposedly had hatched to turn the city upside down. And it all fitted perfectly with what he had been investigating and the solution to the mystery unfurled like a rolled-up rug.

'Chuck and Severyn found a traitor in the Outfit,' said Ida, 'and between the traitor and Moran and some out-of-town heroin connection, they were going to take out Capone. But something went wrong that night with the stooge, and Gwendolyn stumbled into it.'

'It all makes sense,' said Dante, 'apart from where these two men you're looking for got the idea for it. It doesn't sound like they're the type to be involved in something this high-level.'

'Maybe they've got a connection to someone – Moran, or the traitor, or the heroin dealers.'

'Maybe,' said Dante.

They both fell silent and thought, and after a moment, the girl frowned, as if something had just occurred to her. Then she looked up at him.

'The traitor,' she said. 'I think I know who it is. Someone from the Outfit was following us the last couple of days before Jacob died. Maybe it was him. A man called Sacco. I didn't know him, but Jacob recognized him.'

'Average height, brown mustache?' asked Dante, remembering the name, and the man, from the golf course in Burnham.

Ida nodded.

'Sounds like it's him,' said Dante. 'Did Jacob say anything about him?'

'Just that he saw him getting arrested a few months ago. And that he was in charge of one of the Outfit's whiskey runs.'

'Which one?'

'He didn't say.'

Dante mulled it over and the girl looked at him, puzzled.

'There's something else,' she said. 'If they tried to wipe out Capone once and they failed, it means they'll probably try again.'

And at this they looked at each other, and it seemed to Dante they both felt some new weight pressing down on them.

'So what are you going to do now?' she asked.

If another hit was being planned on Al, he needed to finish it as soon as possible, whether he was implicated or not.

'I need to find out if Sacco really is the traitor. And if he is, track him down,' he said. 'Before anyone else dies. Then I'll go after Severyn. If I find him, I won't save him for you.'

'I kinda figured on that,' she said.

He thought about the men in the forest, and the professional whose hotel room he'd broken into. 'There'll be more people coming,' he said.

'I kinda figured on that, too,' she replied, and took another slow drag on her cigarette and looked at him.

Dante stared back, imagining he was Jacob looking at her, trying to feel what his brother had felt, and in the silence, somewhere in his body, as real as a broken bone or a ripped muscle, the abyss opened up again.

'He forgave you,' she said out of nowhere and Dante frowned. 'Jacob?'

She nodded. 'He said you'd run away after the poisoning and he'd never seen you since. He said he was angry at first, but then the anger dwindled, and he forgave you. He missed you.'

He stared at her, not believing it. It was just what he needed to hear, just what would soothe him, and that must have been why she'd said it – she'd made it up to make him feel better.

He shook his head.

'It's true,' she said. 'He said after the anger and the blame, the sad thing was that he missed you.'

Her look was so earnest, so free of artifice, that he realized she didn't have the guile to lie about something like that, and he began to persuade himself it might be true. He swallowed down the emotion that was welling up inside him, that same despair he'd had since the roadhouse. He couldn't let the feeling take hold of him, not now. He wanted to tell her that he'd promised himself he'd visit Jacob when the case was wrapped up, but he knew how pathetic it would have sounded, and he knew if he tried to explain himself he might break down. So he swallowed the feeling and said nothing, and the two of them looked at each other, each acknowledging wordlessly how broken they were. Two strangers made familiar by grief.

Then her eyes became watery and her cheeks flushed, and something about the intimacy of it made Dante feel wretched that he was trying to suppress his own emotions. She looked at the table and wiped her eyes with her sleeve.

'I can't abide crying in front of a stranger,' she said, her Southern accent stronger in her distress.

'How do I get in contact with you?' he asked, and she opened up her purse and scribbled down a phone number and a name. Dante pocketed it, and told her she could reach him at the Drake. Then he stood and put some change on the table for the drinks. He thought a moment and took the sunglasses from his breast pocket, and held them out to her.

'Take them,' he said. 'They're good for covering tears.'

He left the cafeteria, and as he walked down the street to his car, he suddenly felt alone and the despair came rushing back, and he wished Loretta was there with him. She was supposed to have come to the funeral but hadn't shown up, and for the first time he wondered what had happened to her.

He got into the Blackhawk, wound down the windows, and sat for a moment, and it was then, in the stillness, with nothing to distract him, that it hit him: the loneliness; the horror that his only brother had gone to the grave and they hadn't patched things up; that he had to face what was coming alone, with a ruined ankle and a ruined arm and not much of a hope at all.

His heart raced and panic coursed through him, turning his legs to jelly. In those moments of heaving dread, he realized he was as good as dead, the only thing keeping him going the thought that he had to stop them first.

52

Ida watched Jacob's brother walk out of the cafeteria and she shook her head. They'd had six years to make up, to become brothers again, and now, they would never be reconciled. She downed the last of her coffee and called the waitress over to get the check, and as she did so, she noticed something on her hand: a comet of mud streaking across her palm, soil from the funeral.

The waitress arrived and Ida handed her the change Dante had left on the table. Then she headed to the restrooms, feeling the eyes of the Pinkerton men boring into her. She stepped inside and saw one of the two sinks was occupied by a waitress applying makeup. They caught each other's eyes in the mirror and the waitress smiled at her, a hand raised to her face, thickening her eyelashes with kohl.

Ida smiled back and approached the free sink; she turned on the faucet and the waitress's eyes flicked down to Ida's hands where she spotted the mud.

'Coal?' asked the waitress as she flicked the brush against her lashes.

'Excuse me?'

'Coal dust? On your hand? I get it at home all the time – it's a damn pain.' The waitress smiled at her and Ida peered at her hands. They were under the running water now, the smudge slowly fading into nothingness, black particles streaking along the white porcelain of the sink.

'Oh, no,' said Ida, 'it's mud, from the cemetery.'

'Oh, I'm sorry,' said the woman, abashed, looking once more at Ida's mourning clothes.

'My condolences,' she said, smiling again, before turning back to the mirror. 'Of course,' she added in a mutter. 'Why would you be using coal in this weather?'

She finished with her makeup and sashayed out of the restroom, leaving Ida alone, staring at her hands in the water running from the faucet. She thought about what the woman had said and looked again at the sink – the water was running clear now.

She turned off the faucet, walked out into the cafeteria, past the Pinks in the booth and out onto the street, where Michael was leaning against the bonnet of the car they'd been driven over in, smoking a cigarette.

'I know where Gwendolyn is,' Ida said, her gaze level on Michael. 'You got a car?'

Michael shook his head. 'It's back at the safe house.'

'Let's go pick it up then.'

The Pinks emerged from the cafeteria as she said it and Michael nodded at them, and they all got into the car and drove back to the safe house.

When they got there, the men pulled Michael aside and he spoke to them privately, arranging the details of the story they would be telling HQ. Michael had seniority over the men, and more importantly, their respect, and when the bargaining was done, he came over to Ida and nodded.

'You wanna go and get changed before we leave?' he asked.

'No.'

Michael looked at her a moment, then they headed toward a Chevrolet parked down the street.

'What did you arrange with them?' she asked.

'We lost you in the cemetery. You ran away through the gravestones after the funeral had finished. I chased after you, but you disappeared.'

'No one's going to believe that.'

'No, I don't suppose they will.'

'Plus it makes me sound like a hysteric.'

'I know.'

Michael drove at a clip and as he did she told him everything Jacob's brother had revealed to her, and they discussed it, and both of them agreed he was telling the truth, and they planned what to do next. Then in less than half an hour they were back at Coulton's apartment, back on the muddy street near the Stockyards where they'd been ambushed. The sun was setting by the time they arrived and the murky light lent the place an even more depressing air than it had had on their first visit. They drove round the block a couple of times to make sure no one was lying in wait, then they parked up and went round to the trunk of the car. Inside was a large leather holdall which Michael opened up, allowing Ida to see the stash of guns in it.

'Are you armed?' he asked. Ida shook her head, and Michael took out a .38 and passed it to her, after which he took a flashlight from the trunk and closed it. Ida checked the gun and put it in her handbag. Then they approached the building.

Michael opened up the door while Ida stood guard and they stepped into the dusty old lobby once more. Michael switched on the flashlight and found the door to the basement. He picked it open and they descended a flight of stairs.

He waved the flashlight around, trying to gauge the size of the space they had entered. It looked like the coal store took up the whole floor-plan of the building, and the place was awash with the stuff – a sea of coal covering every inch, rising up in the corners where it was heaped against the walls, so that it almost reached head-height. There was enough here for all the apartments in the building to see out a winter, if any of the apartments were occupied.

Ida should have thought of it earlier; Coulton was the only resident in the building. He and Severyn could come and go there undisturbed, could dump whatever they wanted in that basement. They'd had the apartment cleaned spotless except for that residue in the sink that Ida had mistaken for mud from the day's rain.

It was only the waitress's comment that had made her realize the connection, and the only reason there'd be coal in the sink in the middle of a heatwave.

They stepped carefully off the stairs and onto the bed of coal and looked around. Next to them was an alcove packed with shovels and buckets. They picked up two shovels and turned to look at each other, wordlessly acknowledging the situation. They could smell it on the air, just below the layers of dust and coal, the faint, sour scent of death. They picked their way over the coals to where the smell was worst and Michael put the flashlight down on the surface and they both used the tips of their shovels to scrape away the top layers of coal.

After a few minutes, the smell getting steadily worse, a piece of dirty white cloth came into view. Then within that cloth, an arm, a sleeve, a broken gold bracelet, a manicured hand, all of it covered in a layer of soot. Beneath the one hand was the other hand, the two of them clasped together.

Ida turned to look at Michael and they put down the shovels and carried on removing the coals by hand, piece by piece, until they could see her face, grimy, swollen from the strangulation, robbed of its beauty. Michael sighed and picked up the flashlight and shone it down on their discovery. It was then that they noticed how she had been buried: on her side; her hands raised in front of her face, palms together, the posture of someone in prayer. Her eyes had been closed, and her hair was laid away from her face. They'd placed her down there with care, with remorse, with love, and Ida tried to tally that with what she knew of Coulton and Severyn, and it didn't quite make sense.

'Look how she's been laid out,' said Ida. 'Like they cared.'

'Maybe they did,' Michael said. 'It's a good place to hide a body. Coulton and Severyn's names aren't on the lease, there're no other tenants, the carbon in the coals would keep the smell filtered in, and even if it didn't, the whole neighborhood reeks of the Stockyards anyway. She could be down here for years before anyone stumbled across her. But, still . . . you'd think at some point they'd come back and move her.'

'Maybe they were going to but something went wrong,' said Ida.

They looked over Gwendolyn's body once more, her hands clasped together in prayer, her blonde hair breaking over the coals. Ida started to feel sick, disgusted and angered by what they'd done to the girl.

'Let's cover her back up,' she said. 'I don't want the rats to get to her.'

Michael nodded.

'And then let's go and find out what happened,' she added.

'Go and talk to the boy?' Michael asked, and Ida nodded in turn.

A grim determination to bring it all to a close had seized her, and this boy whom Michael had found, the one who'd helped ambush them, who'd helped dispose of the dancer's body, they'd get him to talk.

As they carefully replaced the coals over Gwendolyn's body, Ida thought about Jacob's funeral, about his death and the way in which Gwendolyn's life and dignity had been stripped from her, too – all of it done by a group of men in search of nothing more than money.

The anger that had been building up in her had turned into a desire for vengeance, the same desire that had seized her in the Stockyards just after Jacob had died, the desire that over the last few days had all but disappeared. Now she wanted to find Severyn more than ever, make him pay for what he'd done to Gwendolyn and Jacob. She remembered what Jacob had said about having the courage to not look away. She'd closed her eyes in the Stock-yards, but not anymore.

53

Five minutes into the drive from the cemetery to the Metropole Dante spotted a tail – a black sedan, three or four cars back, switching lanes a little too eagerly. He turned left off his route, and left again, and the sedan followed him all the way, and when he made a third left so he was back on the road where he'd started the manoeuvre, the black sedan turned the corner behind him once more. Either they were amateur shadows, or they were sending him a message, or they just didn't care.

He parked up in front of the Metropole and ran into it as fast as the pain in his ankle would allow. He caught the elevator up to the top floors and when the doors opened they revealed Al's suites in a state of half-emptied disarray. Packing crates were stacked up in the hallway and a chain of removal men were lugging boxes toward the service lift.

Dante pushed past the men and into the main suite, but the room was empty save for a gaggle of Al's captains and some kids, and a few removal men. Dante saw Frank Nitti locking documents into a strongbox. He limped over and Frank looked up at him.

'What the fuck happened to you?' he asked.

'I got shot.'

'They didn't do a good job.'

'Where's Al?'

At this Frank frowned. 'He's over at the Lexington. We're moving.'

'To the Lexington?'

'Al didn't tell you? He's taken ten rooms. He's getting scared about all this Moran stuff. Reckons he'll be safer there when the war kicks off.'

Dante noted the use of *when*.

'What's so safe about the Lex?' he asked, the Lexington only being a couple of blocks further down the street.

'The coal tunnels,' said Frank. 'In the basement. They come up all over the neighborhood. Al reckons we can use them as escape routes. Who shot you?'

'I dunno,' said Dante. 'How do I contact Al?'

'Hobble over there.'

'You got phones there yet?'

'Sure. Call up and ask for George Phillips. Now, you gonna tell me what happened to you?'

'Not just yet. Who's in charge of the Minneapolis–Milwaukee whiskey run these days?'

'Sacco. George Sacco,' said Frank.

'What's his story?'

'Nothing much. He's a local hood. Him and his kid brother have worked for us for years.'

'How long's he been in charge of the run?'

'A couple of years, maybe,' Frank said, shrugging.

It was all the confirmation Dante needed, and it fitted with what the girl had told him. Sacco was the traitor.

'Where is he? I need to get hold of him.'

'This about the poison booze or about you getting shot?' asked Frank.

'Maybe both.'

'You're pegging him for the poisoning?' Frank asked.

'Maybe. Where is he, Frank?'

'I don't know. He was supposed to be here today to help with the move but he never showed up. You want me to ask his brother?'

'His brother's here?'

Frank nodded and gestured to a group of men on the other

side of the room, a cadre of young guns heaving file binders into a trunk for the trip down the road.

'Which one is he?' Dante asked.

Frank frowned.

'Shit. He was there just a minute ago,' he said, before shouting at the men on the other side of the room, 'Hey! Where'd Sacco go?'

'He just left,' one of the men shouted back. 'Didn't say where.'

Frank turned to look at Dante, finally realizing the urgency of the situation.

'If I wanted to get hold of him where'd I go?' asked Dante quickly.

'He works out of a bar in the Near West Side. Schiller's. You want a home address, I can ask around.'

'Do it. Leave a message at the Drake. And stay close to Al, I think someone's going to try and whack him. Maybe Sacco.'

Dante turned and ran out of the place as best he could. When he got into the hallway, he checked the elevator needle – it was going down, a couple of floors below him. He took the stairs, trying to put the pain in his ankle out of his mind, and he rushed into the lobby as a silhouette flittered through the revolving doors into the sunlight outside.

Dante made it to the street to see a man run across the road and get into a cream-colored coupe. Sacco's younger brother. Dante hobbled over to the Blackhawk, punched the ignition, gunned the gas, and managed to get into lane just a couple of cars behind him.

Then Dante spotted the shadow car from earlier – the sedan – behind him again. Sacco turned left into a narrow side street, and Dante followed, and it was only when Sacco slowed down in front of him that Dante realized his mistake. The shadow car turned in behind him, and Dante was trapped on the quiet street between the two cars, a sitting duck.

He floored the gas and his car lurched forward, mounted the sidewalk with one set of wheels, and rammed past the coupe in front, the sides of the cars scraping and screeching, a door handle popping into the air. Then Dante was through and he swerved back onto the road half a second before he would have smashed into a lamppost. His car fishtailed but he got it under control and ripped a left at the next junction, but then he lost control again, crashed into the back of a parked car and smacked his head against the steering wheel.

The world spun about him, his vision a kaleidoscope of fuzz and glinting blur. Then he got his brain into gear, opened the door and tumbled out of the car onto the sidewalk. A few yards back, on the other side of the road, he saw the sedan screech to a halt and the men step out, two of them with Colts, one with a tommy gun, and all of a sudden the street was ringing with bullets and pandemonium; people screaming and running for cover; drivers braking to avoid the gunmen; slugs ripping holes into Dante's car in a roar of fire and noise.

He looked up and down the street and saw a drugstore a little further up: *Jones & Sons Drugstore – Medications, Ointments, Firearms, Sundries*. Between him and it, a row of parked cars. He fumbled his Beretta from his pocket, got into a crouch and ran half bent to the store and pulled himself in.

He looked about the place and saw it was empty. He locked the door and hobbled toward the counter, behind which the tommy guns were lined up in a display case on a high shelf. As he tried to get to the guns he was brought up short by the sight of an elderly man and a girl cowering in the space behind the counter.

'I need a tommy gun. And magazines. Now.'

The old man stared at him, frozen in fear, then he collected himself and stood and hustled across the floor. Dante peered at the girl who was staring at him, terrified, then he moved back to the front of the store and peeked around the window. The men were walking across the street to where they guessed he was lying behind his car, to finish him off. Dante recognized one of them – the man in the suit from the forest up in Millersville. Dante studied him carefully, looking for signs of a bullet wound, of the injury Dante had caused when he'd shot the man in the woods, but he couldn't find any.

He turned back around to see the old man put the gun on the counter, and haul a crate of drum magazines up next to it. Dante hobbled over to him, took out his wallet.

'How much?' he asked.

The man looked surprised. 'The gun's two hundred and ten. The magazines are three dollars for a twenty-shot, twenty-two dollars for a fifty-shot.'

Dante laid three hundred on the counter.

'Keep the change.'

He loaded a fifty-shot onto the gun and walked back to the front of the store. He looked through the glass again and saw the three men had ceased turning their bullets loose, and were scrambling back to their car. Dante opened the door and the little girl stared at him.

'What did they do?' she asked, and Dante thought a moment.

'Killed my dog,' he said.

He stepped out into the street and walked across the road as the men were approaching the sedan. They were turned away from him, but in that moment, he didn't care. He lowered the tommy gun and squeezed the trigger, and the burn of bullets seared the air. He'd never fired a tommy before and wasn't prepared for the kickback, so fearsome and wild he lost control. A salvo of bullets skipped off the road and bounced into the air. Then he got a fix on it, lifted the gun upwards, and saw just how wildly inaccurate a weapon it was; why the army and police had refused to use it for so many years; why the gun companies ended up selling them all to gangsters. As the bullets pumped out he had to sway the gun back and forth to find his mark and the men's car pinged and sparked. He caught one of them in the back and he dropped to the ground, and the remaining two turned tail and ran.

Dante eased off the trigger, and the bullets and noise stopped and an eerie quiet descended onto the street, silent except for the sound of the men's frantic footsteps pounding up the road and the hiss of the damaged cars. He ran after them, the pain in his ankle no more than a dullness now.

They turned a corner onto a side street, and then onto a main road, this one roofed by elevated railroad tracks up above, the planks and gaps casting the street into zebra stripes which shuttered and flickered as Dante ran through them – light, dark, light, dark. As people saw the tommy in Dante's hand they cleared the street with screams and gasps. Then there was an L train passing on the tracks above them, rattling like a slot-machine jackpot, an explosion of sound and noise.

The men turned into a station on the corner, up two flights of stairs, bursting into the ticket hall, hopping the turnstiles, more stairs and then they were out on the platform, jumping onto the tracks, running along them. Dante paused, took a moment to catch his breath, checked the line and jumped onto the tracks too, his ankle searing with pain as he landed. Finally, there was empty space between them. He leveled the gun and squeezed off a few rounds, which skittered into the planks near the men's feet. Too far away now to get a good shot.

He ran after them along the boards and tried not to look down at the gaps between the planks, the two-story drop to the road below, where cars were zooming up and down the street.

In front of them was a bend in the tracks, and the two men disappeared behind it and when Dante turned the bend too he saw a train bearing down on them, a roaring cavalcade of metal and weight, enough to rattle his bones from yards away. The driver blasted his horn, deafening them, the ear-shattering squeal of the brakes like nails on a blackboard. The man from the forest leapt out of its path, and then Sacco jumped, too.

Just a second too late.

The train caught him while he was in the air, swatting him like a fly. His body seemed to compact as it was hit by the onrushing train, and then it bounced upwards, arced over the tracks and the guardrails, into the air above the street, and hung there for what seemed like forever, limbs as splayed as a doll's.

And then he dropped, plunging two stories down to the street, where he landed with a crash on the asphalt just as a car reached the spot, not braking fast enough.

Dante stopped running, thoughts helter-skelter. His stomach seemed to drop out of him and the muscles in his gut wrenched. The train had stopped a dozen or so yards in front of him. He saw the driver through the glass of the cab, shock on his face, and next to the stopped train, on the other set of tracks, was the man from the forest. Down below a woman was screaming.

Then the train-driver clambered out of his cab, and Dante saw the blood smeared along the front of the train's metal face and he thought again of a swatted fly.

The man from the forest looked up and they made eye contact, and then the man burst into a run, and Dante followed. He ran on the tracks, past the halted train, and all the passengers in the windows were staring. Ahead he saw the tracks widening out, a bulge where two lines crossed each other, and beyond them, a station, the start of a new line, where a train was turning, looping from one set of tracks to another. Dante skipped onto the opposite track and the man did likewise, but as he did, he stumbled, fell forwards and disappeared from sight.

Dante ran over. The man was lying on the tracks, squirming, his leg caught between two of the planks. Dante approached and the man looked up at him. They were both breathless from the chase, horrified by what they'd seen. Dante looked at the man's foot, and made a judgment on how long it would take for the cops to get there and find them.

'It's gonna be painful getting out of that,' said Dante.

'Fuck you,' hissed the man, and he tried again to pull his foot out of the gap. Dante sat on the rail next to him, put a hand on his racing heart. His lungs burned and his breath was labored; he was dizzy from blood loss, his ankle was throbbing and he hadn't shot up since that morning.

'Even if you get your foot out, I'm sitting here with a gun,' he said. 'I give it five minutes before the next train comes, less before the cops show up. Tell me what I want to know and I'll help you out.'

'Bullshit,' said the man.

Dante shrugged. He took out his cigarettes and lit one up, despite his breathlessness and the burning in his lungs. The man was squirming desperately now, trying to wrench his ankle free, and Dante could see from the gritted expression on his face how much it was costing him in pain. Dante looked at his own ankle, tried to rotate it, wondered if he'd done himself permanent damage, and thought of his dead brother. Then he caught sight of the man out of the corner of his eye, saw that he'd stopped struggling, and they stared at each other, an endless moment.

'What do you want to know?' he said eventually, and Dante took a drag on his cigarette, making sure he didn't reply too quickly.

'Who's running the operation up in Millersville?'

'George Sacco.'

'I already know that. Who's he working for? There's a New York connection.'

'I don't know.'

'Yes, you do.'

'I swear.'

'What do you know then?'

'Nothing. Just that Sacco came up with the idea of piggy-backing the whiskey run to distribute dope.'

'And you never asked who he was getting the dope from?'

'No.'

'What do you know about the poison booze at the Ritz?'

At this the man flinched, then tried to play it off with a grin. 'Nothing,' he said, unnaturally.

Dante took a puff on his cigarette and looked down the line again.

'Well, would you look at that,' he said. 'The train's early . . .' And he nodded to his left, and the man turned to see another train turning slowly through the loop, about to head in their direction. The man looked back at him, genuine fear in his eyes.

'I got something,' he said. 'Help me outta here and I'll spill.'

'Tell me first.'

'I know who Sacco was working for.'

'Who?'

'Charles Coulton.'

'The kid?'

'His father. Coulton Senior. He had the connection to New York. Through someone he knew in Washington. The kid and his friend were just along for the ride.'

Dante stared at the man, thoughts pell-mell, skittering off into different directions, then zoning back in on what the man had said, and his memories started to coalesce.

'Charles Coulton?' he said, even though he knew what he had heard was the truth. He knew the name, but when the girl had mentioned a Chuck Coulton in the cafeteria, a rich-kid wastrel, a prep-school kid who'd stumbled onto a criminal buddy in the war, Dante hadn't thought to connect it to the Charles Coulton he'd heard about in New York. A racketeer from Newark, born Charles Ferguson, who'd headed off to Washington years back to ride the Capitol Hill gravy train. A man who'd moved to a new city and changed his name, just like Dante had.

'Coulton went to Capone with the dope-distribution deal months back but Capone wasn't interested,' the man said. 'So then he approached Sacco with the idea of doing it on the hush, piggybacking the Outfit's van. He hooked us all into it – me, Sacco,

Sacco's kid brother, the hillbillies that run the roadhouse. Some boat captain brought the stuff in from Canada, same place New York got their stuff from, all the way from France.'

'Who was the connection in New York?'

'I told you, I don't know. Coulton never said. Coulton was the middle man. He didn't want Sacco finding out and cutting him out of the deal. I swear that's it.'

'And what about Moran?'

'What about him?'

'How was he involved?'

A bemused look crossed the man's face.

'Moran wasn't involved. I swear. Now help me outta here. Please!'

Dante stared at the man. Moran had to be involved. The dead stooge in the alleyway proved it. The man turned to look at the train, and Dante followed his gaze: it was at the station now, picking up passengers. In the distance he could hear police sirens.

'Come on . . .' the man pleaded.

Dante flicked his cigarette away, stood, and held out his hand for the man to take. The man grabbed his wrist. But instead of pulling himself up, he pulled Dante down, lifted a knee into his chest, made a grab for the tommy. They both fell forward toward the gap and Dante saw the dead space looming up at him, the cars, the street. The man kneed him in the gut, winding him. Through the pain Dante caught sight of the man's foot: he must have gotten it free while they were talking.

The man got on top of him, tried to grab the gun, one hand on the barrel, the other trying to pull Dante's fingers off the handle, and Dante realized he wasn't the only one making stupid moves. Then the train's horn blasted and they turned to see it getting closer.

'Fucking idiot,' hissed the man as they tussled. Then a grin formed on his face. 'We took out insurance on you.'

'I'm not the idiot,' said Dante. 'I'm not the one holding a gun by the barrel.'

Dante put his hand over the man's and squeezed the trigger, and the tommy sprayed bullets into the air, and the barrel instantly glowed hot, scorching, and the smell of cooked meat sizzled into the air, and the man shrieked and rolled onto his side, clutching his hand, and Dante caught a glimpse of it: the palm burned brown, smoldering, black. The man stumbled backward just as the train rushed past. Dante watched, the driver braking too late.

The train eventually stopped a few yards further down, a gust of wind swirling after it, a cyclone of warm air, scented with the smell of burned flesh and engine grease. Dante took a few steps forward, and through the track he could see the man from the forest, lifeless on the street below.

He used his sleeve to wipe down the tommy, left it on the side of the tracks and ran for the station, wondering what the man meant by the last thing he'd said, the insurance they had taken out on him, the smile on his face when he said it. And then Dante prayed it had nothing to do with Loretta not turning up to the funeral.

54

As Michael and Ida drove over to the apartment, he filled her in on how he'd managed to track down Arturo Vargas, the boy who had helped ambush them. He had sought out the boy's known associates from the list Walker had provided, finding them one by one, pressing them for information in a daisy chain of threats and intimidation. He'd visited three different tenements, two bars, and a palm-reader's shop. Eventually he'd been directed to a flophouse in the Spaghetti Zone where he unearthed Vargas in a basement dormitory.

After a brief chase, Michael and Walker had cornered the boy and persuaded him to come with them. They told him they had a witness who would testify to seeing him throw the dancer's body off the bridge, they said they'd pin the ambush on him as an accomplice, and they informed him that both Severyn and Capone had taken a contract out on him. They told him, in short, that he was a dead man. Unless he went with them to a safe house, and told them everything he knew. Then they'd offer him protection and a means to escape the city, and they'd never breathe a word to the police.

Vargas agreed, warily, and they took him over to an empty apartment the State's Attorney's used for putting up witnesses. Once he was settled in, Michael had gone to the funeral to get Ida, leaving the boy with Walker and some men from the SA's.

As Michael filled her in on all of it, he watched her closely, noticing how different she looked since they'd discovered Gwendolyn's body: more focused, more sharp. When he'd walked into the safe house earlier that day he'd been shocked to see how fragile and meek she looked. She'd always had an air of self-doubt about her, a shaky mistrust of her own resilience, but in the safe house that afternoon, she'd looked broken. Now it seemed like her resolve was creeping back.

They parked the Chevrolet on a nondescript street in Pilsen and approached a run-down tenement. The sun had set and the street was dark except for the lights shining in from the windows in the buildings above. Michael pressed the buzzer four times – long, short, long, short. The buzzer echoed back and they stepped inside.

They walked up to the second floor, where a man was standing by an entrance to an apartment, a service revolver in his hand. Michael nodded, and the man knocked three times on the door behind him and the door opened, revealing Walker, who beckoned for them to enter.

It was a railroad apartment, the rooms arranged in a line without a corridor, just one room leading into the next, into the next, into the next, until the last one, a living room, where there was finally a window, and some light.

It was cramped and messy. Vargas was sitting on a sofa, in front of a coffee table loaded with food they'd brought back from a Chinese restaurant. A man from the State's Attorney's was leaning against the counter of the adjoining kitchenette, keeping an eye on him. Vargas looked up at them as they entered, and in the harsh light of the bare bulb, he looked even younger than he had early that morning, when Michael and Walker were talking to him in the gloom of an alleyway behind the flophouse.

'You wanna drink?' Walker asked them, and both Ida and Michael shook their heads. Walker got them some chairs from the kitchenette and they all sat around the coffee table.

'We got ourselves some food,' said Walker, picking up a fork and a carton of noodles. 'You eaten?'

Michael's gaze drifted over the cartons of rice and pork, and even though he hadn't eaten in what felt like days, and was nauseous from lack of food, he shook his head, and lit a Virginia Slim.

'Arturo, this is my colleague from the Pinkertons, Ida Davis,' said Michael. 'I told you about her. We were hired together by Gwendolyn's mother.'

Vargas looked at Ida and smiled and nodded, and Ida stared back at him coldly.

'Let's start with the ambush. What were you doing going to Coulton's apartment?'

'What's everyone doing? Looking for money. Business gets kinda slow this time o' year,' Vargas said in an adenoidal voice. 'Chuck had a stash over there and I figured the place was empty.'

'You just happened to turn up at the same time we did?' asked Michael.

'Yeah,' said Vargas, picking up on the sarcasm in Michael's tone, and responding to it with some of his own. 'Wrong place, wrong time.'

He grinned, picked up a fork and a carton of barbecued pork, and without looking back up, he started to eat. The gesture infuriated Michael. His family had been forced to decamp to Detroit, Ida had seen Jacob murdered, Gwendolyn was dead, and Vargas was treating it all as a joke.

'Put the fucking food down,' said Michael, glaring at him, surprised to hear how much anger there was in his own voice.

Everything seemed to go quiet. Vargas stopped chewing and stared back at Michael, the fork hovering in the air between the carton and his mouth.

'I didn't think I'd need to explain exactly how much shit you're in,' said Michael. 'But it seems I do. We can put you at the Ashland Avenue Bridge where you and Severyn dumped Esther Jones's body. We can pin the ambush on you. You're looking at the electric chair. And when the Outfit finds out what you did, they're gonna put a contract on you. And your pal, Severyn, he's probably already looking to kill you. You don't start cooperating with us, you'll be in a jail cell within the hour, and you'll be a sitting duck for whatever trigger Severyn or Capone have hired to whack you. By this time tomorrow, you'll be dead. But if you tell us what you know, we'll drive you to the train station ourselves, and even buy you your goddamn ticket. So put down the food, and start talking. I'm not gonna ask twice.'

Michael kept his gaze fixed on Vargas the whole time he spoke, so he could see how the menace in his words and manner worked on the boy, making the color drain from his face, suffusing it instead with uncertainty and worry, how even, ever so slightly, the carton in his hand started to tremble.

Vargas put down the carton and the fork. Then he swallowed the food that was in his mouth, and nodded at Michael, gesturing that he'd start to cooperate. Michael glared at him for a few moments longer, pressing home the advantage.

'Why'd you think the place was empty?' Michael asked eventually. 'Had you spoken to Chuck since Gwendolyn disappeared?'

'Sure. I spoke to him just after it happened.'

'After what happened?'

'After he killed her.'

Vargas looked uncertainly at Michael, and Michael turned to look at Ida, and saw how she was staring fixedly at Vargas, frozen almost. Michael turned back and gestured for him to continue.

'Lloyd called me that night,' he explained, his gaze flicking between Michael and Ida. 'Said to get round to the apartment. That Chuck was cut up real bad and needed help. I knew about this plan they had, with Capone and Moran and the champagne bottles, and I knew they'd planned it for that night. Chuck used to tell me stuff. We were close. Told me about Lloyd and his father, and how scared he was of them. So when Lloyd called me up I figured it had all gone wrong, but when I got there . . . I could hardly tell it was Chuck, all the blood and cuts on his face.'

'Someone had smashed a bottle into his face?' asked Michael.

'They must have smashed a case of bottles into his face to

make him look like that. And his eyes . . . he couldn't see. And he'd just let it dry there, you know? Hadn't washed it off, taken the glass out. I told him it would get infected but it was like he couldn't hear me. I asked what happened and he just babbled, and that's when I realized how bad it was. His mind was gone. I mean, he was always a little different, you know? Lloyd could switch on you, but Chuck just had this . . . *air* to him. Maybe killing the drivers, or killing Gwendolyn, or what happened to his face, or going blind, or maybe all of it together, it sent him over the edge.'

'Did he tell you what happened to him that night?' Michael asked.

'Kinda. Chuck was babbling. I told you, he'd lost it. But I figured out a few things from what he was saying, you know? And then when Lloyd came back, he told me the rest of it.'

Michael rubbed his temples, wishing the boy would speak in a more logical order. He noticed how strongly the smell of the Chinese food was filling the room, the jasmine and grease growing stronger in the heat.

'Okay. Start from the beginning,' said Michael.

'You know about that plan they had?' said Vargas. 'With the poison booze in the Ritz?'

Michael nodded.

'Well, the night it happened, they'd arranged to meet the delivery drivers there – at the apartment. They'd told them they were going to pay them, but the plan was to snuff them out. And they did. But as they were moving the bodies back into the van Gwendolyn showed up, saw what was happening and ran off. They had to chase after her, but they lost her, and then they caught up with her back at her parents' house. They followed her from there and picked her up somewhere near the station. They brought her back to the apartment. Then Lloyd went out, and while he was gone, Chuck and Gwendolyn argued, and, well, Chuck did it by accident. While they were arguing and he was

trying to explain things to her. I mean, I think that's what happened – it was hard to tell from what he was saying.'

'He strangled her? And where was Severyn?'

'I don't know. Cleaning up the van with the delivery drivers,
maybe. But he wasn't there, because Chuck was ranting about
having hidden something in the coal cellar and I figured he meant
Gwendolyn. And he was babbling about Lloyd and his father not
finding out, so I guess he hid her body without telling anyone cuz
he wasn't thinking straight.'

'And this was before Roebuck smashed a bottle into Chuck's
face?'

Vargas nodded. 'They were supposed to go over to Bronzeville where Roebuck was, over in this buffet flat near Federal
Street. That was the other part of the plan. But this thing with
Gwen slowed them down, so by the time they got there Roebuck had smelled a rat and barreled out of there and on the
way out he smashed up Chuck's face real good, and Lloyd had
to chase him halfway through Bronzeville before he killed him.
And then they went back to the apartment and Lloyd went off to
try and straighten things out now that everything had gone to shit
and he called me to look after Chuck, get a doctor there, see him
fixed up.'

Michael tried to process what he was hearing, and Vargas'
words were raising more questions than answers, making Michael
think what he knew was all wrong. He could understand why they
had killed the drivers – cleaning up loose ends – but he still didn't
know where the stooge in the alley fitted into it all.

'Why did they kill Roebuck?' he asked.

'Because Roebuck worked for Moran,' said Vargas. 'That was
their plan. I thought you knew.'

'Tell me what the plan was.'

'To start a war. Between Capone and Moran. They staged the
poisoning and then the plan was to dump the bodies of the drivers
together with the stooge's. When they all showed up dead together

the next day, Capone would think it was Moran making a move on him and he'd start a war. Except Gwen turned up in the middle of it and it all went to shit.'

Michael turned to look at Ida, and she stared back at him in dismay. Moran wasn't involved in it, and neither was Capone: they were both dupes. And as Michael thought on it, the thousand possibilities coalesced into one, all the evidence locking into a single, logical chain of events. It explained why the Moran stooge died the same night, why Gwendolyn's body was still in the coal cellar, why Capone had employed someone to look into the poisoning, and it explained the poisoning itself. And it fitted with what Jacob's brother had said; if a cartel of heroin dealers wanted free reign in the city, to get rid of the obstacle that was Capone, all they had to do was get Capone and Moran involved in a war, which would weaken them both, and then step in when they'd finished pummeling each other to deliver the killer blow.

He'd come across the tactic before. It was a Sicilian strategy, setting two factions off against each other, letting them kill one another, then walking into the power vacuum left behind. Michael had heard rumors from Pinkerton operatives in New York that two upstarts over there were planning on using the ploy against the Masseria and Maranzano families. And here in Chicago, some-one was employing the same simple, lethal strategy.

Michael stubbed his cigarette out in one of the empty cartons, releasing a smell of burned grease and paper into the air.

'So what happened with Chuck?' he asked, looking up at Vargas.

'I needed to get him to a hospital. Not just for his face, but for his head too, you know. All I could do was call his father. He arranged for someone to come pick him up, the guy with the glass eye, take him to a hospital he was connected with where they wouldn't ask any questions. I don't know where. The guy turned up in a car and took him away and I ain't seen him since.'

'And Severyn? You know where Severyn is now?'

'No.'

Vargas said it so quickly, so forcefully, that Michael knew instantly he was lying.

'Yes, you do.'

'I swear, I don't,' he said, shaking his head.

'I'm not gonna ask you again,' said Michael, glowering at him.

And again Vargas shook his head and the frustration set something off in Michael. In a red haze he jumped out of his seat, grabbed the boy by the collar and hauled him up against the wall, thumping him into it. And somehow Michael's gun was in his hand, pressed against Vargas' neck, and Vargas was sobbing, and behind him, Michael could sense the others had got to their feet too.

'Easy, Michael,' he heard Walker say from behind him.

'Severyn tried to kill us,' said Michael to Vargas. 'He's going to try and kill you too. I had to move my family out of the city. You tell me where he is.'

Vargas stared at him, terrified, and in the stillness, Michael felt the sweat pouring off his forehead, the heat in the room, the slippery metal of the Colt in his hand.

'I don't know where he is,' said Vargas, panic in his voice. 'But I know where he's going. I know where he'll be tonight.'

'Where?'

'Soldier Field. The boxing match. They had a backup plan if it all went wrong. Capone's booked a hundred prime seats for the fight. Most of the Outfit's going to be there. They're going to bomb it. Take them all out in one go.'

55

Dante clambered down to street level, looked for a cafeteria and went to the restrooms to wash the blood from his face and the smell of cordite from his hands. Back out front he asked one of the girls behind the counter if there was a clothes shop thereabouts and was directed to a thrift store a couple of blocks away.

He bought a new shirt and jacket and trousers and changed into them, taking the old clothes with him, dumping them into a trash can on the street.

Then he went into a grocery and got on the phone. He called Loretta's sister's house and Mary answered, said Loretta had left that morning for the funeral, and Dante put the phone down before she asked him too many questions. Then he called the Drake, checked for messages: Frank had left Sacco's home address, which he memorized before ending the call.

Then he retraced his steps back to where the shoot-out had started. Police were milling about, the whole area cordoned off. He looked around and saw Sacco's coupe abandoned in the alleyway around the corner from the main road, a half a block from where the cordon started. He walked in the opposite direction to the crime scene, in a wide circle, and entered the alleyway from the far end. He guessed the man hadn't locked it when he'd jumped out to chase him down. He checked and found he was right: the driver's side door – with great scratches down it from Dante having rammed past him – opened up when he tried the handle.

He sat inside, and saw that the keys had dropped into the footwell. He picked them up and pocketed them and then he searched the car for clues. In the glovebox he found a wallet, money, a cafeteria receipt, and a cellophane wrapper with heroin in it, the same stuff Dante had been buying from the shoeshine man, the same stuff they were importing into the city. Nothing under the seats or in the door pouches except for a book of matches from Schiller's, the bar Frank said they worked out of.

He got out and checked the trunk: a shotgun, shells scattered about. A leather holdall. Sports clothes inside, boxing gloves, boots, all of them with the Illinois Athletic Club crest on them. He closed the trunk and got back in the car.

Through the mouth of the alleyway he could see the main road where the shoot-out had happened, the police cordon, and in the distance, the bullet-ridden wreck of his own car, the once-beautiful Blackhawk, and opposite it the sedan and beyond that, the drugstore, where the old man and the girl were talking to a beat-cop. Dante tried to think what he had left in his car, what the police could use to trace it back to him aside from a week's worth of fingerprints.

Then he started up Sacco's car, reversed it down the alley, and headed off in the direction of the Drake. He ran a mental list of where Loretta could be: Schiller's bar, Sacco's home, the Illinois Athletic Club, Coulton's home, an apartment they had rented for the occasion; absolutely any enclosed space in the vast, endless city of Chicago. The futility of it made his heart wrench. He tried to think of ways to find a woman in the middle of a city, to bargain her back to safety, but he came up blank and cursed his guilt-ridden, drug-addled excuse for a brain.

He pulled up outside the Drake and saw two Cadillacs badly parked on the forecourt, each with curtains pulled over the back window and a bell on the driver's-side running board – police cars. He carried on driving. He drove and smoked and ran through every angle in his head, and every angle ended up with either him dead or Loretta dead or both of them dead. Gangsters normally left women out of the warfare, there being an unspoken agreement between all of them that girlfriends and mistresses, and wives especially, were off limits. The breaking of this code by the people who had taken Loretta disconcerted Dante, made him wonder what else they were capable of.

He thought about Al finding out the traitor was Sacco, and that Sacco's link back to New York was Coulton, and Coulton's link in New York was Luciano and Lansky – Dante's friends – and what Dante's chances were of surviving that. He thought about the chances of surviving an exchange with Coulton. He thought about the unlikely possibility of him getting out of Chicago and what his chances were if he went on the run. He tried to imagine the happy ending, with him and Loretta getting out of it alive, and he couldn't do it.

At some point the adrenaline and the last of the dope wore off, and the pain came on hard, so he pulled up outside a pharmacy somewhere in Pilsen, went in and bought a hypodermic and some needles, then returned to the car, found a quiet road, and prepared a spike with the dope he'd found in Sacco's car, heating it on the end of a tin can he'd found in the street – a trick from his days on the boxcars.

He snapped his lighter shut, sucked the dope into the syringe and spiked himself in the arm. He stared down the empty road in front of him, where in the distance the city shimmered pale in the heat above the asphalt. He saw a playground further up the block, children playing on swings and a dome-shaped climbing frame coated in rust, looking like the skeleton of some long-dead mammoth, half submerged into the earth. They'd never had playgrounds in Little Italy when he was growing up, but the energy of the children, the joyful racket they were sending into the air, reminded him of his own childhood, and his mind went woozy and drifted for a moment from the job at hand.

He remembered playing stickball with Jacob, running down sidewalks, chasing fireflies in the dusk, double-dates, getting into trouble, his father coming home from work, his mother at the stove, birthdays, church parades, schoolrooms, pranks. Another city now, vanished into the past, fully submerged into the underworld, laid to rest.

As his heart pumped the dope through his bloodstream, he felt the pain leaving his body, felt his injuries dissolving one by one: the swollen ankle, an echo of the infirmity he'd given Jacob; the shotgun wounds in his arm and shoulder; the bruises in his armpit from firing the tommy gun; the bruise on his head from the crash; the ruined veins all along his arms and legs.

He'd abused his body well over the years, eked as much pleasure and pain from it as he could, and here were the marks to show for it – a body broken, smashed, in need of repair. *I'm already dead*, he thought. And in that moment he realized why all those years of trying to kill himself hadn't worked. He'd died when his wife had, and ever since he'd just been killing time, waiting to catch up with her, a ghost, or maybe its opposite, a body without a soul, wandering through the world in a daze.

And that was when he realized what he had to do. If Dante was already dead, he might as well sacrifice himself. Then maybe Loretta might survive and maybe he'd finally get to do something noble with the broken half-life that was now his existence.

He opened his eyes and stared at the empty road ahead and he noticed how strangely calm he was, and not just on account of the dope. For the first time that day his heart wasn't racing, he wasn't panicked or remorseful, anxious or filled with dread. He had a purpose, finally. Something that would see him through till the end.

He started the car and drove around the neighborhood till he found a speak-easy. He went in to see if they had a phone he could use, and they did, so he sat and ordered a beer, and dialed the number for Sacco's home address on the phone they had behind the counter.

No answer. The beer arrived and a bowl of peanuts. Dante took a sip of the drink, but when he tried to eat, the peanuts felt like lead in his gut. He called the number he had on the matches from Schiller's bar.

'Schiller's,' said the voice on the other end.

'I want to speak to Sacco.'

'He ain't here.'

'Well, where is he?'

'Who's asking?'

'The man who killed his brother . . .'

The line went quiet, muffled, a hand over the receiver at the other end. A few seconds later the man came back on the line.

'He's not here, but I can get him. What do you want?'

'I want a deal. I'll call back in an hour and he better be there.'

'All right . . .'

Dante passed the hour in a swirl of cigarettes and beer and the sound of the Fletcher Henderson Orchestra fluttering out of the radio behind the bar, a medley of popular songs played tight and precise. When he called back, an agitated voice answered the phone.

'Yeah?'

'Is that Sacco?'

'Yeah. Who's this?'

'You already know.'

There was silence on the line for a moment, then Sacco asked, 'What do you want?' And Dante could feel the pain in the man's voice; Sacco had lost his brother, but then, so had Dante.

'I want to bargain. I want the girl back.'

'Yeah? What've you got to bargain with?'

Dante had to press home his only advantage, what the hood had said on the railroad tracks before he died – that Coulton was scared of anyone finding out who his New York connection was, lest he as the middle man was squeezed out of the operation.

'I know who Coulton's connection is in New York. I can set you up with them. And once you're set, you can kill Coulton like you've wanted to all along and take over the operation yourself. You'll be the king of Chicago. All I want in return is the girl.'

The line went quiet as Sacco debated whether or not Dante was being honest, and if he was, whether he should enter into a double-cross with a man he didn't even know. As Dante waited for a response, he listened to the electrical rustle of the static going down copper wires, bouncing about the city's exchanges and switchboards.

'And what about Capone?' Sacco asked.

'I haven't breathed a word to him. You let the girl go and he'll never find out about all the dope you've been distributing in his vans, or the fact it was you and your pals behind the poison party at the Ritz.'

Dante paused to let the revelation that he knew all about their schemes sink in. More silence. And as he waited to see if Sacco would buy the bluff, Dante's heart pounded, and the receiver felt heavy in his hand.

'All right,' the man said. 'But if you want the girl, you got a problem. She's with Coulton, not me.'

'Then arrange a meeting. Tell him I want to bargain with him. I don't care if I end up dead. All I want is the girl to walk away.'

There was another long pause as Sacco debated yet another rearrangement of the pieces on the chess board.

'Okay . . .' he said eventually. 'I'll need to check with Coulton first. You got a number I can call you on?'

'I'll call you,' said Dante. 'In an hour.'

He put the phone down, and thought. Sacco had played the calmness well, speaking so levelly to the man who had just killed his brother. Maybe Dante had inflamed Sacco's greed, and the man really was in on the scheme to double-cross Coulton. Or maybe he was bluffing too, pretending he was in on it, whilst actually plotting to double-cross Dante.

The permutations branched off and spun around each other

in so many variations Dante soon realized there was no point trying to account for them all. He'd find out soon enough how it'd go down, and he prayed it would be enough to see Loretta safe.

Another hour, another swirl of alcohol and smoke and the radio program changed to a puff piece on the fight that night, journalists interviewing pundits. The barman and some of the regulars were comparing odds they'd gotten on the fighters, and Dante thought of Michigan Red, who must be in the middle of his busiest day ever, trying to level his book, and Dante remembered his parting words – *He a shaky dog, jus' like you* – and he started laughing till tears formed in his eyes, and the barman and the regulars were looking at him sidelong.

The clock ticked by and he called Schiller's back.

'It's on,' said Sacco. 'Come by Coulton's at ten. The old man wants to see you, and you'll get to see the girl's all right.'

'And then what happens?'

'The girl gets to go free. I'll make sure of it. Then we'll drive you out to the prairie somewheres, and before we put a bullet in your head, you tell us who the New York connection is.'

The image of an endless cornfield flashed into Dante's mind, sun-drenched and serene, caressed by the wind. He'd always thought he'd end up buried near water for some reason, a lake or a sea, but now the thought of the prairie somehow seemed fitting, it being an inland ocean, vast and unknowable and tender in its way.

'Okay. What's the address?'

Sacco gave it to him and Dante memorized it.

'And if you get any ideas,' said Sacco, 'about telling Coulton we had this chat, I'll make sure the girl hurts.'

'Sure,' said Dante, and he put down the phone.

He wondered whether he'd done the right thing by Loretta, then he realized with some sadness that he'd probably never know.

He left the bar and went back to Sacco's car, drove about until he found a fleapit hotel, in a run-down part of Pilsen. He parked the dead man's car a couple of blocks away, walked back and rented a room. It was as depressing a hotel room as he could imagine – grey walls, lumpy bed, low ceiling, stiflingly hot. On the wall opposite the bed there was a print of a sunset over a beach somewhere nice, California maybe, making the room feel even worse by comparison.

Dante took the Suicide Special out of his pocket, tossed it on the bed, took his hat off too. Then he undressed, checked the bleeding from his shoulder, eased the bandages off and took a shower, and thought how it would be the last time he'd ever experience the sensation of water rushing over him.

Then he lay on the bed and shot up one last time, with the heroin supplied by the men who were going to kill him. Through one of the walls he could hear a couple having sex, through the window children playing in the street, from somewhere else far away, the sound of a Victrola, playing a blues. A dead man's blues.

His eyes wandered around the sorry-looking hotel room and he briefly thought of his suite at the Drake, then he looked at the print of the California sunset on the wall, and the actual sunset out of the window, and was unsure which of the two was more dread-inducing. Then the earth got dark and the city lights came on and he rose and went into the bathroom and splashed some water on his face.

Then he came back into the room and searched for his Beretta, sure that he'd left it on the bed. He found it under his hat, and as he was putting the hat on his head, he realized something. He took the hat back off, took the Beretta from his pocket and dropped it into the crown of the hat. A perfect fit. His small, woman's gun fitted into the top of his hat, and that gave him an idea.

Maybe he wasn't a dead man after all.

NATIONAL BROADCASTING CORPORATION

RADIO TRANSCRIPT

Commentary – Graham McNamee

. . . NBC has linked 82 stations together to form a nationwide broadcast that is the largest single broadcast in history, ladies and gentlemen, with over 50 million people listening in. We'd like to say a special hello to those of you listening via the amplifiers set up in public spaces in towns across America. Give yourselves a round of applause, ladies and gentlemen . . . Now the fighters aren't scheduled to enter the ring till 9.45 p.m., so let me take a moment to give you a quick description of Soldier Field . . .

I guess the easiest way to describe it would be to say that it's like a modern-day Roman amphitheater, a coliseum. It's a rectangular-shaped, open-air stadium, right on the lakeside, and it's currently bathed in the light of 44 giant arc lamps set up all around it, each one 1,000 watts strong, turning the night into day . . .

On the north side of the arena, 700 feet from the ring, is a line of 32 giant columns, the portico of the Field Museum. On the south side is a stand where hundreds of rows of people rise into the night, and above them all a row of 26 giant American flags. On the east and west sides are another two great stands rising up into the sky, and above each of those stands are two more porticos, each containing double rows of Doric columns, and it's above these that the 44 great lights are shining down on the stadium, which is filled to capacity. And let me tell you, it's quite a sight . . .

150,000 fight fans have been streaming in through the 50 concrete vents underneath the east and west stands since 6 p.m., helped by 6,000 ushers. Perhaps the most noticeable entry of all was that of the city's own Al Capone, who entered in the center of what I can only describe as a ring of muscle. Mr Capone has apparently bought 100 of the most expensive $40 seats for himself and I have it on good authority that he's got $50,000 riding on Dempsey, ladies and gentlemen . . .

At the moment the ring is occupied by some of Illinois' most prominent politicians, Governor Len Small, Mayor 'Big Bill' Thompson and State's Attorney, Robert E. Crowe. The politicians are addressing the crowd and receiving rapturous applause . . .

56

The roads to the stadium were packed with more people than Ida had ever seen, like Mardi Gras and election night and the Lindbergh parade all rolled into one. Thousands on the streets, even though not one of them had a ticket. But history was in the making, the eyes of the world on their city, their neighborhood, their stadium, and the excitement couldn't be appreciated sitting at home. The buzz in the air, the hubbub, the electric pulse – it had to be shared, so people deluged the streets, the whole of Chicago milling about the sidewalks, arguing, drinking, listening to radio broadcasts that echoed like static down the streets, washed against buildings, followed Ida and Michael as they ran from their abandoned car for Soldier Field.

Then the stadium itself hove into view, a hulking, towering mammoth of stone, slumbering on the lakeshore, topped with Roman columns. Ida saw how the arc lamps on its roof had turned the whole thing into a basin of dazzling golden light, shining unnaturally skyward, as if the glow was the overspill of some miracle taking place inside.

They sprinted across the grounds that ringed the place, carpeted with a debris of peanut bags and sports-paper pages and countless cigarette ends, barreling through the fuzz of people on the grass.

Then they were through the last of the crowds, at an entrance, the beast of the stadium looming high, a line of police and a gaggle of guards stretched across its turnstiles. Walker had called ahead, had hopefully gotten through to the captains that were at the stadium, and the police were already searching the place for rigs or grenade men or Severyn himself, and hopefully the whole thing hadn't been put down to a hoax. Michael flashed his ID and told them who they were and they were waved through, one of the cops coming with them.

They ran through the turnstiles and into an enclosure that funneled people into the stands, and the cop led Michael off to where the captain was, somewhere in the bowels, and Ida nodded best of luck to him and she followed the arrows for the stands, down a corridor, at the end of which, through a square opening, she could see the field, and in it, the boxing ring, elevated, the black shapes of the fighters distorted and floating on an ocean of white light.

She rushed out into it, the stadium proper, and when she looked up and about her, it was as if the world had swung about to accommodate her view. On all sides of the arena the stands towered into the sky, packed full of people, disappearing into a blur, and above them all were the colonnades rising even further, topped with spotlights beaming at the ring, sharp as razors.

She looked at the people stretching up into the heavens and imagined the stands exploding, the indescribable carnage. Glimpses of the bombed-out speak-easy flashed into her mind, the charred bodies, the ripped-off limbs. She looked again at the people about her, men in shirt-sleeves, kids in flat caps, women in their summer dresses. She imagined all of them crushed under an avalanche of cement and twisted girders when the stands came tumbling down.

She ran up the nearest set of steps, got to a decent height, and tried to scan the ringside seats for Capone. But there was too much glare from the spotlights bouncing off the canvas. She saw a kid a few seats away with a pair of viewing glasses and shouted to him over the roar. 'Hey, kid! Kid! I'll give you a buck if you let me look through your glasses.'

The kid looked her up and down. 'Money first,' he shouted back.

Ida fumbled through her purse and gave him a dollar bill and the kid passed her the glasses in return. When she peered through them the figures on the canvas came into view, and in the burning beams she saw one fighter punch another, and as the man's head was flung back, a curve of blood unfurled into the air, and the curve divided, fanned out in an arc, and individual beads of red moisture flashed for a moment in the lights, rotated, then sprayed onto the canvas.

The crowd roared and Ida moved the glasses about, looked around the ringside seats, and found Capone. He was sitting close enough to the ring to make an attack from the top of his own stand possible. If the underneath of the stand wasn't rigged, that's where an assassin would be, up above. She couldn't search the whole stadium, so she had to take a gamble on Severyn being there too, close to the target.

She returned the glasses to the kid, ran back down to ground level, and sprinted around the passage that encircled the stadium. She marked off the stands in her head as she went, and when she'd made a half-lap, she passed two cops standing either side of another walkway, and figured they must be there on account of it being the entrance to where Capone was sitting. She ran past them and they shouted at her, spun round and followed.

She dashed back into the stadium proper. She ran up the stand three steps at a time, darted into a row of seats, pushed her way to another set of steps just as the cops appeared around the corner of the walkway. She turned and looked about the stand, along the stairs, at the gantries, praying she'd see something, that she'd see Severyn. The cops were hustling through the seats now, and her heart was beating faster, and she spun about, looking, praying that something would happen.

And then it did.

And it was on account of the cops.

At the very top of the stand something moved, a blur Ida

caught out of the corner of her eye, a person, moving, hurrying away.

Severyn.

He'd seen the policemen heading up the stand and assumed they were after him.

Ida burst into a run, watched as Severyn jumped over the barrier between Capone's stand and the one adjacent. She reached the top row of seats after what felt like an eternity and vaulted over the barrier into the next stand too. She looked about and saw him jump onto the colonnade at the top of the stand, watched as he disappeared into the shadows between two columns.

She ran after him and hopped onto the colonnade, pressed her back against the nearest column, and pulled the .38 Michael had given her from her handbag. Then she turned to look about the space. Stretching in front of her were the two long lines of columns, the space between them all darkness and shadows, as eerie as an abandoned Roman temple. On the columns' other side, far below, she could see the dark mass of the lake. She stayed still, quiet, listening, waiting.

In the arena, the crowd roared. She heard footsteps against metal. She ran down the colonnade, her black dress as inky as the shadows she was passing through, and at the far end she saw some scaffolding rising all the way up one of the columns, to reach the lights on the roof. She found a ladder attached to the scaffolding and climbed it, knowing she was a sitting duck as she did so; that all Severyn had to do was shoot at her from the top and she'd fall, be smashed against the surface of the asphalt all those feet below.

She scrambled onto the top of the colonnade, on top of all Soldier Field. Along the inner side of the roof were the spotlights, each as tall as a man, buzzing loudly and burning so strongly she could feel their heat from yards away, feel it burning the humidity out of the night, leaving the air dry and charged. She lifted a hand to her eyes, took her .38 from her bag once more and stalked along the roof, guessing Severyn would be in between the spotlights somewhere, looking down on the crowd.

She moved to the edge of the closest one and looked down. Below her she could see the edge of the stand, and what she saw made her heart sink. The two cops who had been chasing her were sprinting across the asphalt below, heading to the next stand along. They'd missed the ladder. They were going the wrong way. She was on her own.

She thought about attracting their attention, screaming at them that the man they were after was up above them. But she doubted they would hear her over the noise of the crowd, and if she did make herself heard, she'd give away her location, just as she had in the Stockyards.

She wondered if she should go back down, call for help. Her blood was heavy with fear, her muscles tense, her heart pumping. She wasn't even sure she could hold the gun straight. But she thought of Jacob and knew she couldn't live with herself if she let Severyn escape. She already felt guilty enough as it was. He was just on the other side of the spotlights. She had to risk it. She flexed the muscles in her fingers, making sure they were ready to shoot, then she spun around the corner.

But he wasn't there.

In front of the spotlights, overhanging the stands, was a metal gangway. She jumped onto it and was immediately blinded by the light beams. Then a shot rang out and something grabbed her and Severyn threw her onto the giant bulbs and she screamed as the heat seared the skin on her back and shoulders, melting the fabric of her dress onto it. She lurched forward and felt her skin rip, peeling away where it remained glued to the glass, smelled the scent of burned meat waft into the air.

She doubled over, heart pounding, pain knocking the breath out of her. In the dazzling snowstorm of light, she could just about discern a grey shape somewhere in front of her, almost indistinguishable in the blaze. He was coming back; she'd be thrown onto the bulbs once more, then tossed over the edge of the gangway and smashed onto the stand below.

She raised her .38 into the air, pointed at him, and pulled the trigger. His grey shape spun through the glare, and something clanged onto the gangway and she prayed it was his gun.

'You don't have it in you,' he shouted, in his disintegrated voice.

She wanted to scream at him, some wail of revenge, but she knew she had to holster her emotions.

'Stay back,' she managed to say, tensing her arm, aiming her gun upwards, toward where she guessed his head was.

'You don't have it in you,' he repeated, taking a step closer.

She knew what he was doing, distracting her with words while he inched closer, close enough to snatch her gun.

'Why all this?' she said. 'For money?'

In the stands far below, the crowd roared, and Ida noticed her eyes were streaming, the tears turning the glare liquid, coating the world in a fluid of light.

'Money is life,' the man said.

She shook her head, ripping the burned skin on her back, the pain causing her hand to drop for a second. And in that second the shape loomed in front of her, and she was thrown onto the bulb itself. And the pain was everything, obliterating all reality.

She collapsed onto the gangway, and he was on top of her, trying to roll her over, to get at her gun. She turned and tossed it away from her, and through the fog she saw him stumble away to get it.

She lay on the floor and her muscles woke up and she breathed in finally, gulping at the air, knowing it was just a matter of time before he killed her. Then, through the pain, she realized something was pressing into her hip, something in the pocket of her dress, the edge of the sunglasses Jacob's brother had given her.

She fumbled them onto her face and opened her eyes, and she could actually see through the glare, the dark discs dimming the light to something bearable. Now she had the advantage. She could make out Severyn in front of her, blinded by the light, on all fours, looking for her gun. She turned around and suddenly saw Severyn's gun where he had dropped it when she'd shot him.

She tried to get up and the flayed skin on her shoulder rippled in pain, making her wince and collapse once more onto the floor. She looked up – Severyn was just inches from her gun. She forced herself up, stumbled along the gangway till she reached it. A pearl-handled revolver. She picked it up and turned and they both fired together.

Ida's bullet clanged off the gangway next to Severyn. He fired again and the shoulder of her dress burst open in a puff of cotton, and then she felt the pain and stumbled backwards, and Severyn ran at her, one more bullet to finish her off. She raised her weakened hand and fired and caught him in the gut.

He stumbled and fell, and Ida collapsed against the handrail. She took a moment to gather her strength, then she lifted up the gun and pointed it shakily at him. He craned his neck left and right, trying to guess where she was, completely blinded now by the lights.

Ida was so battered and exhausted that she could barely manage to breathe.

It was all she could do to keep her arm up, her hand shaking from the pain of the bullet wound and the agony of the burns rippling down her body.

He raised his gun again and fanned it about. Then he must have heard her rasping breaths somehow, because despite his blindness, his gun swayed in her direction. Just before it reached her, she fired.

Until the chamber was empty, and Severyn was finally still.

57

La Salle Street was dead, the office-workers gone, the cleaners not yet arrived, anyone else who might have been abroad drawn to the commotion at Soldier Field. Dante drove down empty streets, slowly past the front of the building, saw the parked cars opposite, then the figures hunched down low in them. He carried on driving, around the block, checked the service entrance at the back of the building, checked the side streets, and parked up around the corner. He looped around so he walked back onto the street from the opposite direction, making the men in the cars think he'd parked at the other end of the block.

He stepped through the building's revolving doors and into the lobby. It was huge and high-ceilinged, and decorated in ancient Egyptian motifs, so much so that it felt like some abandoned movie set, the stage for *The Ten Commandments* or *The King of Kings*.

There were no guards, no doormen, no one manning the reception desk, and therefore no one to remember him ever being there. He saw one of the elevators had its doors open, so he walked over to it, and as he did so, he stared at the mural above, and the eye of Horus stared back at him.

He got into the elevator, and there being no boy to operate it for him, he pulled the door shut, and pressed the only button inside it – the one for the twenty-fourth floor – and it jolted into action.

The doors opened onto a dimly lit, eerie corridor in which three men were waiting for him. The first was Sacco, whom Dante recognized from the golf course. He had his brown suit and bowler hat on, and a Smith & Wesson .45 in his hand. The second man looked like hired muscle, big and surly. And the third man looked like an accountant, dressed in a smart suit, with one of his eyes moving slightly off, glassy, glinting a little too much in the gloom.

Sacco nodded at Dante to raise his hands, and he did so, and the muscle came over and frisked him, and Dante's heart went haywire and he panicked they'd find his gun, even though he knew nobody ever searched people's hats.

After a few seconds, the muscle gave Sacco the all-clear and Dante relaxed a touch and Sacco flicked the .45 sideways a couple of times, and Dante walked down the corridor in the direction indicated, and the three men followed him wordlessly.

Up ahead, Dante could see light coming through a glass door, spilling a rectangle of lemon yellow onto the corridor's murky carpet. Then he could hear a voice emanating faintly from the room on the other side of the door, a radio, the boxing match, the commentator's words cutting through the silence on a wave of static.

'In,' said Sacco from behind him.

Dante opened the door and stepped into an office. Floor-to-ceiling windows looked south over Chicago, with the lake on one side, and the city lights gleaming on the other. Directly in front of the window was a mahogany desk, and behind it sat Coulton, a cigar clenched in his teeth, listening to the radio which had been placed between a pair of Ming vases on a sideboard.

And next to the sideboard, sitting on a sofa, was Loretta, still dressed in her funeral clothes, looking disconsolate but unharmed. Dante threw her a questioning glance, and she nodded in response that she was okay.

Opposite the desk were a couple of empty chairs. Coulton held a hand out to them and Dante sat. Then Coulton nodded at Sacco and the other men.

'Wait outside,' he said, and Dante turned to see a grimace creep onto Sacco's face. Coulton wanted the men out of the way in case Dante revealed who the New York connection was during their chat. Dante wondered if this meant Sacco hadn't told Coulton about his offer. If Sacco really was going to double-cross his boss.

After a moment, Sacco nodded and did as he was commanded, and the three of them left the office.

Dante took his hat off, carefully, turned it so its lining was facing upwards, the Beretta just there, snug in the strips of cloth he'd hastily sewn into the crown to keep it in place. Could he kill Coulton with his first shot? Unlikely. Two bullets for Coulton, maybe? Saving the other four for the men outside? Even more unlikely. And after that, could he find the service elevator and get Loretta out of there before the men parked up in front of the building realized?

He ran his fingers around the brim of his hat.

'Just in case you thought you might get the opportunity . . .' said Coulton, and he lifted a Colt 1911 off the desktop, raised his eyebrows, then rested it back down, the business end pointed at Dante.

'You said to Sacco on the phone you had a deal to make?' he said. 'That you know certain things . . .'

Dante nodded and told Coulton what he knew. He laid it on thick with how clever he thought Coulton's plan was, and Coulton lapped it up, listening eagerly, taking long puffs on his cigar.

'It was a nice plan,' said Dante, wrapping things up, 'but you got something wrong.'

'Oh? What was that?' said Coulton, leaning forward.

'You didn't offer me a job.'

Coulton laughed, but Dante kept his eyes on him and carried on talking.

'I'm the best fixer this city ever had,' he said. 'You let me and the girl walk out of here and I'll take care of the New York side for you. Make sure Lansky and Luciano don't short-change you.'

At the mention of the names Coulton flinched, and Dante had his proof.

'They're friends of mine,' continued Dante. 'I can keep them in check, and you know I'll do a better job of it than anyone else you could hire. And I won't say a word to your men outside. Both of us know if Sacco found out who the connection is, he'd cut you out of the action in a heartbeat. And I'll keep Capone off your back until you make your next attempt to take him out.'

Dante looked at Coulton, wondering if he'd buy it. But there wasn't the slightest hint of emotion on the old man's face. He leaned back in his chair and took a puff on his cigar before speaking again.

'You don't share Capone's objection to the dope trade?' he asked.

Dante shook his head. 'Capone's a dinosaur,' he said. 'You think I want to be working for a man like that? I'm paying off a debt. Prohibition's coming to an end. In a year or two, it'll have been repealed, and then what'll happen to bootleggers like Capone? No hotel chains or restaurants will want to deal with gangsters anymore. Only a fool like Capone can't see the end coming, the need to switch into something new. We take those distribution channels the bootleggers set up and use them for narcotics. That's the future. And I wanna be a part of it. I wanna be in business with you.'

Coulton stared at him, mulling over Dante's offer, sifting through the angles. In the stillness, the only movement was the flow of cigar smoke, the flicker of the city lights outside, the boats along the dark surface of the lake; the only sound was the buzz of the radio. In a ring in another part of the city, some elegant act of violence occurred, one man got the better of another, and the country roared.

'I went to Capone with the idea months ago and he turned me down,' said Coulton. 'Explain that to me – a man who snorts cocaine and drinks like a fish and sleeps with half the girls in his brothels – a man like that turning his nose up at heroin.'

Coulton shrugged, indicating that he still found Capone's decision perplexing.

'You're right,' he continued. 'Narcotics are the future. Easier to smuggle than booze, easier to transport, a million times more addictive and profitable. The government gave us a gift with prohibition, but by banning narcotics, they're ushering in a golden age. Unfortunately, Dante, that golden age doesn't include you. If you'd have come to me a few weeks ago, we could have worked something out. But now . . .' He shook his head.

'Then why did you let me come here?'

'We have something planned tonight. Something we wanted you out of the way for. When you called suggesting to meet, well, it was a happy coincidence. For us. Plus we didn't know if you'd told Capone about us. Judging from your little speech back there, you haven't.'

'And the New York connection?'

Coulton shrugged. 'So you know who I'm buying from in New York? That won't matter when you're dead.'

And he grinned, and Dante knew that there was no point talking to the man, that he had badly misjudged the situation, and his thoughts crept to his backup plan, to the Saturday Night Special stitched into his hat.

'What about the girl? You could let her go,' said Dante. 'Do what you want with me, but let her go.'

Coulton sighed. 'She's just been witness to our meeting,' he said. 'What can I do?' And he raised his hands suggesting there was nothing to be done, and Dante's heart sank and a grim resolution filled his being. Coulton's hands were in the air: the furthest they had been from the gun on his desk the whole time they'd been speaking.

Dante's eyes darted from the man's hands to the man's gun, calculating the distance, and Coulton frowned, followed Dante's gaze, sensed something was up. The old man lurched forward, grabbing for his Colt. Dante ripped the snub-nose from his hat and fired it twice. The first shot shattered the window; the second left a penny-sized hole in the old man's forehead, and a bewildered expression on his face. He slumped onto the desktop, his fingers an inch or so from his gun. Then the window exploded outwards in a roar, glass fragments sucked out into the night, the papers rising up from the desk and swirling into the air, Loretta screaming over the rush of the wind.

Dante leapt forward and grabbed the Colt from Coulton's desk and spun about just as Sacco and the muscle burst in, guns raised, and a deafening volley of bullets rattled around the room. The two men dropped to the floor and Dante felt a wave of relief, and then he felt the dullness in his gut and wondered why he was pushed up against the desk, and he looked down and saw the bullethole in his shirt, the blood pumping out of it, and for some reason all he could think to focus on as the pain cascaded through his body was the voice of the commentator over the roar of the wind . . .

Cuts have formed above Dempsey's eyes. His face is swollen, he's bleeding from his mouth . . .

Then he was on the floor, and somewhere in the distance Loretta was screaming. He could see Sacco and the other man splayed out on the floor, and the perspective lines began to swirl, the world beginning to tumble. He closed his eyes and there was the roar of the wind. He heard a bell ringing, a crowd somewhere cheering, frantic voices.

And the round ends, and Teddy Haines is quick to smear Vaseline all over Dempsey's face . . .

Then a woman's voice, a woman's hands helping him up and he opened his eyes and saw the room in disarray, his view lopsided. Loretta was dragging him to the door, now just a wooden frame holding a hundred glass shards.

Dante fumbled about in his pocket, slippery with blood, and

pulled out his lighter and waved it about for Loretta to take. She frowned a moment, then caught his meaning. She left him leaning against the frame of the glass door and she went over to the drinks stand and poured a decanter of whiskey over the sofa, then used the lighter to set it on fire.

Dante turned his head to watch, and he caught a glimpse of Coulton, slumped over the desk, the papers on it soaking up his blood. Then the sofa was aflame, and the carpet, and the paintings nailed to the wall, the horsemen and hunting parties and the green hills they were riding over, all turning to black in the blaze.

Loretta put her arm under Dante's shoulder and they hobbled through the glass-fanged mouth of the shattered door. They stepped into the corridor, and the third man was there, pinning himself against the wall, crying.

'Please don't kill me . . . Please . . . I'm just a secretary . . . Please . . .' Dante looked at the man, at how red his good eye was, raw and streaming tears, and how his glass eye was still perfectly clear, and how bizarre that was.

'Please don't kill me . . .'

They left him there, sobbing in a fit of despair, and they moved off, Loretta following the signs for the elevator. Dante shook his head.

The service elevator . . .

And he wasn't sure if he'd said it out loud until they changed direction, heading the other way down the long dark corridor. They reached a wall and slumped against it and Loretta was bashing a button on the wall and there was a wrenching sound as the elevator came to life, and when the doors opened and they stepped inside, Dante saw the great blood smear on the wall where he'd been slumped, and he looked down and saw his shirt and trousers were red, blood congealing in clots in the spaces between the laces of his shoes, and he knew he was dead, but that maybe he had saved Loretta.

He slumped against one of the metal panels that lined the

interior of the elevator, and slid down it till he was sitting on the floor. The burning sensation in his stomach seared through the shock and he realized his hands were cupped around the hole in his gut and he thought of pregnant women, cupping their hands around new life.

Loretta had tears falling down her face and he realized he didn't have much time and he realized he was muttering, babbling, slurring. He fumbled the car keys from his pocket, raised them up, saw a drop of blood drip off the end of them as he held them aloft.

. . . Leave me here – run away – there's men in the cars in front – there'll be glass on the street from the window – go round the back – and run . . .

He wondered if he'd actually said the words, or just thought them. He babbled on, muttering, and he wondered if she'd heard him, if she'd get away. If he'd told her what Sacco's car looked like.

And at some point there was a great thud and the vibrations stopped. The lights flickered off, and then on again, and he saw he was alone in the elevator, and his stomach was no longer hurting, and then the great mechanism started up again and he moved on, past the ground floor, past the basement, continuing on into the darkness, falling through the universe to the city of ghosts entombed in the past, to join his parents and his siblings and his wife, all of them waiting for him at his sister's graduation party.

CONCLUSION

CODA

'You were best. You fought a smart fight, kid.'

Chicago Herald Tribune

THE WORLD'S GREATEST NEWSPAPER

TUNNEY WINS BY DECISION

NEWS SUMMARY

Tunney wins decision by unanimous verdict of judges. *Page 1.*

James O'Donnell Bennett describes intense drama of battle. *Page 1.*

Dempsey camp protest slow count in seventh round. *Page 1.*

Society women and shop girls go see, and learn all about fighting. *Page 2.*

Tunney 11-to-10 choice in fistic mart at eleventh hour. *Page 4.*

Hits and misses all looked alike from the way-back seats. *Page 5.*

Trains, planes and autos bring fans to fight. *Page 5.*

CROWD SCREAMS AT TENSE DRAMA AS GENE RISES

(A page of pictures of the fight, showing the action in the various rounds, is on page 3.)

BY JAMES O'DONNELL BENNETT

In a prize fight with terrific ebb and flow in it Gene Tunney held his world's championship against Jack Dempsey's ferocious assaults on Soldier's Field last night. The moment of high drama came in the seventh round at 10:34 when Dempsey knocked Tunney down to a count of nine, but referee Dave Barry was accused of starting the count late as under new rules . . .

PINKERTON'S NATIONAL DETECTIVE AGENCY, INC.

FOUNDED BY ALLAN PINKERTON, 1850

ALLAN PINKERTON, NEW YORK

OFFICES:

ATLANTA	CLEVELAND	HOUSTON	MONTREAL	PORTLAND, ORE	SEATTLE
BALTIMORE	DALLAS	INDIANAPOLIS	NEW ORLEANS	PROVIDENCE	SPOKANE
BOSTON	DENVER	KANSAS CITY	NEW YORK	RICHMOND	ST. LOUIS
BUFFALO	DETROIT	LOS ANGELES	OMAHA	SALT LAKE CITY	ST. PAUL
CHICAGO	HARRISBURG	MILWAUKEE	PHILADELPHIA	SAN FRANCISCO	SYRACUSE
CINCINNATI	HARTFORD	MINNEAPOLIS	PITTSBURGH	SCRANTON	TORONTO

137 South Wells Street,

Chicago, July 16th, 1928

Disciplinary hearing: #1928-C-IL-04b

Operatives: Davis, Ida #713, Talbot, Michael #442

Dear Sir and Madam,

We write to inform you of the decision of the disciplinary hearing held on July 13th into your conduct with regards to case #103-455-28 – H. Van Haren.

The arbiters decided that on all counts the claims of gross misconduct and willful disregard of orders were valid, and the hearing recommended dismissal; a recommendation which was taken up by the Executive Committee.

This ruling is not subject to appeal and enforcement is immediate. Any personal possessions left in your former offices will be forwarded to you

by post. We would like to remind you that the
privacy agreements you signed at the commencement
of your employment with the firm are binding in
perpetuity.

    Respectfully,

    David G. Trainor,

    Chair, Executive Committee

PINKERTON'S NATIONAL DETECTIVE AGENCY
WE NEVER SLEEP

58

Michael took the eight-fifteen *Wolverine* out to Ann Arbor, and from there he caught a taxi the last six miles to where the asylum was located, on the Huron River, a little outside Ypsilanti. When he arrived at the building, a pleasant-looking, neo-classical mansion, the doctor was on the steps to meet him. He was in his fifties, bearded and portly, and he greeted Michael with a cautious smile and a firm handshake, before leading him through reception, up some stairs, and down a maze of corridors.

He described the facility's unique character, how it was funded through the School of Medicine at Michigan University, the groundbreaking research that was conducted there; trying to underline, Michael saw, that if anything they spoke about became public, it would cause harm to the institution, and the vulnerable patients they were trying so hard to treat.

It had taken weeks of research to find the place. The day after Coulton and Severyn had died and Ida had been hospitalized, Michael had been informed that they were being suspended from the Pinkertons, pending a disciplinary hearing. So he had called up Walker and explained to him what he wanted to do, and Walker had presented him with a six-week contract that attached him to the State's Attorney's office as a temporary investigator. It meant he could conduct his research with the weight of the SA behind him, and that sped things up no end, as did the fact that Charles Coulton Senior's business empire had been left in a tattered and tangled mess. With the man dead, and his son and business secretary missing, and his office burned down, a swarm of lawyers had taken control of his estate, and it was to them that Michael made his semi-official requests.

He pored over the dead man's accounts, discovered he'd made an endowment to the university, and that his secretary had taken a trip out there the day after Gwendolyn died. He went through the employee records, found the relevant driver and interviewed him; he confirmed the trip, the timing, the passengers, and the bonus he'd received for keeping his mouth shut.

After that it was just a case of coercing the people that ran the asylum into talking to him. He called the university and gave them a story about Coulton's death and his suspected criminality, and said that an official probe into his financial affairs was underway, including looking at any charitable endowments the man had made. He sent them a request letter on government-headed paper, and received in return a list of the asylum's employees. These he ran through the Bureau of Identification in Chicago, and the Bureau of Investigation in Washington, and he found a match – one of the doctors at the facility had an outstanding arrest warrant from California, having been caught, thirty years earlier, peddling abortion drugs to prostitutes in Santa Barbara, just a few months after he'd graduated from UCLA.

Michael called him and explained the situation, that all he wanted in return for not telling the university administration about his outstanding warrant for the distribution of abortifacient drugs was some information on one of his patients. The doctor agreed, and Michael booked a ticket on the *Wolverine*, and twenty-four hours later the doctor was leading him down the corridors of the asylum, looking only faintly put out to be in the company of the man who was blackmailing him.

They stopped at a locked and bolted door that reminded Michael of a solitary-confinement cell, and he noted the slate square to one side, with the patient's name written on it in chalk: *Charles Cooper*. The doctor opened up the viewing hatch, and Michael stepped forward to peer inside.

It was a nice cell, as far as cells went: it had a bed in it and a barred window looking out onto the river and the cornfields beyond, a table and a bucket, and walls painted a soothing shade of pale green. And then Michael noticed the force-feeding chair in the corner, with buckles at its feet and on its arms, and blocks either side of the headrest, making it look like an electric chair.

He turned his gaze from the chair to the bed, where, lying down, in a straitjacket and pyjamas, was Charles Coulton Junior. His head was propped up on a pillow, allowing Michael to see his face, or what was left of it. Arturo Vargas had not exaggerated when he said that Coulton had been left unrecognizable after Benny Roebuck had smashed a champagne bottle into his face. Great scars pitted his skin and his nose had been partly sliced off, and there was an awful, lopsided quality to the structure of what was left. Michael doubted even the boy's closest friends would recognize him.

And in the midst of all that scarred, lumpen flesh were two hollows where a pair of eyes should have been.

'The eyes?' Michael asked.

'Infected. They were removed in the trauma center.'

So Roebuck had blinded Coulton, causing Severyn to exact revenge when he finally caught up with the man in the alley-way. Maybe because of the angle of Coulton's head, it looked to Michael as if he was staring at the ceiling above him, at the waves of dust floating about in the afternoon sunlight. He made no motion the whole time Michael was studying him, seemed completely oblivious to the world, and Michael wondered how much of it was catalepsy and how much of it was medication.

He took a last look at the killer of Gwendolyn Van Haren, the boy onto whom Coulton Senior had pinned his dreams of an empire, and he stepped away from the viewing grate, and the doctor closed it gently.

'We can talk in my office,' he said.

*

Ten minutes later they were sitting in a bright room which, like Coulton's cell, had a view over the river and cornfields. A secretary had brought them cups of mint tea and the scent of it filled the air.

'I'm not in charge of his case,' said the doctor, 'but after your call, I looked at the boy's case notes, spoke to my colleagues and acquainted myself with his history.'

Michael nodded and looked at the man, and he tried to match up the fifty-something bearded doctor with the graduate in California thirty years previously who had been caught selling abortions to prostitutes.

'What is it you'd like to know?' he asked Michael.

'Is there a chance he'll ever leave here?'

'I don't think he'll ever be cured, if that's what you're asking. If you decide to reveal his identity he might be sent to another facility, but I doubt he'll ever end up in a prison, even if he's tried for the girl's murder. No judge would send him anywhere but a hospital. He's catatonic, may as well be in a coma. We have to force-feed him, clean him up. He's doubly incontinent. I've never heard of a single instance of someone coming back to normal function after such a complete shutdown.'

'And who's paying for him to be here?'

'The boy's care will be paid for out of the endowment – a certain portion of it is ring-fenced for the patients here, and there's a good few years of it still to run. After that, if there's no financing left, he'll be put into a state lunatic asylum. They're building a new one over in Ypsilanti.'

'So he'll always be like that? How I saw him in the cell?'

'We prefer to call them rooms. But yes, he's yet to show any lucidity. Like I said, if we didn't feed him, he'd starve. In that respect, he's only a danger to himself.'

'You have any idea what caused it?'

The doctor shifted in his seat. 'There's perhaps something you don't know about the boy. This isn't the first time he's been a patient here. This is his third visit. He stayed here briefly during his time at college, when his homosexual tendencies became apparent. Then he came again more recently, a year ago, after he'd suffered a nervous collapse. We treated him with psycho-analysis and electro-shock therapy. My colleague in charge of his case, Dr Munroe, has built up a comprehensive psychopathology of the boy. If you'd like, I could précis it?'

'Please . . .'

'The patient has been through a number of significant traumas. The death of his mother in childbirth meant he grew up motherless with a father who blamed him for her death. Then came the manifestation of his homosexual tendencies, and his experiences during the war. These most recent traumas – the death of his fiancée, and the facial injuries – were, to put it in layman's terms, the final straw. Most of Dr Munroe's notes deal with the relationship to the patient's father. He raised the patient to be cultured, literate, genteel, and then lambasted him for possessing those very same qualities, blaming them for what he saw as his son's spoiled, enfeebled nature, his effeminacy. On the one hand he was criticized for being too soft, but when he tried to act like his father, replicated his roughness, he was criticized for being uncouth.

'And so the patient grew up confused, unloved, unable to rec-oncile the two contradictory people his father wanted him to be. He began engaging in behavior patterns designed to display and prove his masculinity – troublemaking at school, volunteering to fight in the war in Europe, associating with low-lifes. In the war he met Lloyd Severyn, the criminal type the patient had already been attracted to in the past. With Severyn he was accepted by someone similar to his father, and this assuaged some of his feel-ings of worthlessness, the patient seeing him as a bridge between the two worlds he'd always been torn between. The patient's wishes to become involved in the father's schemes stem from this, too, I suppose. That need to live up to those expectations.

'But on that final night the boy realized he had failed the father again, and the reason for that failure was the appearance of his fiancée, and by extension his sexuality. He suffered a relapse, took out his anger and frustration on the girl, killing her in the process, and then he shut down. Maybe before he was attacked and his face was destroyed, maybe after. He finally realized he could not be the two different people he had spent his life trying to be, and so he became neither, without personality, unable to respond to stimulus, unsure of who or what he was.

'That is Dr Munroe's assessment, at least. Perhaps at some point some new persona might arise, some third personality he can use to interact with the world, but given the severity of the trauma, I doubt it. I fear he'll be like this for life, a body without a person inside.'

The doctor held up his hands, then placed them on the desk in front of him. Michael nodded, and stared at the untouched cups of tea.

'So,' said the doctor after a moment, 'will you reveal his whereabouts? Or let us continue to treat him? I don't see any benefit to anyone in forcing him through the court system. Dr Munroe will testify to the patient's total inability, and the judge will send him back to an asylum, and all that will happen will be a waste of taxpayers' money.'

'I agree with you, doctor. But I'll need to discuss it with my partner first. There's the dead girl's mother to think about, too. She has a right to know the truth. Perhaps, in the end, the decision is hers.'

'I see,' said the doctor, with cold formality. 'Please let me know of her decision.'

Michael left the office shortly after that, and stood on the front steps of the building while he waited for his car. He looked up at the great white mansion behind him, shining in the afternoon sunlight, and he thought about the room at its rear, where Gwendolyn's killer was strapped into a straitjacket, his face shorn of its eyes, his body shorn of its mind. It made him think about New Orleans, about folk tales of voodou priests bringing corpses back to life, and he thought of what Coulton Senior had told him in his office about voodou and money.

Then Michael's car arrived, and he got in, and was driven through the arsenic green of the fields, back to the station, back to Chicago, mulling over voodou and the dreams of empires lying in tatters, and the residue and weight of the shadows that passed silently through the world.

Dear Mrs Van Haren,

We would firstly like to offer to you our condolences on the loss of your daughter. This case was the most troubling and distressing we have had to investigate in our time with the Pinkertons and it affected us both deeply. We have put much thought into our decision to write to you, weighing your right to know the truth about what happened to Gwendolyn against the heartbreak we know it will cause you. As you have this letter in your hand, you already know our decision. What has been printed in the newspapers and in the Pinkertons' own reports is somewhat true, but it does not tell the full story; below is what we believe to be the truth. We uncovered these details in painful circumstances, and at great personal cost, so we felt it only right that we present them to you, whether or not you choose to read them.

Your daughter spent the day of her disappearance trying to find Charles Coulton Junior so that she could tell him she was breaking off their engagement. She went to Bronzeville and met a man called Randall Taylor, a go-between, who gave her the address of an apartment Coulton rented, where he thought Coulton might be. The apartment was on a desolate road to the south of the Stockyards and Coulton used it as pied-à-terre.

Gwendolyn arrived there at some point after ten o'clock. But on her arrival, she happened to interrupt Coulton and his companion, Lloyd Severyn, as they were involved in cleaning up a violent crime. When she saw what they were doing, she rushed back home and, fearing for her life, attempted to leave the country. She packed a bag and caught a taxi to Illinois Central station, but en route, a few blocks from the station, Severyn caught up with her, abducted her, and took her back to the apartment.

While she was there, Coulton and she argued, and Coulton strangled and killed her. We do not believe her murder was premeditated, and Severyn was not involved in her death. In a panic, Coulton moved her body to the basement and hid it under the coals in the cellar and, later that night, fled the scene.

These are the broad details of what happened to your daughter, much of which overlaps with what you already know. Attached are copies of our personal case files, which detail the larger context of the events, the crime Gwendolyn stumbled upon that night, and how it was part of a conspiracy set up by Charles Coulton Senior whose aim was the establishment of a heroin distribution network in the city.

We thought we would write you these details personally so that you knew from us first-hand what we had uncovered, and would not have to rely on newspapers and the skewed reports of the police and our former colleagues in the Pinkertons.

My father, Peter Davis, often used to say that it's best to know the truth, no matter how upsetting that truth may be. Throughout my life I have believed this to be valid and well-founded, but in writing this letter, I am no longer sure.

If you have any questions or would like to discuss anything in relation to this, we are always available to talk, and can be reached via the return address. Again, we offer you our condolences on your loss and hope you may find some measure of consolation.

With deepest sympathy,
    Ida Davis and Michael Talbot

59

Footsteps echoed along the corridor of the hospital, and the man in the bed propped himself up, grimacing against the pain ripping through his stomach. There was a knock, and the door swung open, and the nurse leaned in and smiled.

'A Mr Halpert here to see you,' she said.

The man in the bed frowned, not recognizing the name.

'Says he's a movie producer,' the nurse added, 'from Hollywood . . .' She rolled her eyes and grinned and the man in the bed smiled back at her and a memory rose up in his mind from what seemed like an age ago – a hotel bar, a Jewish man, suntanned, in Chicago looking for gangsters.

'Ask him in,' he said, and the nurse nodded and disappeared behind the door and a few seconds later Halpert stepped into the room. He had his hat in one hand, a briefcase in the other, and a broad smile on his face.

'Mr Sanfelippo?' he said, and Dante nodded.

'We met at the bar of the Drake . . .'

'Yes, I remember. Please, take a seat.'

Halpert smiled and sat, drummed his fingers on the crown of his hat.

'How are the injuries?' he asked.

'Mending,' said Dante. 'The doctors had to remove four feet of intestines, but there's been no infection, and the morphine keeps the worst of the pain at bay.' The last of these statements was not strictly true, but Dante had found his visitors were more comfortable in his presence if they thought he was comfortable, too.

Halpert smiled and opened up his briefcase, took out a brown paper bag full of grapes and passed it to Dante.

'Thank you,' said Dante, stretching painfully to put the grapes on the bedside table. Halpert took a handful of them out of the bag and began popping them into his mouth.

'How's your hunt for actors been going?' asked Dante.

'My boss is recalling me to California.'

'I'm sorry to hear it.'

'On the plus side, I managed to read that book on Capone – an early draft – and I think we're going to go ahead and film it.'

'That's very brave. So what can I do for you, Mr Halpert?'

'Well, after we had our chat at the bar, your line of work was pointed out to me by a third party, and that set me off to tracking you down. I'd like to offer you a job, Mr Sanfelippo.'

'Thanks for the offer but I'm not an actor.'

'Not that kind of a job, although you've got the face for it. As you know, we've got these gangster films coming up, and we need someone to act as an . . . overseer of authenticity. A consultant. To help keep them realistic.'

'I see,' said Dante, not quite convinced that such a job could exist. 'The job title would be?'

'Consultant,' said Halpert, popping another grape into his mouth.

'And what would my actual job be?'

Halpert grinned, as if the two had just shared a secret. 'You'd be a fixer. For the studio. You've quite the reputation for it. Perhaps Hollywood is a more . . . relaxed . . . environment to pursue your talent.'

'Which studio is this?'

'Silly me.' Halpert rummaged around his pockets and produced a card and passed it to Dante.

SAM HALPERT

Executive Producer, Howard Hughes Movie Productions
Santa Monica Boulevard, Los Angeles, Cal.

'We're raring to go on *Scarface* – that's the Capone film. It'd be a nice easy start for you. And after that, whatever Mr Hughes thinks you'd be good at. You'll find Mr Hughes to be a very generous man. You'd have your accommodation paid for, first-class travel wherever you went, and the retainer would be substantial. Mr Hughes would even pay for you to visit the city of angels for a few weeks to see how you like it before you commit. We'll get you on the Santa Fe *Chief*. It's an all-Pullman – I came on it myself – buffet cars, lounge cars, dining cars. Only takes sixty-eight hours but you'll wish it took more.'

Dante had heard of the train, 'the rolling boudoir of the film set'. He thought of the last time he had taken a train to California, sleeping in a boxcar with three other hobos, freezing through the Sierra Nevada mountains, burning up through the desert.

'Mr Halpert, would you like a first piece of advice? A freebie? Change the name from *Scarface* to something else. Al's very sensitive about those scars.'

Halpert grinned. 'See, Mr Sanfelippo, you're proving your worth already.'

He got out a pen and pad and made like he was jotting down what Dante had said and Dante realized why the man was producing movies and not acting in them.

'Your confidence in me,' said Dante, 'your job offer – is based on what you heard about me after meeting me in a bar?'

'We've been looking for someone to come and work for us in this capacity for a while now. That was also one of my reasons to be in Chicago, though I couldn't admit it last time we met. I made substantial inquiries about you. We're sure you'll be a good fit. Like I said, the age of the celluloid gangster is here, and maybe you could be a part of it.'

Halpert smiled and his hand went rummaging through the brown paper bag for more grapes.

'Well, that's a mighty fine offer. How long do I get to decide?'

'As long as you want. Take some time to think it over and let me know. I'm leaving town in a couple of days, but you can contact me at the Drake before then, and via the Hollywood office after I leave.'

'Thank you, Mr Halpert. I'll have a think about it.'

'You do that, and get well soon.'

The man rose, nodded a quick goodbye and walked out of the room, and Dante listened to his footsteps echoing along the corridor and into nothingness. He looked at the card again, tapped his fingers against it and tried to imagine California. Then he looked up at the drab hospital room. The afternoon sun was slanting in through the window, turning a section of the bed and the floor a golden orange. Loretta would be here soon, and he'd show her the card for the fun of it.

She'd been here every day over the last month. She was the face he had seen when he'd awoken after the surgery, and he'd felt her presence when he was drifting in and out of consciousness in the days just after the operation, strung out on hospital morphine while simultaneously withdrawing from the heroin. It was the longest he'd ever gone without it. The morphine helped; the fact that he was bedridden and couldn't score helped even more. But for the first time in years, he actually wanted to quit. A strange feeling after all that time in the wilderness.

He looked at the bag of grapes, leaned over to pluck a couple out and as he shifted, he felt the pull of his skin against the stitches in his stomach and an avalanche of pain ran through him, and his mind jumped back to the night in the building.

He could only remember snatches of what had happened, but Loretta had filled him in. She had gotten him out of the building, found the car, somehow managed to get him into it, driven him to a hospital. She'd called around and managed to get Al there within a few hours, and he'd taken care of the rest – arranging for Dante to be moved to the hospital he was in now, where the doctors were on the payroll.

They'd kept watch on the newspapers for reports about Coulton's death – all of them described it as an accident, a freak office fire responsible for the death of the financier and two of his associates. No mention of the bodies having bullets in them. Al claimed he'd done nothing to suppress any Coroner's reports so they'd put the hush job down to someone in City Hall or the State's Attorney's office or maybe the attorneys that were crawling all over the remains of the man's business empire.

Aside from that, Al put his weight behind getting evidence to disappear from the shoot-out on the elevated tracks. Heavy kickbacks for the officers investigating not to pursue who the mystery fourth man in the shoot-out was, to lose all evidence of Dante's presence there. Fingerprint samples from the bullet-riddled car by the drugstore vanished from the file before they could be cross-checked.

When Dante had gotten some of his energy back and was a little more lucid, he'd explained to Al what had happened. He told him almost everything – that Coulton wanted to take out Al so he could take over his distribution network, that he'd teamed up with Sacco, who was his man on the inside. He didn't mention the New York connection, not wanting to implicate himself. Al must have known, though, must have linked Coulton's plan to the man coming to see him months earlier with a scheme to bring heroin into the city. Al had thanked him, told him he'd done a good job, and proceeded to make cracks about Loretta, and that's when Dante knew he was in the clear.

Then he'd had the first of his unexpected visitors – Jacob's girlfriend. She'd come by and sat awkwardly in the guest chair and they'd talked just as awkwardly, an odd, stilted conversation. She told him how she'd dealt with Severyn, how the police had found the nitroglycerin strapped to the top of a stand in Soldier Field. How the authorities, knowing the man who'd put it there was dead, were happy to keep it quiet, nip any outrage in the bud.

In a way, Dante was glad it was her who had taken care of

Jacob's killer. Between them they'd put the last few details in their place. He felt a chill run through him when she told him about Coulton's plan to set Capone and Moran against each other; it was exactly the same plan Lansky and Luciano had talked about using on New York's two biggest crime families – the Masserias and Maranzanos.

The news left Dante in no doubt as to the identity of the New York connection – it had to be his two friends, and it made him think of what Red had said, about the way Chicago ran on each man's need to get one over on the next man, that the world turned on the friction of conflicting interests. Coulton and his friends had been using exactly that to further their ends, twisting that sad, simple truth about humanity to wreak a terrible violence on the city, and Dante and Jacob and the girl had all been dragged into the center of the storm.

Through all of it he and the girl had managed to survive, and now the two of them talked about it with the distant intimacy of veterans. They spoke haltingly and he realized that just like him, the girl was a traumatized soul, one who had difficulty expressing her troubles. But Dante had Loretta for support, and as he looked at the girl, he wondered who she had, and he felt sorry for her.

Then out of the blue she asked him if he was sticking around in Chicago, and he said he probably wasn't. And when she asked him where he was going, he surprised himself by saying he wasn't sure.

The girl left him her card, and told him to stay in touch, and he thought it was a strange thing for her to do until she explained why and it made Dante happy. And then she took the sunglasses out of her bag and gave them back to him and told him she didn't need them anymore, and they both smiled.

Looking back on the meeting now, he wished the movie man had come a few days earlier, and he could have told the girl he was going to Hollywood. The more he thought about it, the more he realized it was as good a place as any for a new start. He looked at the movie man's card once more, flicked it through his fingers. He'd call up the fisherman out on Long Island, tell him that he could keep the boat, keep the business, do whatever he wanted with it. He smiled at the thought of telling them, when they asked, that he'd decided to go out west to make movies. The age of the celluloid gangster was here.

Despite the pain, he leaned over and grabbed the bag of grapes, eating them as he watched the sun move lower through the window, unfurling a fan of golden light across the room. Just before it finally set, he picked up the card once more and looked at it, at the address on Santa Monica Boulevard, and then he heard footsteps approaching and Loretta stepped into the room, all long legs in the setting sun, her hair the red of furnaces and prairie fires.

'What's with the card?' she asked, taking off her coat.

He thought a moment, and grinned.

60

The offices were small, and if she was being honest, dingy, but the rent was cheap and the location was central. She'd paid six months in advance, bought a desk and chairs, an electric fan, a pot plant, a radio, and an Artophone suitcase record player. She'd installed a phone line, and paid a stenciler to paint the name on the glass of the outer door in Times New Roman, gold with black trim: *Ida Davis, Private Investigations.*

She'd placed ads in newspapers and magazines and business directories and told her old colleagues back at the Pinkertons, and the courthouses and the State's Attorney's and the police stations and the Detective Division that she was open for business, and asked them to send people her way if they could.

Now it was just a question of waiting, and she surprised herself by not getting too anxious while she did. She had a feeling that bad times were coming, and bad times were good for detectives. Plus she still had most of the money left over from Mrs Van Haren's check, enough to see her through years of bad times if she was careful and considered.

She'd thought about Mrs Van Haren often in the weeks that had passed; she thought about the letter she and Michael had written, about what the letter didn't say, about where the boy was, locked up in a lunatic asylum somewhere in Michigan. She'd had to convince Michael not to mention it, that no good could possibly come of it. She also thought about what the letter implied – that it was Mrs Van Haren's actions in trying to marry her daughter off that had ultimately been the cause of her death. Mrs Van Haren must have been clever enough to spot the implication, and she'd still sent them the reward money out of her personal savings, despite the swirl of debts that was engulfing her family. Maybe it was the woman's guilt at work, Ida had thought; maybe the money was her penance.

Michael had taken his half of the cash and put it in trust for Tom and Mae's education. Now Michael was semi-retired, taking up a consultant's role at the Department of the Treasury. His refusal to be bribed by the State's Attorney's office had apparently caught the attention of some officials in the department who were looking for incorruptible men to assist in the training of new agents. Michael had offered Ida a job there, too, but she'd had enough of working for other people, had developed a distrust of large organizations. Her apprenticeship had come to an end and it was time for her to step out on her own. Although that wasn't quite true just yet. Michael would be sticking around for a little bit, to help her out, especially in seven months or so when she'd need time off. She wasn't sure how she'd deal with the business and the child, but she had Michael and Annette to help her out, Louis too, and she guessed that was enough.

At the thought, she rose and walked over to the table in the corner where the Artophone was. She picked up the record Louis had dropped off, stared at the label, gold writing on black: *Okeh Electric – West End Blues – Louis Armstrong and His Hot Five.*

He had come by a few days previously with the record and a bottle of bourbon to christen the new office. It was unusual for him to bring her a record; he had released dozens of them over the years and he rarely made a point of giving her a copy. She'd put it on and they'd listened to it and she could tell at once why he'd made an exception for this one; it was something special, something she'd never heard the like of before. Whatever it was Louis had been searching for, the perfect form, he'd found it, pulled it into existence, and captured it on wax.

They'd listened to it three times over before either of them spoke, then Louis told her how it took six weeks to get the records back from the pressing plant, so he'd had to wait that long to finally get to listen to what they'd recorded, and when he'd eventually gotten his hands on it, he and Earl couldn't quite believe it. They'd spent hours hunched over the record player at the Ranch, smoking and listening to it on a loop, praising their good luck that it had turned out so well.

Now she put the record on the platter and started it up, and then she went over to the open window and leaned against the frame, hoping the breeze would cool her down. The heatwave showed no signs of abating, and day after day the city still blazed with the sun, steeping them in sweat and sleeplessness. Her insomnia was exacerbated by the burns all along her back. Six weeks on and they were still tender and sore, and she had to apply ointment every four hours, and if she followed doctor's orders, would continue to do so for the next two months. The gunshot wound wasn't as bad, the bullet having passed through the flesh at the top of her shoulder, just grazing the bone. She'd come out of it all alive, mostly in one piece, and the experience of having survived it had shown her that she was tougher than she'd thought, just as Michael had always told her. There wasn't any reason to worry; there never had been.

Now she was on the mend, and the office was set up, and all there was left to do was wait for September to roll around, for the kick of autumn to shatter the pitiless heat.

She looked down on the city below, at the busy streets, the traffic, the sunlight pooling on the windows of the skyscraper opposite, turning its facade into a honeycomb of yellow quartz. Then the music started up, with its distinctive fanfare, and a great hypnotic calm came over her, just as it always did when she listened to the song, as if the music was releasing into the air the drowsiness of a late summer afternoon, the mood of what it meant to be alive at that particular time, in that particular place. And it made Ida think of every summer that had ever been, and ever would be.

And in that moment of stillness, she rubbed her belly where the bulge would form and knew that no matter what, the baby would be a perfect thing, as perfect as Louis' song, because in nature as in art, perfect things were inevitable.

She smiled to herself, and a warmth ran through her, and she thought how if the baby was a boy, she'd name it Jacob, and she drifted off into daydreams and after a minute or two, the song finished and the needle scratched around the final groove and the noise of the streets floated in once more from the window. She picked up the needle, returned it to its holder and stopped the record.

And then there was a knock at the door.

She paused a moment, put the record back in its sleeve, straightened herself up and turned around.

'Come in,' she said, and the door opened, and a tall, blonde woman stepped in, a guarded expression on her face, a blue-and-white sports dress hanging off her frame.

'Hello, are you Miss Davis?'

'Yes,' said Ida, stepping forward to greet her. 'How may I help?'

'I was looking to hire you. You're the private detective, right?'

Ida smiled and nodded and gestured to the chair at the desk and the woman sat, and Ida studied her first-ever customer, and her smile broadened; a blonde woman, it was always a blonde.

Ida took her seat at the desk.

'So what's the problem?' she asked.

The woman paused a moment, and then she began to tell her story, and as she did so, Ida felt the promise of a new adventure in the air, as tangible as the roar of the city outside, as electric as Chicago forging ever on into the future.

'I heard a record Louis Armstrong made called "West End Blues". And he doesn't say any words, and I thought, this is wonderful, and I liked the feeling he got from it. Sometimes the record would make me so sad I'd cry up a storm. Other times the same damn record would make me so happy.'

BILLIE HOLIDAY, c.1956

AFTERWORD

I have tried to make this book as factually accurate as possible, but as always with historical fiction, I sometimes had to choose between historical accuracy and telling the story I most wanted to tell. In some cases, different histories contradicted each other, or there was not enough evidence to determine what had actually happened. Below are some notes on where I deviated from established fact, or made calls between opposing accounts; any other deviations were either too minor to include here, or are my own errors or omissions, for which I apologize.

Louis Armstrong's journey to Chicago in the prologue is based on his description of that journey in his autobiography (*Satchmo: My Life in New Orleans*). I deviated from the story to include elements from other people's accounts of their journeys northwards as part of the Great Migration, so that the episode became something of an amalgam.

The Mafia funeral that starts the book is also an amalgam, in this instance of a number of Chicago gangster funerals: most notably those of Dean O'Banion and Mike Merlo in 1924 (the latter is the source of the blue-flower theme). The planes full of flower petals are also based on fact. For 'Diamond' Joe Esposito's funeral in 1928 two planes were indeed loaded with flowers to create a rain of roses; on the day, however, due to bad weather, the planes never took flight.

Sherlock Jr., the Buster Keaton film Ida and Louis go to see, was actually released four years earlier in 1924. Keaton's film of 1928 was *Steamboat Bill Jr*, perhaps his masterpiece. I chose the earlier, less well-regarded film as it closer fitted the book's themes.

Perhaps my greatest sin against history was the inclusion of the Long Count Fight between Gene Tunney and Jack Dempsey. This fight actually occurred in September 1927, some nine months before the events of the book. I wanted to include both this and another landmark event – Louis Armstrong's recording of 'West End Blues'. The latter, though, occurred in 1928. In deciding to fit both into one summer, I had to choose between misrepresenting the history of boxing, or of jazz, and ended up choosing the former.

The recording is a seminal one, not only in Louis Armstrong's life, but also in the history of jazz and popular music. Armstrong had spent years experimenting with song structures and forms for the solo (the form he established back then is still used across genres today). In the recordings he made in the summer of 1928 his achievements in these areas found their perfect expression. The 1920s was a decade of modernism and artistic avant-gardism – Armstrong's radical innovation and experimentation means there is a case to be made for adding him to the pantheon of 1920s modernist stars, a case eloquently made in Thomas Brothers' *Louis Armstrong: Master of Modernism* and Kevin Jackson's *Constellation of Genius: 1922: Modernism and All That Jazz*.

Some readers may have noticed that the structure of this book copies the structure of Armstrong's recording of 'West End Blues' as depicted in one of the later chapters. It was my intention to have this book completely follow the arrangement of the song, so that each character became a different part of the instrumentation. Unfortunately, I was not wholly successful; earlier drafts that faithfully followed the song's structure had issues with plot and pacing, so I had to deviate slightly. I guess it's best to say this book is *almost* structured according to the song.

The arrival of the Paul Whiteman Orchestra in Chicago, and the subsequent jam sessions between them and Louis and his bandmates, actually occurred a few months earlier as well, in November 1927.

Throughout this entire period, Armstrong and Capone were indeed on familiar and friendly terms. The two got on so well together that their closeness was remarked upon by other jazz musicians who were in Chicago at the time.

Poison booze was a widespread phenomenon during prohibition. The inspiration for the batch of champagne in the book was the real-life case of amateur chemists Harry Gross and Max Reisman, who developed an adulterant that would allow Jamaican Ginger extract (a medicine that was 70% ethanol) to pass Treasury Department tests while preserving its drinkability. Unfortunately, the adulterant they developed turned out to be a neurotoxin. Poisoned Jamaican Ginger led to thousands of cases of paralysis and death. The most common effect was a withering of the muscles in the foot and ankle, causing victims to walk with a peculiar limp or shuffle. The infirmity was so widespread, a number of blues songs were written and recorded about it.

The conspiracy at the heart of the book – heroin dealers attempting to make inroads into Chicago – is based on fact. The 'French Connection' (the route through which heroin made its way from Turkey to the United States) was already well established in the late 1920s. New York gangsters (notably 'Lucky' Luciano) were already involved in the distribution and sale of the drug, whilst the older guard were against it. Capone was content to keep his focus where he had originally made his money – alcohol, gambling and prostitution.

Luciano and his associate Meyer Lansky used the tactic of letting rival factions attack each other before stepping into the breach in the Castellammarese War in New York in 1930–1. The war was fought by the Masseria and Maranzano crime families for control of the city. Almost as soon as Salvatore Maranzano won and declared himself *capo di tutti capi*, Luciano stepped in, assassinated him, and set up a power-sharing commission. I thought it possible that if New York gangsters were looking to wrestle back control of Chicago in 1928 (as indeed they were), they might use the same tactic. Due to the timing of the Castellammarese War, however, Michael's knowledge that it was brewing in 1928 is somewhat fanciful.

Capone's visit to the doctor I invented. Whether he knew about his syphilis in 1928 is hard to confirm, although he was certainly showing signs of it by then, having contracted it as a youth in Brooklyn. The first documented evidence of it is from 1932, when Capone underwent a medical examination on entry to the Atlanta US Penitentiary (the exam also revealed he was suffering from gonorrhea).

The extent of Capone's cocaine use is yet another matter for debate. That he used it is not in doubt, but the evidence that he was a habitual user seems to rest solely on his autopsy in 1947, which revealed that he had a perforated septum, a symptom of heavy cocaine use, but also of syphilis.

Capone's war with Bugs Moran reached its climax about eight months after the end of this book, in the St Valentine's Day Massacre in 1929. Capone hired men to attack Moran's Northside Gang in their Lincoln Park headquarters. Posing as police officers, they lined seven of Moran's men against a wall, then gunned them down. With Moran's customary good luck, he was by chance not on the premises at the time. The massacre was the beginning of the end for Capone. Bloody photos of the incident made front pages around the world, the goodwill of the city turned against him, and the authorities allocated ever more resources toward having him imprisoned. He was convicted of tax evasion in 1931 and released eight years later, by which time he had been ravaged by syphilis, both mentally and physically. He died on his Florida estate in 1947, at the age of forty-eight, an invalid with the mental age of a child.

A great introduction to the era is Bill Bryson's excellent *One Summer: America, 1927*. For more information on the Chicago jazz scene in the 1920s, I would recommend Thomas Brothers' *Louis Armstrong: Master of Modernism* and William Howland Kenney's *Chicago Jazz: A Cultural History 1904–1930*. The most enjoyable of the Capone biographies I read was Laurence Bergreen's *Capone: The Man and the Era*.

*

Dead Man's Blues is intended to be the second in a four-part series which charts the history of jazz and the Mob through the middle fifty years of the twentieth century. In an Oulipo-inspired conceit, each of the four parts will contain a different city, decade, song, season, theme and weather. Part three will be set in 1940s New York in the autumn. The weather, theme and song are yet to be decided, although for the latter, 'Autumn in New York' seems an obvious choice. Maybe too obvious. We'll see. The main characters from the first two books will reappear in the next two.

RAY CELESTIN
London, March 2016

Acknowledgments

Huge thanks to Shemuel Bulgin, Mariam Pourshoushtari,
Ben Maguire, Julia Pye, Tony Hemphill, Jane Finigan,
Juliet Mahony, Susannah Godman, Sophie Orme, Josie Humber,
Maria Rejt, and everyone at L&R, Mantle and Macmillan.

Discover all four novels in Ray Celestin's
award-winning City Blues series

THE AXEMAN'S JAZZ

DEAD MAN'S BLUES

THE MOBSTER'S LAMENT

SUNSET SWING

The City Blues series begins with

THE AXEMAN'S JAZZ

New Orleans, 1919.
As a dark serial killer – the Axeman – stalks the city, three
individuals set out to unmask him . . .

Detective Lieutenant Michael Talbot – heading up the
official investigation, but struggling to find leads, and
harbouring a grave secret of his own.

Former detective Luca d'Andrea – now working for the
Mafia; his need to solve the mystery of the Axeman is
every bit as urgent as that of the authorities.

And Ida – a secretary at the Pinkerton Detective Agency.
Obsessed with Sherlock Holmes and dreaming of a better life, she
stumbles across a clue which lures her and her musician friend,
Louis Armstrong, to the case – and into terrible danger . . .

As Michael, Luca and Ida each draw closer to discovering the
killer's identity, the Axeman himself will issue a challenge to the
people of New Orleans: play jazz or risk becoming the next victim.

OUT NOW IN PAPERBACK.

Discover the second book in the City Blues series,

DEAD MAN'S BLUES

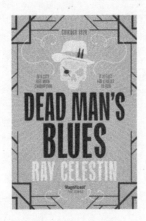

Chicago, 1928.
In the stifling summer heat three investigations begin . . .

Pinkerton detectives Michael Talbot and Ida Davis are
hired to locate a missing heiress. But it proves harder than
expected to find a woman known across the city.

After being called to a gruesome murder in Chicago's
violent Black Belt, crime-scene photographer Jacob Russo
can't get the dead man's image out of his head, and decides
to track down the culprit himself.

And with a group of city leaders poisoned at the Ritz, Dante
Sanfelippo – rum-runner and fixer – is called in by Al Capone to
discover whether someone is trying to bring down his empire.

As the three parties edge closer to the truth, their paths will cross
and their lives will be threatened. But will any of them find the
answers they need in the city of blues, booze and brutality?

OUT NOW IN PAPERBACK.

The City Blues series continues with the third instalment

THE MOBSTER'S LAMENT

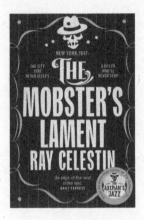

New York, 1947.
A gangster's last chance to escape the clutches of New York's Mafia,
and a ruthless serial killer is tracking his every move . . .

Mob fixer Gabriel Leveson's plans to flee the city are put
on hold when he is tasked with tracking down stolen Mob money
by 'the boss of all bosses', Frank Costello. But while he's busy
looking, he doesn't notice who's watching him . . .

Meanwhile, Private Investigator Ida Young and her old
partner, Michael Talbot, must prove the innocence of
Talbot's son Tom, who has been accused of the brutal
murders of four people in a Harlem flop-house. With all the
evidence pointing towards him, their only chance of
exoneration is to find the killer themselves.

Whilst across town, Ida's childhood friend, Louis Armstrong,
is on the brink of bankruptcy, when a promoter approaches
him with a strange offer to reignite his career . . .

OUT NOW IN PAPERBACK.

The City Blues series comes to an end with

SUNSET SWING

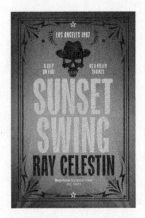

Los Angeles. December, 1967.

A young nurse, Kerry Gaudet, travels to the City of Angels desperate to find her missing brother, fearing that something terrible has happened to him: a serial killer is terrorizing the city, picking victims at random, and Kerry has precious few leads.

Ida Young, recently retired Private Investigator, is dragged into helping the police when a young woman is discovered murdered in her motel room. Ida has never met the victim but her name has been found at the crime scene and the LAPD wants to know why . . .

Meanwhile Mob fixer Dante Sanfelippo has put his life savings into purchasing a winery in Napa Valley, but first he must do one final favour for the Mob before leaving town: find a bail jumper before the bond money falls due, and time is fast running out.

Ida's friend, Louis Armstrong, flies into the city just as her investigations uncover mysterious clues to the killer's identity. And Dante must tread a dangerous path to pay his dues, a path which will throw him headlong into a terrifying government conspiracy and a secret that the conspirators will do anything to protect . . .

OUT NOVEMBER 2021 AND AVAILABLE TO PRE-ORDER NOW.